MARY WILKIN

A Humble Romance
and Other Stories

The American Short Story Series

VOLUME 52

GARRETT PRESS

512-00202-9

Library of Congress Catalog Card No. 69-11894

*This volume was reprinted from the 1887 edition
published by Harper & Bros.*

First Garrett Press Edition published 1969

The American Short Story Series
Volume 52
©1969

Manufactured in the United States of America

GARRETT PRESS, INC.
Publishers

250 West 54th Street, New York, N.Y. 10019

LIST OF STORIES.

iv   *LIST OF STORIES.*

A HUMBLE ROMANCE.

SHE was stooping over the great kitchen sink, washing
the breakfast dishes. Under fostering circumstances, her
slenderness of build might have resulted in delicacy or
daintiness; now the harmony between strength and task
had been repeatedly broken, and the result was ugliness.
Her finger joints and wrist bones were knotty and out of
proportion, her elbows, which her rolled-up sleeves displayed, were pointed and knobby, her shoulders bent, her
feet spread beyond their natural bounds—from head to
foot she was a little discordant note. She had a pale,
peaked face, her scanty fair hair was strained tightly back,
and twisted into a tiny knot, and her expression was at
once passive and eager.

There came a ringing knock at the kitchen door, and a
face of another description, large, strong-featured, and assured, peered out of the pantry, which was over against the
sink.

"Who is it, Sally?"

"I don' know, Mis' King."

"Well, go to the door, can't you, an' not stan' thar gapin'.
I can't; my hands are in the butter."

Sally shook the dish-water off her red, sodden fingers,
and shuffled to the door.

A tall man with a scraggy sandy mustache stood there. He had some scales in his hand.

"Good - mornin', marm," he said.   "Hev you got any rags?"

"I'll see," said the girl.   Then she went over to the pantry, and whispered to her mistress that it was the tin-peddler.

"Botheration !" cried Mrs. King, impatiently; "why couldn't he hev come another day? Here I am right in the midst of butter, an' I've got lots of rags, an' I've got to hev some new milk-pails right away."

All of this reached the ears of the tin-peddler, but he merely stood waiting, the corners of his large mouth curving up good-naturedly, and scrutinized with pleasant blue eyes the belongings of the kitchen, and especially the slight, slouching figure at the sink, to which Sally had returned.

"I s'pose," said Mrs. King, approaching the peddler at length, with decision thinly veiled by doubt, "that I shall hev to trade with you, though I don' know how to stop this mornin', for I'm right in the midst of butter-making. I wish you'd 'a happened along some other day."

"Wa'al," replied the peddler, laughing, "an' so I would, marm, ef I'd only known.   But I don't see jest how I could hev, unless you'd 'a pasted it up on the fences, or had it put in the newspaper, or mebbe in the almanac."

He lounged smilingly against the door-casing, jingling his scales, and waiting for the woman to make up her mind.

She smiled unwillingly, with knitted brows.

"Well," said she, "of course you ain't to blame.   I guess I'll go an' pick up my rags, up in the garret. There's quite a lot of 'em, an' it 'll take some time.   I don't know as you'll want to wait."

"Lor', I don't keer," answered the peddler. "I'd jest as soon rest a leetle as not. It's a powerful hot mornin' for this time o' year, an' I've got all the day afore me."

He came in and seated himself, with a loose-jointed sprawl, on a chair near the door.

After Mrs. King had gone out, he sat a few minutes eying the girl at the sink intently. She kept steadily on with her work, though there was a little embarrassment and uncertainty in her face.

"Would it be too much trouble ef I should ask you to give me a tumbler of water, miss?"

She filled one of her hot, newly-washed glasses with water from a pail standing on a shelf at one end of the sink, and brought it over to him. "It's cold," she said. "I drawed it myself jest a few minutes ago, or I'd get some right out of the well for you."

"This is all right, an' thanky kindly, miss; it's proper good water."

He drained the glass, and carried it back to her at the sink, where she had returned. She did not seem to dare absent herself from her dish-washing task an instant.

He set the empty glass down beside the pail; then he caught hold of the girl by her slender shoulders and faced her round towards him. She turned pale, and gave a smothered scream.

"Thar! thar! don't you go to being afeard of me," said the peddler. "I wouldn't hurt you for the whole world. I jest want to take a squar look at you. You're the worst-off-lookin' little cretur I ever set my eyes on."

She looked up at him pitifully, still only half reassured. There were inflamed circles around her dilated blue eyes.

"You've been cryin', ain't you?"

The girl nodded meekly. "Please let me go," she said.

"Yes, I'll let you go; but I'm a-goin' to ask you a few questions first, an' I want you to answer 'em, for I'll be hanged ef I ever see— Ain't she good to you?"—indicating Mrs. King with a wave of his hand towards the door through which she had departed.

"Yes, she's good enough, I guess."

"Don't ever scold you, hey?"

"I don' know; I guess so, sometimes."

"Did this mornin', didn't she?"

"A little. I was kinder behind with the work."

"Keeps you workin' pretty stiddy, don't she?"

"Yes; thar's consider'ble to do this time o' year."

"Cookin' for hired men, I s'pose, and butter an' milk?"

"Yes."

"How long hev you been livin' here?"

"She took me when I was little."

"Do you do anything besides work?—go round like other gals?—hev any good times?"

"Sometimes." She said it doubtfully, as if casting about in her mind for reminiscences to prove the truth of it.

"Git good wages?"

"A dollar, a week sence I was eighteen. I worked for my board an' close afore."

"Got any folks?"

"I guess I've got some brothers and sisters somewhar. I don' know jest whar. Two of 'em went West, an' one is married somewhar in York State. We was scattered when father died. Thar was ten of us, an' we was awful poor. Mis' King took me. I was the youngest; 'bout four, they said I was. I 'ain't never known any folks but Mis' King."

The peddler walked up and down the kitchen floor twice; Sally kept on with her dishes; then he came back to her.

"Look a-here," he said; "leave your dish-washin' alone a minute. I want you to give me a good look in the face, an' tell me what you think of me."

She looked up shyly in his florid, freckled face, with its high cheek-bones and scraggy sandy mustache; then she plunged her hands into the dish-tub again.

"I don' know," she said, bashfully.

"Well, mebbe you do know, only you can't put it into words. Now jest take a look out the window at my tin cart thar. That's all my own, a private consarn. I ain't runnin' for no company. I owns the cart an' horse, an' disposes of the rags, an' sells the tin, all on my own hook. An' I'm a-doin' pretty well at it; I'm a-layin' up a leetle money. I ain't got no family. Now this was what I was a-comin' at: s'pose you should jest leave the dishes, an' the scoldin' woman, an' the butter, an' everything, an' go a-ridin' off with me on my tin-cart. I wouldn't know you, an' *she* wouldn't know you, an' you wouldn't know yourself, in a week. You wouldn't hev a bit of work to do, but jest set up thar like a queen, a-ridin' and seein' the country. For that's the way we'd live, you know. I wouldn't hev you keepin' house an' slavin'. We'd stop along the road for vittles, and bring up at taverns nights. What d'ye say to it?"

She stopped her dish-washing now, and stood staring at him, her lips slightly parted and her cheeks flushed.

"I know I ain't much in the way of looks," the peddler went on, "an' I'm older than you—I'm near forty—an' I've been married afore. I don't s'pose you kin take a likin' to me right off, but you might arter a while. An' I'd take keer of you, you poor leetle thing. An' I don't b'lieve you know anything about how nice it is to be taken keer of, an' hev the hard, rough things kep' off by somebody that likes yer."

Still she said nothing, but stood staring at him.

"You ain't got no beau, hev you?" asked the peddler, as a sudden thought struck him.

"No." She shook her head, and her cheeks flushed redder.

"Well, what do you say to goin' with me? You'll hev to hurry up an' make up your mind, or the old lady'll be back."

The girl was almost foolishly ignorant of the world, but her instincts were as brave and innocent as an angel's. Tainted with the shiftless weariness and phlegm of her parents, in one direction she was vigorous enough.

Whether it was by the grace of God, or an inheritance from some far-off Puritan ancestor, the fire in whose veins had not burned low, she could see, if she saw nothing else, the distinction between right and wrong with awful plainness. Nobody had ever called her anything but a *good* girl. It was said with a disparagement, maybe, but it was always "a good girl."

She looked up at the man before her, her cheeks burning painfully hot, her eyes at once drooping and searching. "I—don't know jest—how you mean," she stammered. "I wouldn't go with the king, if—it wasn't to—go honest—"

The peddler's face flushed as red as hers. "Now, look a-here, little un," he said, "You jest listen, an' it's God's own truth; ef I hadn't 'a meant all right I wouldn't 'a come to you, but to some other gal, hansumer, an' pearter, an'—but, O Lord! I ain't that kind, anyway. What I want is to merry you honest, an' take keer of you, an' git that

look off your face. I know it's awful sudden, an' it's askin'
a good deal of a gal to trust so much in a fellow she never
set eyes on afore. Ef you can't do it, I'll never blame you ;
but ef you kin, well, I don't b'lieve you'll ever be sorry.
Most folks would think I was a fool, too, an' mebbe I am,
but I wanted to take keer on you the minute I set eyes on
you ; an' afore I know it the wantin' to take keer on you
will be growin' into lovin' you. Now you hurry and make
up your mind, or she will be back."

Sally had little imagination, and a loving nature. In her
heart, as in all girls' hearts, the shy, secret longing for a
lover had strengthened with her growth, but she had never
dreamed definitely of one. Now she surveyed the homely,
scrawny, good-natured visage before her, and it filled well
enough the longing nature had placed in her helpless heart.
His appearance dispelled no previous illusion, for previous
illusion there had been none. No one had ever spoken to
her in this way. Rough and precipitate though it was, it
was skilful wooing ; for it made its sincerity felt, and a girl
more sophisticated than this one could not have listened to
it wholly untouched.

The erratic nature of the whole proceeding did not dismay her. She had no conscience for conventionalities ;
she was too simple ; hers only provided for pure right and
wrong. Strange to say, the possible injury she would do
her mistress by leaving her in this way did not occur to
her till afterwards. Now she looked at her lover, and began to believe in him, and as soon as she began to believe
in him — poor, unattractive, ignorant little thing that she
was !—she began to love just like other girls. All over her
crimson face flashed the signs of yielding. The peddler
saw and understood them.

"You will—won't you, little un?" he cried. Then, as her eyes drooped more before his, and her mouth quivered between a sob and a smile, he took a step forward and stretched out his arms towards her. Then he stepped back, and his arms fell.

"No," he cried, "I won't; I'd like to give you a hug, but I won't; I won't so much as touch that little lean hand of yours till you're my wife. You shall see I mean honest. But come along now, little un, or she will be back. I declar' ef I don't more'n half believe she's fell in a fit, or she'd ha' been back afore now. Come now, dear, be spry!"

"Now?" said Sally, in turn.

"Now! why, of course now: what's the use of waitin'? Mebbe you want to make some weddin' cake, but I reckon we'd better buy some over in Derby, for it might put the old lady out;" and the peddler chuckled. "Why, I'm jest a-goin' to stow you away in that 'ere tin-cart of mine— there's plenty of room, for I've been on the road a-sellin' nigh a week. An' then I'm a-goin' to drive out of this yard, arter I've traded with your missis, as innocent as the very innocentest lamb you ever see, an' I'm a-goin' to drive along a piece till it's safe; an' then you're a-goin' to git out an' set up on the seat alongside of me, an' we're goin' to keep on till we git to Derby, an' then we'll git married, jest as soon as we kin find a minister as wants to airn a ten-dollar bill."

"But," gasped Sally, "she'll ask whar I am."

"I'll fix that. You lay there in the cart an' hear what I say. Lor', I'd jest as soon tell her to her face, myself, what we was goin' to do, an' set you right up on the seat aside of me, afore her eyes; but she'd talk hard, most likely, an' you look scared enough now, an' you'd cry, an' your eyes would git redder; an' she might sass you so you'd be ready to back out, too. Women kin say hard things to other women, an' they ain't likely to understan' any woman but themselves trustin' a man overmuch. I reckon this is the best way." He went towards the door, and motioned her to come.

"But I want my bonnet."

"Never mind the bunnit; I'll buy you one in Derby."

"But I don't want to ride into Derby bare-headed," said Sally, almost crying.

"Well, I don't know as you do, little un, that's a fact; but hurry an' git the bunnit, or she *will* be here. I thought I heard her a minute ago."

"Thar's a leetle money I've saved, too."

"Well, git that; we don't want to make the old lady vallyble presents, an' you kin buy yourself sugar-plums with it. But be spry."

She gave him one more scared glance, and hastened out of the room, her limp calico accommodating itself to every ungraceful hitch of her thin limbs and sharp hips.

"I'll git her a gown with puckers in the back," mused the peddler, gazing after her. Then he hastened out to his tin-cart, and arranged a vacant space in the body of it. He had a great-coat, which he spread over the floor.

"Thar, little un, let me put you right in," he whispered, when Sally emerged, her bonnet on, a figured green delaine shawl over her shoulders, and her little hoard in an old stocking dangling from her hand.

She turned round and faced him once more, her eyes like a child's peering into a dark room. "You mean *honest?*"

"Before God, I do, little un. Now git in quick, for she *is* comin'!"

He had to lift her in, for her poor little limbs were too

1*

weak to support her. They were not a moment too soon, for Mrs. King stood in the kitchen door a second later.

"Here! you ain't goin', air you?" she called out.

"No, marm; I jest stepped out to look arter my hoss; he was a trifle uneasy with the flies, an' thar was a yaller wasp buzzin' round." And the peddler stepped up to the door with an open and artless visage.

"Well, I didn't know but you'd git tired waitin'. You spoke so about not bein' in a hurry that I stopped to pick my white rags out from the colored ones. I knew they'd bring more ef I did. I'd been meanin' to hev 'em all sorted out afore a peddler come along. I thought I'd hev Sally pick 'em over last week, but she was sick— Why, whar is Sally?"

"Who?"

"Sally—the girl that was washin' dishes when you come —she went to the door."

"Oh, the gal! I b'lieve I saw her go out the door a minute afore I went out to see to my hoss."

"Well, I'll call her, for she'll never git the dishes done, I guess, an' then we'll see about the rags."

Mrs. King strode towards the door, but the peddler stopped her.

"Now, marm, ef you please," said he, "I'd a leetle rayther you'd attend to business first, and call Sally arterwards, ef it's jest the same to you, for I am gittin' in a leetle of a hurry, and don't feel as ef I could afford to wait much longer."

"Well," said Mrs. King, reluctantly, "I don't suppose I orter ask you to, but I do hev such discouragin' times with help. I declare it don't seem to me as ef Sally ever would git them dishes done."

"Wa'al, it don't seem to me, from what I've seen, that she ever will, either," said the peddler, as he gathered up Mrs. King's rag-bags and started for the cart.

"Anybody wouldn't need to watch her for more'n two minutes to see how slow she was," assented Mrs. King, following. "She's a girl I took when she was a baby to bring up, an' I've wished more'n fifty times I hadn't. She's a good girl enough, but she's awful slow—no snap to her. How much is them milk pans?"

Mrs. King was reputedly a sharp woman at a bargain. To trade with her was ordinarily a long job for any peddler, but to-day it was shortened through skilful management. The tinman came down with astonishing alacrity from his first price, at the merest suggestion from his customer, and, in a much shorter time than usual, she bustled into the house, her arms full of pans, and the radiant and triumphant conviction of a good bargain in her face.

The peddler whirled rapidly into his seat, and snatched up the lines; but even then he heard Mrs. King calling the girl as he rattled around the corner.

A quarter of a mile from Mrs. King's there was a house; a little beyond, the road ran through a considerable stretch of woods. This was a very thinly settled neighborhood. The peddler drove rapidly until he reached the woods; then he stopped, got down, and peered into the cart.

Sally's white face and round eyes peered piteously back at him.

"How're you gittin' along, little un?"

"Oh, let me git out an' go back!"

"Lor', no, little un, you don't want to go back now! Bless your heart, she's all primed for an awful sassin'. I tell you what 'tis, you sha'n't ride cooped up in thar any longer; you shall git out an' set up here with me. We'll keep our ears pricked up, an' ef we hear anybody comin', I'll stow you in the box under the seat afore you kin say Jack Robinson, an' thar ain't any houses for three mile."

He helped the poor shivering little thing out, and lifted her up to the high seat. When he had seated himself beside her, and gathered up the lines, he looked down at her curiously. Her bonnet the severe taste of Mrs. King had regulated. It was a brown straw, trimmed with brown ribbon. He eyed it disapprovingly. " I'll git you a white bunnit, sich as brides wear, in Derby," said he.

She blushed a little at that, and glanced up at him, a little grateful light over her face.

"You poor little thing!" said the peddler, and put out his hand towards her, then drew it back again.

Derby was a town with the prestige of a city. It was the centre of trade for a large circle of little country towns ; its main street was crowded on a fair day, when the roads were good, with any quantity of nondescript and antediluvian-looking vehicles, and the owners thereof presented a wide variety of quaintness in person and attire.

So this eloping pair, the tall, bony, shambling man, and the thin, cowed-looking girl, her scant skirts slipping too far below her waist-line in the back, and following the movements of her awkward heels, excited no particular attention.

After the tin-cart had been put up in the hotel stable, and the two had been legally pronounced man and wife, or, specifically, Mr. and Mrs. Jake Russell, they proceeded on foot down the principal street, in which all the shops were congregated, in search of some amendments to the bride's attire.

If it was comparatively unnoticed, Sally was fully alive
to the unsuitableness of her costume. She turned around,
and followed with wistful eyes the prettily dressed girls
they met. There was a great regret in her heart over her
best gown, a brown delaine, with a flounce on the bottom,
and a shiny back. She had so confidently believed in its
grandeur so long, that now, seen by her mental vision, it
hardly paled before these splendors of pleating and draping.
It compared, advantageously, in her mind, with a brown
velvet suit whose wearer looked with amusement in her
eyes at Sally's forlorn figure. If she only had on her
brown delaine, she felt that she could walk more confidently through this strangeness. But, nervously snatching her
bonnet and her money, she had, in fact, heard Mrs. King's
tread on the attic stairs, and had not dared to stop longer
to secure it.

She knew they were out on a search for a new dress for
her now, but she felt a sorrowful conviction that nothing
could be found which could fully make up for the loss of
her own beloved best gown. And then Sally was not very
quick with her needle ; she thought with dismay of the
making up ; the possibility of being aided by a dressmaker,
or a ready-made costume, never entered her simple mind.

Jake shambled loosely down the street, and she followed
meekly after him, a pace or two behind.

At length the peddler stopped before a large establishment, in whose windows some ready-made ladies' garments
were displayed. "Here we air," said he, triumphantly.

Sally stepped weakly after him up the broad steps.

One particular dress in the window had excited the peddler's warm admiration. It was a trifle florid in design,
with dashes of red here and there.

2

Sally eyed it a little doubtfully, when the clerk, at Jake's request, had taken it down to show them. Untutored as her taste was, she turned as naturally to quiet plumage as a wood-pigeon. The red slashes rather alarmed her. However, she said nothing against her husband's decision to purchase the dress. She turned pale at the price; it was nearly the whole of her precious store. But she took up her stocking-purse determinedly when Jake began examining his pocket-book.

"I pays for this," said she to the clerk, lifting up her little face to him with scared resolve.

"Why, no you don't, little un!" cried Jake, catching hold of her arm. "I'm a-goin' to pay for it, o' course. It's a pity ef I can't buy my own wife a dress."

Sally flushed all over her lean throat, but she resolutely held out the money.

"No," she said again, shaking her head obstinately, "*I* pays for it."

The peddler let her have her way then, though he bit his scraggy mustache with amaze and vexation as he watched her pay the bill, and stare with a sort of frightened wistfulness after her beloved money as it disappeared in the clerk's grasp.

When they emerged from the store, the new dress under his arm, he burst out, "What on airth made you do that, little un?"

"Other folks does that way. When they gits merried they buys their own close, ef they kin."

"But it took pretty nearly all you'd got, didn't it?"

"That ain't no matter."

The peddler stared at her, half in consternation, half in admiration.

"Well," said he, "I guess you've got a little will o' your own, arter all, little un, an' I'm glad on't. A woman'd orter hev a little will to back her sweetness; it's all too soft an' slushy otherways. But I'll git even with you about the dress."

Which he proceeded to do by ushering his startled bride into the next dry-goods establishment, and purchasing a dress pattern of robin's-egg blue silk, and a delicate white bonnet. Sally, however, insisted on buying a plain sun-hat with the remainder of her own money. She was keenly alive to the absurdity and peril of that airy white structure on the top of a tin-cart.

The pair remained in Derby about a week; then they started forth on their travels, the blue silk, which a Derby dressmaker had made up after the prevailing mode, and the white bonnet, stowed away in a little new trunk in the body of the cart.

The peddler, having only himself to consult as to his motions, struck a new route now. Sally wished to keep away from her late mistress's vicinity. She had always a nervous dread of meeting her in some unlikely fashion.

She wrote a curious little ill-spelled note to her, at the first town where they stopped after leaving Derby. Whether or not Mrs. King was consoled and mollified by it she never knew.

Their way still lay through a thinly settled country. The tin-peddler found readier customers in those farmers' wives who were far from stores. It was late spring. Often they rode for a mile or two through the lovely fresh woods, without coming to a single house.

The girl had never heard of Arcadia, but, all unexpressed to herself, she was riding through it under gold-green boughs, to the sweet, broken jangling of tin-ware.

When they stopped to trade at the farmhouses, how proudly she sat, a new erectness in her slender back, and held her husband's horse tightly while he talked with the woman of the house, with now and then a careful glance towards her to see if she were safe. They always contrived to bring up, on a Sabbath-day, at some town where there was a place of worship. Then the blue silk and the white bonnet were taken reverently from their hiding-place, and Sally, full of happy consciousness, went to church with her husband in all her bridal bravery.

These two simple pilgrims, with all the beauty and grace in either of them turned only towards each other, and seen rightly only in each other's untutored, uncritical eyes, had journeyed together blissfully for about three months, when one afternoon Jake came out of a little country tavern, where they had proposed stopping for the night, with a pale face. Sally had been waiting on the cart outside until he should see if they could be accommodated. He jumped up beside her and took the lines.

"We'll go on to Ware," he said, in a dry voice; "it's only three mile further. They're full here."

Jake drove rapidly along, an awful look on his homely face, giving it the beauty of tragedy.

Sally kept looking up at him with pathetic wonder, but he never looked at her or spoke till they reached the last stretch of woods before Ware village. Then, just before they left the leafy cover, he slackened his speed a little, and threw his arm around her.

"See here, little un," he said, brokenly. "You've—got—consider'ble backbone, 'ain't you? Ef anything awful should happen, it wouldn't—kill you—you'd bear up?"

"Ef you told me to."

He caught at her words eagerly. "I would tell you to, little un—I do tell you to," he cried. "Ef anything awful ever should—happen—you'll remember that I told you to bear up."

"Yes, I'll bear up." Then she clung to him, trembling. "Oh, what is it, Jake?"

"Never mind now, little un," he answered; "p'rhaps nothin' awful's goin' to happen; I didn't say thar was. Chirk up an' give us a kiss, an' look at that 'ere sky thar, all pink an' yaller."

He tried to be cheerful, and comfort her with joking endearments then, but the awful lines in his face stayed rigid and unchanged under the smiles.

Sally, however, had not much discernment, and little of the sensitiveness of temperament which takes impressions of coming evil. She soon recovered her spirits, and was unusually merry, for her, the whole evening, making, out of the excess of her innocence and happiness, several little jokes, which made Jake laugh loyally, and set his stricken face harder the next minute.

In the course of the evening he took out his pocket-book and displayed his money, and counted it jokingly. Then he spoke, in a careless, casual manner, of a certain sum he had deposited in a country bank, and how, if he were taken sick and needed it, Sally could draw it out as well as he. Then he spoke of the value of his stock in trade and horse and cart. When they went to bed that night he had told his wife, without her suspecting he was telling her, all about his affairs.

She fell asleep as easily as a child. Jake lay rigid and motionless till he had listened an hour to her regular breathing. Then he rose softly, lighted a candle, which he shaded from her face, and sat down at a little table with a pen and paper. He wrote painfully, with cramped muscles, his head bent on one side, following every movement of his pen, yet with a confident steadiness which seemed to show that all the subject-matter had been learned by heart beforehand. Then he folded the paper carefully around a little book which he took from his pocket, and approached the bed, keeping his face turned away from his sleeping wife. He laid the little package on his vacant pillow, still keeping his face aside.

Then he got into his clothes quickly, his head turned persistently from the bed, and opened the door softly, and went out, never once looking back.

When Sally awoke the next morning she found her husband gone, and the little package on the pillow. She opened it, more curious than frightened. There was a note folded around a bank-book. Sally spelled out the note laboriously, with whitening lips and dilating eyes. It was a singular composition, its deep feeling pricking through its illiterate stiffness.

"DEAR WIFE,—I've got to go and leve you. It's the only way. Ef I kin ever come back, I will. I told you bout my bizness last night. You'd better drive the cart to Derby to that Mister Arms I told you bout, an' he'll help you sell it an' the hoss. Tell him your husband had to go away, an' left them orders. I've left you my bank-book, so you can git the money out of the bank the way I told you, an' my watch an' pocket-book is under the pillow. I left you all the money, cept what little I couldn't git long without. You'd better git boarded somewhar in Derby. You'll hev enough money to keep you awhile, an' I'll send you some more when thet's gone, ef I hev to work my fingers to the bone. Don't ye go to worryin' an' workin' hard. An' bear up. Don't forgit thet you promised me to bear up. When you gits to feelin' awful bad, an' you will, jest say it over to yourself—'He told me to bear up, an' I said as I would bear up.' Scuse poor writin' an' a bad pen.

"Yours till death, JAKE RUSSELL."

When Sally had read the letter quite through, she sat still a few minutes on the edge of the bed, her lean, round-shouldered figure showing painfully through her clinging night-dress, her eyes staring straight before her.

Then she rose, dressed herself, put the bank-book, with the letter folded around it, and her husband's pocket-book, in her bosom, and went down-stairs quietly. Just before she went out her room door she paused with her hand on the latch, and muttered to herself, " He told me to bear up, an' I said as I would bear up."

She sought the landlord to pay her bill, and found that it was already paid, and that her recreant husband had smoothed over matters in one direction for her by telling the landlord that he was called away on urgent business, and that his wife was to take the tin-cart next morning, and meet him at a certain point.

So she drove away on her tin-cart in solitary state without exciting any of the wondering comments which would have been agony to her.

When she gathered up the lines and went rattling down the country road, if ever there was a zealous disciple of a new religion, she was one. Her prophet was her raw-boned peddler husband, and her creed and whole confession of faith his parting words to her.

She did not take the road to Derby ; she had made up her mind about that as she sat on the edge of the bed after reading the letter. She drove straight along the originally prescribed route, stopping at the farmhouses, taking rags and selling tin, just as she had seen her husband do. There were much astonishment and many curious questions among her customers. A woman running a tin-cart was an unprecedented spectacle, but she explained matters, with meek

dignity, to all who questioned her.   Her husband had gone
away, and she was to attend to his customers until he should
return.   She could not always quite allay the suspicion that
there must needs be something wrong, but she managed the
trading satisfactorily, and gave good bargains, and so went
on her way unmolested.   But not a farmyard did she enter
or leave without the words sounding in her beating little
heart, like a strong, encouraging chant, " He told me to
bear up, an' I said as I would bear up."

When her stock ran low, she drove to Derby to replenish
it.   Here she had opposition from the dealers, but her almost abnormal persistence overcame it.

She showed Jake's letter to Mr. Arms, the tin-dealer with
whom she traded, and he urged her to take up with the ad-
vice in it, promising her a good bargain ; but she was resolute.

Soon she found that she was doing as well as her husband had done, if not better.   Her customers, after they
had grown used to the novelty of a tinwoman, instead of a
tinman, liked her.   In addition to the regular stock, she
carried various little notions needed frequently by house-
wives, such as pins, needles, thread, etc.

She oftener stayed at a farmhouse overnight than a tavern, and frequently stopped over at one a few days in severe
weather.

After her trip to Derby she always carried a little pistol,
probably more to guard Jake's watch and property than
herself.

Whatever money she did not absolutely require for cur-
rent expenses went to swell Jake's little hoard in the Derby
bank.   During the three years she kept up her lonely travelling little remittances came directed to her from time to

time, in the care of Mr. Arms. When one came, Sally cried pitifully, and put it into the bank with the rest.

She never gave up expecting her husband. She never woke up one morning without the hope in her heart that he would come that day. Every golden dawn showed a fair possibility to her, and so did every red sunset. She scanned every distant, approaching figure in the sweet country roads with the half conviction in her heart that it was he, and when nearness dispelled the illusion, her heart bounded bravely back from its momentary sinking, and she looked ahead for another traveller.

Still he did not come for three years from the spring he went away. Except through the money remittances, which gave no clew but the New York postmark on the envelope, she had not heard from him.

One June afternoon she, a poor lonely pilgrim, now without her beloved swain, driving through her old Arcadian solitudes, whose enchanted meaning was lost to her, heard a voice from behind calling to her, above the jangling of tin, "Sally! Sally! Sally!"

She turned, and there he was, running after her. She turned her head quickly, and, stopping the horse, sat perfectly still, her breath almost gone with suspense. She did not dare look again for fear she had not seen aright.

The hurrying steps came nearer and nearer; she looked when they came abreast the cart. It was he. It always seemed to her that she would have died if it had not been, that time.

"Jake! Jake!"

"Oh, Sally!"

He was up on the seat before she could breathe again, and his arms around her.

"Jake, I did—bear up—I did."

" I know you did, little un. Mr. Arms told me all about
it. Oh, you dear little un, you poor little un, a-drivin' round
on this cart all alone !"

Jake laid his cheek against Sally's and sobbed.

" Don't cry, Jake. I've airned money, I hev, an' it's in
the bank for you."

" Oh, you blessed little un ! Sally, they said hard things
'bout me to you in Derby, didn't they ?"

She started violently at that. There was one thing which
had been said to her in Derby, and the memory of it had
been a repressed terror ever since.

" Yes : they said as how you'd run off with—another
woman."

" What did you say ?"

" I didn't believe it."

" I did, Sally."

" Well, you've come back."

" Afore I married you I'd been merried afore. By all
that's good an' great, little un, I thought my wife was dead.
Her folks said she was. When I come home from peddlin'
one time, she was gone, an' they said she was off on a visit.
I found out in a few weeks she'd run off with another fellow. I went off peddlin' agin without carin' much what become of me. 'Bout a year arterwards I saw her death in a
paper, an' I wrote to her folks, an' they said 'twas true.
They were a bad lot, the whole of 'em. I got took in. But
she had a mighty pretty face, an' a tongue like honey, an' I
s'pose I was green. Three year ago, when I went into
that 'ere tavern in Grover, thar she was in the kitchin a-
cookin'. The fellow she run off with had left her, an' she'd
been trying to hunt me up. She was awful poor, an' had

come across this place an' took it. She was allers a good
cook, an' she suited the customers fust-rate. I guess they
liked to see her pretty face 'round too, confound her!

"Well, little un, she knew me right off, an' hung on to
me, an' cried, an' begged me to forgive her; and when she
spied you a-settin' thar on the cart, she tore. I hed to hold
her to keep her from goin' out an' tellin' you the whole
story. I thought you'd die ef she did. I didn't know then
how you could bear up, little un. *Ef* you 'ain't got backbone !"

"Jake, I did bear up."

"I know you did, you blessed little cretur. Well, she said
ef I didn't leave you, an' go with her, she'd expose me. As
soon as she found she'd got the weapons in her own hands,
an' could hev me up for bigamy, she didn't cry so much, an'
wa'n't quite so humble.

"Well, little un, then I run off an' left you. I couldn't
stay with you ef you wa'n't my wife, an' 'twas all the way to
stop her tongue. I met her that night, an' we went to New
York. I got lodgin's for her; then I went to work in a
box factory, an' supported her. I never went nigh her from
one week's end to the other; I couldn't do it without hevin'
murder in my heart; but I kep' her in money. Every scrap
I could save I sent to you, but I used to lay awake nights,
worryin' for fear you'd want things. Well, it's all over. She
died a month ago, an' I saw her buried."

"I knowed she was dead when you begun to tell about
her, because you'd come."

"Yes, she's dead this time, an' I'm glad. Don't you look
scared, little un. I hope the Lord 'll forgive me, but *I'm
glad*. She was a bad un, you know, Sally."

"Was she sorry?"

"I don' know, little un."

Sally's head was resting peacefully on Jake's shoulder; golden flecks of light sifted down on them through the rustling maple and locust boughs; the horse, with bent head, was cropping the tender young grass at the side of the road.

"Now we'll start up the horse, an' go to Derby an' git married over agin, Sally."

She raised her head suddenly, and looked up at him with eager eyes.

"Jake."

"Well, little un?"

"Oh, Jake, my blue silk dress an' the white bonnet is in the trunk in the cart jest the same, an' I can git 'em out, an' put 'em on under the trees thar, an' wear 'em to be married in!"

TWO OLD LOVERS.

LEYDEN was emphatically a village of cottages, and each
of them built after one of two patterns: either the front
door was on the right side, in the corner of a little piazza
extending a third of the length of the house, with the main
roof jutting over it, or the piazza stretched across the front,
and the door was in the centre.

The cottages were painted uniformly white, and had
blinds of a bright spring-green color. There was a little
flower-garden in front of each; the beds were laid out artis-
tically in triangles, hearts, and rounds, and edged with
box; boys'-love, sweet-williams, and pinks were the fash-
ionable and prevailing flowers.

There was a general air of cheerful though humble prosperity about the place, which it owed, and indeed its very
existence also, to the three old weather-beaten boot-and-
shoe factories which arose stanchly and importantly in the
very midst of the natty little white cottages.

Years before, when one Hiram Strong put up his three
factories for the manufacture of the rough shoe which the
working-man of America wears, he hardly thought he was
also gaining for himself the honor of founding Leyden.
He chose the site for his buildings mainly because they
would be easily accessible to the railway which stretched

to the city, sixty miles distant. At first the workmen came on the cars from the neighboring towns, but after a while they became tired of that, and one after another built for himself a cottage, and established his family and his household belongings near the scene of his daily labors. So gradually Leyden grew. A built his cottage like C, and B built his like D. They painted them white, and hung the green blinds, and laid out their flower-beds in front and their vegetable-beds at the back. By and by came a church and a store and a post-office to pass, and Leyden was a full-fledged town.

That was a long time ago. The shoe-factories had long passed out of the hands of Hiram Strong's heirs ; he himself was only a memory on the earth. The business was not quite as wide-awake and vigorous as when in its first youth ; it droned a little now ; there was not quite so much bustle and hurry as formerly. The factories were never lighted up of an evening on account of overwork, and the workmen found plenty of time for pleasant and salutary gossip over their cutting and pegging. But this did not detract in the least from the general cheerfulness and prosperity of Leyden. The inhabitants still had all the work they needed to supply the means necessary for their small comforts, and they were contented. They too had begun to drone a little like the factories. "As slow as Leyden " was the saying among the faster-going towns adjoining theirs. Every morning at seven the old men, young men, and boys, in their calico shirt-sleeves, their faces a little pale—perhaps from their in-door life—filed unquestioningly out of the back doors of the white cottages, treading still deeper the well-worn foot-paths stretching around the sides of the houses, and entered the factories. They were great,

ugly wooden buildings, with wings which they had grown
in their youth jutting clumsily from their lumbering shoulders. Their outer walls were black and grimy, streaked
and splashed and patched with red paint in every variety
of shade, accordingly as the original hue was tempered
with smoke or the beatings of the storms of many years.

The men worked peacefully and evenly in the shoe-shops
all day; and the women stayed at home and kept the little white cottages tidy, cooked the meals, and washed the
clothes, and did the sewing. For recreation the men sat
on the piazza in front of Barker's store of an evening, and
gossiped or discussed politics ; and the women talked over
their neighbors' fences, or took their sewing into their
neighbors' of an afternoon.

People died in Leyden as elsewhere; and here and there
was a little white cottage whose narrow foot-path leading round to its back door its master would never tread
again.

In one of these lived Widow Martha Brewster and her
daughter Maria. Their cottage was one of those which
had its piazza across the front. Every summer they trained
morning-glories over it, and planted their little garden
with the flower-seeds popular in Leyden. There was not
a cottage in the whole place whose surroundings were
neater and gayer than theirs, for all they were only two
women, and two old women at that; for Widow Martha Brewster was in the neighborhood of eighty, and her
daughter, Maria Brewster, near sixty. The two had lived
alone since Jacob Brewster died and stopped going to
the factory, some fifteen years ago. He had left them
this particular white cottage, and a snug little sum in the
savings - bank besides, for the whole Brewster family had

worked and economized all their long lives. The women had corded boots at home, while the man had worked in the shop, and never spent a cent without thinking of it overnight.

Leyden folks all thought that David Emmons would marry Maria Brewster when her father died. "David can rent his house, and go to live with Maria and her mother," said they, with an affectionate readiness to arrange matters for them. But he did not. Every Sunday night at eight o'clock punctually, the form of David Emmons, arrayed in his best clothes, with his stiff white dickey, and a nosegay in his button-hole, was seen to advance up the road towards Maria Brewster's, as he had been seen to advance every Sunday night for the last twenty-five years, but that was all. He manifested not the slightest intention of carrying out people's judicious plans for his welfare and Maria's.

She did not seem to pine with hope deferred; people could not honestly think there was any occasion to pity her for her lover's tardiness. A cheerier woman never lived. She was literally bubbling over with jollity. Round-faced and black-eyed, with a funny little bounce of her whole body when she walked, she was the merry feature of the whole place.

Her mother was now too feeble, but Maria still corded boots for the factories as of old. David Emmons, who was quite sixty, worked in them, as he had from his youth. He was a slender, mild-faced old man, with a fringe of gray yellow beard around his chin; his head was quite bald. Years ago he had been handsome, they said, but somehow people had always laughed at him a little, although they all liked him. "The slowest of all the slow Leydenites" outsiders called him, and even the "slow Leydenites" poked fun at this exaggeration of themselves. It was an old and well-worn remark that it took David Emmons an hour to go courting, and that he was always obliged to leave his own home at seven in order to reach Maria's at eight, and there was a standing joke that the meeting-house passed him one morning on his way to the shop.

David heard the chaffing of course—there is very little delicacy in matters of this kind among country people— but he took it all in good part. He would laugh at himself with the rest, but there was something touching in his deprecatory way of saying sometimes, " Well, I don't know how 'tis, but it don't seem to be in my natur' to do any other way. I suppose I was born without the faculty of gittin' along quick in this world. You'll have to git behind and push me a leetle, I reckon."

He owned his little cottage, which was one of the kind which had the piazza on the right side. He lived entirely alone. There was a half-acre or so of land beside his house, which he used for a vegetable garden. After and before shop hours, in the dewy evenings and mornings, he dug and weeded assiduously between the green ranks of corn and beans. If David Emmons was slow, his vegetables were not. None of the gardens in Leyden surpassed his in luxuriant growth. His corn tasselled out and his potato patch was white with blossoms as soon as anybody's.

He was almost a vegetarian in his diet ; the products of his garden spot were his staple articles of food. Early in the morning would the gentle old bachelor set his pot of green things boiling, and dine gratefully at noon, like mild Robert Herrick, on pulse and herbs. His garden supplied also his sweetheart and her mother with all the vegetables

3

they could use.   Many times in the course of a week could
David have been seen slowly moving towards the Brewster
cottage with a basket on his arm well stocked with the ma-
terials for an innocent and delicious repast.

But Maria was not to be outdone by her old lover in
kindly deeds.   Not a Saturday but a goodly share of her
weekly baking was deposited, neatly covered with a white
crash towel, on David's little kitchen table.   The surrepti-
tious air with which the back-door key was taken from its
hiding-place (which she well knew) under the kitchen blind,
the door unlocked and entered, and the good things deposited, was charming, although highly ineffectual.   "There
goes Maria with David's baking," said the women, peering
out of their windows as she bounced, rather more gently
and cautiously than usual, down the street.   And David
himself knew well the ministering angel to whom these
benefits were due when he lifted the towel and discovered
with tearful eyes the brown loaves and flaky pies—the
proofs of his Maria's love and culinary skill.

Among the younger and more irrevent portions of the
community there was considerable speculation as to the
mode of courtship of these old lovers of twenty-five years'
standing.   Was there ever a kiss, a tender clasp of the
hand, those usual expressions of affection between sweet-
hearts?

Some of the more daring spirits had even gone so far as
to commit the manifest impropriety of peeping in Maria's
parlor windows ; but they had only seen David sitting quiet
and prim on the little slippery horse-hair sofa, and Maria
by the table, rocking slowly in her little cane-seated rocker.
Did Maria ever leave her rocker and sit on that slippery
horse-hair sofa by David's side?   They never knew ; but

she never did. There was something laughable, and at the same time rather pathetic, about Maria and David's courting. All the outward appurtenances of "keeping company" were as rigidly observed as they had been twenty-five years ago, when David Emmons first cast his mild blue eyes shyly and lovingly on red-cheeked, quick-spoken Maria Brewster. Every Sunday evening, in the winter, there was a fire kindled in the parlor, the parlor lamp was lit at dusk all the year round, and Maria's mother retired early, that the young people might "sit up." The "sitting up" was no very formidable affair now, whatever it might have been in the first stages of the courtship. The need of sleep over-balanced sentiment in those old lovers, and by ten o'clock at the latest Maria's lamp was out, and David had wended his solitary way to his own home.

Leyden people had a great curiosity to know if David had ever actually popped the question to Maria, or if his natural slowness was at fault in this as in other things. Their curiosity had been long exercised in vain, but Widow Brewster, as she waxed older, grew loquacious, and one day told a neighbor, who had called in her daughter's absence, that "David had never reely come to the p'int. She supposed he would some time ; for her part, she thought he had better ; but then, after all, she knowed Maria didn't care, and maybe 'twas jest as well as 'twas, only sometimes she was afeard she should never live to see the weddin' if they wasn't spry." Then there had been hints concerning a certain pearl-colored silk which Maria, having a good chance to get at a bargain, had purchased some twenty years ago, when she thought, from sundry remarks, that David was coming to the point ; and it was further inti-mated that the silk had been privately made up ten years since, when Maria had again surmised that the point was about being reached. The neighbor went home in a state of great delight, having by skilful manœuvring actually obtained a glimpse of the pearl-colored silk.

It was perfectly true that Maria did not lay David's tardiness in putting the important question very much to heart. She was too cheerful, too busy, and too much interested in her daily duties to fret much about anything. There was never at any time much of the sentimental element in her composition, and her feeling for David was eminently practical in its nature. She, although the woman, had the stronger character of the two, and there was something rather mother-like than lover-like in her affection for him. It was through the protecting care which chiefly characterized her love that the only pain to her came from their long courtship and postponement of marriage. It was true that, years ago, when David had led her to think, from certain hesitating words spoken at parting one Sunday night, that he would certainly ask the momentous question soon, her heart had gone into a happy flutter. She had bought the pearl-colored silk then.

Years after, her heart had fluttered again, but a little less wildly this time. David almost asked her another Sunday night. Then she had made up the pearl-colored silk. She used to go and look at it fondly and admiringly from time to time ; once in a while she would try it on and survey herself in the glass, and imagine herself David's bride—a faded bride, but a happy and a beloved one.

She looked at the dress occasionally now, but a little sadly, as the conviction that she should never wear it was forcing itself upon her more and more. But the sadness was always more for David's sake than her own. She saw him growing an old man, and the lonely, uncared-for life that he led filled her heart with tender pity and sorrow for him. She did not confine her kind offices to the Saturday baking. Every week his little house was tidied and set to rights, and his mending looked after.

Once, on a Sunday night, when she spied a rip in his coat, that had grown long from the want of womanly fingers constantly at hand, she had a good cry after he had left and she had gone into her room. There was something more pitiful to her, something that touched her heart more deeply, in that rip in her lover's Sunday coat than in all her long years of waiting.

As the years went on, it was sometimes with a sad heart that Maria stood and watched the poor lonely old figure moving slower than ever down the street to his lonely home ; but the heart was sad for him always, and never for herself. She used to wonder at him a little sometimes, though always with the most loyal tenderness, that he should choose to lead the solitary, cheerless life that he did, to go back to his dark, voiceless home, when he might be so sheltered and cared for in his old age. She firmly believed that it was only owing to her lover's incorrigible slowness, in this as in everything else. She never doubted for an instant that he loved her. Some women might have tried hastening matters a little themselves, but Maria, with the delicacy which is sometimes more inherent in a steady, practical nature like hers than in a more ardent one, would have lost her self-respect forever if she had done such a thing.

So she lived cheerfully along, corded her boots, though her fingers were getting stiff, humored her mother, who was getting feebler and more childish every year, and did the best she could for her poor, foolish old lover.

When David was seventy, and she sixty-eight, she gave
away the pearl-colored silk to a cousin's daughter who was
going to be married.   The girl was young and pretty and
happy, but she was poor, and the silk would make over into
a grander wedding dress for her than she could hope to
obtain in any other way.

Poor old Maria smoothed the lustrous folds fondly with
her withered hands before sending it away, and cried a
little, with a patient pity for David and herself.   But when
a tear splashed directly on to the shining surface of the
silk, she stopped crying at once, and her sorrowful expression changed into one of careful scrutiny as she wiped the
salt drop away with her handkerchief, and held the dress
up to the light to be sure that it was not spotted.   A practical nature like Maria's is sometimes a great boon to its
possessor.   It is doubtful if anything else can dry a tear
as quickly.

Somehow Maria always felt a little differently towards
David after she had given away her wedding dress.   There
had always been a little tinge of consciousness in her manner towards him, a little reserve and caution before people.
But after the wedding dress had gone, all question of marriage had disappeared so entirely from her mind, that the
delicate considerations born of it vanished.   She was uncommonly hale and hearty for a woman of her age ; there
was apparently much more than two years' difference between her and her lover.   It was not only the Saturday's
bread and pie that she carried now and deposited on David's little kitchen table, but, openly and boldly, not caring
who should see her, many a warm dinner.   Every day,
after her own house-work was done, David's house was set
to rights.   He should have all the comforts he needed in

his last years, she determined. That they were his last years was evident. He coughed, and now walked so slowly from feebleness and weakness that it was a matter of doubt to observers whether he could reach Maria Brewster's before Monday evening.

One Sunday night he stayed a little longer than usual— the clock struck ten before he started. Then he rose, and said, as he had done every Sunday evening for so many years, " Well, Maria, I guess it's about time for me to be goin'."

She helped him on with his coat, and tied on his tippet. Contrary to his usual habit he stood in the door, and hesitated a minute—there seemed to be something he wanted to say.

" Maria."

" Well, David ?"

" I'm gittin' to be an old man, you know, an' I've allus been slow-goin' ; I couldn't seem to help it. There has been a good many things I haven't got around to." The old cracked voice quavered painfully.

" Yes, I know, David, all about it ; you couldn't help it. I wouldn't worry a bit about it if I were you."

" You don't lay up anything agin me, Maria ?"

" No, David."

" Good-night, Maria."

" Good-night, David. I will fetch you over some boiled dinner to-morrow."

She held the lamp at the door till the patient, tottering old figure was out of sight. She had to wipe the tears from her spectacles in order to see to read her Bible when she went in.

Next morning she was hurrying up her housework to go

over to David's—somehow she felt a little anxious about him this morning—when there came a loud knock at her door. When she opened it, a boy stood there, panting for breath; he was David's next neighbor's son.

"Mr. Emmons is sick," he said, "an' wants you. I was goin' for milk, when he rapped on the window. Father an' mother's in thar, an' the doctor. Mother said, tell you to hurry."

The news had spread rapidly; people knew what it meant when they saw Maria hurrying down the street, without her bonnet, her gray hair flying. One woman cried when she saw her. "Poor thing!" she sobbed, "poor thing!"

A crowd was around David's cottage when Maria reached it. She went straight in through the kitchen to his little bedroom, and up to his side. The doctor was in the room, and several neighbors. When he saw Maria, poor old David held out his hand to her and smiled feebly. Then he looked imploringly at the doctor, then at the others in the room. The doctor understood, and said a word to them, and they filed silently out. Then he turned to Maria. "Be quick," he whispered.

She leaned over him. "Dear David," she said, her wrinkled face quivering, her gray hair straying over her cheeks.

He looked up at her with a strange wonder in his glazing eyes. "Maria"—a thin, husky voice, that was more like a wind through dry corn-stalks, said—"Maria, I'm—dyin', an'—I allers meant to—have asked you—to—marry me."

A SYMPHONY IN LAVENDER.

IT was quite late in the evening, dark and rainy, when I arrived, and I suppose the first object in Ware, outside of my immediate personal surroundings, which arrested my attention was the Munson house. When I looked out of my window the next morning it loomed up directly opposite, across the road, dark and moist from the rain of the night before. There were so many elm-trees in front of it and in front of the house I was in, that the little pools of rain-water, still standing in the road here and there, did not glisten and .shine at all, although the sun was bright and quite high. The house itself stood back far enough to allow of a good square yard in front, and was raised from the street-level the height of a face-wall. Three or four steps led up to the front walk. On each side of the steps, growing near the edge of the wall, was an enormous lilac-tree in full blossom. I could see them tossing their purple clusters between the elm branches: there was quite a wind blowing that morning. A hedge of lilacs, kept low by constant cropping, began at the blooming lilac-trees, and reached around the rest of the yard, at the top of the face-wall. The yard was gay with flowers, laid out in fantastic little beds, all bordered trimly with box. The house was one of those square, solid, white-painted, green-blinded edi-

fices which marked the wealth and importance of the
dweller .therein a half-century or so ago, and still cast a
dim halo of respect over his memory. It had no beauty
in itself, being boldly plain and glaring, like all of its kind ;
but the green waving boughs of the elms and lilacs and
the undulating shadows they cast toned it down, and gave
it an air of coolness and quiet and lovely reserve. I began to feel a sort of pleasant, idle curiosity concerning it
as I stood there at my chamber window, and after breakfast, when I had gone into the sitting-room, whose front
windows also faced that way, I took occasion to ask my
hostess, who had come in with me, who lived there.

"Of course it is nobody I have ever seen or heard of,"
said I ; "but I was looking at the house this morning, and
have taken a fancy to know."

Mrs. Leonard gazed reflectively across at the house, and
then at me. It was an odd way she always had before
speaking.

"There's a maiden lady lives there," she answered, at
length, turning her gaze from me to the house again, "all
alone ; that is, all alone except old Margaret. She's always been in the family—ever since Caroline was a baby,
I guess : a faithful old creature as ever lived, but she's
pretty feeble now. I reckon Caroline has to do pretty
much all the work, and I don't suppose she's much company, or much of anything but a care. There she comes
now."

"Who ?" said I, feeling a little bewildered.

"Why, Caroline—Caroline Munson."

A slim, straight little woman, with a white pitcher in her
hand, was descending the stone steps between the blooming lilac-trees opposite. She had on a lilac-colored calico

dress and a white apron. She wore no hat or bonnet, and
her gray hair seemed to be arranged in a cluster of soft
little curls at the top of her head. Her face, across the
street, looked like that of a woman of forty, fair and pleas-
ing.

"She's going down to Mrs. Barnes's after milk," Mrs.
Leonard explained. "She always goes herself, every
morning just about this time. She never sends old Margaret; I reckon she ain't fit to go. I guess she can do
some things about the house, but when it comes to travelling outside Caroline has to do it herself."

Then Mrs. Leonard was called into the kitchen, and I
thought over the information, at once vague and definite, I
had received, and watched Miss Caroline Munson walk
down the shady street. She had a pretty, gentle gait.

About a week later I received an invitation to take tea
with her. I was probably never more surprised in my
life, as I had not the slightest acquaintance with her. I
had sometimes happened to watch her morning pilgrimages down the street after milk, and occasionally had observed her working over her flower-beds in her front yard.
That was all, so far as I was concerned; and I did not suppose she knew there was such a person as myself in existence. But Mrs. Leonard, who was also bidden, explained
it.

"It's Caroline's way," said she. "She's always had a
sort of mania for asking folks to tea. Why, I reckon
there's hardly a fortnight, on an average, the year round,
but what she invites somebody or other to tea. I suppose
she gets kind of dull, and there's a little excitement about
it, getting ready for company. Anyhow, she must like it,
or she wouldn't ask people. She probably has heard you

were going to board here this summer—Ware's a little place you know, and folks hear everything about each other—and thought she would invite you over with me. You had better go; you'll enjoy it. It's a nice place to go to, and she's a beautiful cook, or Margaret is; I don't know which does the cooking, but I guess they both have a hand in it. Anyhow, you'll have a pleasant time. We'll take our sewing, and go early—by three o'clock. That's the way people go out to take tea in Ware."

So the next afternoon, at three o'clock, Mrs. Leonard and I sallied across the street to Miss Caroline Munson's. She met us at the door, in response to a tap of the old-fashioned knocker. Her manner of greeting us was charming from its very quaintness. She hardly said three words, but showed at the same time a simple courtesy and a pleased shyness, like a child overcome with the delight of a tea-party in her honor. She ushered us into a beautiful old parlor on the right of the hall, and we seated ourselves with our sewing. The conversation was not very brisk nor very general so far as I was concerned. There was scarcely any topic of common interest to the three of us, probably. Mrs. Leonard was one of those women who converse only of matters pertaining to themselves or their own circle of acquaintances, and seldom digress. Miss Munson I could not judge of as to conversational habits, of course; she seemed now to be merely listening with a sort of gentle interest, scarcely saying a word herself, to Mrs. Leonard's remarks. I was a total stranger to Ware and Ware people, and consequently could neither talk nor listen to much purpose.

But I was interested in observing Miss Munson. She was a nice person to observe, for if she was conscious of being an object of scrutiny, she did not show it. Her eyes never flashed up and met mine fixed upon her, with a suddenness startling and embarrassing to both of us. I could stare at her as guilelessly and properly as I could at a flower.

Indeed, Miss Munson did make me think of a flower, and of one prevalent in her front yard, too—a lilac : there was that same dull bloom about her, and a shy, antiquated grace. A lilac always does seem a little older than some other flowers. Miss Munson, I could now see, was probably nearer fifty than forty. There were little lines and shadows in her face that one could not discern across the street. It seemed to me that she must have been very lovely in her youth, with that sort of loveliness which does not demand attention, but holds it with no effort. An exquisite, delicate young creature, she ought to have been, and had been, unless her present appearance told lies.

Lilac seemed to be her favorite color for gowns, for she wore that afternoon a delicious old-fashioned lilac muslin that looked as if it had been laid away in lavender every winter for the last thirty years. The waist was cut surplice fashion, and she wore a dainty lace handkerchief tucked into it. Take it altogether, I suppose I never spent a pleasanter afternoon in my life, although it was pleasant in a quiet, uneventful sort of a way. There was an atmosphere of gentle grace and comfort about everything: about Miss Munson, about the room, and about the lookout from the high, deep-seated windows. There was not one vivid tint in that parlor ; everything had the dimness of age over it. All the brightness was gone out of the carpet. Large, shadowy figures sprawled over the floor, their indistinctness giving them the suggestion of grace, and the polish on the mahogany furniture was too dull to reflect the light. The gilded scrolls on the wall-paper no longer shone, and over some of the old engravings on the walls a half-transparent film that looked like mist had spread. Outside, a cool green shadow lay over the garden, and soft, lazy puffs of lilac-scented air came in at the windows. Oh, it was all lovely, and it was so little trouble to enjoy it.

I liked, too, the tea which came later. The dining-room was as charming in its way as the parlor, large and dark and solid, with some beautiful quaint pieces of furniture in it. The china was pink and gold ; and I fancied to myself that Miss Munson's grandmother had spun the table-linen, and put it away in a big chest, with rose leaves between the folds. I do believe the surroundings and the circumstances imparted a subtle flavor to everything I tasted, which gave rise to something higher than mere gustatory delight, or maybe it was my mood ; but it certainly seemed to me that I had never before enjoyed a tea so much.

After that day, Miss Munson and I became very well acquainted. I got into the habit of running over there very often ; she seldom came to see me. It was tacitly understood between us that it was pleasanter for me to do the visiting.

I do not know how she felt towards me—I think she liked me—but I began to feel an exceeding, even a loving, interest in her. All that I could think of sometimes, when with her, was a person walking in a garden and getting continually delicious little sniffs of violets, so that he certainly knew they were near him, although they were hidden somewhere under the leaves, and he could not see them. There would not be a day that Miss Munson would not say things that were so many little hints of a rare sweetness and beauty of nature, which her shyness and quietness did not let appear all at once.

She was rather chary always of giving very broad glimpses of herself. I was always more or less puzzled and evaded by her, though she was evidently a sincere, childlike woman, with a liking for simple pleasures. She took genuine delight in picking a little bunch of flowers in her garden for a neighbor, and in giving those little tea-parties. She was religious in an innocent, unquestioning way, too. I oftener than not found an open Bible near her when I came in, and she talked about praying as simply as one would about breathing.

But the day before I left Ware she told me a very peculiar story, by which she displayed herself to me all at once in a fuller light, although she revealed such a character that I was, in one way, none the less puzzled. She and I were sitting in her parlor. She was feeling sad about my going, and perhaps that led her to confide in me. Anyway, she looked up, suddenly, after a little silence.

" Do you," she said, " believe in dreams ?"

"That is a question I can't answer truthfully," I replied, laughing. " I don't really know whether I believe in dreams or not."

"I don't know either," she said, slowly, and she shuddered a little. " I have a mind to tell you," she went on, " about a dream I had once, and about something that happened to me afterwards. I never did tell any one, and I believe I would like to. That is, if you would like to have me," she asked, as timidly as a child afraid of giving trouble.

I assured her that I would, and, after a little pause, she told me this:

"I was about twenty-two," she said, "and father and mother had been dead, one four, the other six years. I was living alone here with Margaret, as I have ever since. I have thought sometimes that it was my living alone so much, and not going about with other girls more, that made me dream as much as I did, but I don't know. I used always to have a great many dreams, and some of them seemed as if they must mean something; but this particular one, in itself and in its effect on my after-life, was very singular.

"It was in spring, and the lilacs were just in bloom, when I dreamed it. I thought I was walking down the road there under the elm-trees. I had on a lilac muslin gown, and I carried a basket of flowers on my arm. They were mostly white, or else the very faintest pink—lilies and roses. I had gone down the street a little way, when I saw a young man coming towards me. He had on a broad-brimmed soft hat and a velvet coat, and carried something that looked odd under his arm. When he came nearer I could see that he had a handsome dark face, and that he was carrying an artist's easel. When he reached me he stopped and looked down into my face and then at my basket of flowers. I stopped too—I could not seem to help it in my dream—and gazed down at the ground. I was afraid to look at him, and I trembled so that the lilies and roses in my basket quivered.

Finally he spoke. 'Won't you give me one of your flowers,' he said—'just one?'

"I gathered courage to glance up at him then, and when his eyes met mine it did seem to me that I wanted to give him one of those flowers more than anything else in the world. I looked into my basket, and had my fingers on the stem of the finest lily there, when something came whirring and fanning by my face and settled on my shoulder, and when I turned my head, with my heart beating loud, there was a white dove.

" But, somehow, I seemed in my dream to forget all about the dove in a minute, and I looked away in the young man's face again, and lifted the lily from the basket as I did so.

" But his face did not look to me as it did before, though I still wanted to give him the lily just as much. I stood still, gazing at him, for a moment ; there was, in my dream, a sort of fascination over me which would not let me take my eyes from him. As I gazed, his face changed more and more to me, till finally—I cannot explain it—it looked at once beautiful and repulsive. I wanted at once to give him the lily and would have died rather than give it to him, and I turned and fled, with my basket of flowers and my dove on my shoulder, and a great horror of something, I did not know what, in my heart. Then I woke up all of a tremble."

Miss Munson stopped. "What do you think of the dream ?" she said, in a few minutes. "Do you think it possible that it could have had any especial significance, or should you think it merely a sleeping vagary of a romantic, imaginative girl ?"

" I think that would depend entirely upon after-events," I answered ; "they might or might not prove its significance."

"Do you think so ?" she said, eagerly. "Well, it seemed to me that they did, but the worst of it has been I have never been quite sure—never quite sure. But I will tell you, and you shall judge. A year from the time I dreamed that dream, I actually met that same young man one morning in the street. I had on my lilac gown, and I held a sprig of

4

lilac in my hand ; I had broken it off the bush as I came
along. He almost stopped for a second when he came up
to me, and looked down into my face. I was terribly
startled, for I recognized at once the man of my dream, and
I can't tell you how horrible and uncanny it all seemed for
a minute. There was the same handsome dark face ; there
were the broad hat, and the velvet coat, and the easel under the arm. Well, he passed on, and I did ; but I was in
a flutter all day, and his eyes seemed to be looking into
mine continually.

"A few days afterwards he called upon me with Mrs.
Graves, a lady who used to live in Ware and take boarders :
she moved away some years ago. I learned that he was
an artist. His name was—no, I will not tell you his name :
he is from your city, and well known. He had engaged
board with Mrs. Graves for the summer. After that there
was scarcely a day but I saw him. We were both entirely
free to seek each other's society, and we were together a
great deal. He used to take me sketching with him, and
he would come here at all hours of the day as unconcernedly as a brother might. He would sit beside me in
the parlor and watch me sew, and in the kitchen and watch
me cook. He was very boyish and unconventional in his
ways, and I used to think it charming. We soon grew to
care a great deal about each other, of course, although he
said nothing about it to me for a long time. I knew from
the first that I loved him dearly, but from the first there
was, as there was in my dream, a kind of horror of him
along with the love: it kept me from being entirely happy.
The night before he went away he spoke. We had been
to walk, and were standing here at my door. He asked
me to marry him. I looked up in his face, and felt just as

I did in my dream about giving him the flower, when all of
a sudden his face looked different to me, just as it did in
the dream. I cannot explain it. It was as if I saw no
more of the kindness and the love in it, only something else
—evil—and the same horror came over me.

"I don't know how I looked to him as I stood gazing
up at him, but he turned very pale, and started back. 'My
God! Caroline,' he said, 'what is it?'

"I don't know what I said, but it must have expressed
my sudden repulsion very strongly; for, after a few bitter
words, he left me, and I went into the house. I never saw
him again. I have seen his name in the papers, and that
is all.

"Now I want to know," Miss Munson went on, "if you
think that my dream was really sent to me as a warning,
or that I fancied it all, and wrecked — no, I won't say
wrecked—dulled the happiness of my whole life for a nervous whim?"

She looked questioningly at me, an expression at once
serious and pitiful on her delicate face. I hardly knew
what to say. It was obvious that I could form no correct
opinion unless I knew the man. I wondered if I did.
There was an artist of about the right age whom I thought
of. If he were the one—well, I think Miss Munson was right.

She saw that I hesitated. "Never mind," she said, rising
with her usual quiet, gentle smile on her lips, "you don't
know any more than I do, and I never shall know in this
world. All I hope is that it was what God meant, and not
what I imagined. We won't talk any more about it. I
have liked to tell you, for some reason or other, that is all.
Now I am going to take you into the garden and pick your
last posy for you."

After I had gone down the stone steps with my hands full of verbenas and pansies, I turned and looked up at her standing so mild and sweet between the lilac-trees, and said good-bye again. That was the last time I saw her.

The next summer when I came to Ware the blinds on the front of the Munson house were all closed, and the little flower-beds in the front yard were untended; only the lilacs were in blossom, for they had the immortal spring for their gardener.

"Miss Munson died last winter," said Mrs. Leonard, looking reflectively across the street. "She was laid out in a lilac-colored cashmere gown; it was her request. She always wore lilac, you know. Well" (with a sigh), "I do believe that Caroline Munson, if she is an angel—and I suppose she is—doesn't look much more different from what she did before than those lilacs over there do from last year's ones."

A TARDY THANKSGIVING.

"I s'POSE you air goin' down to Hannah's to spend Thanksgivin', Mis' Muzzy?"

The old lady who asked the question was seated in Mrs. Muzzy's best hair-cloth rocking-chair, which had been brought out of the parlor for the occasion. She had a mild, tiny-featured old face, wore a false front of auburn hair, and a black lace cap decorated with purple ribbons, and was knitting—putting new heels into some blue yarn stockings.

The answer she got to her question, delivered in her prim, purring, company tone, made her jump nervously.

"No; I ain't goin' a step—not if I know what I'm about."

The words shot out of Mrs. Muzzy's mouth as if each one had had a charge of powder in its rear, and the speaker went on jerking the stout thread viciously through the seam she was sewing.

She was a squarely built woman, compactly fleshy. There was a bright red color on each of her firm, round cheeks; there was not a vague line in her whole face; her mouth opened and shut unhesitatingly and fairly; and she looked out of her small brown eyes directly, with no circumlocution.

"Mebbe you air goin' up to your brother Andrew's then?" ventured the old lady, feebly.

" No, Mis' Field, I ain't a-goin' to Andrew's nuther.   I ain't a-goin' nowheres."

" But," purred the old lady, " ain't you afeard you'll be awful lonesome ?   Lor', I don't know what I should do ef it warn't for Serrah an' her childern on a Thanksgivin'-day. To be sure, you ain't got any childern an' grandchildern to go to, but thar's your sister Hannah an' hers, an' Andrew an' his, an' it kinder seems as if brothers and sisters come next."

" Thar ain't no use talkin'," said Mrs. Muzzy, in a loud, clear-cut voice.   " I ain't a-goin' to Hannah's to Thanks-givin', an' I ain't a-goin' to Andrew's to Thanksgivin', an' I ain't agoin' to hev any Thanksgivin' to hum.   I ain't got nothin' to give thanks fur, as I see on.   I s'pose ef I could go to meetin' Thanksgivin' mornin', an' hear the sermon, an' then set down to turkey and plum-puddin',' an' be a-thankin' the Lord in my heart for lettin' my husband fall off the scaffold in the barn an' git killed last summer, an' for lettin' my daughter Charlotte die of a quick consump-tion last spring, an' my son John two year ago this fall, I might keep Thanksgivin' as well as other folks.   But I can't, an' I ain't a-goin' to purtend I do.   Thar's one thing about it—I ain't a hypocrite, an' never was."

" What air you a-goin' to do, Mis' Muzzy ?"

" Do !" Mrs. Muzzy sniffed.   " Do ! I'm a-goin to stay to hum, an'—do my pig-work."

The old lady's small-featured countenance, from its very mechanism, was incapable of expressing any very strong emotion, but it took on now a look of gentle horror.   She dropped her knitting-work, and her dim blue eyes seemed to take up the whole of her spectacles.

" Lor' sakes, Mis' Muzzy !   Pig-work on Thanksgivin'-day !   I never heerd anything like it !"

"I don't keer. The pig-work has got to be done, an' I might jest as well do it Thanksgivin'-day as any other. I feel enough sight more like it than eating turkey an' plum-puddin', with all I've been through."

"Ain't you a-goin' to meetin'?"

"No."

"Lor' sakes!"

The old lady fell to knitting again in a mild daze. Mrs. Muzzy would have been too much for her in her best days; now she almost reduced her to lunacy. Still, this old lady, who was a neighbor, living about a quarter of a mile distant, felt for her the attraction which weak natures often feel for the strong. She was very fond of dropping in of an afternoon with her knitting-work. There was not so much difference in their ages as one might think at first, either, although Mrs. Muzzy was so much younger-looking. Her daughter, who had died the spring before, had been a schoolmate of Mrs. Field's Sarah.

The old lady often accepted the invitation to stay and take a cup of tea, but to-day she shortened her call a little. The "pig-work" on Thanksgiving-day rankled in her mind, and she wanted to go home and tell her daughter Sarah.

After she had gone, Mrs. Muzzy went from the warm sitting-room into her cold, exquisitely neat kitchen, and kindled a fire in the cooking-stove, and made herself a cup of tea. Though she was living alone, every meal was prepared and eaten with religious exactitude. She spread a white cloth over the table, put on some slices of bread, a little dish of quince sauce, and some custard-pie. Then she sat down with a sort of defiant appetite.

She had finished her bread and sauce, and begun on her

pie, when the kitchen-door, which led directly out-doors, opened, and a girl of twenty or so walked in.

"How d'ye do, Lizzie?" said Mrs. Muzzy.

"Pretty well, Aunt Jane," replied the girl, listlessly, and she sank down in the nearest chair.

She was a tall, slender girl, with dun-colored hair. She had delicate features, and would have been pretty if it had not been for a pitiful droop at the corners of her mouth, the dullness of her eyes, and the dark rings under them.

"Hev some custard-pie?"

"No, thank you; I am not hungry."

"Hev you eat any supper?"

"I don't know—yes, I think so—some bread and butter."

"I saw young Allen go by here 'bout three o'clock, ridin' with that Hammond girl," remarked Mrs. Muzzy, eying her niece sharply.

She only looked at her aunt in the same way she had done before, with an expression of misery too helpless and settled to be augmented.

"Yes," she replied; "I saw them."

"She's a pretty-looking gal. Her cheeks air as red as roses, an' she had on a handsome bunnit."

"Yes."

"It's quite a long time since he's been to see you."

"Yes."

Never was such complete unresistance to a tormentor, if tormentor she meant to be.

"Well, I wouldn't mind anyhow, ef I was you," said Mrs. Muzzy, looking at the girl's weary face, and changing her tone a little. "Let him go ef he wants to. Jest show him you don't keer."

The girl woke up a little at that. "Show him I don't

care!" she cried, passionately. "He knows I care. It would be a disgrace to me if I didn't care, after I've been going with him for three years, and he leaving me for a new face. It's no use pretending I don't. I don't see why folks tell me to. My heart ought to be broken, and it is."

"I'd hev more sperrit."

"Would you? Well, I'm made different, I suppose," said the girl; and her face took on its listless expression again.

Her aunt finished her second cup of tea, and began to clear away the table.

"Are you coming over to our house Thanksgiving, or Uncle Andrews?" asked Lizzie, after a little, with some faint appearance of interest.

"I ain't a-goin' nowheres; I'm a-goin' to stay to hum an' do my pig-work."

"Pig-work?"

"Yes; I'm a-goin' to hev 'em killed Tuesday."

Her surprise made Lizzie for a minute look like another girl. "But, Aunt Jane, why? I never heard of such a thing! Pig-work on Thanksgiving-day!"

Mrs. Muzzy braced herself up defiantly. "Look a-here, Lizzie Munroe," quoth she; "you think you're down as fur as anybody kin be, because you've lost your beau. Well, I've lost my husband, that I'd lived with forty year, an' that was more than any beau, an' I've lost my daughter, both of 'em this year, an' two year ago this fall my son John, an' I don't see as I've got anything to be thankful for. I ain't a-goin' to keep Thanksgivin'-day, an' eat turkey an' plum-puddin'. I feel enough sight more like doin' pig-work, an' I'm a-goin' to."

The girl's dull eyes seemed to catch a gleam from her aunt's. For a minute she looked strangely like her. Mrs.

Muzzy's passionate, defiant nature fired her niece's more unresisting, hopeless one.

"Well, Aunt Jane," she said, in a tone like an echo of her aunt's, "I don't wonder you feel so. And—I don't care about eating turkey and plum-pudding either — I'll come over and help you."

Mrs. Muzzy looked startled for a minute. Perhaps her own spirit reflected in another looked differently to her.

"Well, Lizzie, jest as you like," she said then. "I'll be glad of your help; it's consider'ble to do pig-work all alone, an' I've never been used to it"—with a sigh.

"Well, I'll come, Aunt Jane."

There was a long silence; then the girl took her sad face out of the door, and her aunt, having set away the last of her tea things, went back into her warm sitting-room; the kitchen fire was going out, and it was growing cold.

Thanksgiving morning, a week later, was gray and cloudy, and the air felt like snow. Mrs. Muzzy's kitchen was full of steaming, glowing heat. She had two immense iron kettles on her stove, and was busily cutting pork into small square bits to try out.

Lizzie was there helping, too. She had come over early. Her sad young face looked sadder this morning. The cold, gray light brought out all the pitiful, drooping lines more plainly. She had probably been weeping instead of sleeping the night before. Her dun-colored hair was put back plainly and neatly; grief did not with her manifest itself in untidiness, though she never crimped her hair now. Lizzie looked like another girl with her hair crimped. Her dark print fitted over her slender shoulders trimly, and she wore a little white ruffle in the neck. She was cutting pork too; her wrists, though small, were muscular, and she worked steadily and effectively, though with a pathetic indifference. Mrs. Muzzy's firmly set face betrayed little of it, but she really eyed her niece from time to time with furtive uneasiness.

She had an inner consciousness, ever present to herself, that her state of mind was highly culpable, but she undertook the responsibility for herself with sullen defiance. It was another thing, however, to be responsible for a similar state in another. Lizzie, standing there, with her dull, hopeless face, indefatigably cutting pork, seemed to her like the visible fruit of her own rebellious nature.

"Hev you seen Jenny Bostwick lately !" asked she, with a desperate determination to alter her niece's expression.

"No," replied Lizzie, slowly. "Joe hasn't left her. They're always together. I can't bear to go there."

"I know," said Mrs. Muzzy, with quick, sympathetic recognition of the feeling. "I felt that way after John died. I couldn't bear to go into Mis' Mann's, because there was her Edward — she'd had him spared, an' my boy'd been taken."

There was something startling in the frankness, almost shamelessness, of the girl's avowal of envious misery, and her aunt's instantaneous sympathy with it. It was as if their two natures were growing more and more into an evil accord.

About ten o'clock the front-door bell rang. "You go to the door, Lizzie," said Mrs. Muzzy ; "you look better'n I."

Lizzie took off her apron, and went obediently. Time was when the tinkle of a door-bell could make her tremble all over, but she was calm enough now. It was six months since George Allen had been to see her, and she had given up all hope of his ever coming again.

Mrs. Muzzy heard the doors open and shut, then a mur-mur of voices in the sitting-room. One of the voices was unquestionably a man's, low-pitched and earnest. Lizzie's seemed to break into sobs now and then, and once she laughed. Mrs. Muzzy started when she heard that; she had almost forgotten how Lizzie's laugh sounded.

"Who on earth has Lizzie got in there?" she muttered to herself; but she was a woman who could keep her curi-osity in check. She went steadily on with her work till the sitting-room door opened and Lizzie came out.

But was it Lizzie?—the girl with those pink cheeks and radiant eyes, and that dimpling mouth? Mrs. Muzzy laid her knife down and stared at her.

"It's George! George!" said Lizzie, in a happy, trem-bling whisper that seemed almost ready to break out into a scream of joy. "He's come to—to take me up to his house to dinner. I'm going home to change my dress and get ready." She was trembling so she could hardly move, but she began pinning on her shawl in joyful haste.

"Lizzie Munroe," said her aunt, sternly, "you don't mean to say you're goin' on with that fellow after all that's happened?"

"Yes, I am; he's come for me." Great tears of pure delight rolled down her cheeks. She had her hood on now, and turned impatiently towards the sitting-room door.

"Come for you! I s'pose ef he'd got married to that Hammond girl an' come for you, you'd gone jest the same!" cried her aunt, with coarse sarcasm.

"Yes, I would!" cried Lizzie, recklessly, her hand on the door-knob.

"I don't b'lieve but what that Hammond girl's given him the mitten, else he wouldn't 'a come. I wouldn't play second fiddle for any feller."

"I would for *him!*" cried Lizzie, as shameless in her happiness as she had been in her misery. She opened the door a crack and peeped in ; then she turned to her aunt, her eyes like stars, her cheeks fairly ablaze.

"Good-bye, Aunt Jane," she said. "I'm sorry to leave you alone with the pig-work. You'd better change your mind an' go over to mother's to dinner."

Mrs. Muzzy vouchsafed no reply, and Lizzie went into the sitting-room and shut the door.

Pretty soon her aunt watched her and her truant sweetheart walking down the street. Lizzie was actually hanging on to his arm, in broad daylight.

"I don't see where she took such a disposition," muttered Mrs. Muzzy. "Not from my side. I'd never have made such a fool of myself over a feller."

Then she went on with her pig-work, righteous indignation and scorn against Lizzie mingling in her bosom with rebellion against the will of the Lord.

It had always been her boast that she wasn't one of the kind of women who are forever dropping things, and getting burned and scalded, and cutting their fingers. She thought there was no kind of need of it, if anybody had her wits about her, and didn't fly about like a hen with her head cut off.

She was to prove, however, to-day that her boasting, for one occasion at least, was vain.

She had lifted the first kettle of boiling lard off the stove in safety, and deposited it in the sink. The second—how she did it she never knew, whether the sudden weakening of a muscle or the slipping of a finger occasioned it—she dropped bodily as she was lifting it from the fire.

None of the hot fat went on the stove, or there would

have been a worse complication of disasters. It landed on the floor and Mrs. Muzzy's right foot. She lost none of her resolute coolness, with the sudden shock and agony. The kettle was scorching the floor; you could smell the burning paint. She lifted it on to the stove hearth, and cast a distrustful and indignant glance at the molten grease spreading over the floor.

Then she had luckily a pair of scissors within reach. She sat down and cut off, with convulsive shivers of pain, but grim determination, her shoe and stocking. The foot was shockingly burned. She set her lips hard when she saw it.

"A half-winter's job," said she. "Well!"

She dragged herself in her chair with one foot, hitching herself along, into the buttery, to the flour barrel. She powdered the wounded foot thickly with flour, and hitched back.

"There," said she, "that's all I can do. There ought to be oil and bandages and things; but I've got to set still. I wish somebody would come."

Then she sat there in silent endurance, in the midst of the grease, which had cooled, and formed a white coating over the kitchen floor. Her foot was a mass of torture. She did not have long to wait for help, however; she had not been sitting there half an hour when she heard quick steps on the frozen ground outside.

"Open the door, Jane," called the voice of her sister Hannah, Lizzie's mother. "I've got my hands full."

"I can't," responded Mrs. Muzzy, "you'll hev to do it yourself."

The door opened after a second. The caller, who had a large plate in each hand, stopped short in utter dismay as she took in the aspect of things—her sister, with her floury foot and pale face, and the lard on the floor.

"Why, what hev you done, Jane?" she cried.

Mrs. Muzzy looked up, and actually smiled, the first time her sister had seen her for many a day. "What hev you got thar, Hannah?" asked she.

"Why, I brought you over some Thanksgivin' dinner; but I guess you won't feel like eatin' any now."

"Yes, I do. Bring it here."

"But you want somethin' done more for your foot. Did you tip the hot lard right on to it? Don't it ache? Hadn't you better wait an' eat your dinner after the foot's been seen to?"

"No, Hannah; I want it now. I want to eat some turkey an' plum-puddin' afore I'm an hour older, an' keep Thanksgivin'. I said I wouldn't, but the Lord got ahead of me, an' I'm glad he has. Bring it here an' I'll eat my dinner, an' then, mebbe, I kin hev somethin' more done for my foot."

Her sister gave in then, and Mrs. Muzzy, her forehead wrinkled with pain, sat there and ate her Thanksgiving dinner to the very last mouthful.

"Lizzie's feelin' happier," she remarked once.

"Yes; George came to take her to his folks' to dinner."

"Well, I'm glad of it, ef she's goin' to feel any better."

"You would be, ef you was her mother," said her sister, simply.

A MODERN DRAGON.

It was a hot Sunday in June. The bell was ringing for the morning service in the Dover orthodox church, and the people were flocking up the hill on which the sacred edifice stood. The farmers' wives and daughters wore their thinnest dresses, and were armed with stout fans and sun-umbrellas; the men looked wretched and steaming in their Sunday coats. The sun beat fiercely down on Dover village, on its white houses and clover fields. The bees and insects were droning so loud that people could hear them inside the church. In there it was cooler, though still warm enough: everybody was fanning.

The bell tolled, and the people kept coming up the aisles. David Ayres, in his place in the second row of the singing seats, watched them soberly. He was a tall, stoutly built young man; his face was brown and heavy-featured, but handsome. He had a fine bass voice.

A titter and whisper spread through the row of female singers before him. "Look at Almira King!" The flower-wreathed bonnets shook with mirth.

"What are the girls laughing at?" thought David Ayres.

A girl was tripping up the aisle below, dressed in a pink silk gown, bewilderingly draped and pleated. She wore a little white crape bonnet with a knot of crushed roses.

The young man thought she looked beautiful, and saw nothing laughable about it. All he wondered at was how the Kings could afford such a fine dress, and how the girl happened to come to church anyway. He had never seen her there before.

The girl entered a pew well towards the front, and settled down, like a bird, with a pretty flutter. All David could see of her between the people were her shapely pink shoulders and knot of yellow hair below the little bonnet. When the choir sang the first hymn, however, all the congregation rose and turned about to face the singing seats, and he took a good look at her as he rolled out his sonorous bass notes. She had a charming, round, childish face, simple and sweet. She was looking down at her pretty gown with an innocent simper. She pulled the drapery in the back a little ; then she glanced over her shoulder to see if it was right ; then she smoothed the front of the overskirt tenderly. " She's mighty tickled with her new dress," reflected David Ayres, sagely ; but he felt none of the sharp-eyed female singers' contempt at the girl's silly vanity.

All at once Almira looked up and met the young man's eyes fixed full upon her. Her eyelids dropped, and she crimsoned to the lace round her white throat. He could see, even at that distance, that she was confused and disturbed. " I won't look at her again, if it makes her act that way," resolved he ; and forthwith fixed his eyes on his book as he sung.

After the service was over he went down to the vestry to Sunday-school. He had a class. The session occupied about an hour. Coming out, he fell in with his cousin Ida Babcock.

" Ida," said he, abruptly, " I wish you'd tell me why
5

folks were laughing when Almira King came in this morning. I didn't see anything to laugh at. Did you?"

"Why, David Ayres, that dress was perfectly ridiculous for a girl to wear to meeting. Don't you know it was? I don't wonder folks laughed."

"I do," quoth David, stoutly. "I think the dress was all right. She looked like a doll in it, anyway. I guess you girls were jealous."

Ida colored up. She was a plain girl herself. "I guess we weren't jealous," returned she, with spirit. "You men will overlook anything for a pretty face, and that's all there is about it. Every blessed thing that girl came to meeting for this morning was to show her dress."

"I don't see," said her cousin, with slow emphasis, "what does make you girls forever pick on each other. I should think, when you saw one of your own kind look as pretty and sweet as Almira King did this morning, you'd feel proud of her in one way, and say the nicest things about her that you could."

"Well, the dress was all out of place, and I don't think that's very bad to say," said Ida, trying to keep her temper. "But it's no use arguing with you about it, David: men don't look at such things like women."

"I don't think they do," replied David.

When Ida got home she told her mother that she didn't know whether David was luny or meant to be aggravating.

"I suppose I made Ida mad," reflected David, as he sped along the dusty road in his open buggy, keeping a tight rein on his smart horse; "but I don't care. If there's anything I hate, it's one girl picking on another. Ida ought to be broken of it."

The Ayres farm was situated about a mile and a half out of Dover village. About half a mile out David passed the King place. The house was poor—a low red cottage—but there were some fertile fields about it. The King farm was small, but, as far as it went, productive.

David, as he whirled by, caught a glimpse of a woman coming round the corner of the house from the garden with a pan in her hand full of beans. She was an odd figure, short and stout, with a masculine width of shoulders. Her calico dress cleared her thick ankles, her black hair was cut short, and she wore a man's straw hat.

" Pity such a pretty girl as Almira King has got such a mother !" David thought, after his swift glance at her.

When he got home he found dinner all ready. Everything was on time in the Ayres household. David's mother sat by the sitting-room window, fanning herself and reading her Bible, while she waited for her son. She was a fair, stout woman, in an old-fashioned muslin gown. The ground was white, with a brown vine straggling thickly over it. She looked up pleasantly as David entered, after putting up his horse : he was his own hostler. There were soft curves in her face, which were deceptive. Mrs. Ayres was not just such a woman as her looks denoted. Strangers generally found themselves taken aback by her, after a little. She was a very devout woman, but she had not been to church to-day : she had been afraid to undertake the ride in the hot sun. Her health was not very good.

They had dinner directly in the large room, running the width of the house, which served as dining-room and kitchen in the winter, and dining-room alone in the summer; there was an unfinished back room, into which the cooking-stove was then moved. The Ayres farmhouse was extremely substantial and comfortable, but the old-time notions of David's ancestors were still prevalent in it.

The hired girl sat down to the table with David and his mother. She was about forty, as plump as Mrs. Ayres, though not as fair. There was a cast in her eyes. She had lived in the Ayres family ever since David was born. She had the reputation of being none too strong-minded, but that had never been any objection to her in Mrs. Ayres's opinion. If anything, she enjoyed the prestige which her own superior intellect gave her, cheap triumph though it was ; and Susan Means had always been faithful, reliable help.

There was cold meat for dinner. Mrs. Ayres was conscientious about any unnecessary cooking on the Sabbath.

"Who was at church, David," asked his mother, watching him carve.

"Oh, the folks who usually go ; except—well, that King girl was there. I never saw her in church before."

"You don't say so ! I wonder how her mother happened to let her, she's such a strong spiritualist. Well, the girl can't amount to much, with that kind of bringing up, poor thing."

"She looked real pretty, mother ; and she was dressed pretty too."

"What did she have on ?"

"Something pink—silk, I guess."

"Pink silk ! I never—"

Mrs. Ayres went on with the subject, finding it interesting ; but David soon contrived to change it. For some reason he did not feel as hot to take up the cudgels for Almira with his mother as he had with his cousin Ida.

After dinner he went up-stairs. Instead of entering his

own room, he stole stealthily into the large front chamber over the parlor. It was not occupied. The best bedstead and feather-bed were in there, and the best bureau. The windows were open, and a cool green light came in through the blinds. He sat down by one of them, and fell into a young man's day-dream, with him as shy and innocent as a girl's. "I suppose," said he to himself, "if I ever—get married, we could have this chamber fitted up, and—some new furniture in it. Almira King did look pretty to-day."

He had seen her dozens of times before, and admired her, but not as he had to-day. It seemed a pity that such a foolish thing as a pink silk dress should swerve such a mighty thing as a human heart. But feathers might fly along to paradise, if the wind happened to be that way, and point out its direction, to things more important.

As for the girl herself, it was perfectly true that she had been to church merely to show herself in her new dress. The dress had to be worn and shown, else what was the good of having it at all, and the church was the only available place in which to display it at present.

When Almira returned that morning her mother was out in the garden picking vegetables for dinner. She followed her there. "Mother," she called, "I've got home!"

The woman looked up and saw the rosy creature standing there with the most intense and unselfish pleasure. "Well," said she, smiling till she looked foolish, she was so pleased, "what did the folks say to you, Almiry?"

"They didn't say anything, mother; but—they stared, I can tell you."

"I'll warrant they did! Now, deary, you'd better not stand there so close to the beans, or you'll get somethin' on your dress.   You'd better go in an' change it, an' git rested, while I git dinner."

"David Ayres sits up in the singing seats, and—you'd ought to have seen him look at me, mother, once."

"I'll warrant he did."

The mother stared fondly after the girl as she went off across the green field.   "I wish David Ayres would take a shine to Almiry," said she.   "He's a good, stiddy young man, an' there ain't anybody but him an' his mother an' Caleb, now Mr. Ayres is gone, an' there's a good deal of money there.   Almiry would be well purvided for.   P'r'aps he will."

When Almira came into the house she went straight to her own room.   It was a bedroom opening out of the parlor.   Both rooms had been fitted up for her with a daintiness strange to the rest of the house.   Her sleeping-room had a pretty set in it, and a lace curtain at the window; the parlor a real Brussels carpet and stuffed chairs.   Mrs. King had worked hard for it, but she was amply paid by the feeling that her "Almiry had as pretty a room to set in as any girl in Dover."

The glass on Almira's bureau would not tip far enough for her to see her whole figure, so she stood on a chair before it, and turned round and round admiring herself.   She was radiant with the simplest and most unconcealed vanity.   "I do look so beautiful!" she said, quite out loud.   The memory of David Ayres's admiring gaze underlaid her delight in herself, and strengthened it.   Presently she changed the beloved dress reluctantly for a blue muslin which was trimmed with lace, and pretty too.   She had a good many dainty appointments.   Everything about her, to the embroidery on her under-clothing, was nice, through her homely mother's care. She lay down on the lounge in her parlor then, with a paper of sugar-plums and a child's paper. She dearly loved little pretty, simple tales and sugar-plums. She heard her mother in the kitchen moving about, getting dinner, but she never thought of such a thing as helping her. Still, she was not selfish. She had only been brought up in unconsciousness of her own obligations, and she had not keenness of wit to see them for herself.

Once in a while she stopped reading, and thought about David Ayres. She wondered, should she go to evening meeting, whether he would ever wait on her home. Pretty as Almira was, no Dover young man had ever paid her the slightest attention, beyond admiring looks. They were kept aloof by the peculiarities of her mother. "I've a great mind to go to meeting to-night," reflected Almira. "I can't wear my pink silk in the evening, but I've a good mind to go."

Two weeks from that day there was a disturbance on her account in the Ayres household.

It was a little cooler than Sunday, and Mrs. Ayres had been to church—to morning and afternoon service too—and she had spent the nooning at her married son's, Caleb, who lived in the village. David had driven home. He had some things to see to, and Susan got his dinner for him.

When the mother and son rode home together finally, after the second service was through, he knew by certain infallible signs in her face that something was wrong, and he felt guiltily what it was. She said nothing about it till they reached home : then, when he had put his horse up, and she had changed her best black silk, the reckoning came.

He started off for a stroll across the pasture ; but she had kept her eyes on him, and called him back, thrusting her head out of the sitting-room window. "Come here, David," said she ; " I want to speak to you."

He tried to have the talk standing outside the window, but she made him come in. So he stood leaning against the sitting-room door, fingering the latch impatiently, while she sat facing him in her big rocking-chair by the window.

" David," she began, " I heard something about you over to Caleb's to-day, and I want to know if it's true. I heard you were going with that King girl ; that you've been waiting on her home from meeting, and taking her to ride, and that that's where you were so late last Sunday night, when I thought you were over to Caleb's. I want to know if it's true."

The stout young fellow had been brought up with a dread of his fair-faced, firm-handed mother ; he looked boyish and blushing. Then his manhood asserted itself, as it should now, if ever. "Yes, mother," he replied, his sober eyes fixed on her ; "it's true."

" You don't say you mean to marry that King girl, David Ayres ?"

" I think I shall, mother—if she'll have me."

" There ain't any doubt of that, I guess. David, if you marry that girl, with her Spiritualist mother, you'll kill me."

" Oh, mother, don't !"

" I mean what I say, David. You'll kill me. You'll have to choose between your mother and that girl."

The hard jaws seemed to show through Mrs. Ayres's soft cheeks. A blue tinge appeared round her mouth and nostrils. There was an ever-present dread in the Ayres family. Healthy as Mrs. Ayres looked, she had an organic heart trouble, and doctors had said a good deal about the danger of over-excitement.

David looked at her changing face in alarm. "Don't let's talk about it any more now, mother," said he, soothingly. "Don't you worry over it."

But she was not to be put off. She realized the ghastly vantage-ground on which she stood, and she was the kind of woman to make the most of it.

"David, you won't marry that girl?"

"I'll tell you whether I will or not in a week, mother, and that's the best I can do." He looked astonishingly like his mother as he said it. His face had the same determination, almost obstinacy, of hers.

She eyed him sharply, and gave in. "Well," said she.

All that week she hardly seemed like the same woman to him. She petted and caressed him as she had never done before. She descended to womanish wiles to accomplish her ends, for the first time in her life. But, if she had known it, all this had no effect whatever on her son. He had too much shrewd sense not to see through it, and feel almost an angry contempt for his mother in consequence. Her health and the fear of injuring her were the only things which moved him.

The next Sunday he told her, with inward shame and bitterness, that he would give up the girl. He felt as if he was giving up his manhood at the same time. He had tried arguing with his mother a little, but found it useless. The girl's mother was her ground of objection, and she stood firmly on it, no matter how plainly her unreasonableness was shown to her.

"I'd rather you'd die than marry into such a family, David," she had said once.

So David kept aloof from pretty Almira, and the girl began to fret. She did not conceal her grief from her mother—she was too dependent on her, and she was not that kind of a girl. When she came home from meeting alone she cried on her mother's shoulder, and many a time the two watched hand in hand by the parlor window for the lover who did not come.

Almira had really reason to feel aggrieved. David's courtship, though so short, had been precipitate, after the artless country fashion. Enough had been done to raise her expectations, though there was nothing binding.

As the weeks went by, and she received no attention from David beyond an occasional evasive nod as he drove past, her spirits drooped more and more. She had never had any trouble, and she was bewildered. This was her first lover, and she had not known any better than to begin loving him vehemently.

She tried to attract him back in all the pretty, silent little ways she could think of; she could not take any bold step, she was too modest. She would sit on the door-step, in a pretty dress, with her hair carefully done up, when she thought he might pass by.

She went to church in her pink silk, and glanced timidly and wistfully up at him when the choir was singing; but David would sing sternly on and never look at her.

Then she would go home feeling that there was no use in having a pink silk dress or a pretty face. This poor little rose of a girl, of a Sunday night, after her lover had slighted her still once more, might as well have been a burdock weed or a ragged robin for all the satisfaction she took in being a rose.

She altered in her looks; her simple, smiling face grew

thin and pitiful. Her mother studied it like a chapter in which her own future sorrows were written out.

Mrs. King worked in the field and garden like a man, and many a time she tramped home through the hot sun just to get one look at Almira, then back again. She was an energetic woman. For years before the death of her husband, who had been an invalid a long time, she had managed the little farm herself, and successfully too. She had petted and taken care of her husband, who had been a gentle, slow-motioned man, as she petted and took care of Almira now. He was some ten years younger than she. She had assumed the management of affairs from the first, after he married her, a stout hired girl in a neighboring farmhouse. He had really been incapable himself of carrying on this little farm, which his father had left him.

Every little luxury which she could procure for Almira she always had from her earliest childhood. Now that this trouble had come upon her, she did more ; she relinquished for the time a habit of depositing small sums from her earnings in the savings-bank, at fixed intervals, for future emergencies. She planned many a surprise for Almira in the way of new gowns and trinkets. The girl was young and trifling enough to brighten momentarily at the sight of them, and that was ample payment for her mother. But as soon as she had worn them, and found that David did not notice her any more on their account, the brightness died away. Mrs. King spent money recklessly in those days, such hard-earned money too. " What's the use of my layin' up money," she asked herself, an' Almiry lookin' like that ?"

Finally the mother grew almost desperate. She suffered far more than her daughter ; she watched for David's coming with a stronger anxiety. She began to form wild plans for bettering matters. She even thought of arresting the young man, on his way past the house some day, and freeing her mind to him. She thought of going to see his mother. But, coarse and unwomanly as she was in appearance, there was a good deal of womanly modesty in her; she shrank from those measures, though sometimes, watching David ride by, she felt as if she could kill him.

One day she spied Susan Means, the Ayres' hired woman, walking past, and she called her in. She was just up from the potato-field herself; Almira had gone to the village on an errand.

"Susan," she called, standing in the door, "come in here a minute; I want to see you."

The woman looked wonderingly at a point a foot or more to the left of her with her crooked eyes; then she came up the walk.

"Come in," said Mrs. King. "I want to ask you some-thin'. I want to ask you," she went on, outwardly defiant, when the two stood together in the kitchen, "ef you know what Mis' Ayres's David has been treating my Almiry so fur?"

"I don' know what you mean, as I knows on," replied the other, smiling strangely at the cupboard-door. She was a good-humored soul, but the twist in her eyes gave her an appearance of uncanniness and mystery. Mrs. King, direct and fierce, fired up in unreasonable wrath.

"I guess you know," said she; "everybody knows. I'll warrant you've heerd it talked about enough. I want to know what David Ayres has been foolin' round Almiry King fur, an' gittin' her all upset, an' then leavin' her—that's what I want to know."

It was perfectly true that Susan had known what Mrs.

King meant, but she had been scared, and her little wits had taught her to evade the question. She probably knew much more about the state of affairs than either David or his mother thought. She often imbibed more than her mental capacity was considered equal to. It takes a wise person to gauge another's mind and find the true bottom. She kept on smiling strangely at the cupboard-door.

"I've heerd a little," said she, "ef you want to know."

"I do want to know. I'll let 'em know they can't go foolin' 'round my girl."

"You'll be mad."

"No, I won't be mad. Out with it."

"I don' know as it's anythin' Mis' Ayres has got agin Almiry, but she's kinder sot agin you."

"What's she sot agin me fur?"

"Wa'al, I guess it's on account of your wearin' your dresses half-way up to your knees, and them cowhide shoes, and that hat, and hevin' your hair cut so short. But I guess it's mainly 'cause you air a Spiritualist."

"I don't believe a word of it."

"Accordin' to what I've heerd, it's so."

Mrs. King did not know when the woman went. She stood leaning against the wall, dazed, till Almira came in. "Is it me?" she had muttered once; "an' I willin' to die for her! O Lord!"

Almira stared at her when she entered the kitchen.

"What's the matter, mother?"

"Nothin', deary."

Next Sunday there was a greater sensation in the orthodox church than there had been over Almira in her pink silk. The girl was not there—she was hardly well enough that day—but her mother walked up the aisle when the bell

first began to toll. People stared, doubtful if they knew
her. She had on a decent long black dress and a neat bonnet. Her short hair had given way to a braided knot. She
sat in the pew and listened solemnly to the sermon, regard-
less of the attention she excited. All she took pains to notice was that David Ayres and his mother were there. She
made sure of that, and that they were looking at her.

When she got home, Almira was lying on the lounge in
her room. She had been crying; her eyes were red with
tears. Her mother sat down, and looked at her with wonderful love and hope. "Don't cry, deary," said she. " I
shouldn't wonder a bit if he came to-night. That's been
all the trouble, the girl said, an' now I've fixed that all right.
I let my dress down, an' got the switch, an' I've been to
meetin'. He'll be along to-night."

But he was not. Through the next week Mrs. King toil-
ing in her field, of a necessity still in the short dress and
heavy shoes, had a demeanor like a hunted criminal. She
kept a constant lookout on the road; if she caught a glimpse
of David Ayres coming, she hid. He should never see her
again in the costume which had weaned him from Almira.
If she had been able she would have hired a man for this
work now; but she had spent too much money in other
ways of late. She thought surely the young man would
come on the next Sabbath. But he did not. Then she
ventured on a decisive step, goaded on by Almira's pitiful
face. There really was occasion for alarm on the girl's account. She inherited a weak, spiritless constitution from
her father, and a slight cause might exhaust what little
stamina she possessed. She might drift into nervous inva-
lidism, if she did not die.

Mrs. King tied on her new switch with infinite difficulty,

arrayed herself in her long skirts, and walked a mile and a half to see David Ayres's mother. The interview between the two women was at once pitiful and comical. Mrs. Ayres, her whole soul set against the marriage of her son with this woman's daughter, was immovably hard. She sat like a stone, and listened to the other's rough eloquence. " I've done the best I could," said Mrs. King, humbling herself unshrinkingly. " I know I ain't looked an' dressed jest like other folks ; but now I'm a-doin' different. I've got a switch, an' done up my hair like other women, an' I've let down my dress. I've been to meetin' too, an' I'm goin' right along. I ain't ever been much of a Spiritualist. I got led into it a leetle after Samuel died, an' I've took some papers. But I ain't goin' to any more."

It was all of no use. Mrs. Ayres hardly gave any response at all ; she was almost wordless. All her anxiety was lest David should come in while Almira's mother was there ; but he did not. Finally the poor woman went home. She had gotten no satisfaction at all. She had humbled herself, at the last she had stormed, all to no purpose. Now she was hopeless. She had a rude physical sturdiness about her that had seemed to extend to her inmost nature. But it hardly had. If it had, it was by reason of her unselfish affections. At heart she had always been almost as simple and yielding as Almira herself. She was a thoroughly feminine creature in her masculine attire, with her rough voice. As the days went on, and she saw her daughter fretting, and felt helpless to aid her, her own strength failed slowly, though she did not know it. There had probably been some weak fibre in her, which could not stand a hard strain, in spite of her appearance of strength. She had never been ill in her life ; she felt new sensations now, without realizing what they meant. She was worrying herself to death without knowing it. She worked harder and harder. She had never toiled in her life as she did in the late summer and early autumn of that year, with Almira's sad young face taking all the sweetness out of the labor.

At last she came in one afternoon, and fainted on the threshold. Almira, almost beside herself, called in a neighbor and sent for the doctor. It was a sudden, violent attack, induced finally, perhaps, by an error in diet, or a cold, but superinduced by her wearing anxiety. She never got off the bed in her poor little bedroom again. Her room opened out of the kitchen, and was not much like Almira's.

After she came out of her first swoon, she was conscious till she died—the next day. She knew how it was going to end with her from the first, though she made the doctor tell her the next afternoon. Then, with a sudden resolution, she asked him to go for David Ayres. "Thar's been trouble betwixt him and my girl," said she, "that has got to be set right afore I go."

So David came, and stood with Almira beside her bed. She was suffering a good deal of pain, but she had nerve enough to disregard it.

"I've been betwixt you an' Almiry," said she, "an' thar didn't seem to be no way of settin' it right but this, though I tried. I've heerd how you felt about it, an' I dare say it was nateral. I don't lay up nothin'. All is, ef you don't marry Almiry now, an' take care of her, an' make her happy, may the Lord never forgive you for triflin' with her !"

"Oh," cried David, "I will never think of anybody but Almira all my life. I'll marry her to-morrow."

"Then it's all right," said Mrs. King, and ended the word with a groan.

The young man stood there, his face white through the tan. He was beside himself with pity and shame ; but he could not say a word. He almost hated his narrow-minded mother.

"I'd like to see you take hold on Almiry's hand," said Mrs. King, gasping again. "I want to see you look happy and smilin' agin, deary, the way you used to."

David caught hold of Almira's hand with a great sob. But she threw his away, and flung herself down on her knees by her mother's bed.

"Oh, mother! mother! mother!" she sobbed. "I love you best! I do love you best! I always will! I never will love him as much as I did you. I promise you."

6

AN HONEST SOUL.

"Thar's Mis' Bliss's pieces in the brown kaliker bag, an' thar's Mis' Bennet's pieces in the bed-tickin' bag," said she, surveying complacently the two bags leaning against her kitchen - wall. "I'll get a dollar for both of them quilts, an' thar'll be two dollars. I've got a dollar an' sixty-three cents on hand now, an' thar's plenty of meal an' merlasses, an' some salt fish an' pertaters in the house. I'll get along middlin' well, I reckon. Thar ain't no call fer me to worry. I'll red up the house a leetle now, an' then I'll begin on Mis' Bliss's pieces."

The *house* was an infinitesimal affair, containing only two rooms besides the tiny lean-to which served as wood-shed. It stood far enough back from the road for a pretentious mansion, and there was one curious feature about it—not a door nor window was there in front, only a blank, unbroken wall. Strangers passing by used to stare wonderingly at it sometimes, but it was explained easily enough. Old Simeon Patch, years ago, when the longing for a home of his own had grown strong in his heart, and he had only a few hundred dollars saved from his hard earnings to invest in one, had wisely done the best he could with what he had.

Not much remained to spend on the house after the spacious lot was paid for, so he resolved to build as much house as he could with his money, and complete it when better days should come.

This tiny edifice was in reality simply the L of a goodly two-story house which had existed only in the fond and faithful fancies of Simeon Patch and his wife. That blank front wall was designed to be joined to the projected main building ; so, of course, there was no need of doors or windows. Simeon Patch came of a hard-working, honest race, whose pride it had been to keep out of debt, and he was a true child of his ancestors. Not a dollar would he spend that was not in his hand ; a mortgaged house was his horror. So he paid cash for every blade of grass on his lot of land, and every nail in his bit of a house, and settled down patiently in it until he should grub together enough more to buy a few additional boards and shingles, and pay the money down.

That time never came : he died in the course of a few years, after a lingering illness, and only had enough saved to pay his doctor's bill and funeral expenses, and leave his wife and daughter entirely without debt, in their little fragment of a house on the big, sorry lot of land.

There they had lived, mother and daughter, earning and saving in various little, petty ways, keeping their heads sturdily above water, and holding the dreaded mortgage off the house for many years. Then the mother died, and the daughter, Martha Patch, took up the little homely struggle alone. She was over seventy now—a small, slender old woman, as straight as a rail, with sharp black eyes, and a quick toss of her head when she spoke. She did odd housewifely jobs for the neighbors, wove rag-carpets, pieced bed-quilts, braided rugs, etc., and contrived to supply all her simple wants.

This evening, after she had finished putting her house to rights, she fell to investigating the contents of the bags which two of the neighbors had brought in the night before, with orders for quilts, much to her delight.

" Mis' Bliss has got proper handsome pieces," said she— " proper handsome ; they'll make a good-lookin' quilt. Mis' Bennet's is good too, but they ain't quite ekal to Mis' Bliss's. I reckon some of 'em's old."

She began spreading some of the largest, prettiest pieces on her white-scoured table. " Thar," said she, gazing at one admiringly, " that jest takes my eye ; them leetle pink roses is pretty, an' no mistake. I reckon that's French caliker. Thar's some big pieces too. Lor', what bag did I take 'em out on ! It must hev been Mis' Bliss's. I mustn't git 'em mixed."

She cut out some squares, and sat down by the window in a low wooden rocking-chair to sew. This window did not have a very pleasant outlook. The house was situated so far back from the road that it commanded only a rear view of the adjoining one. It was a great cross to Martha Patch. She was one of those women who like to see everything that is going on outside, and who often have excuse enough in the fact that so little is going on with them.

" It's a great divarsion," she used to say, in her snapping way, which was more nervous than ill-natured, bobbing her head violently at the same time—" a very great divarsion to see Mr. Peters's cows goin' in an' out of the barn day arter day ; an' that's about all I do see—never git a sight of the folks goin' to meetin' nor nothin'."

The lack of a front window was a continual source of grief to her.

" When the minister's prayin' for the widders an' orphans

he'd better make mention of one more," said she, once, "an' that's women without front winders."

She and her mother had planned to save money enough to have one some day, but they had never been able to bring it about. A window commanding a view of the street and the passers-by would have been a great source of comfort to the poor old woman, sitting and sewing as she did day in and day out. As it was, she seized eagerly upon the few objects of interest which did come within her vision, and made much of them. There were some children who, on their way from school, could make a short cut through her yard and reach home quicker. She watched for them every day, and if they did not appear quite as soon as usual she would grow uneasy, and eye the clock, and mutter to herself, "I wonder where them Mosely children can be?" When they came she watched their progress with sharp attention, and thought them over for an hour afterwards. Not a bird which passed her window escaped her notice. This innocent old gossip fed her mind upon their small domestic affairs in lieu of larger ones. To-day she often paused between her stitches to gaze absorbedly at a yellow-bird vibrating nervously round the branches of a young tree opposite. It was early spring, and the branches were all of a light-green foam.

"That's the same yaller-bird I saw yesterday, I do b'lieve," said she. "I recken he's goin' to build a nest in that ellum."

Lately she had been watching the progress of the grass gradually springing up all over the yard. One spot where it grew much greener than elsewhere her mind dwelt upon curiously.

"I can't make out," she said to a neighbor, "whether

that 'ere spot is greener than the rest because the sun shines brightly thar, or because somethin's buried thar."

She toiled steadily on the patchwork quilts. At the end of a fortnight they were nearly completed. She hurried on the last one morning, thinking she would carry them both to their owners that afternoon and get her pay. She did not stop for any dinner.

Spreading them out for one last look before rolling them up in bundles, she caught her breath hastily.

"What hev I done?" said she. "Massy sakes! I hevn't gone an' put Mis' Bliss's caliker with the leetle pink roses on't in Mis' Bennet's quilt? I hev, jest as sure as preachin'! What shell I do?"

The poor old soul stood staring at the quilts in pitiful dismay. "A hull fortni't's work," she muttered. "What shell I do? Them pink roses is the prettiest caliker in the hull lot. Mis' Bliss will be mad if they air in Mis' Bennet's quilt. She won't say nothin', an' she'll pay me, but she'll feel it inside, an' it won't be doin' the squar' thing by her. No; if I'm goin' to airn money I'll airn it."

Martha Patch gave her head a jerk. The spirit which animated her father when he went to housekeeping in a piece of a house without any front window blazed up within her. She made herself a cup of tea, then sat deliberately down by the window to rip the quilts to pieces. It had to be done pretty thoroughly on account of her admiration for the pink calico, and the quantity of it—it figured in nearly every square. "I wish I hed a front winder to set to while I'm doin' on't," said she; but she patiently plied her scissors till dusk, only stopping for a short survey of the Mosely children. After days of steady work the pieces were put together again, this time the pink-rose calico in Mrs. Bliss's

quilt. Martha Patch rolled the quilts up with a sigh of relief and a sense of virtuous triumph.

"I'll sort over the pieces that's left in the bags," said
she, "then I'll take 'em over an' git my pay. I'm gittin'
pretty short of vittles."

She began pulling the pieces out of the bed-ticking bag,
laying them on her lap and smoothing them out, prepara-
tory to doing them up in a neat, tight roll to take home—
she was very methodical about everything she did. Suddenly she turned pale, and stared wildly at a tiny scrap of
calico which she had just fished out of the bag.

"Massy sakes!" she cried; "it ain't, is it?" She clutched
Mrs. Bliss's quilt from the table and laid the bit of calico
beside the pink-rose squares.

"It's jest the same thing," she groaned, "an' it came out
on Mis' Bennet's bag. Dear me suz! dear me suz!"

She dropped helplessly into her chair by the window,
still holding the quilt and the telltale scrap of calico, and
gazed out in a bewildered sort of way. Her poor old eyes
looked dim and weak with tears.

"Thar's the Mosely children comin'," she said; "happy
little gals, laughin' an' hollerin', goin' home to their mother
to git a good dinner. Me a-settin' here's a lesson they
ain't larned in their books yit; hope to goodness they never
will; hope they won't ever hev to piece quilts fur a livin',
without any front winder to set to. Thar's a dandelion
blown out on that green spot. Reckon thar *is* somethin'
buried thar. Lordy massy! *hev* I got to rip them two
quilts to pieces agin an' sew 'em over?"

Finally she resolved to carry a bit of the pink-rose calico
over to Mrs. Bennet's and find out, without betraying the
dilemma she was in, if it were really hers.

Her poor old knees fairly shook under her when she entered Mrs. Bennet's sitting-room.

"Why, yes, Martha, it's mine," said Mrs. Bennet, in response to her agitated question. "Hattie had a dress like it, don't you remember? There was a lot of new pieces left, and I thought they would work into a quilt nice. But, for pity's sake, Martha, what is the matter? You look just as white as a sheet. You ain't sick, are you?"

"No," said Martha, with a feeble toss of her head, to keep up the deception; "I ain't sick, only kinder all gone with the warm weather. I reckon I'll hev to fix me up some thoroughwort tea. Thoroughwort's a great strengthener."

"I would," said Mrs. Bennet, sympathizingly; "and don't you work too hard on that quilt; I ain't in a bit of a hurry for it. I sha'n't want it before next winter anyway. I only thought I'd like to have it pieced and ready."

"I reckon I can't get it done afore another fortni't," said Martha, trembling.

"I don't care if you don't get it done for the next three months. Don't go yet, Martha; you ain't rested a minute, and it's a pretty long walk. Don't you want a bite of something before you go? Have a piece of cake? You look real faint."

"No, thanky," said Martha, and departed in spite of all friendly entreaties to tarry. Mrs. Bennet watched her moving slowly down the road, still holding the little pink calico rag in her brown, withered fingers.

"Martha Patch is failing; she ain't near so straight as she was," remarked Mrs. Bennet. "She looks real bent over to-day."

The little wiry springiness was, indeed, gone from her

gait as she crept slowly along the sweet country road, and there was a helpless droop in her thin, narrow shoulders. It was a beautiful spring day; the fruit-trees were all in blossom. There were more orchards than houses on the way, and more blooming trees to pass than people.

Martha looked up at the white branches as she passed under them. " I kin smell the apple-blows," said she, " but somehow the goodness is all gone out on 'em. I'd jest as soon smell cabbage. Oh, dear me suz, kin I ever do them quilts over agin ?"

When she got home, however, she rallied a little. There was a nervous force about this old woman which was not easily overcome even by an accumulation of misfortunes. She might bend a good deal, but she was almost sure to spring back again. She took off her hood and shawl, and straightened herself up. " Thar's no use puttin' it off; it's got to be done. I'll hev them quilts right ef it kills me !"

She tied on a purple calico apron and sat down at the window again, with a quilt and the scissors. Out came the pink roses. There she sat through the long afternoon, cutting the stitches which she had so laboriously put in—a little defiant old figure, its head, with a flat black lace cap on it, bobbing up and down in time with its hands. There were some purple bows on the cap, and they fluttered ; quite a little wind blew in at the window.

The eight-day clock on the mantel ticked peacefully. It was a queer old timepiece, which had belonged to her grandmother Patch. A painting of a quaint female, with puffed hair and a bunch of roses, adorned the front of it, under the dial-plate. It was flanked on either side by tall, green vases.

There was a dull-colored rag-carpet of Martha's own

manufacture on the floor of the room.   Some wooden chairs
stood around stiffly ; an old, yellow map of Massachusetts
and a portrait of George Washington hung on the walls.
There was not a speck of dust anywhere, nor any disorder.
Neatness was one of the comforts of Martha's life.   Putting and keeping things in order was one of the interests
which enlivened her dulness and made the world attractive
to her.

The poor soul sat at the window, bending over the quilt,
until dusk, and she sat there, bending over the quilt until
dusk, many a day after.

It is a hard question to decide, whether there were any
real merit in such finely strained honesty, or whether it were
merely a case of morbid conscientiousness.   Perhaps the
old woman, inheriting very likely her father's scruples, had
had them so intensified by age and childishness that they
had become a little off the bias of reason.

Be that as it may, she thought it was the right course for
her to make the quilts over, and, thinking so, it was all that
she could do.   She could never have been satisfied otherwise.   It took her a considerable while longer to finish the
quilts again, and this time she began to suffer from other
causes than mere fatigue.   Her stock of provisions commenced to run low, and her money was gone.   At last she
had nothing but a few potatoes in the house to eat.   She
contrived to dig some dandelion greens once or twice ;
these with the potatoes were all her diet.   There was really
no necessity for such a state of things ; she was surrounded
by kindly well-to-do people, who would have gone without
themselves rather than let her suffer.   But she had always
been very reticent about her needs, and felt great pride
about accepting anything for which she did not pay.

But she struggled along until the quilts were done, and no one knew. She set the last stitch quite late one evening; then she spread the quilts out and surveyed them. "Thar they air now, all right," said she; "the pink roses is in Mis' Bennet's, an' I ain't cheated nobody out on their caliker, an' I've airned my money. I'll take 'em hum in the mornin', an' then I'll buy somethin' to eat. I begin to feel a dreadful sinkin' at my stummuck."

She locked up the house carefully—she always felt a great responsibility when she had people's work on hand— and went to bed.

Next morning she woke up so faint and dizzy that she hardly knew herself. She crawled out into the kitchen, and sank down on the floor. She could not move another step.

"Lor sakes!" she moaned, " I reckon I'm 'bout done to !"

The quilts lay near her on the table ; she stared up at them with feeble complacency. " Ef I'm goin' to die, I'm glad I got them quilts done right fust. Massy, how sinkin' I do feel ! I wish I had a cup of tea."

There she lay, and the beautiful spring morning wore on. The sun shone in at the window, and moved nearer and nearer, until finally she lay in a sunbeam, a poor, shrivelled little old woman, whose resolute spirit had nearly been her death, in her scant nightgown and ruffled cap, a little shawl falling from her shoulders. She did not feel ill, only absolutely too weak and helpless to move. Her mind was just as active as ever, and her black eyes peered sharply out of her pinched face. She kept making efforts to rise, but she could not stir.

"Lor sakes !" she snapped out at length, " how long *hev* I got to lay here ? I'm mad !"

She saw some dust on the black paint of a chair which stood in the sun, and she eyed that distressfully.

"Jest look at that dust on the runs of that cheer!" she muttered. "What if anybody come in! I wonder if I can't reach it!"

The chair was near her, and she managed to stretch out her limp old hand and rub the dust off the rounds. Then she let it sink down, panting.

"I wonder ef I *ain't* goin' to die," she gasped. "I wonder ef I'm prepared. I never took nothin' that shouldn't belong to me that I knows on. Oh, dear me suz, I wish somebody would come!"

When her strained ears did catch the sound of footsteps outside, a sudden resolve sprang up in her heart.

"I won't let on to nobody how I've made them quilts over, an' how I hevn't had enough to eat—I won't."

When the door was tried she called out feebly, "Who is thar?"

The voice of Mrs. Peters, her next-door neighbor, came back in response: "It's me. What's the matter, Marthy?"

"I'm kinder used up; don't know how you'll git in; I can't git to the door to unlock it to save my life."

"Can't I get in at the window?"

"Mebbe you kin."

Mrs. Peters was a long-limbed, spare woman, and she got in through the window with considerable ease, it being quite low from the ground.

She turned pale when she saw Martha lying on the floor. "Why, Marthy, what is the matter? How long have you been laying there?"

"Ever since I got up. I was kinder dizzy, an' hed a

dreadful sinkin' feelin'. It ain't much, I reckon. Ef I
could hev a cup of tea it would set me right up. Thar's
a spoonful left in the pantry. Ef you jest put a few kindlin's in the stove, Mis' Peters, an' set in the kettle an'
made me a cup, I could git up, I know. I've got to go an'
kerry them quilts hum to Mis' Bliss an' Mis' Bennet."

"I don't believe but what you've got all tired out over
the quilts. You've been working too hard."

"No, I 'ain't, Mis' Peters ; it's nothin' but play piecin'
quilts. All I mind is not havin' a front winder to set to
while I'm doin' on't."

Mrs. Peters was a quiet, sensible woman of few words ;
she insisted upon carrying Martha into the bedroom and
putting her comfortably to bed. It was easily done ; she
was muscular, and the old woman a very light weight.
Then she went into the pantry. She was beginning to suspect the state of affairs, and her suspicions were strengthened when she saw the bare shelves. She started the fire,
put on the tea-kettle, and then slipped across the yard to
her own house for further reinforcements.

Pretty soon Martha was drinking her cup of tea and eating her toast and a dropped egg. She had taken the food
with some reluctance, half starved as she was. Finally she
gave in—the sight of it was too much for her. "Well, I
will borry it, Mis' Peters," said she ; "an' I'll pay you jest
as soon as I kin git up."

After she had eaten she felt stronger. Mrs. Peters had
hard work to keep her quiet until afternoon ; then she would
get up and carry the quilts home. The two ladies were
profuse in praises. Martha, proud and smiling. Mrs. Bennet noticed the pink roses at once. "How pretty that calico did work in," she remarked.

"Yes," assented Martha, between an inclination to chuckle and to cry.

"Ef I ain't thankful I did them quilts over," thought she, creeping slowly homeward, her hard-earned two dollars knotted into a corner of her handkerchief for security.

About sunset Mrs. Peters came in again. "Marthy," she said, after a while, "Sam says he's out of work just now, and he'll cut through a front window for you. He's got some old sash and glass that's been laying round in the barn ever since I can remember. It'll be a real charity for you to take it off his hands, and he'll like to do it. Sam's as uneasy as a fish out of water when he hasn't got any work."

Martha eyed her suspiciously. "Thanky; but I don't want nothin' done that I can't pay for," said she, with a stiff toss of her head.

"It would be pay enough, just letting Sam do it, Marthy; but, if you really feel set about it, I've got some sheets that need turning. You can do them some time this summer, and that will pay us for all it's worth."

The black eyes looked at her sharply. "Air you sure?"

"Yes; it's fully as much as it's worth," said Mrs. Peters. "I'm most afraid it's more. There's four sheets, and putting in a window is nothing more than putting in a patch—the old stuff ain't worth anything."

When Martha fully realized that she was going to have a front window, and that her pride might suffer it to be given to her and yet receive no insult, she was as delighted as a child.

"Lor sakes!" said she, "jest to think that I shall have a front winder to set to! I wish mother could ha' lived to see it. Mebbe you kinder wonder at it, Mis' Peters—you've allers had front winders; but you haven't any idea what a great thing it seems to me. It kinder makes me feel younger. Thar's the Mosely children; they're 'bout all I've ever seen pass *this* winder, Mis' Peters. Jest see that green spot out thar; it's been greener than the rest of the yard all the spring, an' now thar's lots of dandelions blowed out on it, an' some clover. I b'lieve the sun shines more on it, somehow. Law me, to think I'm going to hev a front winder!"

"Sarah was in this afternoon," said Mrs. Peters, further (Sarah was her married daughter), "and she says she wants some braided rugs right away. She'll send the rags over by Willie to-morrow."

"You don't say so! Well I'll be glad to do it; an' thar's one thing 'bout it, Mis' Peters—mebbe you'll think it queer for me to say so, but I'm kinder thankful it's rugs she wants. I'm kinder sick of bed-quilts somehow."

A TASTE OF HONEY.

THE long, low, red-painted cottage was raised above the level of the street, on an embankment separated into two terraces. Steep stone steps led up the terraces. They were covered with green, slimy moss, and little ferns and weeds sprang out of every crack. A walk of flat slate stones led from them to the front door, which was painted green, sagged on its hinges, and had a brass knocker.

The whole yard and the double banks were covered with a tall waving crop of red-top and herds-grass and red and white clover. It was in the height of haying-time.

A grassy wheel-track led round the side of the house to a barn dashed with streaks of red paint.

Off to the left stretched some waving pasture-land, and a garden-patch marked by bean-poles and glancing corn-blades, with a long row of beehives showing in the midst of it.

A rusty open buggy and a lop-eared white horse stood in the drive opposite the side door of the house.

An elderly woman with a green cotton umbrella over her head sat placidly waiting in the buggy. She had on a flat-tish black straw bonnet with purple strings, and wore a dull-green silk shawl sprinkled with little bright palm leaves over her broad shoulders.

She had a large, smiling face, crinkly gray hair, and quite a thick white beard cropped close on her double chin.

The side door stood open, and a young woman kept coming out, bringing pails and round wooden boxes, which she stowed away in the back of the buggy and under the seat. She was a little round-shouldered, her face with its thick, dull-colored complexion was like her mother's, just as pleasant and smiling, only with a suggestion of shrewd sense about it which the older woman's did not have.

When the pails and boxes were all in the buggy, she locked the door, got in herself, and drove carefully out of the yard.

The road along which they proceeded lay between waving grain fields. The air was full of the rattle of mowing-machines this morning; nearly every field had its broad furrows where they had passed.

The old white horse jogged slowly along; the two women sat behind him in silence, the older one gazing about her with placid interest, the younger one apparently absorbed in her own thoughts. She was calculating how much her butter and eggs and berries would bring in Bolton, the large market town towards which they were travelling.

Every week, Inez Morse and her mother drove there to sell the produce of their little farm. Her father had died three years before; ever since, the daughter had carried on the farm, hiring very little help. There was a six-hundred-dollar mortgage on it, which she was trying to pay up. It was slow work, though they saved every penny they could, and denied themselves even the fruit of their own land.

Inez had a mild joke about the honey which her bees made. She and her mother scarcely tasted it; it all went to the Bolton markets.

7

" I tell you what 'tis, mother," Inez used to say, " the day the mortgage is paid off we'll have warm biscuit and honey for supper."

Whenever her mother looked wistfully at the delicacies which they could not keep for their own enjoyment, Inez would tell her to never mind—by and by they would eat their own honey. The remark grew into a sort of household proverb for them.

The mother felt their privations much more keenly than the daughter. She was one of those women for whom these simple animal pleasures form a great part of life. She had not much resource in her mind. The payment of the mortgage did not afford her the keen delight in anticipation that it did Inez ; she was hardly capable of it, though she would be pleased enough when the time came. Now she thought more about eating the honey. However, she had never grumbled at any of her daughter's management. In her opinion, Inez always did about right.

When they reached Bolton, Inez drove about the village from house to house, selling her wares at the doors, while her mother sat in the buggy and held the horse. She had a good many regular customers : her goods were always excellent, and gave satisfaction, though she had the name of being a trifle exacting in her bargains, and asking as much as she possibly could.

To-day one of her customers in making change did not give her enough by a cent. Inez, when she discovered it, drove back a quarter of a mile to have the error rectified.

The woman looked amused and a trifle contemptuous when she asked her for the missing penny. Inez saw it. " You think it is queer that I came back for one cent," said she, with slow dignity, " but cents are my dollars."

"Yes, I suppose so," assented the woman, hastily, changing her expression.

Inez, driving through Bolton streets, looked at the girls of her own age, in their pretty street suits, in grave feminine admiration. She herself had never had anything but the very barest necessaries in the way of clothes. Lately a vain desire had crept into her heart for a bright ribbon bow to wear at the throat, as some of those girls did. She never dreamed of gratifying the desire, but it remained. She thought of it so much that, before she knew, she mentioned it to her mother on their way home.

"Mother," said she, "a red ribbon bow with long ends like those girls wore would be pretty for me, wouldn't it?"

Her mother stared at her in amazement. It did not sound like Inez. "Real pretty, child," said she. "I'd hev one ef I was you; you're young, an' you want sech things. I hed 'em when I was a girl."

"Oh, no, mother," cried Inez, hastily. "Of course I never thought of such a thing really. I only spoke of it. We've got to wait till the mortgage is paid to eat our honey, you know."

That evening, after the mother and daughter had eaten their supper, and were sitting in the kitchen in the twilight, there came a knock at the door.

Inez answered it. Willy Linfield stood there.

"How do you do, Willy?" said she.

"Pretty well, thanky, Inez."

Then there was a pause. Inez stood looking gravely at the young man. She wondered what he wanted, and why he did not tell his errand.

"Nice evening?" said he, finally.

"Beautiful."

Then there was another pause. The young fellow stood on one foot, then on the other, and got red in the face.

Inez could not imagine why he did not tell her what he wanted. At last she grew desperate.

"Did your mother want to buy some eggs, Willy?" she asked.

"No-o," he faltered, looking rather taken aback. "I don't—she does—leastways she didn't say anything about it."

"Was it butter, then?"

"No—I guess not. I rather think she's got plenty."

Inez stared at him in growing amazement—what did he want?

He was a fair-complexioned young man, and he looked as if the blood were fairly bursting through his face.

"Good-night, Inez," said he, finally.

"Good-night, Willy," she responded. Then he walked off.

Inez went into the kitchen, entirely mystified. She told her mother about it. "What do you suppose he wanted?" asked she.

Mrs. Morse was an obtuse woman, but Inez's father had come courting her in by-gone days. She caught the clew to the mystery quicker than her daughter.

"Why, I guess he come to see you, Inez, most likely."

"Come to see me! Why, what for?"

"Why, 'cause he wanted to. Why does any feller go to see a girl?"

It was Inez's turn to color then. "I never thought of such a thing as that," said she. "I don't believe it, mother."

"He did, sure's preachin'."

"I never thought of asking him to come in. I guess you are mistaken, mother. Nobody ever came to see me *so*."

Inez kept thinking about it uneasily. It was a new uneasiness for her.

The next day she met Willy Linfield in the village store. She stepped up to him at once.

"Willy," said she, "I didn't ask you to come in last night, and I thought, p'rhaps, afterwards, I'd ought to. I never thought of your wanting to come in. I supposed you'd come on an errand."

The young fellow had looked stiff and offended when she first approached him, but it was impossible to doubt her honest apology.

"Well, I kinder thought of making a little call on you, Inez," he owned, coloring.

"I'm very sorry, then ; but no young man ever came to see me before, and I never thought of such a thing."

She looked into his face pleasantly. He gained courage. "Say, Inez," said he, "the bell-ringers are going to perform in the hall to-morrow night. Wouldn't you like to go with me?"

"Yes, I'd like to. Thank you, Willy."

Inez was not easily perturbed, but she went home now in a flutter. Such a thing as this had never happened to her before. Young men had never shown much partiality for her. Now she was exceedingly pleased. She had never realized that she cared, because she had not had the experiences of other girls ; but now her girlish instincts awoke. She really had a good deal of her mother's simplicity about her, though it was redeemed by native shrewdness.

Now she began to revolve in her mind again the project of the red ribbon. She did want it so much, but she felt as if it was such a dreadful extravagance. At last she decided to get it. She actually looked pale and scared

when she stood buying it at the counter in the little millinery shop.

She went home with it, feeling a guilty delight, and showed
it to her mother, and told her of Willy Linfield's invitation.
She had not before.   This was on the afternoon of the concert day.

" My !" said her mother, elated, " you've got a beau, Inez,
as sure as preachin', an' the red ribbon's beautiful."

Inez could not, however, rid herself of the guilty feeling.
She gave her mother a piece of honeycomb for her supper.
" It ain't fair for me to be buying ribbon out of the mort-
gage money, and mother have nothing," said she to herself.
" So she must have the honey, and that makes two things
out."

But when Inez, with the crisp red bow at her throat, followed her escort awkwardly through the lighted hall, and
sat by his side listening to the crystal notes of the bell-
ringers, the worry about the ribbon and the weight of the
mortgage seemed to slip for a moment from her young,
bowed shoulders.   She thought of them, only to look at
some other girls with ribbons, and to be glad that she had
one too.   She was making a grasp, for a few minutes, at
the girlhood she had never had.

The concert was Wednesday.   Saturday she and her
mother drove again to Bolton to sell their butter and eggs.
When they got home, Inez opened the parlor, which was
never used, and swept and dusted it.   It was a grand apart-
ment to her and her mother.   It had never been opened
since her father's funeral.   When she first unclosed the door
to-day she seemed to see the long coffin in the middle of
the floor, where it had rested then.

She shuddered a little.   " Folks that have had troubles

do see coffins afterwards, even when they're happy, I suppose," muttered she to herself.

Then she went to work. There was a large mahogany bureau in one corner of the room ; some flag-bottomed chairs stood stiffly around ; there was an old-fashioned card-table, with Mrs. Heman's poems and the best lamp in a bead lamp-mat on it, between the two front windows. A narrow gilt-framed looking-glass hung over it.

Mrs. Morse heard Inez at work, and came in. "What *air* you doin' on, Inez ?" she asked in wonder.

"I just thought I'd slick up here a little. Willy Linfield said—he might—drop in awhile Sunday night." Inez did not look at her mother. Somehow she felt more ashamed before her than she would have before a smarter woman.

"My sakes, Inez, you don't say so ! You have got a beau as sure as preachin'. Your father kept right on reg'lar, after we once set up of a Sunday night. You'll have to put a new wick in that lamp, Inez."

"I'll see to it, mother," replied Inez, shortly. She was delighted herself, but she felt angry with her mother for showing so much elation ; it seemed to cheapen her happiness.

Sunday, Inez went with her mother to church in the morning and afternoon. She went to Sabbath-school after the morning service too. She was in a class of girls of her own age. She had never felt, someway, as if she was in the least one of their kind. She never had the things they had, or did anything which they were accustomed to do. To-day she looked at them with a feeling of kinship. She was a girl too. Three or four of them had lovers. Inez eyed them, and thought how she had one too, and he was coming to-night as well as theirs.

She had work to do Sundays as well as week-days. There were cows to milk and hens to feed. But she changed her dress after supper, and put on the new red-ribbon bow. She picked a little nosegay of cinnamon roses out in the front yard (there were a few of these little dwarf roses half buried in the tall grass there), and arranged them in an old wine-glass on the parlor mantel. When she heard Willy's feet on the slate walk and his knock on the front door, her heart beat as it never had before.

"There's your beau, Inez!" cried her mother; "he's come!"

Inez was terribly afraid Willy would hear what her mother said; the windows were all open. She went trembling to the door, and asked him into the garnished parlor.

Mrs. Morse stayed out in the kitchen. The twilight deepened. She could hear the soft hum of voices in the parlor. "Inez is in there courtin'," said she. "Her father an' me used to court, but it's all over. There's something queer about everything."

Willy Linfield came many a Sunday night after that. It was said all around that Willy Linfield was "going" with Inez Morse. Folks wondered why he fancied her. He was a pretty, rather dandified young fellow, and Inez was so plain in her ways. She looked ten years older than he, though she was about the same age.

One Monday afternoon, she told her mother that Willy, the night before, had asked her to marry him. The two women sat at the kitchen windows, resting. They had been washing, and were just through. The kitchen floor was freshly scoured; everything looked damp and clean.

"You don't say so, Inez!" cried her mother, admiringly. "What did you tell him? Of course you'll have him; he's a real nice feller; an' I don't believe you'll ever get any-body else."

"I told him I'd have him if he'd wait three years for me to pay off the mortgage," replied Inez, quietly.

"Did he say he would?"

"Yes."

"It's a long time for a feller to wait," said her mother, shaking her head dubiously. "I'm afeard you'll lose him, Inez."

"Then I'll lose him," said Inez. "I'm going to pay off that mortgage before I marry any man. Mother, look here," she went on, with a passion which was totally foreign to her, and showed how deeply she felt about the matter. "You know a little how I feel about that mortgage. It ain't like any common mortgage. You know how father felt about it."

"Yes, I know, Inez," said her mother, with a sob.

"Many's the time," Inez went on, "that father has talked about it to me over in the field there. He'd been trying all his life to get this place clear; he'd worked like a dog; we all worked and went without. But to save his life he couldn't pay it up within six hundred dollars. When the doctor told him he couldn't live many months longer, he fretted and fretted over it to me. I guess he always talked more about his troubles to me, mother, than he did to you."

"I guess he did, Inez."

"Finally I told him one day—it was when he was able to be about, just before he gave up; I was out in the garden picking peas, and he was there with his cane. 'Inez,' says he, 'I've got to die an' leave that mortgage un-paid, an' I've been workin' ever since I was a young man to do it.' 'Father,' says I, 'don't you worry. *I'll* pay up that mortgage.' 'You can't Inez,' says he. 'Yes, I will,' says I ; 'I promise you, father.' It seemed to cheer him up. He didn't fret so much about it to me afterwards, but he kept asking me if I thought I really could. I always said, 'Yes.'

"Now, mother, if I marry Willy now, nobody knows what's going to be to hinder my keeping my promise to father. Willy ain't got anything laid up, and he ain't very strong. Besides, he's got his mother and sister to do for. Hattie's just beginning to help herself a little, but she can't do much for her mother yet. Mrs. Linfield ain't able to work, and Willy's got to look out for her. Then I've got you. And there might be more still to do for in the course of two or three years ; nobody knows. If I marry Willy now, I shall never pay off that mortgage, that I promised poor father I would, and I ain't going to do it. It'll take just three years to pay it every cent; and then I'll marry him, if he's willing to wait. If the mortgage was just for me I wouldn't care, though I don't think it would be very wise, anyway. But it's for father."

Mrs. Morse was crying. " I know you're jest right about the mortgage, Inez," she sobbed ; "but you'll lose your beau as sure as preachin'."

Nevertheless, it seemed for a long time as if she would not. Willy kept faithful. He was a good sort of young fellow, and very fond of Inez, though he hardly entered into her feelings about the mortgage. There was at times a perfect agony of pity in her heart over her father. It made no difference to her that all his earthly troubles were over for him now. When she thought over how he had toiled and worried and denied himself for the sake of owning their little farm clear, and then had to die without seeing it accomplished, it seemed as if she could not bear it. The pitiful spectacle of her poor, dull father working all his life for such a small aim in such small ways, in vain, haunted her.

During the next three years she strained every nerve. She denied herself even more than she had formerly. Sometimes she used to think her clothes were hardly fit for her to appear in beside Willy, he always looked so nice. But she thought he knew why she dressed so poorly, and would not mind. "It brings the time when we can eat our honey nearer," she said.

Willy was faithful for a long time ; but, the last six months of the third year, he began to drop off a little. Once in a while he would miss a Sunday night. Inez fretted over it a little ; but she did not really think of doubting him, he had been constant to her so long. Besides, there was only one more payment to be made on the mortgage, and she was so jubilant over this that she was hopeful about everything else.

Still, it was not with an altogether light heart that she went to the lawyer's office one afternoon and made the last payment. She was not so happy as she had anticipated. Willy had not been near her for three weeks now. She had not seen him even in church.

Still, she went straight to his house from the lawyer's office ; that had been the old laughing bargain between them. She was to go and tell him the good news ; then he was to go home with her, and help eat the festive supper of warm biscuits and honey.

She walked right in at the side door, and entered the sitting-room. She was familiar with the place. In the sitting-room sat Willy's mother and sister. They both started when they saw her.

"Oh, mother, here she is!" cried Hattie, without speaking to Inez.

Inez's heart sank, but she tried to speak naturally.

"Where's Willy?" asked she. "He's home from the shop, ain't he? I've made the last payment on the mortgage, and I've come to tell him."

The mother and daughter made no reply, but gazed at each other in silent distress.

"Oh, Inez!" cried Hattie, at length, as if she had nothing else to say. "Come into the parlor a minute with me, Inez," she added, after a little.

Inez followed her trembling.

Hattie shut the door, and threw her arms around Inez. "Oh, Inez!" she cried again, and began weeping; "I don't know how to tell you. Willy has treated you awful mean. We've all talked to him, but it didn't do any good. Oh, Inez, I can't tell you! He's—gone over to West Dorset this afternoon—to get married! Oh, Inez?"

"Who is he going to marry?"

"Her name's Tower—Minnie Tower. Oh, Inez, we're so awful sorry! He hasn't known her long. We never dreamed of such a thing."

"Never mind," said Inez, quietly. "Don't take on so, Hattie. Perhaps it's all for the best."

"Why, don't you *care*, Inez?"

There was a pitiful calm on Inez's dull face. "There's no use fretting over what can't be helped," said she. "I don't think Willy has acted bad. I made him wait a long time."

"That was the trouble, Inez."

"I couldn't help it. I should do it over again."

Inez took it so calmly that the other girl brightened. She

had felt frightened and distressed over this, but she had not a very deep nature.

"Inez," said she, hesitatingly, when she made a motion to go; "they've got a room fixed up-stairs, you know; would you like to see it? It looks real pretty."

Inez shuddered. This fine stab served to pierce the deepest, though she knew the girl meant all right.

"No, thank you, Hattie, I won't stop."

Inez was thankful when she got out in the air. She felt a little faint. She had to walk a mile before she reached home. Once she stopped and rested, sitting on a stone beside the road. She looked wearily around at the familiar landscape.

"The mortgage is paid," said she, "but I'll never eat my honey."

Her mother was watching at the kitchen window for her when she entered the yard.

"Is it paid, Inez?" asked she, eagerly, when the door opened.

"Every cent, mother," replied the daughter, kissing her—something she seldom did; she was not given to caresses.

"Where's your beau?" was the next question. "I thought you was going to bring him home."

"He ain't coming, mother. He's gone over to West Dorset to get married."

"Inez Morse, you don't mean to say so! You don't mean you've really lost your beau? Wa'al, I told you you would."

Mrs. Morse sat down and began to cry.

Inez had taken her things off, and now she was getting out the moulding-board and some flour.

"What air you doin' on, Inez?"

"I'm making the warm biscuit for supper, mother, to eat with the honey."

"You ain't goin' to make warm biscuit when you've lost your beau?"

"I don't see why that need to cheat us out of our supper we've talked about all these years."

"I do declar', I don't believe you mind it a bit," said the poor, simple mother, her sorrow for her daughter lighting up a little.

"I don't care so much but what I've got enough comfort left to live on, mother."

"Wa'al, I'm glad you kin look at it so, Inez; but you air a queer girl."

The biscuit were as light as puffs. Inez's face was as cheerful as usual when she and her mother sat down at the little table, with the biscuit and golden honey-comb in a clear glass dish between them. The mother looked placidly happy. She was delighted that Inez could "take it so."

But when she saw her help herself to the biscuit and honey, she said again; "You air a queer girl, Inez. I know the mortgage is paid, an' I only wish your poor father knew, an' here we sit eatin' the warm biscuit and honey. But I should think losin' your beau would take all the sweetness out of the honey."

The pleasant patience in Inez's face was more pathetic than tears. "I guess there's a good many folks find it the same way with their honey in this world," said she. "To-morrow, if it's pleasant, we'll drive to Bolton, and get you a new dress, mother."

BRAKES AND WHITE VI'LETS.

ONE afternoon Marm Lawson had company to tea. There were three women near her own age—she was seventy. Her withered, aged figure sat up pert and erect at the head of the table, pouring the tea from the shiny britannia teapot into the best pink china cups. She never leaned back in a chair : there seemed to be a kind of springy stiffness about her spine which forbade it. Her black cashmere gown fitted her long, shrunken form as tightly and trimly as a girl's ; she had on her best cap, made of very pretty old figured lace, with bows of lavender satin ribbon. She wore her iron-gray hair in two little thin dancing curls, one on each side of her narrow, sallow face, just forward of her cap.

In some other positions she would have been called a stately old lady ; she could be now with perfect truth. Her old character had in itself a true New World stateliness and aristocratic feeling wholly independent of birth or riches or education.

Marm Lawson was not a duchess ; but she was Marm Lawson. The " Marm " itself was a title.

In a more ambitious and cultured town than this it would have been Madam ; but the Marm proved just as well her simple neighbors' recognition of her latent dignity of character.

Her three guests sat, each at one of the three remaining

sides of the square table.   Levina sat meekly, half trans-
fixed, apparently, at a corner.

She was a slender young girl, Marm Lawson's granddaughter, her son Charles's daughter.   She had lived with
her grandmother ever since the death of her mother, some
ten years since. Her fair, colorless hair was combed smooth-
ly straight back from her pale, high forehead ; her serious
blue eyes looked solemnly out from beneath it.   She ate
her warm biscuit and damson sauce decorously, never
speaking a word in the presence of her elders : she had
been taught old-fashioned manners, and they clung to her,
though she was important fifteen.

Conversation did not flow very glibly among the guests,
though they were ordinarily garrulous enough old souls.
When they spoke, it was precisely, and not like themselves.
Every nerve in them was braced up to meet the occasion
with propriety. This state afternoon, Marm Lawson's china
tea-cups, and company damson sauce and pound-cakes,
coming right in the midst of their common everydays,
were embarrassing and awe-inspiring. They were like
children ; they regarded Marm Lawson, as children will a
suddenly elevated playmate, with a feeling of strangeness
and respect.   The one who felt this the least was a pretty,
silly old woman, with a front piece of reddish-brown hair.
She crimped it every night.   Her cheeks were as fair and
pink as a young girl's, her china-blue eyes as bright.

She ate her supper with a relish, and now and then eyed
Marm Lawson with a pleased consciousness of her own
pinky cheeks. " How awful yaller she is !" she thought.
But there was never any evidence of the thought in her
placid blue eyes, nor about her tiny mouth, into which she
was stuffing great pieces of cake like a greedy baby.

The one next her, who looked younger than she was, from being fleshy, and so having no deep wrinkles, was a widow, who lived with her married daughter ; the fair old woman was a widow too, and so was Marm Lawson ; but the fourth had an old husband living. He was a deacon of the orthodox church. He had been asked to tea, but had been too busy planting to come. "I'm dretful sorry the deacon couldn't come," Marm Lawson had said, when she was seating her guests at the table. The pink old lady mentally resolved that she wouldn't have sat at a corner if he had ; she was jealous, and always on the lookout for slights, and careful of her own interests. She had fixed on the largest piece of cake in the plate before it was passed ; then she took it, defiantly.

After tea, when they all sat in the north room with their knitting, they felt more at ease, and their tongues moved faster. Marm Lawson had opened the north room to-day. The south, on the opposite side of the entry, was her usual sitting-room. The north one was shut up except on occasions.

The china closet, where she kept her best china, was in there, the best hair-cloth rocking-chairs, and Mrs. Hemans and Mrs. Sigourney in red and gold on the mahogany work-table. Everything—the hair-cloth furniture, the books, the beaded lamp-mat—had a peculiar north-room smell, not disagreeable, but characteristic, as much the room's own odor as a flower's. It clung to the things when long removed from it, too. Levina, years afterwards, and far away, putting her face down to the red-and-gold Hemans book, could smell the north room.

She overheard the old ladies speaking her name several times as she went about clearing away the tea-things, which

8

was her work ; but she paid no heed. She had no morbid interest in herself, and therefore no unlawful curiosity. She was a quietly strong-minded, conscientious girl ; but she was too delicate. That was what her elders were talking about.

"Seems to me Leviny's lookin' kinder pindlin', ain't she ?" said the fleshy old lady, who was Mrs. Potter ; she had buried a good many children of her own, years ago. There had been two young daughters about Levina's age.

"I thought so too," agreed the deacon's wife. "I couldn't keep my eyes off her when we was havin' tea. She made me think a sight of your Jenny, Mis' Potter."

Marm Lawson sat up straighter and knitted firmly. "I don't see any reason why Leviny ain't well. She allers looks pale ; it's her nateral color."

"It ain't so much the pale," said Mrs. Potter, "but thar's somethin' else, a kind of a look around the nose an' the mouth that I've seen a good many times," and she sighed. "*Don't* you think it's jest a leetle damp here, Miss Lawson ? Do you s'pose it altogether suits Leviny ?"

Marm Lawson's knitting-needles clicked furiously, and the lavender bows on her cap trembled. "No, I don't think this house is any damper than any other house. I've heard 'bout 'nough 'bout it. I've lived here all my life, an' been well 'nough. I don't see why Leviny can't."

"*Now*, Mis' Lawson," said the fair old lady, "how kin you say it ain't damp ? Jest look at all them brakes under the winders ; they allers grow whar it's damp, an' the whole medder out this side is too wet to walk in, an' jest kivered with white vi'lets."

"Thar's a good many other houses in town got brakes under the winders, an' medders of white vi'lets pretty near 'em."

"Leviny's mother died here, you know," added the fair old lady.

" She'd 'a died anywhar ; consumption was in the Crane family. Leviny's well 'nough ; guess I'd know if she wasn't. I've got 'bout as good opportunities of jedgin' as anybody."

The others subsided under this thrust. Poor Marm Lawson was so excited as to be near forgetting her hospitality. But the subject was revived among themselves on their way home.

" Marm Lawson was dretful riled 'cause I said what I did," said the fair old lady ; " but I don't keer. I b'lieve that gal's goin' jest like her mother."

" I wish her father'd take her away," said Mrs. Potter, "somewhar whar it's drier."

" Talk about that house not bein' damp ! Jest look at that great streak of mildew on the front of it ; they can't keep it off. It comes right through the paint every time."

" She won't ever own it."

But poor Marm Lawson had to succumb to it, if she would not own it. Six months later she was living alone in the beloved old house, which sat closely down on the ground, with no foundation stones showing, and had, indeed, its great blotch of mildew ever present on its white-painted front. The grass in the little front yard was always rank and short, and a lighter green than elsewhere ; a thick row of trees stood just outside it, along the sidewalk.

" Of course it's damp, mother," Charles Lawson had said, looking in dismay at his fading daughter, whom he had come to see from his home in Lincoln, a town fifty miles distant ; and he took her away with him on the next train in spite of all his mother's objections. He had a good deal of her own decision of character. He had a second wife now, a good woman, so Levina would be well cared for, and have a home. He urged his mother very strongly to sell the house and go to live with him ; but she scorned the idea.

Give up her home ! she said ; she'd like to see herself : she knew all about old women livin' with their sons' wives. No : she'd lived fifty year in the old place, if it was damp, an' she guessed she could stan' it a while longer. Thar wa'n't no need of Leviny's goin'.

She kept up a stern, indignant front till the coach containing Levina and her father had rumbled out of sight ; then she went back into the house, into her south room, and sat down and cried. "Charles might hev let me keep her ; she wa'n't sick much ; she'd been pickin' up an' eatin' a good deal more lately ; she'd get well here jest as well as anywhar. Charles might hev let me keep her. He's got a wife now. I'll warrant she don't understand nothin 'bout nursin'. Poor lonesome old woman I be ! Oh dear ! oh dear !"

The poor old woman did have a hard, solitary life through the next winter. Charles was a good son, and it troubled him ; he wrote to her again and again, begging her to come to him. His wife wrote, and Levina, who was mending, wrote little, loving, precise letters. But the old lady stayed resolutely where she was. She wouldn't leave her home— no, not for a short visit. She knew all about that ; the house would be sold afore she knew it, if she left it, if 'twa'nt fur more'n a week, an' then she wouldn't hev any home.

Early in spring, however, her resolution seemed to give way. The longing to see her granddaughter grew stronger and stronger. Just before the ferns and white violets came up around the house she wrote to her son, and told him she would come an' stay just one week, an' not any more ; they needn't tease her to.

The morning she started, Mrs. Potter and her daughter came in to help her off. They lived opposite, in a house a little back from the road, on a hill. She had to ride ten miles in a stage-coach to a little isolated station to take the cars. When she got into the coach there was a queer expression on her face. Mrs. Potter's daughter, Mrs. Cartwright, noticed it, and spoke about it to her mother.

"Marm Lawson looked sort of funny to me when she went off," she told her mother.

"She felt awfully 'bout leavin' the place."

"Twa'n't that. She had a look as if she was makin' up her mind to something."

The poor old woman was making up her mind all that long ten-mile drive, between the budding willows and maples, to Cold Brook. She was torn betwixt two loves and two longings : one for her dear Levina, and one for her dear home, with its setting of green brakes and white violets. She was the only passenger. Sitting up straight in the lumbering coach, clutching her valise and her bandbox, she argued with herself : "Here's Leviny, poor child, expectin' to see grandma—wonder if she's growed any? An' here's the old place —seems as ef 'twas tearin' of me in two to leave it. Oh dear ! I know I sha'n't sleep a wink at Charles's, nor eat a morsel ; I never could eat strange cookin.' But, my sakes, seems to me I don't keer, ef I kin only see Leviny, dear child. S'pose the house should ketch fire while I was gone? Oh dear !"

Her mind was not made up when she arrived at Cold Brook, where she was to take the cars. The train was late. She sat down in the little station, and watched the coach

roll off. Should she go, or stay? The station was nothing more than a long bench with a roof over it as a
shelter from the rain. One side was entirely open. She
was all alone there. In two or three minutes she heard
the far-off whistle of the train. Should she go or stay?
Oh, Levina! Oh, the old house! Even while she was
asking herself she was dragging her little trunk around to
the rear of the station. Then she carried her valise and
bandbox round, and crouched down there with them, a
wretched, determined, guilty little old lady. She had decided: the house had triumphed over Levina. The train
came nearer and nearer, the engine-bell ringing. It gave a
half-halt at the little station; then, as there were no passengers in sight, went on. Days passed sometimes without
any passengers at this little out-of-the-way place.

When the train had gone, the old lady dragged her baggage round to the front of the station again, and sat down.
She hoped vaguely that a coach would come before long
and take her home ; but she knew nothing about it. There
she sat, hour after hour ; freight trains thundered past, and
one or two passenger trains ; none of them stopped. She
could see people looking curiously at her sitting there,
and then they were gone. She had some gingerbread and
cheese in her valise, and she took them out and ate them.
It grew dusky, and no coach had come ; she began to realize that none would come that night. Marm Lawson had
a great deal of spirit. When she understood that she would
either have to remain where she was through the night, or
strike off into the woods until she came to the road and a
house, she faced the situation bravely. She did not really
think of the latter alternative for a minute. She would not
have left her trunk unguarded there for anything. She was

always accustomed to retire early. She opened her valise, took out her Bible, and read a chapter ; then she went down on her knees beside the rough bench and said her prayers. Then she made up a bed on the bench, with her shawl and cloak, and a folded dress for a pillow, and lay quietly down. She looked across and saw the railroad track in the dusk, and the fringe of low woods on the other side.

"It's a queer place to go to sleep in," said she ; "but I s'pose His overrulin' providence is jest as strong here as anywhar. I only hope I 'ain't committed a sin agin Him in not goin' to see Leviny."

The soft spring twilight deepened ; when the stars had come out faintly, the poor, strong old soul, wearied out, had fallen asleep.

The stage-driver in the morning found her seated there, erect and pert as ever, waiting for him. He eyed her curiously ; she was a stranger to him ; but he had not a suspicion that she had stayed in the station all night. He thought she had been brought early that morning from one of the neighboring farms to take the stage.

Marm Lawson got home about noon. She went into her own house defiantly. She almost felt as if she had no right there. The neighbors, who saw her come, came running in, wild with curiosity. But they got very little satisfaction out of her. All she would say was that she had made up her mind not to go any farther when she had got to Cold Brook, and she s'posed she had a perfect right to. She could not help owning that she had stayed all night there— they knew when the stages ran. She met their consternation on this point with the same severe self-possession, however. It was a strong proof of Marm Lawson's obstinate force of character that she went erectly through this without the slightest abatement of her dignity or self-confidence.

She did not falter at all even when her son Charles came a few days later. He was more severe with her for her folly and imprudence than he had ever been in his life. If she cared more for that damp, musty old place than she did for Levina or himself, or her own life, she had better say so, and have done with it.

She eyed him with stern indignation. "Charles," said she, "your mother has got all her faculties *yet*, an' she knows what's best for her a leetle better'n you kin tell her. 'Tain't for you to dictate, yet a while."

Still, in spite of her defiance, she was wretched after her son had gone away. Even the meadow of white violets and the brakes could not console her. She hungered pitifully after Levina. Still, she could not make up her mind to leave home to go to her. She complained bitterly because they would not let her granddaughter come back; she "knowed" it wouldn't hurt her, she said. It wa'n't any damper here than anywhere else; she hadn't seen a speck of mould on her bread all summer. Without any doubt, her constant struggle with herself wore on her. Being away from what she loved was the very bitterness of death to this strong-affectioned old woman; and when the being away was voluntary, and something for which she had to blame herself, it was bitterness on bitterness.

Towards the last of August she was taken ill — quite alarmingly so — and they sent for her son. He came, and brought Levina, who would not be left behind.

When the coach stopped, Marm Lawson, who was perfectly conscious all the while, heard it. Then she heard Levina's voice. "Who's that?" she said, with a startled look, to Mrs. Cartwright, who was taking care of her. " 'Tain't Leviny?"

In another minute Levina was in the room.

" Oh, dear grandma!"

Her grandmother gave one hungry look at her; then she turned her face on the pillow. " Now, Levina Lawson, you ain't goin' to stay in this damp house one minute, an' git to coughin' agin. You kin go right over to Mis' Cartwright's, on the hill, an' stay to-night, an' to-morrow mornin' you take the stage an' go home. I won't hev you here. You've just got a leetle better. Go right away! Levina Lawson, why don't you *mind?*"

Her grandmother sat straight up in bed with a ghastly expression of anger. The poor little girl ran out of the room then, sobbing. She stayed in the house, but they had to hide her being there from her grandmother. All that night and the next day, she kept listening suspiciously.

"Charles," she would say, "you wouldn't keep Leviny here when you know it's as much as her life's worth, I know; but I keep thinkin' I hear her."

Towards night she grew worse; indeed, she died about one in the morning. A little before, she stretched out a withered hand and beckoned her son to her.

" Charles," whispered she, huskily, " I want—to tell you —somethin'. I've made up my mind to—sell the place, an'—go to live with you an' Leviny—only—I want you to go out in the mornin' an' dig up a root of white vi'lets an' some brakes, so—I kin take 'em with me."

ROBINS AND HAMMERS.

IT was Monday morning; Lois had her washing all done and her kitchen cleaned up, and it was yet not ten o'clock; the dew had not dried off the grass, and the surprise of the morning had not worn off in her heart. Lois was a girl who felt such things. After she had finished her kitchen-work, she came with her broom into the front entry, with its unpainted, uneven floor; she was going to sweep that out; then her work in the lower part of the house was done, and she had nothing more to do before dinner except to put her own room up-stairs in order.

She opened the front door after she had come the length of the narrow entry, then she could not help standing there a little while and staring out, leaning on her broom. It was beautiful outside, and, apart from that, the out-doors gave her somehow a sweet sense of companionship. The soft wind, and the sunshine, and the sweet spring smells came in by the open door like people. Lois felt it, though she did not get so far as thinking it. She had been lonesome, without knowing she was so till then. She was always alone in the house all day while her father was at work. Her mother was dead, and she had no brothers nor sisters.

The house faced southeast, and there was a weeping-willow tree in front of it. Its long boughs, which were more like tender green garlands than branches, swayed gently in the wind, and the sun shone through them. Lois looked at it radiantly. The spring birds were singing very shrill and sweet. There were bluebirds and orioles, and, more than anything else, robins. Lois always seemed to hear the robins plainest, maybe because she loved them best. She had always liked robins ever since she was a child. But now there was something else she liked to listen to better than the robins, and that was the sound of the carpenters' hammers on a house over the way. She could see its pinky unpainted pine walls through the trees. That was to be her house, where she and John Elliot were to live when they should be married in the autumn. The taps of the hammers seemed to Lois to harmonize sweetly with the calls of the bluebirds and the robins; they were of the same kind to her; both sounds belonged to love and hope and the spring.

Lois was small and compact in figure; her light-brown hair crinkled closely around her forehead and hung in tight curls on her neck. She had a pretty, thin face, with bright eyes, sensitive lips, and a clear skin. She was neat in her poor calico dress. There was no money in the Arms family, though once they had been comfortably off. Hiram Arms had been a prosperous farmer on his own account up in Rowe; now he was renting this great, unpainted, weather-beaten old house in Pawlet, and letting himself out to other farmers for low hire. A good many causes had brought it about: fire and mortgages and sickness. It had not happened until after Sarah Arms's death—that was always a comfort to her daughter Lois. Sarah Arms had been a high-spirited woman; there were people who said that her ambition and extravagance had brought about her husband's

failure. There had been a bay-window and a new piazza
on that snug farmhouse in Rowe, of which the old neighbors spoke dubiously now.   " Hiram Arms never ought to
have put on them additions," said they ; " but Mis' Arms
would hev 'em, poor woman."

So now the father and daughter grubbed along in Pawlet,
the daughter uncomplainingly, the father complainingly. He
was naturally a nervous man, and trouble had shaken him.
But at last, since Lois's engagement to John Elliot, their
affairs began to look brighter. John had not much money ;
he would have to mortgage his new house ; but he had
steady work and good pay, and a prospect of better. Hiram
Arms was to give up, on his daughter's marriage, the desolate
old house which he rented, and go to live with her in her
new one.   He was very proud and happy about it, and
talked it over a good deal among the neighbors ; he had
always been almost foolishly fond of his daughter, and he
was growing garrulous.

Finally Lois took her broom and went about her work.
She had been brought up on the rigid New England plan,
and had a guilty feeling that it was a waste of time if she
stopped a minute to be happy. There was very little furniture in these large, square, low-walled rooms, but everything
was scrupulously clean.   After her sweeping was done and
her own room put in order, Lois had a little time to sit
down and sew before she got dinner ; after dinner, when
the dishes were put away and her father gone back to his
work, she had a long quiet spell the whole afternoon till
six o'clock.

There Lois sat in the one of the two square front apart-
ments which they used for a sitting-room, sewing. She was
making a kind of coarse cotton edging. She could not

think of such things as boughten trimming for her poor little wedding outfit; but it was no matter, for she thought this was beautiful. Hattie Smith had taught her how to do it. She was her nearest girl neighbor, and she lived a quarter of a mile away, with no houses between. Lois, as she sat there, wished Hattie would come over that afternoon, and by three o'clock she did come in sight: a stout, girlish figure, in an ugly light-brown woollen dress fitting tightly over her curving shoulders. She had her plaid shawl over her arm, the afternoon was so warm.

"Oh, Hattie," cried Lois, running to the door and opening it, "I am so glad you've come! I was awful lonesome."

"Well, I thought I'd come over two or three minutes. Mother an' I got our washin' out of the way real early to day, and there wasn't anything to do at home, an' I thought I'd bring my sewing over here."

The two girls sat peacefully down at their work in the sitting-room. Hattie was running up some breadths of a dress, and Lois kept on with her edging.

"You get along real fast with that edging, don't you?" said Hattie.

"Well, I don't know. I haven't worked on it very steady."

"I think it's real pretty."

"So do I; beautiful."

Hattie dropped her sewing after a little, and stared at Lois with an odd expression on her large face, half of con- cealed pleasure, half of doubt and commiseration.

"Lois," said she, "I heard something to-day, an' I don't know whether to tell you of it or not. I told mother I was half a mind to, for I thought you ought to know it. It made me real mad."

"What is it, Hattie?"

"Why, I don't know as I ought to tell. I'm afraid it'll make you feel bad."

"No, it won't."

"Well, if you're sure it won't. I wouldn't mind it a bit if I was you. It made me real mad. I think she was just as mean as she could be. You see, old Mis' Elliot run over to borrow some soap this morning, an' she sat down a minute, an' we got to talkin' about John, an' his new house, an' you. I don't believe I'd better tell you, Lois."

"Yes: I won't mind. Go on."

"Well, mother said something about what a pretty girl you was, an' Mis' Elliot said, yes, you was pretty enough, but she couldn't help wishing sometimes that you had something to help John along with a little. She always thought the woman ought to furnish the house—she did when she was married—an' it was a dreadful hinderance to a young man to have to do everything. John worked terrible hard, an' she was afraid he'd get sick. And then she said she always thought a girl ought to have at least two silk dresses when she was married, a black one an' a colored one, and a good stock of clothes, so her husband wouldn't have to buy anything for her for two years certain. Now, Lois, you won't feel bad? Why, Lois, don't cry!"

Lois's poor little cotton edging lay unnoticed in her lap, and she was sobbing pitifully in her little coarse handkerchief.

"Now, Lois, I wouldn't have told you if I'd thought you'd felt so bad."

Lois wiped her eyes, and raised her head bravely. "I don't feel bad," said she; "only I wouldn't have believed that Mis' Elliot would have spoken so, when she knew I was doing the best I could."

"Well, *I* wouldn't; I think she was awful mean. I wouldn't mind it a bit, Lois."

"I don't," said Lois, and took up the cotton edging again and went on working, trying to look pleasant and unconcerned with her red eyes. She would talk no more on the subject, however, though Hattie kept alluding to it.

Hattie went home a little before tea-time, saying to herself she didn't know what to make of Lois Arms. Lois felt nothing but honest distress; no anger against any one— none against Hattie, nor even against Mrs. Elliot. Her mother, before she died, had told her a good many times that she had not enough spirit, and would have a hard time going through the world, and she would have told her that now had she been alive.

After Hattie went she sat there listening to the carpenters' hammers and the birds, but they no longer sounded to her as they had done. She kept saying it over to herself in a discordant refrain that drowned everything else, and took away the sweetness of it, with a bitter after-taste:

"Two silk dresses, a black one and a colored one; and I ought to furnish the house, and it's going to be a burden to John if I don't."

She had her father's supper all ready for him when he came from his work, though, in spite of her trouble; and they ate it peacefully together in the great barnlike kitchen, which stretched the width of the house behind the other rooms.

It was odd enough that her father, of his own accord, should broach the subject of her anxiety that night; but he did, after supper, in the sitting-room.

"Lois," said he, "don't you want something to buy you some clothes with? 'Ain't you got to make some new things before fall?"

Lois choked a little before she answered. "I guess you've got about ways enough for your money, father."

"Well, I could let you hev a leetle. I ain't got much jest now. Ef two or three dollars would do you any good—"

"I really don't need it now, father. I've got plenty."

"Well, you know best. I got to thinkin' 'bout it this afternoon—I don't know what put it into my head—when I was ploughin'. Ef things were as they was once, you'd hev enough. When I look back I wish your mother hadn't been quite so set 'bout hevin them bay-winders and piazzas."

"Oh, father, don't."

"No, I won't. I don't mean to find fault. Your mother was a good woman and a smart one, and she meant all right. Sometimes I can't help thinkin' it over ; that's all."

Lois kept thinking it all over and over and over. Sunday night John Elliot came ; that was his regular courting night. He came early, long before dusk ; everything, down to his love-making, was prompt, and earnest, and day-lighted with John Elliot. He looked just as he was. His tall, stout figure bore his ill-fitting Sunday clothes so sturdily that it made up for their want of grace ; his large face, with firm, brown cheeks, and heavy but strong mouth and chin, fronted Lois, and her father, and life, squarely.

The three sat solemnly in the front room for a little while after he came. Then Mr. Arms went out into the kitchen, and sat down patiently iı. his old arm-chair, drawn into the back doorway, and listened to the frogs, and the low hum of voices in the next room. Both sounds seemed to belong to a spring he had left behind. He generally went to bed, in his little room which opened out of the kitchen, long before John left, though this sober young man never kept his love up late. But to-night he still sat there in his chair, though half asleep, when the front door closed. He wondered dreamily why John went so soon—an hour earlier than usual. Then he heard Lois go up the front stairs to her room, and then he locked the door and went to bed himself.

Next morning he looked curiously at Lois a good many times, when she was going about getting breakfast for him in the early light. He thought she looked very sober. Once he asked her if she did not feel well, and she said yes. After breakfast, however, she said more. He was just putting on his hat to go to his work when she stopped him.

"Father," said she, "I s'pose you ought to know it; John and I ain't going to get married in the fall."

"You don't mean you've broke it off?"

"No; I haven't broke it off, father. I hope some time it'll be all right, and that's all I can say about it. *Don't* talk any more about it, father. I tell you this, for I think you ought to know."

It was not so easy, however, to stop her nervous, distressed father in his wonderment and conjecturing. He lingered and talked and questioned, but Lois would say no more than she had said, and he went off to work in an anxious bewilderment.

He had been very confidential about his daughter's prospects with the farmer whom he was helping. He had said a good deal about the new house, and how likely the young man was. To-day he said nothing. When he came home he looked very old and dejected.

Lois saw it, with an awful sinking at her heart, but she never faltered in her purpose. A corner of her resolute mother's mantle seemed to have fallen upon her gentle,

9

humble little daughter. She never would marry John Elliot until she could go to him well enough provided with
womanly gear not to be a burden at the outset. There
was no anger in her determination, and no pride deserving
the name.

She had asked him the night before to defer their marriage a year. She gave him no reason; she thought she
could not, without, perhaps, having his mother's remarks
traced back and trouble made; then, too, she knew he
would not consent to the plan.

The result was inevitable with a young man of John
Elliot's turn of mind. He broke the engagement squarely
and went home. Next day the carpenters stopped working
on the new house. The silence of the hammers smote
Lois with a dreadful sense of loneliness all day. Her
father did not notice it till Tuesday night; then he asked
her abruptly, "Have they stopped work on the house?"

"Yes," said Lois, with a great sob. Then she ran up-
stairs, threw herself on her bed, and cried bitterly. She
could not help it. Still, strangely enough, she was very far
from giving up all hope. She had never believed more
firmly in her life that the new house would be finished and
she and John live in it some day. She was going to work
and earn some pretty dresses and some furniture; then
John would come back, and it would be all right. In spite
of her yielding nature there was in her a capability of fine
concentration of purpose, which she might not use more
than once in her life, but which would work wonders then.
Whether it would work wonders with a practical, unimagi-
native, evenly resolute nature like John's, remained to be
seen. Some might have questioned if her subtle fineness
of strength was on a plane equal enough to admit of any
struggle.

She had not a doubt about it. John loved her, and by and by, when she had earned enough money, and had her clothes and her furniture, they would be married, and the carpenters would finish the new house.

Her greatest present distress was her father's dejection and her not seeing John Sunday nights, and she made the best of that. It was odd that she did not worry much over poor John's possible unhappiness; but she was so engaged in acting against her own heart for his happiness that she did not think of that consideration.

So she got the district school to teach, and passed the summer that way, instead of making edging and listening to the carpenters' hammers. The school was half a mile from her home, and she had to keep the house tidy and get meals for her father, besides teaching, so she had to work hard. Back and forth she went, passing first the wild roses and then the golden-rod on the country road, morning and noon and night, never faltering. Her pretty face got a strained, earnest look on it, but never a hopeless one. If John had only known—but he worked on in the shop over in Pawlet village, and never came near Lois. If she were in his thoughts, he kept her there so secretly that nobody knew. He went to work on week-days and to meeting on Sundays just as usual. He never alluded to Lois, or his broken engagement, or his unfinished house, and silenced his mother with, "I don't want to hear a word about this, mother; you may as well understand it first as last."

She never mentioned the matter to him afterwards, though she got a good deal of comfort from talking it over among her neighbors. She was not sorry, on the whole, she said, that the match was broken off. She had nothing against

Lois Arms ; she was a real pretty little thing, and a good girl too, she guessed ; but she always thought John might do a little better.

Then, on John's marriage, she was to have been left alone in her neat cottage house, which her husband had bequeathed her ; and although she had not wanted to live with the young couple and sell her house, or have the young couple live with her, she did not altogether wish to be left alone. If she had told the whole truth, she would have said that she was jealous of her son, and did not really want him to get married at all.

Lois used to meet John's mother sometimes, and would return her stiff bow wistfully. She never thought of being angry with her. John she never met. She used to glance timidly across the church of a Sunday sometimes, and see him upright and grave in his pew ; but he never turned his head her way, and never seemed to see her.

Lois taught all that year till the next spring ; then she had two hundred dollars in money. She had not spent one cent of her salary, but had saved it jealously. She had not given any to her father ; that troubled her most. To see him coming home from his hard, pitiful jobs of wood-cutting and hauling through the winter, his shoulders bent, his thin, nervous face with its white beard growing thinner and more anxious, and she with her little hoard, worried her. But she kept thinking it would be all right soon. She knew his disappointment was wearing on him ; but soon it would be over, and this precious money would bring it about.

Lois had it all planned, just what she would do with her money. Seventy-five dollars would buy her dresses, she thought, and one hundred and twenty-five her furniture.

She anticipated a sumptuous housekeeping outfit from that. She was as innocent as a child about the cost of things. Then John would come back to her, and the taps of the hammers on the new house would chime in again with the songs of the robins.

Lois was thinking what day she should go over to the village to buy her dresses, and how she should send a little note to John, when one day, shortly after her school closed, her father was brought home with a broken arm. That settled the matter. The dresses were not bought, the note was not written, and the carpenters' hammers remained silent when the robins began to sing. Lois's school money paid the rent and the doctor's bill, and bought food for herself and father. She nursed her father till he was about again, and then she took up her school-work and began anew. She went without everything. She wore her poor little shoes out at the toes ; in the winter she wrapped her shawl round her little red fingers and went without gloves. She went past the wild roses again, then the golden-rod and asters, then the red maple boughs, then the snow-drifts, back and forth between her home and the schoolhouse, with her pretty, enduring, eager face, till spring came once more.

A few weeks after her school closed, John Elliot, coming home from the shop at dusk one rainy Saturday night, met a girl on the covered bridge just before he got to his home. She had been standing motionless at the farther entrance till she had seen him enter at the other ; then she had walked forward towards him rapidly. She extended her hand, with something white in it, when she reached him.

"Mr. Elliot," said she, trembling, "here's a note for you, if you'll please read it when you get home."

Then he saw it was Lois.

"How do you do?" said he, stiffly, and took the note and went on.

When he got home he opened it and read, holding it under the light on the kitchen shelf, when his mother was out of the room.   It did not take long to read.   It was only:

"DEAR JOHN,—Will you please come over to my house a little while to-morrow night?   I want to see you about something.   LOIS."

He folded the note then, put it in his pocket, and asked his mother if supper were ready.

The next evening he was so long about getting ready for meeting, and brushed his coat and blacked his boots so punctiliously, that his mother noticed it and wondered. Was he going to see Lois Arms?   But he did not go.   He only went to meeting, and straight home afterwards.

If he had only known how Lois was watching for him— though then it was doubtful if he could have gone at once. The limitations of his convictions would always be stronger than his own inclination with him.   He could not slacken his own tight rein over himself very easily at his own command.   He had made up his mind never to go near Lois again, and he could not break his resolve.   He tried, though.   Many an evening in the following weeks he dressed himself in his Sunday suit, and even started to go to see Lois ; but he never went.

Meanwhile it was too much for Lois.   It began to be whispered about the neighborhood that Lois Arms was very poorly ; she was going into a decline.   John heard nothing of it, however ; not till his mother told him one evening, about the first of June.

"John," said she—they were sitting at the tea-table— "I'm goin' to tell you, for I think you'd ought to know it.

I've been over to see Lois Arms this afternoon. I heard she wa'n't well, an' I thought I'd ought to ; an' I think she's goin' the way your sister Mary did."

John sat perfectly still, staring at his mother.

"She looks awfully. She was layin' on the settee in the sittin'-room when I went in. She was all alone. An' that ain't all, John ; I know she's a-frettin' over you. I sat down there side of her, you know, an' she looked up at me so kind of wishful. I can't help cryin' now when I think of it."

" 'You ain't feeling very well, Lois?' says I.

" 'No,' says she, and tried to smile. But she couldn't ; she bust right out cryin'. How she did cry ! She sobbed an' sobbed till I thought she'd kill herself. She shook all over, and there ain't anything to her. I put my face down close to her."

" 'What's the matter, you poor child ?' says I.

" 'Oh, Mis' Elliot !' says she, and she put up her poor little thin arms round my neck an' cried harder.

" 'Lois,' says I, ' is it anything about John ?'

" 'Oh,' says she—' oh, Mis' Elliot !' again.

" 'Do you want to see him ?' says I.

"She didn't say anything, only jest held me tighter and cried harder ; but I knew as well's I wanted to. I wish you'd go over there, John ; I think you'd ought to. It's accordin' to what you profess. I'll own I wa'n't jest pleased with the idea of it at first ; but she's a real good girl, an' she's seemed real smart lately 'bout teachin' school. An' she did make me think so much of your sister Mary, the way she looked. Mary didn't hev anything of that kind on her mind, poor child, I'm thankful to say ; but she looked jest like her. I declare I can't bear to think of it."

Mrs. Elliot broke down and cried. John said nothing,

but rose and went away from the table, leaving his supper untasted. Even then he could not bring himself to go and see Lois that night; he had to wait till the next; but he went then.

It was hardly dark. Lois was lying on the settee in the sitting-room when he went in without knocking.

"Lois!"

"Oh, John!"

"How do you do to-night, Lois? I didn't know you were sick till mother told me last night."

"I'm better. Oh, John!"

He pulled a chair up beside her, and sat down. "See here, Lois, I read your note you gave me, you know; but— I couldn't bring myself to come, after all that had happened, to tell the truth. I'm sorry enough I couldn't, now."

"It's all right, John; never mind."

"Now, Lois, what has all the trouble been about?"

"What trouble?"

"The whole of it from the first. What made you do the way you did, an' put off gettin' married?"

"Don't make me tell you, John."

"Yes, I'm going to make you. I know you're sick, an' it seems cruel to bother you; but it's the only way. It ain't in me to go on an' pretend everything's all right when it ain't. I can do everything else for you but that, an' I can't do that if it's to save your life. "You've got to be open with me now, an' tell me."

"John, if I do, will you promise me, *solemn*, that you won't ever tell anybody else?"

"Yes, I'll promise."

"Well, I thought it wasn't doing right by you if I got married that fall. I didn't have anything hardly, not one silk dress, and I couldn't do anything towards furnishing the house. I thought if I should earn some money it would make it easier for you. I didn't want to begin to be a burden to you right off, John."

"But— Why, I don't know what to make of you, Lois. What put such a thing into your head all of a sudden?"

"I ought to have thought of it before."

"Why didn't you tell me?"

"I couldn't. You wouldn't have let me do it."

"Lois, I never saw a girl like you. Here you've been working hard these two years, an' 'most killing yourself, an' never letting me know, an' me not knowing what to think."

"John, I've got a beautiful black-silk dress and a blue one and lots of other things. Then I've got more'n a hundred dollars saved to buy furniture."

"What do you think I care about the dresses and the furniture? I wish they were in Gibraltar!"

"Don't scold me, John."

"Scold you? There! I guess I won't. Poor Lois! poor girl! You meant all right, but it was all wrong. You've 'most killed yourself. But it'll be all right now. Shall I set the carpenters to work to-morrow, darlin'?"

"Oh, John!"

"I'll speak to 'em bright and early, an' you must hurry an' get well. You worryin' about being a burden! Oh, my Lord! Lois, I'll never get over it. You silly, blessed little girl! There's your father coming."

The next morning Lois did not wake very early, she had slept so soundly; but when she did she heard—incredulously at first, then in a rapture of conviction—the carpenters' hammers. The robins were singing, too.

Then her father called up the stairs: "Lois! Lois! John's begun work on the new house again!"

ON THE WALPOLE ROAD.

WALPOLE was a lively little rural emporium of trade ;
thither the villagers from the small country hamlets thereabouts went to make the bulk of their modest purchases.

One summer afternoon two women were driving slowly
along a road therefrom, in a dusty old-fashioned chaise,
whose bottom was heaped up with brown-paper parcels.

One woman might have been seventy, but she looked
younger, she was so hale and portly. She had a double,
bristling chin, her gray eyes twinkled humorously over her
spectacles, and she wore a wide-flaring black straw bonnet
with purple bows on the inside of the rim. The afternoon
was very warm, and she held in one black-mitted hand a
palm-leaf fan, which she waved gently, now and then, over
against her capacious bosom.

The other woman was younger—forty, perhaps ; her face
was plain-featured and energetic. She wore a gray serge
dress and drab cotton gloves, and held tightly on to the
reins as she drove. Now and then she would slap them
briskly upon the horse's back. He was a heavy, hard-
worked farm animal, and was disposed to jog along at an
easy pace this warm afternoon.

There had not been any rain for a long time, and everything was very dusty. This road was not much travelled,

and grass was growing between the wheel-ruts; but the soil flew up like smoke from the horse's hoofs and the wheels. The blackberry vines climbing over the stone walls on either side, and the meadow-sweet and hardhack bushes were powdered thickly with dust, and had gray leaves instead of green. The big-leaved things, such as burdock, growing close to the ground, had their veins all outlined in dust.

The two women rode in a peaceful sort of way; the old lady fanned herself mildly, and the younger one slapped the horse mechanically. Neither spoke, till they emerged into a more open space on a hill-crest. There they had an uninterrupted view of the northwest sky; the trees had hidden it before.

"I declare, Almiry," said the old lady, "we air goin' to hev a thunder-shower."

"It won't get up till we get home," replied the other, "an' ten chances to one it'll go round by the north anyway, and not touch us at all. That's the way they do half the time here. If I'd 'a seen a cloud as black as that down where I used to live, I'd 'a known for sure there was goin' to be a heavy tempest, but here there's no knowin' anything about it. I wouldn't worry anyway, Mis' Green, if it should come up before we get home: the horse ain't afraid of lightnin'."

The old lady looked comical. "He ain't afraid of anything, is he, Almiry?"

"No," answered her companion, giving the horse a spiteful slap; "he don't know enough to get scared even, that's a fact. I don't believe anything short of Gabriel's trumpet would start him up a bit."

"I don't think you ought to speak that way, Almiry,"

said the old lady ; " it's kinder makin' light o' sacred things, seems to me. But as long as you've spoke of it, I don't believe that would start him up either. Though I'll tell you one thing, Almiry: I don't believe thar's goin' to be anything very frightful 'bout Gabriel's trumpet. I think it's goin' to come kinder like the robins an' the flowers do in the spring, kinder meltin' right into everything else, sweet an' nateral like."

" That ain't accordin' to Scripture," said Almira, stoutly.

" It's accordin' to my Scripture. I tell you what 'tis, Almiry, I've found out one thing a-livin' so long, an' that is, thar ain't so much difference in things on this airth as thar is in the folks that see 'em. It's me a-seein' the Scripturs, an' it's you a-seein' the Scripturs, Almiry, an' you see one thing an' I another, an' I dare say we both see crooked mostly, with maybe a little straight mixed up with it, an' we'll never reely know how much is straight till we see to read it by the light of the New Jerusalem."

" You ought to ha' ben a minister, Mis' Green."

" Wa'al, so I would ha' ben ef I had been a man ; I allers thought I would. But I s'pose the Lord thought there was more need of an extra hand just then to raise up children, an' bake an' brew an' wash dishes. You'd better drive along a leetle faster ef you kin, Almiry."

Almira jerked the reins viciously and clucked, but the horse jogged along undisturbed. " It ain't no use," said she. " You might as well try to start up a stone post."

" Wa'al, mebbe the shower won't come up," said the old lady, and she leaned back and began peacefully fanning herself.

" That cloud makes me think of Aunt Rebecca's funeral,"

she broke out, suddenly. "Did I ever tell you about it, Almiry?"

"No; I don't think you ever did, Mis' Green."

"Wa'al, mebbe you'll like to hear it, as we're joggin' along. It'll keep us from getting aggervated at the horse, poor, dumb thing!"

"Wa'al, you see, Almiry, Aunt Rebecca was my aunt on my mother's side—my mother's oldest sister she was—an' I'd allers thought a sight of her. This happened twenty year ago or more, before Israel died. She was allers such an own-folks sort of a woman, an' jest the best hand when any one was sick I'll never forgit how she nussed me through the typhus fever, the year after mother died. Thar I was took sick all of a sudden, an' four leetle children cryin', an' Israel couldn't get anybody but that shiftless Lyons woman, far and near, to come an' help. When Aunt Rebecca heerd of it she jest left everything an' come. She packed off that Lyons woman, bag an' baggage, an' tuk right hold, as nobody but her could ha' known how to. I allers knew I should ha' died ef it hadn't been for her.

"She lived ten miles off, on this very road, too, but we allers used to visit back an' forth. I couldn't get along without goin' to see Aunt Rebecca once in so often; I'd get jest as lonesome an' homesick as could be.

"So, feelin' that way, it ain't surprisin' that it gave me an awful shock when I heerd she was dead that mornin'. They sent the word by a man that they hailed, drivin' by. He was comin' down here to see about sellin' a horse, an' he said he'd jest as soon stop an' tell us as not. A real nice sort of a man he was—a store-keeper from Comstock. Wa'al, I see Israel standin' out in the road an' talkin' with the man, an' I wondered what it could be about. But when he came in an' told me that Aunt Rebecca was dead, I jest sat right down, kinder stunned like. I couldn't ha' felt much worse ef it had been my mother. An' it was so awful sudden! Why, I'd seen her only the week before, an' she looked uncommon smart for her, I thought. Ef it had been Uncle Enos, her husband, I shouldn't ha' wondered. He'd had the heart-disease for years, an' we'd thought he might die any minute; but to think of her—

"I jest stared at Israel. I felt too bad to cry. I didn't, till I happened to look down at the apron I had on. It was like a dress she had; she had a piece left, an' she gave it to me for an apron. When I saw that, I bust right out sobbin'.

"'O Lord,' says I, 'this apron she give me! Oh dear! dear! dear!'

"'Sarah,' says Israel, 'it's the will of the Lord.'

"'I know it,' says I, 'but she's dead, an' she gave me this apron, dear blessed woman,' an' I went right on cryin', though he tried to stop me. Every time I looked at that apron, it seemed as if I should die.

"Thar wa'n't any particulars, Israel said. All the man that told him knew was that a woman hailed him from one of the front windows as he was drivin' by, and asked him to stop an' tell us. I s'posed most likely the woman that hailed him was Mis' Simmons, a widder woman that used to work for Aunt Rebecca busy times.

"Wa'al, Israel kinder hurried me to get ready. The funeral was app'inted at two o'clock, an' we had a horse that wa'n't much swifter on the road than the one you're drivin' now.

"So I got into my best black gown the quickest I could. I had a good black shawl, and a black bunnit too; so I looked quite decent. I felt reel glad I had em'. They were things I had when mother died. I don't see hardly how I had happened to keep the bunnit, but it was lucky I did. I got ready in such a flutter that I got on my black gown over the caliker one I'd been wearin', an' never knew it till I came to go to bed that night, but I don't think it was much wonder.

"We'd been havin' a terrible dry spell, jest as we've been havin' now, an' everything was like powder. I thought my dress would be spoilt before we got thar. The horse was dreadful lazy, an' it was nothin' but g'langin' an' slappin' an' whippin' all the way, an' it didn't amount to nothin' then.

"When we'd got half-way thar or so, thar come up an awful thunder-shower from the northwest, jest as it's doin' to-day. Wa'al, thar wa'n't nowhar to stop, an' we driv right along. The horse wa'n't afraid of lightnin', an' we got in under the shay top as far as we could, an' pulled the blanket up over us ; but we got drippin' wet. An' thar was Israel in his meetin' coat, an' me in my best gown. Take it with the dust an' everything, they never looked anyhow again.

"Wa'al, Israel g'langed to the horse, an' put the whip over her, but she jest jogged right along. What with feelin' so about Aunt Rebecca, an' worryin' about Israel's coat an' my best gown, I thought I should never live to git thar.

"When we driv by the meetin'-house at Four Corners, where Aunt Rebecca lived, it was five minutes after two, an' two was the time sot for the funeral. I did feel reel worked up to think we was late, an' we chief mourners. When we got to the house thar seemed to be consider'ble goin' on around it, folks goin' in an' out, an' standin' in the yard, an' Israel said he didn't believe we was late, after all. He hollered to a man standin' by the fence, an' asked him if they had had the funeral. The man said no ; they was goin' to hev it at the meetin'-house at three o'clock. We was glad enough to hear that, an' Israel said he would drive round an' hitch the horse, an' I'd better go in an' get dried off a little, an' see the folks.

"It had slacked up then, an' was only drizzlin' a leetle, an' lightnin' a good ways off now an' then.

"Wa'al, I got out, an' went up to the house. Thar was quite a lot of men I knew standin' round the door an' in the entry, but they only bowed kinder stiff an' solemn, an' moved to let me pass. I noticed the entry floor was drip-pin' wet too. 'Been rainin' in,' thinks I. 'I wonder why they didn't shet the door.' I went right into the room on the left-hand side of the entry—that was the settin'-room—an' thar, a-settin' in a cheer by the winder, jest as straight an' smart as could be, in her new black bunnit an' gown, was—Aunt Rebecca.

"Wa'al, ef I was to tell you what I did, Almiry, I s'pose you'd think it was awful. But I s'pose the sudden change from feelin' so bad made me kinder highstericky. I jest sot right down in the first cheer I come to an' laughed ; I laughed till the tears was runnin' down my cheeks, an' it was all I could do to breathe. There was quite a lot of Uncle Enos's folks settin' round the room—his brother's family an' some cousins—an' they looked at me as ef they thought I was crazy. But seein' them look only sot me off again. Some of the folks came in from the entry, an' stood starin' at me, but I jest laughed harder. Finally Aunt Re-becca comes up to me.

"'For mercy's sake, Sarah,' says she, 'what air you doin' so for ?'

"'Oh, dear!' says I. 'I thought you was dead, an' thar you was a-settin'. Oh dear!'

"And then I begun to laugh again. I was awful 'shamed of myself, but I couldn't stop to save my life.

"'For the land's sake, Aunt Rebecca,' says I, 'is thar a funeral or a weddin'? An' ef thar is a funeral, who's dead?'

"'Come into the bedroom with me a minute, Sarah,' says she.

"Then we went into her bedroom, that opened out of the settin-room, an' sot down, an' she told me that it was Uncle Enos that was dead. It seems she was the one that hailed the man, an' he was a little hard of hearin', an' thar was a misunderstandin' between 'em some way.

"Uncle Enos had died very sudden, the day before, of heart-disease. He went into the settin'-room after breakfast, an' sot down by the winder, an' Aunt Rebecca found him thar dead in his cheer when she went in a few minutes afterwards.

"It was such awful hot weather they had to hurry about the funeral. But that wa'n't all. Then she went on to tell me the rest. They had had the awfulest time that ever was. The shower had come up about one o'clock, and the barn had been struck by lightnin'. It was a big new one that Uncle Enos had sot great store by. He had laid out consider'ble money on it, an' they'd jest got in twelve ton of hay. I s'pose that was how it happened to be struck. A barn is a good deal more likely to be when they've jest got hay in. Well, everybody sot to an' put the fire in the barn out. They handed buckets of water up to the men on the roof, an' put that out without much trouble by takin' it in time.

"But after they'd got that put out they found the house

10

was on fire. The same thunderbolt that struck the barn had struck that too, an' it was blazin' away at one end of the roof pretty lively.

"Wa'al, they went to work at that then, an' they'd jest got that fairly put out a few minutes before we come. Nothin' was hurt much, only thar was a good deal of water round: we had hard work next day cleanin' of it up.

"Aunt Rebecca allers was a calm sort of woman, an' she didn't seem near as much flustered by it all as most folks would have been.

"I couldn't help wonderin', an' lookin' at her pretty sharp to see how she took Uncle Enos's death, too. You see, thar was something kinder curious about their gittin' married. I'd heerd about it all from mother. I don't s'pose she ever wanted him, nor cared about him the best she could do, any more than she would have about any good, respectable man that was her neighbor. Uncle Enos was a pretty good sort of a man, though he was allers dreadful sot in his ways, an' I believe it would have been wuss than death, any time, for him to have given up anything he had determined to hev. But I must say I never thought so much of him after mother told me what she did. You see, the way of it was, my grandmother Wilson, Aunt Rebecca's mother, was awful sot on her hevin' him, an' she was dreadful nervous an' feeble, an' Aunt Rebecca jest give in to her. The wust of it was, thar was some one else she wanted too, an' he wanted her. Abner Lyons his name was; he wa'n't any relation to the Lyons woman I had when I was sick. He was a real likely young feller, an' thar wa'n't a thing agin him that any one else could see; but grandmother fairly hated him, an' mother said she did believe her mother would rather hev buried Rebecca than seen her married to him. Well, grandmother took on, an' acted so, that Aunt Rebecca give in an' said she'd marry Uncle Enos, an' the weddin'-day come.

"Mother said she looked handsome as a pictur', but thar was somethin' kinder awful about her when she stood up before the minister with Uncle Enos to be married.

"She was dressed in green silk, an' had some roses in her hair. I kin imagine jest how she must hev looked. She was a good-lookin' woman when I knew her, an' they said when she was young there wa'n't many to compare with her.

"Mother said Uncle Enos looked nice, but he had his mouth kinder hard sot, as ef now he'd got what he wanted, an' meant to hang on to it. He'd known all the time jest how matters was. Aunt Rebecca'd told him the whole story; she declared she wouldn't marry him, without she did.

"I s'pose, at the last minute, that Aunt Rebecca got kinder desp'rate, an' a realizin' sense of what she was doin' come over her, an' she thought she'd make one more effort to escape; for when the minister asked that question 'bout thar bein' any obstacles to their gettin' married, an' ef thar were, let' em speak up, or forever hold their peace, Aunt Rebecca did speak up. Mother said she looked straight at the parson, an' her eyes was shinin' an her cheeks white as lilies.

"'Yes,' says she, 'thar is an obstacle, an' I will speak, an' then I will forever hold my peace. I don't love this man I'm standin' beside of, an' I love another man. Now ef Enos Fairweather wants me after what I've said, I've promised to marry him, an' you kin go on; but I won't tell or act a lie before God an' man.'

"Mother said it was awful. You could hev heerd a pin drop anywheres in the room. The minister jest stopped

short an' looked at Uncle Enos, an' Uncle Enos nodded
his head for him to go on.

"But then the minister begun to hev doubts as to whether
or no he ought to marry 'em after what Aunt Rebecca had
said, an' it seemed for a minute as ef thar wouldn't be any
weddin' at all.

"But grandmother begun to cry, an' take on, an' Aunt
Rebecca jest turned round an' looked at her. 'Go on,'
says she to the minister.

"Mother said ef thar was ever anybody looked fit to be
a martyr, Aunt Rebecca did then. But it never seemed to
me t'was right. Marryin' to please your relations an' dyin'
to please the Lord is two things.

"Wa'al, I never thought much of Uncle Enos after I
heerd that story, though, as I said before, I guess he was a
pretty good sort of a man. The principal thing that was
bad about him, I guess, was, he was bound to hev Aunt
Rebecca, an' he didn't let anything, even proper self-respect stand in his way.

"Aunt Rebecca allers did her duty by him, an' was a good
wife an' good housekeeper. They never had any children.
But I don't s'pose she was ever really happy or contented, an'
I don't see how she could hev respected Uncle Enos, scursly,
for my part, but you'd never hev known but what she did.

"So I looked at her pretty sharp, as we sot thar in her
little bedroom that opened out of the settin'-room ; thar was
jest room for one cheer beside the bed, an' I sot on the bed.
It seemed rather awful, with *him* a-layin' dead in the best
room, but I couldn't help wonderin' ef she wouldn't marry Abner Lyons now. He'd never got married, but lived, all by himself, jest at the rise of the hill from where Aunt Rebecca lived.
He'd never had a housekeeper, but jest shifted for himself,

an' folks said his house was as neat as wax, an' he could cook an' wash dishes as handy as a woman. He used to hev his washin' out on the line by seven o'clock of a Monday mornin', anyhow; that I know, for I've seen it myself; an' the clothes looked white as snow. I shouldn't hev been ashamed of 'em myself.

"Aunt Rebecca looked very calm, an' I don't think she'd ben cryin'. But then that wa'n't nothin' to go by; 'twa'n't her way. I don't believe she'd a cried ef it had been Abner Lyons. Though I don't know, maybe, ef she'd married the man she'd wanted, she'd cried easier. For all Aunt Rebecca was so kind an' sympathizin' to other folks, she'd always seemed like a stone 'bout her own troubles. I don't s'pose, ef the barn an' 'house had both burned down, an' left her without a roof over her head, she'd 'a seemed any different. I kin see her now, jest as she looked, settin' thar, tellin' me the story that would hev flustrated any other woman most to death. But her voice was jest as low an' even, an' never shook. Her hair was gray, but it was kinder crinkly, an' her forehead was as white an' smooth as a young girl's.

"Aunt Rebecca's troubles always stayed in her heart, I s'pose, an' never pricked through. Except for her gray hair, she never looked as ef she'd had one.

"She never took on any more when she went to the funeral, for they buried him at last, poor man. He had 'most as hard a time gittin' buried as he did gittin' married. I couldn't help peekin' round to see ef Abner Lyons was thar, an' he was, on the other side of the aisle from me. An' he was lookin' straight at Uncle Enos's coffin, that stood up in front under the pulpit, with the curiousest expression that I ever did see.

" He didn't look glad reely. I couldn't say he did, but all I could think of was a man who'd been runnin' an' runnin' to get to a place, an' at length had got in sight of it.

" Maybe 'twas dreadful for him to go to a man's funeral an' look that way, but natur' is natur', an' I always felt somehow that ef Uncle Enos chose to do as he did 'twa'n't anythin' more than he ought to hev expected when he was dead.

" But I did feel awful ashamed an' wicked, thinkin' of such things, with the poor man layin' dead before me. An' when I went up to look at him, layin' thar so helpless, I cried like a baby. Poor Uncle Enos! it ain't for us to be down on folks after everything's all over.

" Well, Aunt Rebecca married Abner Lyons 'bout two years after Uncle Enos died, an' they lived together jest five years an' seven months ; then she was took sudden with cholera-morbus from eatin' currants, an' died. He lived a year an' a half or so longer, an' then he died in a kind of consumption.

" 'Twa'n't long they had to be happy together, an' some-times I used to think they wa'n't so happy after all ; for thar's no mistake about it, Abner Lyons was awful fussy. I s'pose his livin' alone so long made him so ; but I don't believe Aunt Rebecca ever made a loaf of bread, after she was married, without his havin' something to say about it ; an' ef thar's anything that's aggervatin' to a woman, it's havin' a man fussin' around in her kitchen.

" But ef Aunt Rebecca didn't find anything just as she thought it was goin' to be, she never let on she was disapp'inted.

" I declare, Almiry, thar's the house in sight, an' the

shower has gone round to the northeast, an' we ain't had a speck of rain to lay the dust.

"Well, my story's gone round to the northeast too. Ain't you tired out hearin' me talk, Almiry?"

"No indeed, Mis' Green," replied Almira, slapping the reins; "I liked to hear you, only it's kind of come to me, as I've been listening, that I *had* heard it before. The last time I took you to Walpole, I guess, you told it."

"Wa'al, I declare, I shouldn't wonder ef I did."

Then the horse turned cautiously around the corner, and stopped willingly before the house.

OLD LADY PINGREE.

It was almost dark at half-past four. Nancy Pingree stood staring out at one of her front windows. Not a person was passing on the wide country road; not one came up the old brick walk between the dry phlox bushes to the house.

It was the same picture out there which the old woman had looked at hundreds of times before in winter twilights like this. The interest in it had died away with the expectation of new developments in it which she had had in her youth. Nature to Nancy Pingree had never been anything but a background for life.

When she had first gone to the window she had said, " I wish I could see somebody comin' that belonged to me."

Then she simply stood thinking. The tall, graceful, leafless trees arching over the quiet snowy road, and the glimpse of clear yellow western sky through them, the whole landscape before her, with all the old lights of her life shining on it, became a mirror in which she saw herself reflected.

She started finally, and went across the room with a long shamble. She was lame in one hip; but, for all that, there was a certain poor majesty in her carriage. Her rusty black dress hung in straight long folds, and trailed a little. She held her head erect, and wore an odd black lace turban.

She had made the turban herself, with no pattern. It was a direct outcome of her own individuality; perched on the top of her long old head it really was—Nancy Pingree.

She took down a plaid shawl which was hanging in a little side entry, pinned it over her head, and opened the outer door into the clear twilight. Straight from the door, on this side of the old house, an avenue of pine-trees led to a hen-coop. Whatever majestic idea had been in the head of Nancy's grandfather, Abraham Pingree, when he had set out these trees, it had come to this.

Nancy went down between the windy pines, over the crusty snow, to the hen-coop. She came back with two eggs in her hand. "They've done pretty well to-day," said she to herself.

When she was in the house again she stood shivering for a little while over her sitting-room air-tight stove. She still held the eggs. A question had come up, the answer to which was costing her a struggle.

"Here's two eggs," said she. "I could have one biled for supper; I kinder feel the need of it too; I ain't had anything hearty to-day. An' I could have the other one fried with a little slice of salt pork for breakfast. Seems to me I should reely relish it. I s'pose Mis' Stevens would admire to have an egg for supper. Jenny ain't had any work this week, an' I know she ain't been out anywhere to buy anything to-day. I should think her mother would actilly go faint sometimes, without meat an' egg an' sech hearty things. She's nothin' but skin an' bone anyway. I've a good mind to kerry her one of these eggs. I would ef I didn't feel as ef I reely needed it myself."

The poor soul stood there looking at the eggs. Finally she put the smaller one in a cupboard beside the chimney,

and went out of the sitting-room into the front hall with the
larger one. She climbed stiffly up the stairs, which were
fine old winding ones. Then she knocked at a door on
the landing.

A thin, pretty-faced young woman opened it. Nancy
proffered the egg. She had a stately manner of extending
her lean arm.

"Here's a new-laid egg I thought your mother might relish for her supper, Jenny," said she.

The young woman's sharp, pretty face grew red. "Oh,
thank you, Miss Pingree ; but I—don't think mother needs
it. I am afraid—you will rob yourself."

Nancy held her wide mouth stiff, only opening it a crack
when she spoke. "I've got plenty for myself, plenty. I
shouldn't use this one before it spiled, mebbe, ef I kep' it.
I thought p'rhaps it would go good for your mother's supper ; but you can do just as you like about takin' it."

The young woman accepted the egg with reserved thanks,
then, and Nancy went stiffly back down-stairs.

"I guess ef Jenny Stevens hadn't took that egg, it would
have been the last thing I'd ever offered her," said she, when
she was in her sitting-room. "I don't see how she ever
got the idea she seems to have that I'm so awful poor."

She made herself a cup of tea, and ate a slice of bread-
and-butter for her supper ; she had resolved to save her
own egg until morning. Then she sat down for the evening
with her knitting. She knitted a good many stockings for
a friend's family. That friend came in at the side door
presently. Nancy heard her fumbling about in the entry,
but she did not rise until the sitting-room door opened.

Then, "Why, how do you do, Mis' Holmes," said she,
rising, in apparent surprise.

"I'm pretty well, thank you, Nancy. How do you do?"

"'Bout as usual. Do take off your things an' set down."

The visitor had a prosperous look; she was richly dressed to country eyes, and had a large, masterly, middle-aged face.

"I just heard some sad news," said she, laying aside her shawl.

"You don't say so!"

"Old Mrs. Powers was found dead in her bed this morning."

Nancy's face took on an anxious look; she asked many questions about the sudden death of Mrs. Powers. She kept recurring to the same topic all the evening. "Strange how sudden folks go nowadays," she often repeated.

At length, just before Mrs. Holmes went, she stood up with an air of resolution. "Mis' Holmes," said she, with a solemn tremor in her voice, "I wish you'd jest step in here a minute."

Mrs. Holmes followed her into her bedroom, which opened out of the sitting-room. Nancy pulled out the bottom drawer in a tall mahogany bureau.

"Look here, Mis' Holmes. I've been thinkin' of it over for some time, an' wantin' to speak about it; an' hearin' old Mis' Powers was took so sudden, makes me think mebbe I'd better not put it off any longer. In case anything happened to me, you'd probably be one to come in an' see to things, an' you'd want to know where everything was, so you could put your hand on it. Well, all the clothes you'd need are right there, folded up in that drawer. An' Mis' Holmes, you'll never speak of this to anybody?"

"No, I won't."

"In this corner, under the clothes, you'll find the money to pay for my buryin'. I've been savin' of it up, a few cents at a time, this twenty year. I calculate there's enough for everythin'. I want to be put in that vacant place at the end of the Pingree lot, an' have a flat stone, like the others, you know. If I leave it with you, you'll see that it's all done right, won't you, Mis' Holmes? I feel pretty perticklar about it. I'm the last of the hull family, you know, an' they were pretty smart folks. It's all run out now. I ain't nothin', but I'd kinder like to have my buryin' done like the others. I don't want it done by the town, an' I don't want nobody to give it to me. I want to pay for it with my own money. You'll see to it, won't you?"

"Of course I will. Everything shall be done just as you say, if I have anything to do about it."

Mrs. Holmes was rarely shocked or painfully touched; but the sight of that poor little hoard of white clothes and burial money called up all the practical kindness in her nature. Every one of Nancy's wishes would be faithfully carried out under her supervision.

"If they put the railroad they're talking about through here, it'll make us rich. The Deacon says it will go through the south part of this land. We'd have enough money for burying and living too," said Mrs. Holmes, as Nancy shut and locked the drawer.

"I ain't no stock in the railroad; all the money would belong to the Deacon ef it was put through this land. I've got all over carin' for riches. All I want is to be buried independent, like the rest of my folks."

"How's the woman up-stairs?" asked Mrs. Holmes when she took leave finally. She had three pairs of Nancy's finished stockings in a bundle.

"She's pretty poorly, I think. She keeps me awake 'most all the time."

Nancy did not go farther than the sitting-room door with her departing visitor. When she had heard the outer door close after her, she went swiftly out into the entry. She held the lamp in her hand, and peered sharply into the corners.

"Yes, she did," said she, and took up a good-sized covered basket from behind the door eagerly.

She carried it into the sitting-room, and opened it; it was packed with eatables. Done up in a little parcel at the bottom was the pay for the three pairs of stockings.

This was the code of etiquette, which had to be strictly adhered to, in the matter of Nancy's receiving presents or remuneration. Gifts or presents openly proffered her were scornfully rejected, and ignominiously carried back by the donor Nancy Pingree was a proud old woman. People called her "Old Lady Pingree." She had not a dollar of her own in the world, except her little hoard of burial money. This immense old mansion, which had been the outcome of the ancient prosperity of the Pingrees, was owned entirely by Mrs. Holmes's husband, through fore-closed mortgages.

"You'd better foreclose, Deacon," Mrs. Holmes had said, "and make sure you've got the place safe in your own hands; an' then you'd better let the poor old lady stay there just the same as long as she lives. She needn't know any difference."

Nancy did know a difference. Down in the depths of her proud old heart rankled the knowledge that an outsider owned the home of her fathers, and that she was living in it on toleration. She let some rooms up-stairs, and received the money for them herself. Mrs. Holmes's benevolence was wide, although it was carefully and coolly calculated.

All Nancy had to live on was the rent of these rooms, be-sides the small proceeds from her three hens and her knit-ting, and neighborly donations. Some days she had not much for sustenance except her pride. She was over eighty.

The people up-stairs were a widow and daughter. The mother, after an absence of many years and much trouble, had turned back, of her nature, to the town in which she had been born and brought up. All her friends were gone now, but they had used to be there. So they came and hired rooms of Miss Pingree, and Jenny did sewing to sup-port herself and her mother. She was a good daughter. They had a hard struggle to live. Jenny did not find work very plentiful ; a good many of the women here did their own sewing. She could scarcely pay the rent of fifty cents per week and buy enough to eat. Her mother was sick now—in consumption, it was thought. Jenny did not re-alize it. She was not confined to her bed.

Jenny came down and knocked at Nancy's door the next morning. She had fifty cents in her hand, with which to pay the rent. She always paid it punctually on Saturday morning.

Nancy cast a glance at the money. "How's your moth-er?" said she. "I heerd her coughin' a good deal last night."

"She had a pretty bad night. I'm going for the doctor. This is the money for the rent."

"Let it go."

"Why, I owe it. I can pay it just as well now as any time."

"I don't want it any time. I don't want any pay for this week. I don't need it. I've got enough."

Jenny's face was crimson. "Thank you, but I'd rather pay what I owe, Miss Pingree."

"I sha'n't take it."

The two poor, proud souls stood confronting each other. Then Jenny laid the fifty cents on the window-seat. "You can do just what you've a mind to do with it," said she. "I certainly sha'n't take it back. Then she went out of the room quickly.

"Strange how she got the idea I was so awful poor!" said Nancy, staring at the money resentfully. "I won't tetch it, anyway. She'll see it layin' there next time she comes in."

The next time poor Jenny came in, it was indeed still lying there on the window-seat, a scanty pile of wealth in five and ten cent pieces and coppers.

But Jenny never noticed it ; she had something else to think of then. It was very early the next morning, but Miss Pingree was up, kindling the fire in her sitting-room stove. Jenny ran right in without knocking ; she had a shawl over her head. "Oh, Miss Pingree," she cried, "can't you go up-stairs to mother while I run for the doctor ?"

Nancy dropped the tongs, and stood up. "Is she—" she began. But Jenny was gone. When the doctor came there was no need for him. Jenny's mother was dead. All that was required now was the aid of some of the friendly, capable women neighbors. Nancy went for them, and they came promptly, Mrs. Holmes and two others.

When they had done all that was necessary they went home. Shortly afterwards Jenny came into Nancy's room ; she had on her shawl and hood. She had been very calm through it all, but her pretty face had a fierce, strained look.

"Miss Pingree," she said, abruptly, "who are the select-men?"

"Why, Deacon Holmes is one. What do you want to know for?"

"I've got to go to them. The town will have to bury mother."

"Oh!" cried Nancy, with two sharp notes, one of pity, one of horror.

Suddenly at that Jenny's forced composure gave way; she sank helplessly into a chair, and began to half sob, half shriek. "Oh, mother! mother! mother! poor mother! To think it has come to this! To think you must be buried by the town. What would you have said? It's the worst of all. Poor mother! poor mother! oh, poor mother."

"Haven't you got any money?"

"No. Oh, mother!"

"An' there ain't any of your folks that could help you?"

"We didn't have any folks."

Then she kept on with her cries and moans. Nancy stood motionless. There is no knowing what a clash of spiritual armies with trumpets and banners there was in her brave old heart; but not a line of her face moved; she hardly breathed.

"Wait a minute, Jenny."

Nancy went into her bedroom and unlocked the lowest drawer in the bureau. She took out all of her little hoard of money except a few cents. She limped majestically across the sitting-room to Jenny.

"Here, child; there ain't any need of your goin' to the town. I've got some money here that I can let you have jest as well as not."

"Miss Pingree!"

"Here."

"Oh, what do you mean? How can I take it? What will you do?"

"I shall do well enough. This ain't all; I've got some more."

When all of Jenny's proud scruples which this terrible emergency had left her had been subdued, and she had gone, Nancy took up the fifty cents on the window-seat.

"Guess she's took this now, an' more too," said she, with an odd tone of satisfaction. Even now, in her splendid self-sacrifice, there was a little leaven of pride. There was no mistaking the fact that it gave her some comfort in this harsh charity, which was almost like giving a piece of her own heart. She inspected the neat appointments of poor Mrs. Stevens's funeral with feelings not wholly of grief at her own deprivation of similar honors, nor yet of honest benevolence. There was a grand though half-smothered consciousness of her own giving in her heart. She felt for herself the respect which she would have felt for an old Pingree in his palmiest days.

As time went on she lost this, however; then the humiliating consciousness of her own condition came uppermost. She dreaded to tell Mrs. Holmes of the change in her resources, and now no vanity over her own benevolence rendered the task easier. She simply felt intense humiliation at having to confess her loss of independence.

However, she never regretted what she had done. She grew very fond of Jenny; indeed, the two had much in common. They generally ate their simple meals together. Jenny had plenty of work to do now; Mrs. Holmes gave her a great deal of sewing. She often told Nancy how she was saving up money to pay her debt; she never suspected

11

the real state of the case.   She had taken to thinking that Miss Pingree must have wider resources than she had known.

Nancy would have died rather than let her know of the meagre sum in that consecrated corner of the bureau drawer.   It seemed to her sometimes that she would rather die than have Mrs. Holmes know, but that was necessary. Suppose she should be taken away suddenly, what surprise, and perhaps even distrust, would be occasioned by the scantiness of the burial hoard !   However, she had not told her when spring came.

At length, she set out after tea one night.   She had resolved to put it off no longer.

The cemetery was on the way.   She lingered and looked in.   Finally she entered.

"I'll jest look around a minute," said she.   "I dare say Mis' Holmes ain't through supper."

The Pingree lot was almost in sight from the street.   Nancy went straight there.   The cemetery was itself a spring garden, blue and white with Houstonias and violets.   The old graves were green, and many little bushes were flowering around them.   The gold-green leaf-buds on the weeping-willows were unfolding.

The Pingree lot, however, partook of none of the general lightness and loveliness.   No blessing of spring had fallen on that long rank of dead Pingrees.   There they lay, in the order of their deaths, men and women and children, each covered with a flat white stone above the grave mould.

Tall, thickly-set evergreen trees fenced in closely the line of graves.   In the midst of the cemetery, where gloom was now rendered tender by the infinite promise of the spring, the whole was a ghastly parallelogram of hopeless death.

Nancy Pingree, looking through the narrow entrance gap in the evergreens on the dark, tomb-like enclosure, had, however, no such impression. She regarded this as the most attractive lot in the cemetery. Its singularity had been in subtle accordance with the Pingree character, and she was a Pingree. At one end of the long row of prostrate stones there was a vacant place : enough for another.

Nancy began with this topic when she was seated, a little later, in Mrs. Holmes's Brussels-carpeted, velvet-upholstered parlor. " I looked in the graveyard a minute on my way here," said she, " an' went over to the Pingree lot. I'd allers calculated to have a stone like the others when I was laid at the end there ; but now I don' know. You remember that money I showed you, Mis' Holmes ? Well, it ain't there now ; I've had to use it. I thought I'd better tell you, in case you wouldn't know what to make of it, if anything happened."

Mrs. Holmes stared at her, with a look first of amazement, then of intelligence. " Nancy Pingree, you gave the money to bury that woman up-stairs."

"Hush ! don't you say anything about it, Mis' Holmes. Jenny don't know the hull of it. She took on so, I couldn't help it. It come over me that I hadn't got anybody to feel bad ef I was buried by the town, an' it wouldn't make so much difference."

" How much money was there ?"

" Eighty dollars," said Nancy, with the tone in which she would have said a million.

Mrs. Holmes was a woman who was seldom governed by hasty impulse ; but she was now. She disregarded the strict regulations attached to giving in Nancy's case, and boldly offered to replace the money out of her own pocket. She could well afford to do it.

Nancy looked majestic with resentment. "No," said she. "If it's got to be done by anybody, I'd enough sight rather 'twould be done by the town. The Pingrees have paid taxes enough in times gone by to make it nothin' more'n fair, after all. Thank you, Mis' Holmes, but I ain't quite come to takin' money out an' out from folks yet."

"Well, I didn't mean to hurt your feelings."

"I know you didn't, Mis' Holmes. You meant it kind enough. We won't say no more about it."

"Don't you believe Jenny will be able to pay you back, some time?"

"I don't know. She says she's goin' to, an' I know she means to—she's awful proud. But she can't save up much, poor child, an' I shouldn't wonder ef I died first. Well, never mind. How's the Deacon?"

"He's well, thank you. He's gone to the railroad meeting. Somebody was telling me the other day that Benny Field was waiting on Jenny."

"Well, I believe he's come home with her from meetin' some lately ; but I don't know."

When Nancy reached home that night she wondered if Benny Field were not really "waiting on Jenny." She found him sitting with her on the front door-step.

Before long she knew that he was. Jenny came to her one afternoon and told her she was going to marry Benny Field. Nancy had previously received another piece of intelligence on the same day.

Early that morning Mrs. Holmes had come over with an important look on her face, and announced to Nancy that the new railroad was indeed going to be laid through the Pingree land.

"They are going to build the depot down on the corner too," said she; "and—the Deacon thinks, seeing the property has come up so much in value, that it isn't any more'n fair that—he should make you a little present."

"I don't want any present."

"Well, I didn't mean to put it that way. It isn't a present. It's no more than your just due. I don't think the Deacon would ever feel just right in his conscience if he didn't pay you a little something. You know the property wasn't considered worth so much when he foreclosed."

"How much did he think of payin'."

"I believe he said—about two hundred dollars."

"Two hundred dollars!"

Nancy had been full of the bliss of it all day, but she had said nothing about it to Jenny.

When the girl told her she was going to be married, Nancy looked at her half in awe.

"Well, I am glad, I'm sure," said she, finally. "I hope you'll be happy ef you reely think it's a wise thing to do to git married." Her tone was almost shamefaced. This old woman, who had never had a lover, regarded this young woman with awe, half as if she had stepped on to another level, where it would be indecorous for her to follow even in thought.

"I suppose I am happy," said Jenny. "I never thought anything of this kind would happen to me. There's one thing, Miss Pingree: I wouldn't think of getting married, I'd never consent to getting married, if I didn't think I could pay up what I owe you, if anything, quicker. Benny says (I've told him about it; I said at first I wouldn't get married anyway till you were paid) that I shall have a sewing-machine, and I can have some help, and set up a little dressmaking shop.　I ain't going to buy a single new thing to wear when I get married.　I told him I wasn't.　I've got a little money for you now, Miss Pingree."

"Oh," said Nancy, looking at her with the ecstatic consciousness of her new wealth in her heart, "I don't want it, child, ever.　I'm glad I could do it for your poor mother. I've got plenty of money.　I wish you'd keep this an' buy yourself some weddin' things with it."

Even Jenny's pride was softened by her happiness.　She looked up at Miss Pingree gratefully ; she would have put her arms around her and kissed her had Miss Pingree been a woman to caress and she herself given to caresses. "You are real good to me," said she, "and you were good to mother.　I do thank you ; but—I should never take a bit of comfort in a new dress until I had paid you every dollar of that money."

There was a beautiful clear sunset that night.　Nancy Pingree sat looking over at it from her sitting-room window. All her heart was full of a sweet, almost rapturous peace. She had had a bare, hard life ; and now the one earthly ambition, pitiful and melancholy as it seemed, which had kept its living fire was gratified.

And perhaps that independent burial in the vacant corner of the ghastly Pingree lot meant more than itself to this old woman, whose great unselfishness had exalted her over her almost cowardly pride.

Perhaps she caught through it more strongly at the only real prospect of delight which all existence could hold for one like her.　Perhaps she saw through it, by her own homely light, the Innocent City and the Angel-people, and the Sweet Green Pastures and Gentle Flocks and Still Waters, and herself changed somehow into something beautiful. Perhaps the grosser ambition held the finer one with its wings.

As she sat there, Benny Field came to the door for Jenny. They were going to walk.

Nancy watched them as they went down the path. "I wonder," said she, "if they are any happier thinkin' about gettin' married than I am thinkin' about gettin' buried?"

CINNAMON ROSES.

THE cottage house had been painted white, but the paint was now only a film in some places. One could see the gray wood through it. The establishment had a generally declining look; the shingles were scaling from the roof, the fences were leaning. All the bit of newness and smartness about it was the front door. That was painted a bright blue.

Cinnamon rose-bushes grew in the square front yard. They were full of their little, sweet, ragged roses now. With their silent, lowly persistency they had overrun the whole yard. There was no stepping-room between them. They formed a green bank against the house walls; their branches reached droopingly across the front walk, and pushed through the fence. Children on the sidewalk could pick the roses.

Four men coming up the street with a business air looked hesitatingly at this rose-crowded front yard when they neared it.

" Thar ain't no use goin' in thar into that mess of prickly roses," said one—a large man with a happy smile and swagger.

" We are obliged by law to have the sale on the premises," remarked another, blandly and authoritatively. He was a light-whiskered young fellow, who wore better clothes than the others, and held a large roll of papers ostentatiously.

"Come round to the side of the house, then," spoke another, with low gruffness. He was a man of fifty. He had a lean, sinewy figure, and a severe, sharp-featured face. His skin was dark reddish-brown from exposure to the sun.

So the four filed around into the side yard, with its short grass and its well and well-sweep. Here a red flag was blowing, fastened to a cherry-tree. The men stood together in close consultation, the light-whiskered young man, who was a lawyer, being chief spokesman.

"We may as well begin," he said, finally, standing off from the others. "The hour has passed; no one else is likely to come."

Then they took their places with a show of ceremony—the large man, who now held the roll of papers, a little aloof, the lawyer, and the fourth man, who was old, and had a stupid, anxious face, at one side, and the man with the severe, red face, leaning carelessly against the cherry-tree.

The large man began to read in a loud voice. As he did so, a loud wail came from the house. He stopped reading, and all turned their faces towards it.

"Oh dear!" they heard distinctly, in a shrill, weak, womanish voice, with an unnatural strain on it—"oh dear! oh dear me! Dear me! dear me! *dear* me!" Then followed loud hysterical sobs; then the voice kept on: "Oh, father, what made you leave me?—what made you die an' leave me? I wa'n't fit to be left alone. Oh, father! oh, mother! oh, Luciny! I 'ain't got anybody—I 'ain't, not anybody. Oh dear! oh dear me! dear me!"

"I heard she took on awfully 'bout it," said the auctioneer.

"Well, you might as well go on," said the lawyer; "duty has to be performed, no matter how unpleasant."

"That's so," assented the auctioneer. Then he proceeded, trying to drown out these distressing cries with his powerful utterance. But the cries rang through and above it always. He kept on smilingly; it was the lawyer who grew impatient.

"For God's sake," cried he, "can't something be done to stop that woman? Why didn't somebody take her away?"

"I guess her brother's wife is in thar with her; I thought I see her at the window a minute ago," said the auctioneer, coming down from his high hill of declamation.

"Well, go on quickly, and have done with it," said the lawyer. "This is awful."

The man at the cherry-tree kept clinching his hands, but he said nothing.

The auctioneer resumed his reading of the long statement of the conditions of the sale, then the bidding began. That was soon over, since there were only two bidders. The old man, who held the mortgage, which had been foreclosed, bid with nervous promptness the exact amount of his claim. Then the man at the cherry-tree made a bid of a few dollars more, and he was pronounced the purchaser.

"Going, going—gone!" said the auctioneer, "to William Havers."

William Havers lingered about his new estate until the others had departed, which they did as soon as the necessary arrangements were completed. They wanted to be out of hearing of those sad cries and complaints.

Havers strolled out to the road with them. When he saw them fairly started, he went swiftly back to the house, to the side door.

He knocked cautiously. Directly the cries broke out louder and shriller. " They've come to order me out. Oh dear ! oh dear ! dear ! dear ! They've come to order me out—they hev, they hev !"

Steps approached the door swiftly ; it opened, and a woman appeared. She looked pale and troubled, but she was not the one in such bitter distress, for the cries still sounded from the interior of the house.

" How do you do, Mr. Havers ?" said the woman, with grave formality.

" Can I see her a minute ?" he asked, hoarsely.

" Elsie ? I don't know. She's takin' on dreadfully. She ain't fit to see anybody. I'm afraid she wouldn't."

" If she'd only see me a minute. I've got something I want to say particular."

" Well, I'll see."

She disappeared, and directly the voice, which had been a little more subdued, waxed louder.

" No, I won't see him ; I won't ; I can't. I won't see anybody. I never want to see anybody again as long as I live. Oh dear ! dear !"

" It ain't any use," said the woman, coming back. " She ain't fit to see anybody ; she's 'most crazy. She don't know what she's sayin', anyhow."

" Then you tell her—you go right in an' tell her now— she kin stay here. It don't make any odds about my buyin' the place ; I won't live here. She kin keep right on stayin' here jest the same."

A door opened suddenly, and another woman appeared. She was a pitiful sight. She had a little, slim, bony figure, which seemed to tremble in every joint. Every line in her small face wavered and quivered ; her blue eyes were wa-

tery and bloodshot; her skin all blotched and stained with
tears. She was so disfigured by grief that it was impossible to judge of her natural appearance. She would have
been hideous, had not her smallness and frailty in her distress made her piteous.

Now, however, something besides sorrow seemed to move
her. She was all alive with a strange, impotent wrath, which
was directed against William Havers.

She clinched her red, bony hands; her poor eyes flashed
with indignation, though the force of it was lost through
their tearful weakness.

"I guess I won't keep on stayin' here," she snapped, in
her thin, hoarse voice. "I guess I won't. You needn't
offer me a home. I've got one pervided. I ain't quite
destitute yet. You needn't think you're goin' to come
round now an' smooth matters over. I know why you've
done it. You can't blind me. You've been watchin' all
the time for a chance to pay us back."

"I don't know what she means," said Havers, helplessly, to the other woman.

"She don't know neither. She's 'most beside herself."

Havers began again, trying to speak soothingly: "Now
don't you go to feelin' so, Miss Mills. You 'ain't got to
leave. I ain't a-goin' to live here myself anyway. I'm
goin'—"

"I ain't goin' to stay here another night. I ain't goin'
to be livin' on you. I guess you'll find out. Oh, Luciny,
what would you have said if you'd knowed what was comin'
twenty year ago! Oh dear! dear!"

The other woman took her by the shoulders. "Now,
Elsie, you've got to walk right in an' stop this. You ain't
talkin' with any reason. You'll be ashamed of yourself
when you come to."

She walked her forcibly out of the entry, and shut the door. Then she turned to Havers.

"You mustn't mind what she says," said she. "She's been about as near crazy as anybody can be, and not be, all day."

"I don't know what she kin mean by my tryin' to pay her back, Mis' Wing."

"Lor', she don't know herself. She's got kind of a notion that you're to blame for buyin' the place. She'll know better to-morrow."

"It's a good deal better for me to buy it than Steadman," said Havers, with a troubled look. "I shall let her keep right on here. To tell the truth, I bought the place more fur—"

"You're a real good man," said Mrs. Wing, warmly. She was Elsie Mills's brother's wife. "She'll be ashamed of herself to-morrow. But she's comin' to live with Silas an' me. She's welcome to a home with us jest as long as she lives. She ain't fit to live alone anyway. We knew when her father died that she'd run the place out in no time. Well, she's takin' on so, I shall have to go in. I don't like to leave her a minute. Don't you mind anything she said."

Contrary to Mrs. Wing's expectations, Elsie Mills was not disposed to retract her words. The next day, when she was peacefully domiciled in her brother's house, and seemed a little calmer, her sister-in-law opened on the subject.

"What in creation made you talk so to William Havers last night?" said she. "Not one man in a hundred would have made you the offer that he did after he'd bought a place."

Elsie fired up at once. " I guess I know why," said she. " Luciny gave him the mitten once—that's why. He's doin' it to show out."

"Why, Elsie Mills, are you in your right mind ?"

"Yes, I am. He acted awful cut up. He never got over it. He always meant to pay us back. Now he's bought the place an' invited me to live on him, he'll feel better."

"Well, I never !"

Mrs. Wing repeated the conversation to her husband, and told him that she was really scared about Elsie : she did not act with any reason.

Silas Wing laughed. " Don't you worry, Maria," said he. " Elsie always had that notion. I never really believed that Luciny give Havers the mitten, myself ; but she did, an' she always went on the notion that he was dreadful upset over it. Elsie's queer. She's mighty meek an' yieldin' generally ; she seems to be kinder goin' sideways at things fur the most part ; but if she ever does git p'inted straight at anything, thar ain't no turnin' her."

" Do you remember anything about William Havers waitin' on Luciny ?"

"Yes. He was round some two years before she died. I didn't think much about it. Luciny was always havin' beaux. An' no wonder ; thar wa'n't many girls like her. Lord ! I kin see her now, jest how she used to look. Poor Elsie wa'n't much beside her, but I don't believe she ever give that a thought. She thought Luciny was beautiful, an' thar wa'n't anything too good fur her. She'd slave herself 'most to death to save her. No ; don't you worry, Maria. Elsie's always run on that notion."

Silas Wing was Elsie Mills's half-brother ; the dead Lu-

cina had been her own sister. The house which had just
been sold was her inheritance from her father.

Silas Wing was an easy, prosperous man, with a shrewd
streak in his character. His sister's property was sadly
deteriorated, and a poor investment. He had no idea of
sinking money to secure it for her, but he was perfectly willing to provide for her, and gave her a most cordial invitation to his home.

He gave her a front chamber in his large, square white
house, and furnished it with her own things, to make it seem
like home.

"Thar ain't any reason why Elsie shouldn't be as happy as
a queen here as long as she lives," he told his wife. "Thar
ain't many women fare any better. She ain't much over
forty. She'd hev to work hard if she was in some places,
an' she ain't fit to. Now she'll jest hev to help you round
a little, an' live jest as comfortable as can be."

Elsie's chamber commanded a good view of her old home,
which was a little farther down on the opposite side of the
street. She could see the yard full of cinnamon roses, and
the blue front door, which stood out bravely. That blue
door was due to her ; she had painted it herself. Silas had
some blue paint left after painting his farm wagon, and she
had begged it. Then she had stood on a chair—a small,
lean figure in clinging calico—and plastered the brilliant
blue thickly over the front door, wielding the brush stiffly in
her little knotty hand, stretching herself up on her slight,
long limbs.

She had always viewed the effect with innocent delight.
The unusualness of a blue front door did not trouble her.
She was as crude and original as a child in her tastes. It
looked bright and fresh in itself, and to her thinking re-

lieved the worn look of the house. She would have painted farther had her paint lasted. After the door was painted blue, she had held up her head better under a neighbor's insinuation that the house was "run down." That, indeed, had led her to do it.

Now she sat forlornly at her chamber window, her elbows on the sill, her sharp chin in her hands, for many an hour, staring over at the blue door and the cinnamon roses, as she might have stared at lost jewels. Nothing about the place seemed so distinctly her own as that blue door; nothing seemed so dear as those cinnamon roses, because her dead sister Lucina had planted them. It is sad work looking at things that were once one's own, when they have not been given away for love, and one still wants them. Elsie was meekly unhappy over it. She was no longer violent and openly despairing, as she had been at first. That had been very unusual with her. She was fond of her brother and his wife, and conformed gently to all the requirements of her new life. She had very little enduring resistance to circumstances in her; she did not kick against the pricks. Still she lay close to them, and was tender enough to be cruelly stung by them.

She grew old, and her friends noticed it.

"It ain't any use," Mrs. Wing told her husband: "Elsie ain't never goin' to be the same as she was before she lost her house. She's grown ten years older in a week."

"She's a silly girl; that's all I've got to say," replied Silas Wing.

One evening Elsie, at her open chamber window, overheard a conversation between her brother and his wife. They were sitting on the doorstep.

"Havers came over to-night," said Silas. "I see him

out at the gate as I come along. He's goin' to let his other house and live here, he says. I declare I'd hardly think he'd want to, this is so much further from town. But the other'll let better, I s'pose. Reckon that's the reason."

"Is he goin' to fix this one up?" asked Mrs. Wing.

"Yes; he's goin' to paint it up some, an' hev the roof shingled. He was kinder laughin' about that blue door, but he didn't seem to think he'd hev it altered afterwards. I told him how poor Elsie painted it herself."

"Lord! I shouldn't think he'd want to keep that blue door."

"He seemed to think it wouldn't look bad if the house was painted new to go with it. He's goin' to cut down all them cinnamon roses in the front yard to-morrow. He's brought over his sickle to-night."

That was all Elsie heard. She did not know how long they talked after that. He was going to cut down Lucina's cinnamon roses!

She kept saying it over to herself, as if it were a task she had to learn, and she could not easily understand. "Luciny's cinnamon roses. He's goin' to cut down all Luciny's cinnamon roses to-morrow."

It was twelve o'clock that night when Elsie crept down the stairs and out the front door. There was no sound, except her brother's heavy breathing, in the house. He and his wife had been asleep three hours. Elsie sidled out of the yard, keeping on the grass, then sped across the road, and down it a little way to her old home. There were only these two houses for a long way; there was not a light visible in either. No one would be passing at this time of the night; there was no danger of her being observed; more-

over, she could not have been very easily.   Great elms grew
on both sides of the street, and they cast broad, flickering
shadows.   Elsie, keeping close with the shadows, as if they
were friends, and progressing with soft starts, after little
pauses to listen and peer, might have passed for a shadow
herself.

She stopped for a minute at the corner of the yard, and
stared fearfully over at the periled roses.   The moon was
coming up, and she could see them distinctly.   She fell to
remembering.   To this innocent, simple-hearted creature,
clinging so closely to old holy loves and loyalties that she
meditated what to her was a desperate deed in defence of
them, that fair dead Lucina became visible among her cinnamon roses.

Elsie for a minute, as she stood there, was all memory ;
the past seemed to come back in pity for her agony of regret, and overshine the present.

The light of an old morning lay on those roses, and young
Lucina stood among them, lovely and triumphant.   She had
just set them in the earth with her own dear hands.

When Elsie moved again she was ready for anything.

Oh, those cinnamon roses !   the only traces which that
beautiful, beloved maiden had left of her presence in the
world !   Oh, those cinnamon roses !   the one little legacy of
grace which she had been able to bequeath to it !

When Elsie came out on the road again she had something carefully covered by her apron, lest the moon should
make it glitter.   She ran home faster than she had come,
with no watchful pauses now.   But she had to make another cautious journey to the Wing barn before she returned
to her room.   Finally she gained it successfully : no one
had heard her.

The next morning some one knocked while the family were at the breakfast table. Silas went to the door.

" The queerest thing," he said, when he returned. " Havers has lost his sickle, the one he brought over last night, an' he wants to borrow mine, an' I can't find that high or low. I would ha' sworn it was hangin' on the hook in the barn. He wants to get them cinnamon roses cut."

" Well, I should think it was queer !" said his wife. " I know I saw it out there yesterday. Are you sure it's gone ?"

" Course I am. Don't you s'pose I've got eyes ?"

Elsie said nothing. She bent her head over her plate and tried to eat. They did not notice how white she was. She kept a sharp watch all day ; she started every time any one spoke ; she kept close to the others ; she dreaded to hear what might be said, but she dreaded more not to hear.

" Has Mr. Havers found his sickle yet ?" Mrs. Wing asked, when her husband came home at night. He had been over to the village. " I see you ridin' home with him."

" No, he 'ain't. He's gone and bought a new one. Says he's bound to hev them roses cut down to-morrow. 'Ain't seen anything of ourn yet, hev ye ?"

" No ; I've been out myself an' looked."

" Well, it beats everything — two sickles right in the neighborhood ! I ruther think some one must ha' took 'em."

" Land ! Silas, nobody's took 'em. I know all about you. I've known you to hev things stole before, an' it always turned out you was the thief. When you lose a thing, it's always stole."

Elsie found it harder to start out to-night; a little of the first impetus was wasted. Still, she did not hesitate. When the house was quiet she crept out again, and went over to the old place.

She did not stop to reflect over the roses to-night. She was braced up to do her errand; but it must be done quickly, or she would give way. She went straight around the house to the woodshed, where she had found the sickle the night before. As she came close to the open arch which served as entrance, there was a swift rush, and William Havers stood beside her holding her arm.

"Oh !" she said, then began feebly gasping for breath.

"Elsie Mills! what in the world are you doin' here?"

She looked up in his face, but did not speak.

"Why, Elsie, what is it? Don't you be afraid, you poor little thing. What was it you wanted? Tell me."

"Let me go !"

"Of course I will, but I think you'd better tell me what you wanted, an' let me get it. I'd be glad enough to. I didn't mean to scare you. I suspected I'd hed a sickle stole, an' I was kinder keepin' a lookout. When I jumped out I didn't see who 'twas."

"I stole your sickle, an' I'll steal it again if you offer to tech Luciny's roses."

"You—stole my sickle—I offer to tech Luciny's roses! I guess I don't know what you mean, Elsie."

"I mean jest what I say. I'll steal your sickle every time you offer to cut down Luciny's roses."

"You mean them roses out in the front yard?"

"Course I do. Didn't she set 'em out?"

"Lord! I didn't know. I didn't know nothin' about it. I hadn't no notion of your feelin' bad. If I had, I guess—

Why didn't you tell me? Why didn't you come right over? I'd hev mown off my own fingers before I'd offered to tech them roses if I'd known."

"Do you s'pose I was goin' to come over here an' ask you not to, when I knew you was jest doin' it for spite 'cause Luciny wouldn't hev you?"

"'Cause Luciny wouldn't hev me?"

"Yes, 'cause Luciny wouldn't hev you."

"I didn't never ask her to hev me, Elsie."

"What?"

"I didn't never ask her."

"I don't see what you mean by that."

"Why, I mean I didn't."

"What was you hangin' round her so fur, then? An' what made you act so awful cut up?"

"Didn't you never know 'twas you, Elsie?"

"Me?"

"Yes, you."

"Well, all I've got to say is, you'd orter to be ashamed of yourself. A girl like Luciny—you wa'n't fit to look at her. I guess there wa'n't many fellers round but would ruther hev hed her than anybody else. I guess it's sour grapes."

"I knew Luciny was the handsomest girl anywheres round, but that didn't make no difference. I always liked you best. I don't think you'd orter be mad, Elsie."

"I ain't; but I don't like to see anybody like Luciny slighted. I wa'n't nothin' side of Luciny."

"Well, I reckon your thinkin' you wa'n't was what made me take to you in the first place. Look a-here, Elsie. I'm a-goin' to tell you. I've been wantin' to, but I didn't know but I'd die before I got a chance. I come over an' bought this place jest on your account, when I heard the mortgage was goin' to be foreclosed. I didn't reely s'pose you'd be willin' to marry me, you treated me so indiff'rent in Luciny's day; but I didn't pay no attention to that. I wanted you to keep on livin' here. When you acted so mad 'cause I spoke about it, I didn't dare to say anything more. But I wish you'd come now. Won't you? I'll go back to my old home; 'twon't put me out a mite. An' I sha'n't do it because I've got any spite, nor want to show out. It'll be because I've always liked you better'n anybody else, an' wanted to do something fur you."

Elsie was crying. "I've got to get used to thinkin' of it," she sobbed.

"Well, you think it over, an' you come back here. It's your home, where you've always lived, an' I know you'll be happier, no matter how much your brother's folks do fur you. You make up your mind an' come back. I'll hev the house painted, an' it 'll look real pretty with the blue door; an' I won't hev a single one of them cinnamon roses cut down, if I find out that their roots are tangled up in a gold mine."

"No; I sha'n't let you give me the house fur nothing; I sha'n't, William."

"Now, Elsie, thar ain't no reason in your feelin' so. When anybody gets to thinkin' a good deal of anybody else, why it don't make so much difference about yourself; the other one stands first. If you kin see the other one happy, you don't know any difference betwixt that an' bein' happy yourself, an' if you kin only *do* something to make the other one happy, why, it comes before anything else. That's jest the way I feel. I've got eddicated up to it. So don't you worry about takin' the house fur nothing. You ain't. Now you'll git cold standin' here. I'm goin' to see you safe to your brother's, an' you think it over."

Her little nervous hand clutched at his coat sleeve to detain him.

"Look-a here a minute. I want to tell you. I ain't never had anything like this to say before, an' I don't know how. When I got to thinkin' about anything of this kind, I always put Luciny in instead of me. But I want to tell you—I'm all took by surprise, an' I don't know—but mebbe, if I could get used to thinkin' of it, I—could—"

"I guess I don't know what you mean, Elsie."

"Well, it don't seem as if thar would be much sense in my gittin' married now, anyway."

Elsie Mills and William Havers were married at the bride's brother's. When the bridal couple went to their own home, they did not enter at the front door. They passed around to the side one, because the front yard was so full of cinnamon roses.

THE BAR LIGHT-HOUSE.

Government had for several years been sadly neglect-
ing a job of mending, in the case of the Bar Light-house
bridge. Here and there boards had begun to spring suspiciously beneath unwary footsteps; then the wind had
begun to tear them off, and the rain to rot and moulder
them down. What was every man's business was nobody's, and no individual was disposed to interfere with
the province of that abstract millionaire, the United States
government. To be sure, the keeper of the Bar Light,
Jackson Reed, who was naturally more solicitous concerning the holding-out of the structure than any one else, had
wildly and fruitlessly patched some of the worst places, off
and on, after a hard "northeaster," when he awoke more
keenly to the exigencies of the case, and the hopeless dila-
toriness of his task-master. But it had amounted to very
little. Long neglect had made something more than mere
patching necessary. Now the quarter-mile bridge leading
to the Bar Light-house, if not in an absolutely unsafe condition, was not calculated to inspire with any degree of
confidence the unaccustomed crosser at least. It was not
quite so bad at low tide, or on a mild, still day. There
was not much to fear then beyond a little fall and a duck-
ing; that is, if one cleared one of those ragged apertures

successfully. But on a dark night, with the winds howling over it, and the ocean thundering beneath it, it was the sort of a bridge that only a disembodied spirit could be supposed to cross with any degree of nonchalance.

The light-house itself was only an ordinary dwelling-house, strongly built, with a tower for the light. It stood on a massive pile of rocks, with little tufts of coarse vegetation in the clefts. Jackson Reed, who had an unfortunate love and longing for a garden spot, had actually wheeled enough earth over from the mainland for a little patch a few yards square, and when he was not engaged in a fruitless struggle with the broken bridge he was engaged in a fruitless struggle with his garden. A pottering old man was Jackson Reed, lacking in nervous force and quickness of intellect; but he had never let the light go out, and the only thing that is absolutely required of a light-house keeper is to keep the light burning for the sailors who steer by it.

The wonder was that his wife Sarah should have been his wife. She was a person not of a different mould merely, but of a different kind; not of a different species, but a different genus. Nervous and alert, what her husband accepted in patient silence she received with shrill remonstrance and questioning. Her husband patched the bridge, crawling over its long reach on his old knees; she railed, as she watched him, at the neglect of government. He uncomplainingly brushed the sand from his little, puny, struggling plants, and she set her thin face against the wind that cast it there.

In both the religious element or cast of mind was strongly predominant, but Jackson Reed simply looked out on nature and into his own soul, and took in as plain incontro-

vertible facts the broken bridge, the tossing sea, his little
wind-swept, sand-strewn garden-patch, and God in heaven.
Neither proved the other or nullified the other; they were
simply *there.* But Sarah Reed, looking out on the frail,
unsafe bridge which connected them with the mainland,
and the mighty, senseless sea which had swallowed up her
father and a brother whom she had idolized, and the poor
little tender green things trying to live under her window,
had seen in them so many denials of either God's love and
mercy, or his existence. She was a rheumatic old woman
now, almost helpless, in fact, unable to step without the
help of her husband. And she sat, day in and day out, at
one of the sea-windows of her sitting-room, knitting, and
holding her defiant old heart persistently against the pricks.

The minister at Rye, a zealous young man, with an innocent confidence in his powers of holy argument, had visited
her repeatedly, with the view of improving her state of
mind. She had joined the church over which he presided
in her youth; indeed, it was the church nearest to the light-
house, and that was three miles distant. The minister had
heard from one of his parishioners, who was a connection
of hers, that Mis' Reed had lost her faith, and straightway
he was fired with holy ardor to do something for her spiritual benefit. But even his tonguey confidence and ingenu-
ousness could glean but little satisfaction from his inter-
views with the rheumatic and unbelieving old woman.

"No, Mr. Pendleton," she used to say, shaking a thin,
rheumatic hand with an impressiveness which her hearer
might have copied advantageously in the pulpit, "it ain't
no use. You kin talk about seein' with the spirit, an' wor-
shippin' with the spirit; anybody needs a little somethin'
to catch hold on with the flesh; when it's all spirit it's too

much for a mortal bein' to comprehend, an' the Lord knows
I ain't never had much of anything but spirit. I ain't
never had any evidence, so to speak; I ain't never had a
prayer answered in my life. If I have, I'd jest like to
know how. You say, mebbe, they've been answered jest
the same, only in a different way from I asked for. Ef you
call it answerin' prayer to give one thing when you ask for
another, I don't. An' I'd ruther not believe thar was any
God than to believe he'd do a thing like that. That's jest
contrary to what he said about himself an' the bread an'
the stone in the New Testament. It's worse to think he'd
cheat anybody like that than to think he ain't anywhar,
accordin' to my mind. No, Mr. Pendleton, a human bein'
needs a little human evidence once in a while to keep up
their faith, an' I ain't never had any. I'll jest let you
know how it's been a leetle. Here I am, an old woman,
an' me an' Jackson's lived here on this rock for forty year.
An' thar's been things I've wanted different, but I ain't
never had 'em—things that I've cried an' groaned an'
prayed to the Lord for—big things an' little things—but I
never got one. Ef the Lord had give me one of the little
things, it seems to me that I might have got a feeling that
he was here.

"Forty year ago, when Jackson an' me was jest married
an' set up housekeepin' here, thar was an awful storm one
night, an' my father an' my brother was out yonder in it.
I stayed on my knees all night prayin'. The next mornin'
their two darlin' bodies was washed ashore. My brother
had only been married a few months—the sweetest, loving-
est little thing she was. She began to pine. I prayed to
hev her spared. She died, an' left her little baby."

"But you had him for your own, did you not?" inter-

rupted Mr. Pendleton, desperately. " He has been a comfort to you. God has displayed his love and mercy in
this case in sparing him to you."

" Mr. Pendleton "—and the rheumatic hand went up
again—" I ain't never asked to hev him spared to me; ef
I had it would hev been different. I ain't got through yet.
Thar's been lots of other things, big ones, that I might jest
as well not speak of, and little ones. Look at that bridge!
I'll ventur' to say that you shook in your shoes when you
came over it, an' wouldn't be sorry this minute ef you was
safe back. Whenever Jackson goes over it my heart is
still an' cold till he comes back, for fear he's fell through.
I've prayed to the Lord about that. Then—you may think
this a little thing—but thar is Jackson's garden. He set
out a rose-bush in it fifteen year ago. Well, it ain't died.
Thar ain't ever been a rose on it, though. An' it seems to
me sometimes that if thar should be jest one rose on that
bush that I should believe that the Lord had been thar.
You wouldn't think I'd been silly enough to pray about
that. I hev. It's fifteen year, an' thar ain't never been a
rose thar. No, Mr. Pendleton, it ain't no use. You mean
well, but it lays with God, ef he's anywhar, to show himself to me in a way I can get hold on."

So the pretty, rosy-faced young minister would go away,
picking his way cautiously over the unstable bridge, after
a somewhat nonplussed prayer, to which Mrs. Reed, inca-
pacitated from kneeling by her rheumatic knees, had sat
and listened grimly.

The Bar Light-house was three miles from Rye. A
sandy, desolate road almost as billowy as the sea stretched
between. The only house in the whole distance was a
little brown one just at the other side of the bridge. The

Weavers lived there, a mother and daughter. They supported themselves by sewing for a shop in Rye. Jackson Reed's nephew, William Barstow, had been engaged to marry the daughter—Abby her name was; but a month ago he had brought a wife home from the city. He had rented a pretty little tenement over in Rye, and gone to housekeeping. Abby Weaver had tied up a few little notes and keepsakes in a neat parcel, and put them away out of sight. Then she went on with her work. She was a plain, trustworthy-looking girl, with no show about her, as different as possible from the one her recreant lover had married. She was pretty, with an entrancing little air of style about everything she wore. Abby had seen her go by a few times in a jaunty velvet jacket and kilted petticoat, with the fair, round face with its fringe of fluffy blond hair smiling up at her husband out of a bewitching little poke. Then she had gone and looked at herself in her poor glass, taking in the old black alpaca, the plain common face with the dull hair combed back from her forehead.

"No wonder," said she, "an' I'm glad it's so, for I don't think the Lord can blame him."

Sarah Reed had found a double trial in the breaking-off of the engagement. In the first place, she had liked Abby. In the second place, this new matrimonial arrangement had taken the darling of her heart from under her immediate supervision. If he had married Abby Weaver, he would have lived either in the light-house, as he had done all his life, or in her mother's cottage. Nothing could suit his pretty city lady but to live in Rye. The bare idea of the light-house terrified her.

Sarah Reed's frame of mind had not improved since the marriage.

One afternoon, a few weeks after the young couple had set up housekeeping, an unexpected deficiency in some household stores sent Jackson Reed to Rye, where the nearest markets were. It was the middle of the afternoon when he went, and there was a storm coming.

"Don't worry, Sarah," his last words were, "an' I'll be back by five to light the lamp. It'll be pretty near dark enough for it then, I reckon, ef it keeps on this way, ef it *is* June."

She sat at her window with her knitting after he had gone, and watched the storm roll up. She had taken a fancy lately to a landward window, the one with the poor little garden-patch under it, and the rose-bush which never blossomed. The bush really looked wonderfully thrifty, considering its many drawbacks to growth. But it was in a sheltered corner, and had all the warmth and mildness that could be had in the bleak place. It was three feet high or so, a hardy little Scotch rose. There certainly seemed no reason in nature why it should not blossom, but blossom it never had. Mrs. Reed never looked at it now for buds. She never even glanced at it to-day; she only looked out uneasily at the darkening sky, and knit on her stocking. She was always knitting stockings; in fact, it was all the kind of work she could do, and she had never been an idle woman with her brain or her fingers. So she knit stout woollen stockings for her husband and William Barstow from morning till night. Her husband kept the house tidy and did the cooking, and he was as faithful at it as a woman. No one looking at the room in which Mrs. Reed sat would have dreamed that it was not the field of action of a tidy housewife. It was a plain, rather cheerless kind of a room. There was a large-figured, dull-colored ingrain carpet on the floor, there was a shiny table, and some flag-bottomed chairs, and a stiff, hair-cloth sofa. A few shells on the mantel-shelf, a lamp-mat that Abby Weaver had made, and a framed wreath which had lain on William Barstow's father's coffin were all the ornaments. Take a room like that and set it on a rock in the ocean, with the wind and the waves howling around it, and there is not anything especially enlivening about it.

Mrs. Reed had been rather good-looking in her youth, and was even rather good-looking now. She had bright, alert blue eyes, and pretty, soft gray hair. But there was an air of keen unrest about her which could jar on nerves like a strident saw. In repose she would have been a sweet old woman. Now she looked and was, as people say, hard to get along with. Jackson Reed's light burning meant more to the Lord, perhaps, than it did to the sailors.

At five o'clock the storm was fairly there, and the old light-house keeper had not come home. A heavy tempest twilight was settling down, and it was almost time the lamp was lighted.

Six o'clock came, and it was darker yet, and still she sat there alone, her knitting dropped in her lap. Seven o'clock, and her old husband had not come. It was quite dark now, and a terrible night, hot and pitchy, and full of mighty electric winds and fires and thunders. A conglomerate roar came from the ocean as from a den of wild beasts. Suddenly an awful thought struck the wretched old woman at the light-house window, and swift on its track rushed another still more awful. The first was, her husband had had a "turn" somewhere on that lonely road from Rye. "Turns," as she called them, Jackson Reed had had once or twice before, but they had never inter-

fered with his duty. He had fallen down insensible, and
lain so for two or three hours. This was what had happened to him now. And the second thought was—her darling. William Barstow was out on that dreadful sea, and
there was no light to guide him to port. Strange that she
had not thought before. Yes, it was Tuesday. Was it
Tuesday? Yes, the very day he was going down to Lock-
port with Johnny Sower. He was out on that sea somewhere in a boat, which could not live in it a minute. Yes,
it was to-day he was going. He and his pretty little wife
were talking it over Sunday night. She was lamenting,
half in sport and half in earnest, over the lonesome day
she would have, and he promised to bring her home a new
bonnet to console her. Yes, it was Tuesday, and Jackson
Reed had told Abby Weaver about it yesterday—that was
Monday. He had forgotten that she was no longer so interested in Willie Barstow's movements. And when he
told his wife what he had done she scolded him for his
thoughtlessness.

Yes, it was Tuesday, and he was out o 'hat sea, and
there was no lamp lighted. Nothing to keep him off these
terrible rocks that the light had been set there to show. In
the morning he would be thrown dumb and cold where she
could almost see him from her window. It would be with
him as it had been with his father and grandfather, and
maybe with his wife as it had been with his poor young
mother. All the strong, baffled, but not suppressed nature
of the woman asserted itself with terrible force.

"Oh, my darling! my darling! my darling!" she shrieked,
in a voice which was in itself both a prayer and a curse.
"You out thar, an' all the love in your mother's heart can't
light ye home! Oh, the black water rollin' over that beau-

tiful face, an' those laughin' blue eyes that looked at me
when you was a baby, an' those black curls I've brushed,
an' those lips I've kissed—puttin' out that lovin' soul! O
Lord! Lord! Lord!"

"He's been a good boy," she went on in a curious tone,
as if the mighty ear of the inexorable God she had half believed in was become now a reality to her, and she was
pouring arguments, unavailing though they might be, into
it—"he's been a good boy; never any bad habits, an',
what's worse than bad habits, never any little mean actions.
There's Abby Weaver, I know; but look at the face of
the girl he's married. O Lord, love is the same behind a
homely face an' a handsome one. But while you keep on
makin' folks that think roses is prettier than potatoes, an'
pearls than oysters, the love that looks out of a pretty
face will hold the longest an' the strongest. He wa'n't to
blame—O Lord, he wa'n't to blame. Abby was a good
girl, but you made this other one as pretty as a pictur'.
He wa'n't to blame, Lord, he wa'n't to blame. Don't drown
him for that. It ain't right to drown him for that. O Lord!
Lord! Lord!"

She sat there shrieking on in a strained, weak voice, half
in prayer, half in expostulation. The wind rose higher and
higher, and the sea thundered louder and longer. A new
terror seized her. If her husband should recover from the
bad turn which she suspected he had had, and attempt to
cross that bridge now, he would be killed too. God knew
what new rents might be in it. When her sitting-room
clock clanged out nine, above the roar of the storm, she
went into a perfect fury of despair. Down she sank on
those old rheumatic knees that had not bent at her bidding
for the last five years, and prayed as she never had before.

13

In the midst of her agony a great calm fell suddenly over her.

"I will go an' light the lamp myself," she said, in an awed voice, "an' He will go with me." Slowly Sarah Reed arose on feet that had not borne her weight for five years. Every movement was excruciating torture, but she paid no heed to it; she seemed to feel it and yet be outside of it. She realized, as it were, the separateness of her soul and her spiritual agony from all bodily pain.

She walked across the floor, went out into the entry, and groped her way up the narrow stairs leading to the tower. She dragged herself up the steep steps with terrible determination. She slid apart the slide at the top, and a blaze of light almost blinded her. *The lamp was lighted.*

Sarah Reed might have floated down those stairs, upborne on angels' wings, for all she knew. Somehow she was back in her sitting-room, on her knees. Her husband found her there, a half-hour later, when he staggered, pale as death and drenched to the skin, into the room.

"Good Lord, Sarah, who lit the lamp?" his first words were.

"The angel of the Lord," she answered, solemnly, raising her gray head.

"I hed a turn over thar on the road, 'bout a mile out of Rye. I've jest come to an' got home. Seemed to me I should die when I thought of William. The bridge is pretty well broke up, but I hung on to the side. And, Lord! when I saw that light burnin' I could ha' come over a cobweb. Who come to light it, Sarah?"

"The angel of the Lord," she said again. "Don't you ever say it ain't so, Jackson; don't you ever dare to try to make me stop thinking it's so. I've been askin' the Lord all these years for something to show me that he was anywhar, an' he has give it to me. I crawled up them stairs—"

"*You* went up them stairs, Sarah?"

"Yes; I went up to light the lamp, an' it was lit. The Lord hed been thar. It's true about him."

The pale old man went up to his kneeling wife and raised her tenderly.

"Don't you believe his angel lit it?" she asked, looking at him with anxious intensity.

"Yes, Sarah, I do," replied Jackson Reed. The thought was steadily recurring to his half-dazed brain, " Abby Weaver, Abby Weaver lit the lamp; but Sarah, Sarah need not know."

The next morning Sarah Reed, looking out of her window, saw a little, pure white rose on the bush beneath it.

"Yes, I meant to have told you it had budded," said her husband, when she exclaimed. "I found it thar yesterday. Thar's another one too."

It was a lovely clear morning. Abby Weaver, looking out of her window, saw William Barstow pass by on his way to the light-house to tell the old folks of his safety.

A LOVER OF FLOWERS.

THERE was no room for any flower-garden in front of the house, it stood so close to the road. The little cottage, unpainted, save for white strips around the windows, had an air of pushing forward timidly. The small, white, sharp-steepled meeting-house stood just opposite. There was a joke prevalent in the town about Silas Vinton's house having once started to go to meeting when the bell rang. The three uneven stone steps before the front door led quite down to the narrow sidewalk, which was scarcely more than a foot-path among grasses and weeds. The little strip of green under the two windows, on each side of the front door, was closed in neatly and trimly by a low fence of two whitewashed rails. Silas Vinton had tried to start some plants in their tiny enclosures, but it was no use. The drip from the eaves directly into the roots kept the earth washed away from them. So there was nothing but the little pebbly strip, where the rain-drops fell, through the close green grass.

Silas had enough land at the rear of his house to make up for the want of it at the front. There were two good acres stretching back to the river-bank. One acre was the flower and vegetable garden, and the other was an apple orchard. There were cherry-trees, but they were scattered about at intervals through the garden. This morning the trees were all in blossom, and some early flowers in the garden, and Silas was out there working. He had taken his coat off, and his blue calico shirt-sleeves showed.

He was a young man under thirty, and he looked still younger. It was not so much because he was short and slender and fair-haired; the effect of childishness he gave came from some inward quality which shaped the outward to itself.

People used to say, "Silas Vinton is a dreadful woman-ish sort of fellar." But it was not womanishness nor boy-ishness, but that childhood which has no sex, which ap-peared in his round, delicate face. When he was a baby he must have had that same look of wonder and inquiry and innocent speculation that he had now.

He was at work near where the garden left off and the orchard began. The flowering apple-trees were full of bees, and there was a cherry-tree near him which swarmed with them. One could hear their murmuring, and through that, between the ranks of rosy trees, the spring rush of the river. The air was very sweet. Silas was setting out some potted plants which he had brought from the house. His windows were rigged with shelves for them from sill to ceiling. His house in winter was like a hothouse.

All this time Silas kept talking to himself, or rather mur-muring. It was the way the bees did, and he too might have been making honey, after a spiritual fashion. "Lilacs and snowballs and almond; apple-blows and cherry-blows and daffodils."

He talked to himself about the plants he was setting out: where this one had better be put, and that one, and how deep to dig the holes for them. But every now and then he cast his eyes about, and repeated, "Lilacs and snowballs and almond : apple-blows and cherry-blows and daffodils." It was like a refrain to his practical musings. These new flowers were in sight around him as he worked, and he kept counting them over as he might have counted jewels.

He was so busy talking and working that he did not hear a girl's footstep on the garden path.

The first he heard was a timid, high-pitched voice, saying, " Silas."

He started, and looked around. "Why, Althea Rose," said he, "you thar? How still you came! I didn't hear you."

"Mother wants to know," the girl said, bashfully, " if you've got any parsnips you could let her have."

"Certain I have ; a good parcel ; and your mother's quite welcome to 'em. They're right over here."

Silas led the way, and the girl followed him. She had a basket in her hand. She was an odd-looking girl. Her face was sweet and fair ; her features were small and delicate, and had that quality which one calls waxen in lilies ; but everything about her which did not depend directly on nature was peculiar. Her thick light hair was cut squarely across her neck, and shelved out around her ears. She had had a little stiff white sun-bonnet on her head, but she had taken it off as she came along, and held it dangling by the strings. Her dark calico dress was so prim in its cut that it almost acquired an individuality from it. She was only sixteen, but the skirt touched the ground, and hid her little, coarsely shod feet. The waist was long and straight, and kept back all her pretty curves.

She stood watching Silas as he got the parsnips. When he had filled her basket, and rose and turned to speak to her, the delicate color flashed up deeper in her cheeks, and her eyes changed like blue flowers when the wind strikes them.

"There," said he, "I've filled the basket full; and tell your mother she can have some more any time she wants 'em."

"Thank you," said Althea. She did not offer to pay him. Silas never would take any pay; he took pride in supplying the neighbors gratuitously with vegetables, and seemed hurt if any remuneration were offered.

Althea reached out her hand for the basket, but Silas kept it. "I'm goin' up to the house," said he, "and I'll carry it as far's the gate; it's kinder heavy."

Passing along by the clumps and little beds of early flowers, a thought struck him. "See here, Althea," said he, "don't you want a bunch of flowers?"

She gave him such a bashful smile that it ran into a silly giggle. "I—don't know."

"I'll pick you a bunch in a minute. I won't keep you waitin', for I suppose your mother wants to cook them parsnips for dinner. I'm goin' to have some for mine; got 'em all dug in the house."

Then he cut lavishly sprays of dioletra, or lady's ear-drop, snowballs, daffodils, flowering almond, and the other spring flowers. He stopped a moment hesitatingly at a lilac bush. "See here," said he, "I don't know as you like lilacs."

"Yes, I like 'em."

"Well, here's a bunch, then. I didn't know but what you mightn't like them; some folks don't. I reckon it's 'most too strong a drink of spring, if I can put it that way, to some. I can stan' it."

When he handed her the enormous nosegay he had cut for her, he looked at her uncovered head. "Ain't you afraid of gettin' burnt, without your bonnet?" asked he.

She gave her sun-bonnet a spiteful little fling. "I hate it!" cried she, with sudden nerve. "Mother makes me wear it, but I pull it off the minute I get out of sight. I want a hat like the other girls. So!"

"I thought the bonnet was real pretty," said Silas, sympathizingly. "I'd wear it, if I was you. You're so light-skinned you'll burn real easy. You're something the color of them apple-blows over there now; it would be a pity if you got brown."

"I don't care if I do! Thank you for the flowers," she added, a little more softly, as she went out of the gate.

Silas stared after her. "She changes round so quick," said he, "as if she was in a gust of wind. First her head a-droppin' down, an' then she goes to dancin'. She's got the prettiest face I ever saw. She's prettier than mother was. I declare I might count her with them flowers I was countin' over when she came. She might come in after the daffodils."

When he went into the house and busied himself about cooking his dinner, he did say the string of flowers over several times, and named Althea after the daffodils. The fancy seemed to please him.

He lived alone now; he had always had his mother with him up to the last two years. Now she was dead. His father had died years before, when Silas was a young boy. He had been a hard-working, penurious man, and had amassed in his lifetime what the townsfolk considered quite a property. He owned his house and land clear, and had, besides, a little sum in the bank.

In his lifetime, Silas and his mother, who was a meek, sickly woman, had been pitifully pinched. After his death, when the restrictive cause had ceased, they found it difficult to rid themselves of the habit of being so. Many a time, Mrs. Vinton would look scared when some extra expenditure came in question, and say, " Oh, Silas, what would your father say?" The old man's iron, grinding will still lived on in his house after he was dead.

Still they made some innovations. Silas took the larger part of the garden for flowers, and cramped the vegetables into a smaller space. Before, Silas and his mother had not been allowed room for one little flower-bed.

After his mother's death Silas went further. He would not sell his vegetables, but gave them away to any one of the neighbors who wanted them. He took the greatest delight in it. The sale of vegetables had always been quite an item to them, but he never thought of missing the money. He was naturally generous, and giving was what singing would have been to him had he been musical.

In apple and cherry time, too, the children swarmed about his place. They were very fond of Silas, and visited him a great deal at all seasons. He seldom had any other visitors.

Silas had never seemed like other young men, whether it was owing to his having been with his mother so much or his own natural disposition. He never had any associates of his own age, of either sex ; nobody ever dreamed of his getting married. People called him a little simple. They were simple country folk themselves. He was probably no simpler than they, only his simplicity took such a different direction that they recognized it as such.

Silas had always loved flowers. As he grew older, and especially after his mother's death, when all direct human interest was gone, the love of them turned his whole self. He was natural enough to grasp after some absorbing inter-

est, and his gentle taste seemed to point that way the easi-
est ; and he might have turned a worse way, though it might
have been a nobler one, than into beds of lilies and thick-
ets of roses. He was so fond of his dainty pursuit that it
was only very dimly that he felt the need of anything else.
He ruminated so heartily and long over his flowers that it
might have been with him as with Marvel's fawn, " Lilies
without, roses within." His very thoughts might have been
tinctured ; he thought principally of his flowers, and his
brain was full of true images of roses and lilies and apple-
blossoms.

But now he began to think of Althea. After she came
for the parsnips she slid continually into his mind along
with the flowers. He hoped every day her mother would
send her again on some errand, but she did not. Silas,
without knowing that he did so, watched and waited every
day for her. Finally, after a week or so, it occurred to him
that Althea's mother might like more parsnips.

So he carried her a great basketful. After he had gone
—he would not come into the house, but lingered a moment in the yard looking wishfully at Althea, who stood in
the door behind her mother—Mrs. Rose eyed her daughter knowingly and sharply.

" Silas Vinton didn't come to bring me parsnips," said she.

Althea looked up at her, frightened. She still stood a
few paces behind her mother ; it was her way. If they
were out on the street together Althea followed after her
always. When her mother attempted to face her, Althea
always stirred softly round behind her.

" He came to see you," said her mother, turning round
again. Althea turned too, and looked more scared than before, and made some unintelligible dissent.

"Yes, he did," said her mother; "don't you contradict me, Althea!"

It was easy enough, after seeing Mrs. Rose, to understand how the daughter got her peculiarities. The mother had moulded the daughter after her own model as exactly as she could, and more exactly than she was herself aware. Mrs. Rose in her youth must have looked very like Althea. She wore her light, partly gray hair cut squarely around her ears, just like Althea's; her dress had the same prim, uncompromising cut.

She was arbitrary, and full of a self-confidence that was absolute power, and so was Althea. But the girl had not yet shown her disposition; her mother, by her older, stronger will, and force of habit, as yet kept her down. She only rebelled furtively. The stern rule she had always been under gave her a shy, almost cowed, demeanor; once in a while the spirit in her gave a flash, as it were, and that was all.

The two were alone; they had no relatives. They had a small pension to live on, and owned a small house besides. Mrs. Rose's husband had died in the army. They never called on the neighbors, and the neighbors never called on them. "Queer folks," they called them.

Mrs. Rose's opinion seemed fortified when Silas came the next Sunday night, and made a call.

He went to evening meeting first, and then walked down the shadowy road towards the Rose house. The Roses were not meeting-folks, and he could not walk home with Althea, and so break the ice. However, Silas was not bashful. It is doubtful if he realized he was going courting at all. He had a great bunch of flowers in his hand, and he was merely going to carry them to Althea; he did not look much beyond that.   His horizon, blue and sunny though it was, came close around him always.

So he sat in Mrs. Rose's sitting-room that evening, and eyed Althea sweetly and kindly, but was not perturbed, though he said very little.

" He's comin' after you, Althea," said her mother, after he had gone.

Althea, slinking behind her mother, burst into tears.

"What are you crying for?" asked her mother, sharply.

" I—don't want him to."

" Get your candle and go to bed."

Silas came regularly every Sunday evening after that, but he met with an obstacle in his wooing which might have nonplussed some lovers—the mother always stayed in the room when he called.   There she would sit, straight and fiercely watchful, her bushy short hair curving around her ears.   However, Silas was not annoyed.   The need of a formal declaration never suggested itself to him ; he supposed Althea *knew,* and there was no need of saying much about it anyway.   It would have puzzled any one to have told Althea's opinion when Silas's attentions became persistent ; she was shy and docile, but never expressive.   Still it was all right with Silas, as long as she did not repulse him.   He had had so much to do with flowers that he derived his notions of girls from them.   He did not look for much return but sweetness and silence.

At last Mrs. Rose grew impatient.   Spring had come round again, and Silas had visited Althea a whole year, and still nothing decisive had been said.   She could not see why.   It was singular that with her keen character she should have been so stupid, but she was.   She did not dream that her own watchfulness and intense interest might delay matters.

One night she spoke out bluntly when he was taking leave. "Look here, Silas Vinton, I think if you an' Althea are goin' to git married, you might as well be about it!"

"I'm ready when Althea is," said Silas. He gave one glance over at her behind her mother, then he did not dare to look again. He was outwardly calm, but the shock of Mrs. Rose's sudden remark was over his very soul. He felt as if he were still in paradise, but as if some angel had given him a rude shake.

"Oh, she's ready enough," said Mrs. Rose. "She don't need to have anything more'n a new dress, an' we can make that in a week."

"A week?" repeated Silas, half in rapture, half in stupidity. "Well, I'm all ready when Althea is. I'm all ready." He kept saying it over as he backed down the steps.

"I'll git the stuff for the dress to-morrow, then," called Mrs. Rose after him, standing in the door.

"I'm all ready when Althea is," Silas's voice answered out of the darkness.

As for Althea, when the door closed after him she began to cry. Her mother turned round and saw her.

"What air you cryin' for!" she demanded.

"Oh, mother, I don't want to get married in a week. I won't! So!"

"Althea Rose," said her mother, "if you don't quit cryin', an' light your candle, an' go to bed an' behave yourself, I'll shake you!"

And Althea lit her candle and went. The old whip-crack was too much for her. But when she was in her room alone, she clinched her fists, and shook her stubborn head at herself in her little looking-glass.

"I won't," muttered she. "*So!*"

The next morning the trees were all in blossom, and
Silas was out in his garden working. He was all over his
excitement of last night. His mind was running in the
larger circle into which Mrs. Rose's proposal, like a stone
in a pond, had thrown it, just as calmly as it had in a
smaller. He felt as if he had always been going to be
married in a week.

"It's jest such a mornin' as 'twas last year," said he,
" when I counted her in after the daffodils."

" Silas !"

"Why, Althea, you've come ag'in !"

She was flushed and trembling, but her eyes were keen.
" I want to tell you something, Silas."

"Why, Althea, what is it ?"

"You won't tell mother? Promise you won't tell ; promise—promise."

"Course I won't, if you don't want me to. Althea, what
is it ?"

"She'd kill me. You won't tell ?"

"No, never, long's I live !"

She gave a scared glance around her. "Mother's making me marry you," said she, bluntly, "an' I don't want
to."

"Oh, Althea !"

"It's the truth."

Silas stood staring at her pitifully. "You was so afraid
of her you didn't dare say anything, weren't you?" said he.

"Yes, I was."

"You poor little thing !" Great tears ran down Silas's
cheeks.

"Then I needn't marry you, need I ?"

"Course you needn't."

"Well, how can we fix it? You know we've got to tell mother something."

"I guess I don't know just what you mean."

"Mother'll make an awful fuss; she's set on my having you; she thinks you've got property. An' if she knew I was the one that broke it off she'd kill me. You've got to make her think you're the one."

"But I ain't."

"That don't make any difference; you've got to make her think so."

"But what shall I say the reason was?"

"Say you've thought it over, and you don't want to support a wife. She'll believe that. They all know your father was awful tight."

The bewilderment in Silas's face almost obscured its awful sadness.

"You won't let her blame me, anyhow, will you, Silas?"

"No; she sha'n't blame you. I'll tell lies before she shall blame you."

"You are awful good, Silas. Say, you don't mind much, do you?"

"No. Don't think nothin' about me; I sha'n't mind; I've got my flowers. Althea—"

"What?"

"I don't know as you'll want to; I jest happened to think of it, that's all. You know folks, when they are goin' to get married, the way we was, kiss each other. You ain't ever kissed me. I never thought much about wantin' you to till now, when you are goin'. Would you mind it to kiss me once? I don't suppose you will want to—"

"Yes, I will," said Althea; and she put up her sweet face and kissed him.

He choked back a sob. " You'd better go now," said he,
" or your mother'll be wonderin' where you are."

She looked frightened. "You be sure not to let her
blame me," she said as she turned to go.

" Yes, I'll be sure. Don't you worry, Althea."

She disappeared among the filmy green bushes, and he
sat down on a stone under the cherry-tree, and held his
head in his hands.

When he got up he looked older. Sorrow at one jerk
had taken him farther out of his long childhood than the
years had. He was a step nearer the rest of the world ;
he would not be so odd, by that much, again. He went
up through the garden to the house ; he looked about
him wonderingly as he went. "Thar's been an awful
change," said he, to himself. " I guess I don't see
straight. The flowers an' things look queer, as if I hadn't
seen 'em before. It's worse than mother's dyin'. Thar
ain't so much God in this. I don't know how to go to
work to stan' it. Poor little thing! she sha'n't have no
more trouble about it, nohow."

Very close to the Rose house stood another, tiny and
modest and white-curtained ; but it had an eye and an ear
ever alert in it. The woman who lived there was sickly,
with too active a mind for her own narrow life, so she fastened it on her neighbors.

This last evening, when Silas went to the Roses she knew
it, as usual. When, by and by, she heard loud talk, she
raised her window softly and listened. The front door of
the Rose house was evidently open, and the talkers were
standing in the hall.

She could hear only one voice to distinguish the words ;
that was Mrs. Rose's. When she was excited she always

spoke very loud. "You're worse than your father was," the listener heard her say, "an' he was tighter than the bark of a tree; but he wa'n't quite so mean but what he could get married. Althea's well rid of such a poor stick as you. Don't s'pose she'd hed 'nough to eat if you'd married her, nor a dress to her back."

The loud talk kept on, and the woman listened greedily. When it had ceased, and Silas had crept down the path, and the door had closed behind him with a great house-shaking slam, she felt more healthily alive than she had for many a day.

Soon all the town knew how Silas Vinton had jilted Althea Rose—because he was too tight to support her. His courtship had made a deal of laughing comment; now he was mercilessly badgered.

He shut himself up with his flowers and bore it as well as he could. Once a neighbor to whom he had given vegetables many a time, offered him pay. That almost broke his heart. Then others no longer asked for them, and he understood why.

He never met Althea at all. For the next two years, except for one or two glimpses of her from his window, he would hardly have known she lived in the same town.

In the winter of the second year, a man who came to his house on an errand asked him if he knew his old girl was going to be married.

Silas turned white. "What do you mean?" asked he.

"Althea Rose is goin' to get married, if the fellar don't back out 'cause he don't want to support her. What do you think of that?"

"I'm glad, if she likes him," said Silas.

14

"Well, mebbe when he comes to count up the cost he'll think better on't."

Silas made no reply to the taunt. He stood behind his window-shelves of plants, and watched the man go down the sidewalk. "I don't wonder he talks so," said he. "But there wa'n't no other way to save her. I had to have some reason. The worst of it is, it ain't true."

Silas's potted plants were very beautiful that year; they were covered with blossoms. Every one stopped to look at his windows.

Silas sat behind them that day after he heard the news, and watched the street. He was hoping Althea would go by; he wanted to see her.

She did come in sight towards night—a slender, girlish figure, in some prim, eccentric winter garb, as noticeable as her summer one.

Silas ran to the door. "Althea!"

"What?" said she, standing at the gate.

He went down the steps and stood beside her.

"See here, Althea. I heard this morning you was going to get married. Is it so?"

Althea looked down. "Yes."

"I jest want to know—it's safe for you to tell me, Althea; I'd die sooner than anybody should know. I jest want to know if it's all right this time; if *you* want him, or it's your mother making you, the way it was before. 'Cause, if it is, don't you marry him. Don't you be afraid of your mother; I'll stan' by you."

"I—guess it's all right, Silas."

"Then your mother ain't making you? Don't you be afraid to tell."

"No, she ain't. She couldn't, really. I'd manage somehow, the way I did before, if I didn't want him."

" I'm glad it's all right, Althea."

She giggled softly. She was fingering a gold locket which she wore outside of her shawl. " See what a pretty locket he give me," said she ; " he's real generous."

" She didn't mean to hurt me when she said that, I know," said Silas, when she had gone on and he was back in the house. And he was right, she did not ; that time she was only a cat's-paw for a scratch of fate.

She was married a couple of weeks later. On the afternoon of the wedding-day one of the neighbor's children came in to see Silas. She was a pretty little thing, and he was very fond of her. She used to tease her mother to let her go over to Silas's.

When she entered Silas's little front room to-day the first thing she did was to stare at the plants in the window. Every blossom was gone.

" Why, Silas," she piped up, " where's all your flowers ?"

" They've gone to a weddin', deary," said Silas.

A FAR-AWAY MELODY.

THE clothes-line was wound securely around the trunks of four gnarled, crooked old apple-trees, which stood promiscuously about the yard back of the cottage. It was tree-blossoming time, but these were too aged and sapless to blossom freely, and there was only a white bough here and there shaking itself triumphantly from among the rest, which had only their new green leaves. There was a branch occasionally which had not even these, but pierced the tender green and the flossy white in hard, gray nakedness. All over the yard, the grass was young and green and short, and had not yet gotten any feathery heads. Once in a while there was a dandelion set closely down among it.

The cottage was low, of a dark-red color, with white facings around the windows, which had no blinds, only green paper curtains.

The back door was in the centre of the house, and opened directly into the green yard, with hardly a pretence of a step, only a flat, oval stone before it.

Through this door, stepping cautiously on the stone, came presently two tall, lank women in chocolate-colored calico gowns, with a basket of clothes between them. They set the basket underneath the line on the grass, with a little

clothes-pin bag beside it, and then proceeded methodically
to hang out the clothes. Everything of a kind went together, and the best things on the outside line, which could
be seen from the street in front of the cottage.

The two women were curiously alike. They were about
the same height, and moved in the same way. Even their
faces were so similar in feature and expression that it might
have been a difficult matter to distinguish between them.
All the difference, and that would have been scarcely apparent to an ordinary observer, was a difference of degree,
if it might be so expressed. In one face the features were
both bolder and sharper in outline, the eyes were a trifle
larger and brighter, and the whole expression more animated and decided than in the other.

One woman's scanty drab hair was a shade darker than
the other's, and the negative fairness of complexion, which
generally accompanies drab hair, was in one relieved by a
slight tinge of warm red on the cheeks.

This slightly intensified woman had been commonly considered the more attractive of the two, although in reality
there was very little to choose between the personal appearance of these twin sisters, Priscilla and Mary Brown. They
moved about the clothes-line, pinning the sweet white linen
on securely, their thick, white-stockinged ankles showing
beneath their limp calicoes as they stepped, and their large
feet in cloth slippers flattening down the short, green grass.
Their sleeves were rolled up, displaying their long, thin,
muscular arms, which were sharply pointed at the elbows.

They were homely women ; they were fifty and over now,
but they never could have been pretty in their teens, their
features were too irredeemably irregular for that. No
youthful freshness of complexion or expression could have

possibly done away with the impression that they gave. Their plainness had probably only been enhanced by the contrast, and these women, to people generally, seemed better-looking than when they were young. There was an honesty and patience in both faces that showed all the plainer for their homeliness.

One, the sister with the darker hair, moved a little quicker than the other, and lifted the wet clothes from the basket to the line more frequently. She was the first to speak, too, after they had been hanging out the clothes for some little time in silence. She stopped as she did so, with a wet pillow-case in her hand, and looked up reflectively at the flowering apple-boughs overhead, and the blue sky showing between, while the sweet spring wind ruffled her scanty hair a little.

"I wonder, Mary," said she, "if it would seem so very queer to die a mornin' like this, say. Don't you believe there's apple branches a-hangin' over them walls made out of precious stones, like these, only there ain't any dead limbs among 'em, an' they're all covered thick with flowers? An' I wonder if it would seem such an awful change to go from this air into the air of the New Jerusalem." Just then a robin hidden somewhere in the trees began to sing. "I s'pose," she went on, "that there's angels instead of robins, though, and they don't roost up in trees to sing, but stand on the ground, with lilies growin' round their feet, maybe, up to their knees, or on the gold stones in the street, an' play on their harps to go with the singin'."

The other sister gave a scared, awed look at her. "Lor, don't talk that way, sister," said she. "What has got into you lately? You make me crawl all over, talkin' so much about dyin'. You feel well, don't you?"

"Lor, yes," replied the other, laughing, and picking up a clothes-pin for her pillow-case; "I feel well enough, an' I don't know what has got me to talkin' so much about dyin' lately, or thinkin' about it. I guess it's the spring weather. P'r'aps flowers growin' make anybody think of wings sproutin' kinder naterally. I won't talk so much about it if it bothers you, an' I don't know but it's sorter nateral it should. Did you get the potatoes before we came out, sister?"—with an awkward and kindly effort to change the subject.

"No," replied the other, stooping over the clothes-basket. There was such a film of tears in her dull blue eyes that she could not distinguish one article from another.

"Well, I guess you had better go in an' get 'em, then; they ain't worth anything, this time of year, unless they soak a while, an' I'll finish hangin' out the clothes while you do it."

"Well, p'r'aps I'd better," the other woman replied, straightening herself up from the clothes-basket. Then she went into the house without another word; but down in the damp cellar, a minute later, she sobbed over the potato barrel as if her heart would break. Her sister's re-marks had filled her with a vague apprehension and grief which she could not throw off. And there was something a little singular about it. Both these women had always been of a deeply religious cast of mind. They had studied the Bible faithfully, if not understandingly, and their relig-ion had strongly tinctured their daily life. They knew al-most as much about the Old Testament prophets as they did about their neighbors; and that was saying a good deal of two single women in a New England country town. Still this religious element in their natures could hardly have been termed spirituality. It deviated from that as much as anything of religion—which is in one way spirituality itself—could.

Both sisters were eminently practical in all affairs of life, down to their very dreams, and Priscilla especially so. She had dealt in religion with the bare facts of sin and repentance, future punishment and reward. She had dwelt very little, probably, upon the poetic splendors of the Eternal City, and talked about them still less. Indeed, she had always been reticent about her religious convictions, and had said very little about them even to her sister.

The two women, with God in their thoughts every moment, seldom had spoken his name to each other. For Priscilla to talk in the strain that she had to-day, and for a week or two previous, off and on, was, from its extreme deviation from her usual custom, certainly startling.

Poor Mary, sobbing over the potato barrel, thought it was a sign of approaching death. She had a few superstitious-like grafts upon her practical, commonplace character.

She wiped her eyes finally, and went up-stairs with her tin basin of potatoes, which were carefully washed and put to soak by the time her sister came in with the empty basket.

At twelve exactly the two sat down to dinner in the clean kitchen, which was one of the two rooms the cottage boasted. The narrow entry ran from the front door to the back. On one side was the kitchen and living-room; on the other, the room where the sisters slept. There were two small unfinished lofts overhead, reached by a step-ladder through a little scuttle in the entry ceiling: and that was all. The sisters had earned the cottage and paid for it years before, by working as tailoresses. They had, besides, quite a snug little sum in the bank, which they had saved out of their hard earnings. There was no need for Priscilla and Mary to work so hard, people said ; but work hard they did, and work hard they would as long as they lived. The mere habit of work had become as necessary to them as breathing.

Just as soon as they had finished their meal and cleared away the dishes, they put on some clean starched purple prints, which were their afternoon dresses, and seated themselves with their work at the two front windows ; the house faced southwest, so the sunlight streamed through both. It was a very warm day for the season, and the windows were open. Close to them in the yard outside stood great clumps of lilac bushes. They grew on the other side of the front door too ; a little later the low cottage would look half-buried in them. The shadows of their leaves made a dancing net-work over the freshly washed yellow floor.

The two sisters sat there and sewed on some coarse vests all the afternoon. Neither made a remark often. The room, with its glossy little cooking-stove, its eight-day clock on the mantel, its chintz-cushioned rocking-chairs, and the dancing shadows of the lilac leaves on its yellow floor, looked pleasant and peaceful.

Just before six o'clock a neighbor dropped in with her cream pitcher to borrow some milk for tea, and she sat down for a minute's chat after she had got it filled. They had been talking a few moments on neighborhood topics, when all of a sudden Priscilla let her work fall and raised her hand. " Hush !" whispered she.

The other two stopped talking, and listened, staring at her wonderingly, but they could hear nothing.

"What is it, Miss Priscilla?" asked the neighbor, with round blue eyes. She was a pretty young thing, who had not been married long.

"Hush! Don't speak. Don't you hear that beautiful music?" Her ear was inclined towards the open window, her hand still raised warningly, and her eyes fixed on the opposite wall beyond them.

Mary turned visibly paler than her usual dull paleness, and shuddered. "I don't hear any music," she said. "Do you, Miss Moore?"

"No-o," replied the caller, her simple little face beginning to put on a scared look, from a vague sense of a mystery she could not fathom.

Mary Brown rose and went to the door, and looked eagerly up and down the street. "There ain't no organ-man in sight anywhere," said she, returning, "an' I can't hear any music, an' Miss Moore can't, an' we're both sharp enough o' hearing'. You're jest imaginin' it, sister."

"I never imagined anything in my life," returned the other, "an' it ain't likely I'm goin' to begin now. It's the beautifulest music. It comes from over the orchard there. Can't you hear it? But it seems to me it's growin' a little fainter like now. I guess it's movin' off, perhaps."

Mary Brown set her lips hard. The grief and anxiety she had felt lately turned suddenly to unreasoning anger against the cause of it; through her very love she fired with quick wrath at the beloved object. Still she did not say much, only, "I guess it must be movin' off," with a laugh, which had an unpleasant ring in it.

After the neighbor had gone, however, she said more, standing before her sister with her arms folded squarely across her bosom. "Now, Priscilla Brown," she exclaimed,

"I think it's about time to put a stop to this. I've heard about enough of it. What do you s'pose Miss Moore thought of you? Next thing it 'll be all over town that you're gettin' spiritual notions. To-day it's music that nobody else can hear, an' yesterday you smelled roses, and there ain't one in blossom this time o' year, and all the time you're talkin' about dyin'. For my part, I don't see why you ain't as likely to live as I am. You're uncommon hearty on vittles. You ate a pretty good dinner to-day for a dyin' person."

"I didn't say I was goin' to die," replied Priscilla, meekly: the two sisters seemed suddenly to have changed natures. "An' I'll try not to talk so, if it plagues you. I told you I wouldn't this mornin', but the music kinder took me by surprise like, an' I thought maybe you an' Miss Moore could hear it. I can jest hear it a little bit now, like the dyin' away of a bell."

"There you go agin!" cried the other, sharply. "Do, for mercy's sake, stop, Priscilla. There ain't no music."

"Well, I won't talk any more about it," she answered, patiently; and she rose and began setting the table for tea, while Mary sat down and resumed her sewing, drawing the thread through the cloth with quick, uneven jerks.

That night the pretty girl neighbor was aroused from her first sleep by a distressed voice at her bedroom window, crying, "Miss Moore! Miss Moore!"

She spoke to her husband, who opened the window. "What's wanted?" he asked, peering out into the darkness.

"Priscilla's sick," moaned the distressed voice; "awful sick. She's fainted, an' I can't bring her to. Go for the doctor—quick! quick! *quick!* The voice ended in a shriek on the last word, and the speaker turned and ran back to the cottage, where, on the bed, lay a pale, gaunt woman, who had not stirred since she left it. Immovable through all her sister's agony, she lay there, her features shaping themselves out more and more from the shadows, the bed-clothes that covered her limbs taking on an awful rigidity.

"She must have died in her sleep," the doctor said, when he came, "without a struggle."

When Mary Brown really understood that her sister was dead, she left her to the kindly ministrations of the good women who are always ready at such times in a country place, and went and sat by the kitchen window in the chair which her sister had occupied that afternoon.

There the women found her when the last offices had been done for the dead.

"Come home with me to-night," one said; "Miss Green will stay with *her*," with a turn of her head towards the opposite room, and an emphasis on the pronoun which distinguished it at once from one applied to a living person.

"No," said Mary Brown; "I'm a-goin' to set here an' listen." She had the window wide open, leaning her head out into the chilly night air.

The women looked at each other; one tapped her head, another nodded hers. "Poor thing!" said a third.

"You see," went on Mary Brown, still speaking with her head leaned out of the window, "I was cross with her this afternoon because she talked about hearin' music. I was cross, an' spoke up sharp to her, because I loved her, but I don't think she knew. I didn't want to think she was goin' to die, but she was. An' she heard the music. It was true. An' now I'm a-goin' to set here an' listen till I hear it too, an' then I'll know she 'ain't laid up what I said agin me, an' that I'm a-goin' to die too."

They found it impossible to reason with her ; there she sat till morning, with a pitying woman beside her, listening all in vain for unearthly melody.

Next day they sent for a widowed niece of the sisters, who came at once, bringing her little boy with her. She was a kindly young woman, and took up her abode in the little cottage, and did the best she could for her poor aunt, who, it soon became evident, would never be quite herself again. There she would sit at the kitchen window and listen day after day. She took a great fancy to her niece's little boy, and used often to hold him in her lap as she sat there. Once in a while she would ask him if he heard any music. " An innocent little thing like him might hear quicker than a hard, unbelievin' old woman like me," she told his mother once.

She lived so for nearly a year after her sister died. It was evident that she failed gradually and surely, though there was no apparent disease. It seemed to trouble her exceedingly that she never heard the music she listened for. She had an idea that she could not die unless she did, and her whole soul seemed filled with longing to join her be-loved twin sister, and be assured of her forgiveness. This sister-love was all she had ever felt, besides her love of God, in any strong degree ; all the passion of devotion of which this homely, commonplace woman was capable was centred in that, and the unsatisfied strength of it was killing her. The weaker she grew, the more earnestly she listened. She was too feeble to sit up, but she would not consent to lie in bed, and made them bolster her up with pillows in a rock-ing-chair by the window. At last she died, in the spring, a week or two before her sister had the preceding year. The season was a little more advanced this year, and the apple-trees were blossomed out further than they were then. She died about ten o'clock in the morning. The day before, her niece had been called into the room by a shrill cry of rapture from her: "I've heard it! I've heard it!" she cried. "A faint sound o' music, like the dyin' away of a bell."

A MORAL EXIGENCY.

At five o'clock, Eunice Fairweather went up-stairs to dress herself for the sociable and Christmas-tree to be given at the parsonage that night in honor of Christmas Eve. She had been very busy all day, making preparations for it. She was the minister's daughter, and had, of a necessity, to take an active part in such affairs.

She took it, as usual, loyally and energetically, but there had always been seasons from her childhood — and she was twenty-five now—when the social duties to which she had been born seemed a weariness and a bore to her. They had seemed so to-day. She had patiently and faithfully sewed up little lace bags with divers-colored worsteds, and stuffed them with candy. She had strung pop-corn, and marked the parcels which had been pouring in since day-break from all quarters. She had taken her prominent part among the corps of indefatigable women always present to assist on such occasions, and kept up her end of the line as minister's daughter bravely. Now, however, the last of the zealous, chattering women she had been working with had bustled home, with a pleasant importance in every hitch of her shawled shoulders, and would not bustle back again until half-past six or so ; and the tree, fully bedecked, stood in unconscious impressiveness in the parsonage parlor.

Eunice had come up-stairs with the resolution to dress herself directly for the festive occasion, and to hasten down again to be in readiness for new exigencies. Her mother was delicate, and had kept her room all day in order to prepare herself for the evening, her father was inefficient at such times, there was no servant, and the brunt of everything came on her.

But her resolution gave way; she wrapped herself in an old plaid shawl and lay down on her bed to rest a few minutes. She did not close her eyes, but lay studying idly the familiar details of the room. It was small, and one side ran in under the eaves; for the parsonage was a cottage. There was one window, with a white cotton curtain trimmed with tasselled fringe, and looped up on an old porcelain knob with a picture painted on it. That knob, with its tiny bright landscape, had been one of the pretty wonders of Eunice's childhood. She looked at it even now with interest, and the marvel and the beauty of it had not wholly departed for her eyes. The walls of the little room had a scraggly-patterned paper on them. The first lustre of it had departed, for that too was one of the associates of Eunice's childhood, but in certain lights there was a satin sheen and a blue line visible. Blue roses on a satin ground had been the original pattern. It had never been pretty, but Eunice had always had faith in it. There was an ancient straw matting on the floor, a homemade braided rug before the cottage bedstead, and one before the stained-pine bureau. There were a few poor attempts at adornment on the walls; a splint letter-case, a motto worked in worsteds, a gay print of an eminently proper little girl holding a faithful little dog.

This last, in its brilliant crudeness, was not a work of

art, but Eunice believed in it. She was a conservative creature. Even after her year at the seminary, for which money had been scraped together five years ago, she had the same admiring trust in all the revelations of her childhood. Her home, on her return to it, looked as fair to her as it had always done; no old ugliness which familiarity had caused to pass unnoticed before gave her a shock of surprise.

She lay quietly, her shawl shrugged up over her face, so only her steady, light-brown eyes were visible. The room was drearily cold. She never had a fire; one in a sleeping-room would have been sinful luxury in the poor minister's family. Even her mother's was only warmed from the sitting-room.

In sunny weather Eunice's room was cheerful, and its look, if not actually its atmosphere, would warm one a little, for the windows faced southwest. But to-day all the light had come through low, gray clouds, for it had been threatening snow ever since morning, and the room had been dismal.

A comfortless dusk was fast spreading over everything now. Eunice rose at length, thinking that she must either dress herself speedily or go down-stairs for a candle.

She was a tall, heavily-built girl, with large, well-formed feet and hands. She had a full face, and a thick, colorless skin. Her features were coarse, but their combination affected one pleasantly. It was a stanch, honest face, with a suggestion of obstinacy in it.

She looked unhappily at herself in her little square glass, as she brushed out her hair and arranged it in a smooth twist at the top of her head. It was not becoming, but it was the way she had always done it. She did not admire

15

the effect herself when the coiffure was complete, neither did she survey her appearance complacently when she had gotten into her best brown cashmere dress, with its ruffle of starched lace in the neck. But it did not occur to her that any change could be made for the better. It was her best dress, and it was the way she did up her hair. She did not like either, but the simple facts of them ended the matter for her.

After the same fashion she regarded her own lot in life, with a sort of resigned disapproval.

On account of her mother's ill-health, she had been encumbered for the last five years with the numberless social duties to which the wife of a poor country minister is liable. She had been active in Sunday-school picnics and church sociables, in mission bands and neighborhood prayer-meetings. She was a church member and a good girl, but the *rôle* did not suit her. Still she accepted it as inevitable, and would no more have thought of evading it than she would have thought of evading life altogether. There was about her an almost stubborn steadfastness of onward movement that would forever keep her in the same rut, no matter how disagreeable it might be, unless some influence outside of herself might move her.

When she went down-stairs, she found her mother seated beside the sitting-room stove, also arrayed in her best—a shiny black silk, long in the shoulder-seams, the tops of the sleeves adorned with pointed caps trimmed with black velvet ribbon.

She looked up at Eunice as she entered, a complacent smile on her long, delicate face ; she thought her homely, honest-looking daughter charming in her best gown.

A murmur of men's voices came from the next room, whose door was closed.

"Father's got Mr. Wilson in there," explained Mrs. Fairweather, in response to Eunice's inquiring glance. "He came just after you went up-stairs. They've been talking very busily about something. Perhaps Mr. Wilson wants to exchange."

Just at that moment, the study door opened and the two men came out, Eunice's father, tall and round-shouldered, with grayish sandy hair and beard, politely allowing his guest to precede him. There was a little resemblance between the two, though there was no relationship. Mr. Wilson was a younger man by ten years; he was shorter and slighter; but he had similarly sandy hair and beard, though they were not quite so gray, and something the same cast of countenance. He was settled over a neighboring parish; he was a widower with four young children; his wife had died a year before.

He had spoken to Mrs. Fairweather on his first entrance, so he stepped directly towards Eunice with extended hand. His ministerial affability was slightly dashed with embarrassment, and his thin cheeks were crimson around the roots of his sandy beard.

Eunice shook the proffered hand with calm courtesy, and inquired after his children. She had not a thought that his embarrassment betokened anything, if, indeed, she observed it at all.

Her father stood by with an air of awkward readiness to proceed to action, waiting until the two should cease the interchanging of courtesies.

When the expected pause came he himself placed a chair for Mr. Wilson. "Sit down, Brother Wilson," he said, nervously, "and I will consult with my daughter concerning the matter we were speaking of. Eunice, I would like to speak with you a moment in the study."

"Certainly, sir," said Eunice. She looked surprised, but she followed him at once into the study. "Tell me as quickly as you can what it is, father," she said, "for it is nearly time for people to begin coming, and I shall have to attend to them."

She had not seated herself, but stood leaning carelessly against the study wall, questioning her father with her steady eyes.

He stood in his awkward height before her. He was plainly trembling. "Eunice," he said, in a shaking voice, "Mr. Wilson came—to say—he would like to marry you, my dear daughter."

He cleared his throat to hide his embarrassment. He felt a terrible constraint in speaking to Eunice of such matters; he looked shamefaced and distressed.

Eunice eyed him steadily. She did not change color in the least. "I think I would rather remain as I am, father," she said, quietly.

Her father roused himself then. "My dear daughter," he said, with restrained eagerness, "don't decide this matter too hastily, without giving it all the consideration it deserves. Mr. Wilson is a good man; he would make you a worthy husband, and he needs a wife sadly. Think what a wide field of action would be before you with those four little motherless children to love and care for! You would have a wonderful opportunity to do good."

"I don't think," said Eunice, bluntly, "that I should care for that sort of an opportunity."

"Then," her father went on, "you will forgive me if I

speak plainly, my dear. You—are getting older ; you have
not had any other visitors. You would be well provided
for in this way—"

"Exceedingly well," replied Eunice, slowly. "There
would be six hundred a year and a leaky parsonage for a
man and woman and four children, and—nobody knows
how many more." She was almost coarse in her slow indignation, and did not blush at it.

"The Lord would provide for his servants."

"I don't know whether he would or not. I don't think
he would be under any obligation to if his servant deliberately encumbered himself with more of a family than he had
brains to support."

Her father looked so distressed that Eunice's heart smote
her for her forcible words. "You don't want to get rid of
me, surely, father," she said, in a changed tone.

Mr. Fairweather's lips moved uncertainly as he answered:
"No, my dear daughter ; don't ever let such a thought enter your head. I only—Mr. Wilson is a good man, and a
woman is best off married, and your mother and I are old.
I have never laid up anything. Sometimes— Maybe I
don't trust the Lord enough, but I have felt anxious about
you, if anything happened to me." Tears were standing in
his light-blue eyes, which had never been so steady and
keen as his daughter's.

There came a loud peal of the door-bell. Eunice started. "There! I must go," she said. "We'll talk about
this another time. Don't worry about it, father dear."

"But, Eunice, what shall I say to him?"

"Must something be said to-night?"

"It would hardly be treating him fairly otherwise."

Eunice looked hesitatingly at her father's worn, anxious

face. "Tell him," she said at length, "that I will give him his answer in a week."

Her father looked gratified. "We will take it to the Lord, my dear."

Eunice's lip curled curiously, but she said, "Yes, sir," dutifully, and hastened from the room to answer the door-bell.

The fresh bevies that were constantly arriving after that engaged her whole attention. She could do no more than give a hurried "Good-evening" to Mr. Wilson when he came to take leave, after a second short conference with her father in the study. He looked deprecatingly hopeful.

The poor man was really in a sad case. Six years ago, when he married, he had been romantic. He would never be again. He was not thirsting for love and communion with a kindred spirit now, but for a good, capable woman who would take care of his four clamorous children without a salary.

He returned to his shabby, dirty parsonage that night with, it seemed to him, quite a reasonable hope that his affairs might soon be changed for the better. Of course he would have preferred that the lady should have said yes directly ; it would both have assured him and shortened the time until his burdens should be lightened; but he could hardly have expected that, when his proposal was so sudden, and there had been no preliminary attention on his part. The week's probation, therefore, did not daunt him much. He did not really see why Eunice should refuse him. She was plain, was getting older ; it probably was her first, and very likely her last, chance of marriage. He was a clergyman in good standing, and she would not lower her social position. He felt sure that he was now about to be relieved from the unpleasant predicament in which he

had been ever since his wife's death, and from which he had
been forced to make no effort to escape, for decency's sake,
for a full year. The year, in fact, had been up five days
ago. He actually took credit to himself for remaining qui-
escent during those five days. It was rather shocking, but
there was a good deal to be said for him. No wife and
four small children, six hundred dollars a year, moderate
brain, and an active conscience, are a hard combination of
circumstances for any man.

To-night, however, he returned thanks to the Lord for his
countless blessings with pious fervor, which would have
been lessened had he known of the state of Eunice's mind
just at that moment.

The merry company had all departed, the tree stood dis-
mantled in the parlor, and she was preparing for bed, with
her head full, not of him, but another man.

Standing before her glass, combing out her rather scanty,
lustreless hair, her fancy pictured to her, beside her own
homely, sober face, another, a man's, blond and handsome,
with a gentle, almost womanish smile on the full red lips,
and a dangerous softness in the blue eyes. Could a third
person have seen the double picture as she did, he would
have been struck with a sense of the incongruity, almost absurdity, of it. Eunice herself, with her hard, uncompromising common-sense, took the attitude of a third person in
regard to it, and at length blew her light out and went to
bed, with a bitter amusement in her heart at her own folly.

There had been present that evening a young man who
was a comparatively recent acquisition to the village society.
He had been in town about three months. His father, two
years before, had purchased one of the largest farms in the
vicinity, moving there from an adjoining state. This son

had been absent at the time; he was reported to be running a cattle ranch in one of those distant territories which
seem almost fabulous to New-Englanders. Since he had
come home he had been the cynosure of the village. He
was thirty and a little over, but he was singularly boyish in
his ways, and took part in all the town frolics with gusto.
He was popularly supposed to be engaged to Ada Harris,
Squire Harris's daughter, as she was often called. Her
father was the prominent man of the village, lived in the
best house, and had the loudest voice in public matters.
He was a lawyer, with rather more pomposity than ability,
perhaps, but there had always been money and influence in
the Harris family, and these warded off all criticism.

The daughter was a pretty blonde of average attainments,
but with keen wits and strong passions. She had not been
present at the Christmas tree, and her lover, either on that
account, or really from some sudden fancy he had taken to
Eunice, had been at her elbow the whole evening. He had
a fashion of making his attentions marked: he did on that
occasion. He made a pretence of assisting her, but it was
only a pretence, and she knew it, though she thought it mar-
vellous. She had met him, but had not before exchanged
two words with him. She had seen him with Ada Harris,
and he had seemed almost as much out of her life as a
lover in a book. Young men of his kind were unknown
quantities heretofore to this steady, homely young woman.
They seemed to belong to other girls.

So his devotion to her through the evening, and his asking permission to call when he took leave, seemed to her
well-nigh incredible. Her head was not turned, in the usual
acceptation of the term—it was not an easy head to turn—
but it was full of Burr Mason, and every thought, no matter

how wide a starting-point it had, lost itself at last in the thought of him.

Mr. Wilson's proposal weighed upon her terribly through the next week. Her father seemed bent upon her accepting it; so did her mother, who sighed in secret over the prospect of her daughter's remaining unmarried. Either through unworldliness, or their conviction of the desirability of the marriage in itself, the meagreness of the financial outlook did not seem to influence them in the least.

Eunice did not once think of Burr Mason as any reason for her reluctance, but when he called the day but one before her week of probation was up, and when he took her to drive the next day, she decided on a refusal of the minister's proposal easily enough. She had wavered a little before.

So Mr. Wilson was left to decide upon some other worthy, reliable woman as a subject for his addresses, and Eunice kept on with her new lover.

How this sober, conscientious girl could reconcile to herself the course she was now taking, was a question. It was probable she did not make the effort; she was so sensible that she would have known its futility and hypocrisy beforehand.

She knew her lover had been engaged to Ada Harris; that she was encouraging him in cruel and dishonorable treatment of another woman; but she kept steadily on. People even came to her and told her that the jilted girl was breaking her heart. She listened, her homely face set in an immovable calm. She listened quietly to her parents' remonstrance, and kept on.

There was an odd quality in Burr Mason's character. He was terribly vacillating, but he knew it. Once he said to Eunice, with the careless freedom that would have been al-

most insolence in another man: "Don't let me see Ada
Harris much, I warn you, dear.   I mean to be true to you,
but she has such a pretty face, and I meant to be true to
her, but you have—I don't know just what, but something
she has not."

Eunice knew the truth of what he said perfectly.   The
incomprehensibleness of it all to her, who was so sensible
of her own disadvantages, was the fascination she had for
such a man.

A few days after Burr Mason had made that remark, Ada
Harris came to see her.   When Eunice went into the sitting-room to greet her, she kept her quiet, unmoved face,
but the change in the girl before her was terrible.   It was
not wasting of flesh or pallor that it consisted in, but something worse.   Her red lips were set so hard that the soft
curves in them were lost, her cheeks burned feverishly, her
blue eyes had a fierce light in them, and, most pitiful thing
of all for another woman to see, she had not crimped her
pretty blond hair, but wore it combed straight back from
her throbbing forehead.

When Eunice entered, she waited for no preliminary
courtesies, but sprang forward, and caught hold of her hand
with a strong, nervous grasp, and stood so, her pretty, desperate face confronting Eunice's calm, plain one.

"Eunice!" she cried, "Eunice! why did you take him
away from me?   Eunice! Eunice!"   Then she broke into
a low wail, without any tears.

Eunice released her hand, and seated herself.   "You had
better take a chair, Ada," she said, in her slow, even tones.
"When you say *him*, you mean Burr Mason, I suppose."

"You know I do.   Oh, Eunice, how could you? how
could you?   I thought you were so good!"

"You ask me why *I* do this and that, but don't you think he had anything to do with it himself?"

Ada stood before her, clinching her little white hands. "Eunice Fairweather, you know Burr Mason, and I know Burr Mason. You know that if you gave him up, and refused to see him, he would come back to me. You know it."

"Yes, I know it."

"You know it; you sit there and say you know it, and yet you do this cruel thing — you, a minister's daughter. You understood from the first how it was. You knew he was mine, that you had no right to him. You knew if you shunned him ever so little, that he would come back to me. And yet you let him come and make love to you. You knew it. There is no excuse for you: you knew it. It is no better for him. You have encouraged him in being false. You have dragged him down. You are a plainer girl than I, and a soberer one, but you are no better. You will not make him a better wife. You cannot make him a good wife after this. It is all for yourself—yourself!"

Eunice sat still.

Then Ada flung herself on her knees at her side, and pleaded, as for her life. "Eunice, O Eunice, give him up to me! It is killing me! Eunice, dear Eunice, say you will!"

As Eunice sat looking at the poor, dishevelled golden head bowed over her lap, a recollection flashed across her mind, oddly enough, of a certain recess at the village school they two had attended years ago, when she was among the older girls, and Ada a child to her: how she had played she was her little girl, and held her in her lap, and that golden head had nestled on her bosom.

"Eunice, O Eunice, he loved me first. You had better have stolen away my own heart. It would not have been so wicked or so cruel. How could you? O Eunice, give him back to me, Eunice, *won't you ?*"

"No."

Ada rose, staggering, without another word. She moaned a little to herself as she crossed the room to the door. Eunice accompanied her to the outer door, and said good-bye. Ada did not return it. Eunice saw her steady herself by catching hold of the gate as she passed through.

Then she went slowly up-stairs to her own room, wrapped herself in a shawl, and lay down on her bed, as she had that Christmas Eve. She was very pale, and there was a strange look, almost of horror, on her face. She stared, as she lay there, at all the familiar objects in the room, but the most common and insignificant of them had a strange and awful look to her. Yet the change was in herself, not in them. The shadow that was over her own soul overshadowed them and perverted her vision. But she felt also almost a fear of all those inanimate objects she was gazing at. They were so many reminders of a better state with her, for she had gazed at them all in her unconscious childhood. She was sickened with horror at their dumb accusations. There was the little glass she had looked in before she had stolen another woman's dearest wealth away from her, the chair she had sat in, the bed she had lain in.

At last Eunice Fairweather's strong will broke down before the accusations of her own conscience, which were so potent as to take upon themselves material shapes.

Ada Harris, in her pretty chamber, lying worn out on her bed, her face buried in the pillow, started at a touch on her shoulder. Some one had stolen into the room unannounced—not her mother, for she was waiting outside. Ada turned her head, and saw Eunice. She struck at her wildly with her slender hands. "Go away!" she screamed.

"Ada!"

"Go away!"

"Burr Mason is down-stairs. I came with him to call on you."

Ada sat upright, staring at her, her hand still uplifted.

"I am going to break my engagement with him."

"Oh, Eunice! Eunice! you blessed—"

Eunice drew the golden head down on her bosom, just as she had on that old school-day.

"Love me all you can, Ada," she said. "I want—something."

A MISTAKEN CHARITY.

THERE were in a green field a little, low, weather-stained cottage, with a foot-path leading to it from the highway several rods distant, and two old women—one with a tin pan and old knife searching for dandelion greens among the short young grass, and the other sitting on the door-step watching her, or, rather, having the appearance of watching her.

"Air there enough for a mess, Harriét?" asked the old woman on the door-step. She accented oddly the last syllable of the Harriet, and there was a curious quality in her feeble, cracked old voice. Besides the question denoted by the arrangement of her words and the rising inflection, there was another, broader and subtler, the very essence of all questioning, in the tone of her voice itself; the cracked, quavering notes that she used reached out of themselves, and asked, and groped like fingers in the dark. One would have known by the voice that the old woman was blind.

The old woman on her knees in the grass searching for dandelions did not reply; she evidently had not heard the question. So the old woman on the door-step, after waiting a few minutes with her head turned expectantly, asked again, varying her question slightly, and speaking louder :

"Air there enough for a mess, do ye s'pose, Harriét?"

The old woman in the grass heard this time. She rose slowly and laboriously; the effort of straightening out the rheumatic old muscles was evidently a painful one; then she eyed the greens heaped up in the tin pan, and pressed them down with her hand.

"Wa'al, I don't know, Charlotte," she replied, hoarsely. "There's plenty on 'em here, but I 'ain't got near enough for a mess; they do bile down so when you get 'em in the pot; an' it's all I can do to bend my j'ints enough to dig 'em."

"I'd give consider'ble to help ye, Harriét," said the old woman on the door-step.

But the other did not hear her; she was down on her knees in the grass again, anxiously spying out the dandelions.

So the old woman on the door-step crossed her little shrivelled hands over her calico knees, and sat quite still, with the soft spring wind blowing over her.

The old wooden door-step was sunk low down among the grasses, and the whole house to which it belonged had an air of settling down and mouldering into the grass as into its own grave.

When Harriet Shattuck grew deaf and rheumatic, and had to give up her work as tailoress, and Charlotte Shattuck lost her eyesight, and was unable to do any more sewing for her livelihood, it was a small and trifling charity for the rich man who held a mortgage on the little house in which they had been born and lived all their lives to give them the use of it, rent and interest free. He might as well have taken credit to himself for not charging a squirrel for his tenement in some old decaying tree in his woods.

So ancient was the little habitation, so wavering and

mouldering, the hands that had fashioned it had lain still
so long in their graves, that it almost seemed to have fallen
below its distinctive rank as a house. Rain and snow had
filtered through its roof, mosses had grown over it, worms
had eaten it, and birds built their nests under its eaves ;
nature had almost completely overrun and obliterated the
work of man, and taken her own to herself again, till the
house seemed as much a natural ruin as an old tree-
stump.

The Shattucks had always been poor people and common
people ; no especial grace and refinement or fine ambition
had ever characterized any of them ; they had always been
poor and coarse and common. The father and his father before him had simply lived in the poor little house,
grubbed for their living, and then unquestioningly died.
The mother had been of no rarer stamp, and the two daughters were cast in the same mould.

After their parents' death Harriet and Charlotte had lived
along in the old place from youth to old age, with the one
hope of ability to keep a roof over their heads, covering on
their backs, and victuals in their mouths—an all-sufficient
one with them.

Neither of them had ever had a lover ; they had always
seemed to repel rather than attract the opposite sex. It
was not merely because they were poor, ordinary, and homely ; there were plenty of men in the place who would have
matched them well in that respect ; the fault lay deeper—
in their characters. Harriet, even in her girlhood, had a
blunt, defiant manner that almost amounted to surliness,
and was well calculated to alarm timid adorers, and Charlotte had always had the reputation of not being any too
strong in her mind.

Harriet had gone about from house to house doing tailor-work after the primitive country fashion, and Charlotte had done plain sewing and mending for the neighbors. They had been, in the main, except when pressed by some temporary anxiety about their work or the payment thereof, happy and contented, with that negative kind of happiness and contentment which comes not from gratified ambition, but a lack of ambition itself. All that they cared for they had had in tolerable abundance, for Harriet at least had been swift and capable about her work. The patched, mossy old roof had been kept over their heads, the coarse, hearty food that they loved had been set on their table, and their cheap clothes had been warm and strong.

After Charlotte's eyes failed her, and Harriet had the rheumatic fever, and the little hoard of earnings went to the doctors, times were harder with them, though still it could not be said that they actually suffered.

When they could not pay the interest on the mortgage they were allowed to keep the place interest free ; there was as much fitness in a mortgage on the little house, any-way, as there would have been on a rotten old apple-tree ; and the people about, who were mostly farmers, and good friendly folk, helped them out with their living. One would donate a barrel of apples from his abundant harvest to the two poor old women, one a barrel of potatoes, another a load of wood for the winter fuel, and many a farmer's wife had bustled up the narrow foot-path with a pound of butter, or a dozen fresh eggs, or a nice bit of pork. Besides all this, there was a tiny garden patch behind the house, with a straggling row of currant bushes in it, and one of goose-berries, where Harriet contrived every year to raise a few pumpkins, which were the pride of her life. On the right

16

of the garden were two old apple-trees, a Baldwin and a Porter, both yet in a tolerably good fruit-bearing state.

The delight which the two poor old souls took in their own pumpkins, their apples and currants, was indescribable. It was not merely that they contributed largely towards their living; they were their own, their private share of the great wealth of nature, the little taste set apart for them alone out of her bounty, and worth more to them on that account, though they were not conscious of it, than all the richer fruits which they received from their neighbors' gardens.

This morning the two apple-trees were brave with flowers, the currant bushes looked alive, and the pumpkin seeds were in the ground. Harriet cast complacent glances in their direction from time to time, as she painfully dug her dandelion greens. She was a short, stoutly built old woman, with a large face coarsely wrinkled, with a suspicion of a stubble of beard on the square chin.

When her tin pan was filled to her satisfaction with the sprawling, spidery greens, and she was hobbling stiffly towards her sister on the door-step, she saw another woman standing before her with a basket in her hand.

"Good-morning, Harriet," she said, in a loud, strident voice, as she drew near. "I've been frying some doughnuts, and I brought you over some warm."

"I've been tellin' her it was real good in her," piped Charlotte from the door-step, with an anxious turn of her sightless face towards the sound of her sister's footstep.

Harriet said nothing but a hoarse "Good-mornin', Mis' Simonds." Then she took the basket in her hand, lifted the towel off the top, selected a doughnut, and deliberately tasted it.

"Tough," said she. "I s'posed so. If there is anything I 'spise on this airth it's a tough doughnut."

"Oh, Harriét!" said Charlotte, with a frightened look.

"They air tough," said Harriet, with hoarse defiance, "and if there is anything I 'spise on this airth it's a tough doughnut."

The woman whose benevolence and cookery were being thus ungratefully received only laughed. She was quite fleshy, and had a round, rosy, determined face.

"Well, Harriet," said she, "I am sorry they are tough, but perhaps you had better take them out on a plate, and give me my basket. You may be able to eat two or three of them if they are tough."

"They air tough—turrible tough," said Harriet, stubbornly; but she took the basket into the house and emptied it of its contents nevertheless.

"I suppose your roof leaked as bad as ever in that heavy rain day before yesterday?" said the visitor to Harriet, with an inquiring squint towards the mossy shingles, as she was about to leave with her empty basket.

"It was turrible," replied Harriet, with crusty acquiescence—"turrible. We had to set pails an' pans everywheres, an' move the bed out."

"Mr. Upton ought to fix it."

"There ain't any fix to it; the old ruff ain't fit to nail new shingles on to; the hammerin' would bring the whole thing down on our heads," said Harriet, grimly.

"Well, I don't know as it can be fixed, it's so old. I suppose the wind comes in bad around the windows and doors too?"

"It's like livin' with a piece of paper, or mebbe a sieve, 'twixt you an' the wind an' the rain," quoth Harriet, with a jerk of her head.

"You ought to have a more comfortable home in your old age," said the visitor, thoughtfully.

"Oh, it's well enough," cried Harriet, in quick alarm, and with a complete change of tone ; the woman's remark had brought an old dread over her. "The old house 'll last as long as Charlotte an' me do. The rain ain't so bad, nuther is the wind ; there's room enough for us in the dry places, an' out of the way of the doors an' windows. It's enough sight better than goin' on the town." Her square, defiant old face actually looked pale as she uttered the last words and stared apprehensively at the woman.

"Oh, I did not think of your doing that," she said, hastily and kindly. "We all know how you feel about that, Harriet, and not one of us neighbors will see you and Charlotte go to the poorhouse while we've got a crust of bread to share with you."

Harriet's face brightened. "Thank ye, Mis' Simonds," she said, with reluctant courtesy. "I'm much obleeged to you an' the neighbors. I think mebbe we'll be able to eat some of them doughnuts if they air tough," she added, mollifyingly, as her caller turned down the foot-path.

"My, Harriét," said Charlotte, lifting up a weakly, wondering, peaked old face, "what did you tell her them doughnuts was tough fur?"

"Charlotte, do you want everybody to look down on us, an' think we ain't no account at all, just like any beggars, 'cause they bring us in vittles?" said Harriet, with a grim glance at her sister's meek, unconscious face.

"No, Harriét," she whispered.

"Do you want *to go to the poor-house ?*"

"No, Harriét." The poor little old woman on the doorstep fairly cowered before her aggressive old sister.

"Then don't hender me agin when I tell folks their doughnuts is tough an' their pertaters is poor. If I don't kinder keep up an' show some sperrit, I sha'n't think nothing of myself, an' other folks won't nuther, and fust thing we know they'll kerry us to the poorhouse. You'd 'a been there before now if it hadn't been for me, Charlotte."

Charlotte looked meekly convinced, and her sister sat down on a chair in the doorway to scrape her dandelions.

"Did you git a good mess, Harriét?" asked Charlotte, in a humble tone.

"Toler'ble."

"They'll be proper relishin' with that piece of pork Mis' Mann brought in yesterday. O Lord, Harriét, it's a chink!"

Harriet sniffed.

Her sister caught with her sensitive ear the little contemptuous sound. "I guess," she said, querulously, and with more pertinacity than she had shown in the matter of the doughnuts, "that if you was in the dark, as I am, Harriét, you wouldn't make fun an' turn up your nose at chinks. If you had seen the light streamin' in all of a sudden through some little hole that you hadn't known of before when you set down on the door-step this mornin', and the wind with the smell of the apple blows in it came in your face, an' when Mis' Simonds brought them hot doughnuts, an' when I thought of the pork an' greens jest now— O Lord, how it did shine in! An' it does now. If you was me, Harriét, you would know there was chinks."

Tears began starting from the sightless eyes, and streaming pitifully down the pale old cheeks.

Harriet looked at her sister, and her grim face softened.

"Why, Charlotte, hev it that thar *is* chinks if you want to. Who cares?"

"Thar *is* chinks, Harriét."

"Wa'al, thar *is* chinks, then. If I don't hurry, I sha'n't get these greens in in time for dinner."

When the two old women sat down complacently to their meal of pork and dandelion greens in their little kitchen they did not dream how destiny slowly and surely was introducing some new colors into their web of life, even when it was almost completed, and that this was one of the last meals they would eat in their old home for many a day. In about a week from that day they were established in the "Old Ladies' Home" in a neighboring city. It came about in this wise: Mrs. Simonds, the woman who had brought the gift of hot doughnuts, was a smart, energetic person, bent on doing good, and she did a great deal. To be sure, she always did it in her own way. If she chose to give hot doughnuts, she gave hot doughnuts; it made not the slightest difference to her if the recipients of her charity would infinitely have preferred ginger cookies. Still, a great many would like hot doughnuts, and she did unquestionably a great deal of good.

She had a worthy coadjutor in the person of a rich and childless elderly widow in the place. They had fairly entered into a partnership in good works, with about an equal capital on both sides, the widow furnishing the money, and Mrs. Simonds, who had much the better head of the two, furnishing the active schemes of benevolence.

The afternoon after the doughnut episode she had gone to the widow with a new project, and the result was that entrance fees had been paid, and old Harriet and Charlotte made sure of a comfortable home for the rest of their lives.

The widow was hand in glove with officers of missionary boards and trustees of charitable institutions. There had been an unusual mortality among the inmates of the "Home" this spring, there were several vacancies, and the matter of the admission of Harriet and Charlotte was very quickly and easily arranged. But the matter which would have seemed the least difficult—inducing the two old women to accept the bounty which Providence, the widow, and Mrs. Simonds were ready to bestow on them—proved the most so. The struggle to persuade them to abandon their tottering old home for a better was a terrible one. The widow had pleaded with mild surprise, and Mrs. Simonds with benevolent determination ; the counsel and reverend eloquence of the minister had been called in ; and when they yielded at last it was with a sad grace for the recipients of a worthy charity.

It had been hard to convince them that the "Home" was not an almshouse under another name, and their yielding at length to anything short of actual force was only due probably to the plea, which was advanced most eloquently to Harriet, that Charlotte would be so much more comfortable.

The morning they came away, Charlotte cried pitifully, and trembled all over her little shrivelled body. Harriet did not cry. But when her sister had passed out the low, sagging door she turned the key in the lock, then took it out and thrust it slyly into her pocket, shaking her head to herself with an air of fierce determination.

Mrs. Simonds's husband, who was to take them to the depot, said to himself, with disloyal defiance of his wife's active charity, that it was a shame, as he helped the two distressed old souls into his light wagon, and put the poor little box, with their homely clothes in it, in behind.

Mrs. Simonds, the widow, the minister, and the gentleman from the "Home" who was to take charge of them, were all at the depot, their faces beaming with the delight of successful benevolence. But the two poor old women looked like two forlorn prisoners in their midst. It was an impressive illustration of the truth of the saying "that it is more blessed to give than to receive."

Well, Harriet and Charlotte Shattuck went to the "Old Ladies' Home" with reluctance and distress. They stayed two months, and then—they ran away.

The "Home" was comfortable, and in some respects even luxurious; but nothing suited those two unhappy, unreasonable old women.

The fare was of a finer, more delicately served variety than they had been accustomed to; those finely flavored nourishing soups for which the "Home" took great credit to itself failed to please palates used to common, coarser food.

"O Lord, Harriét, when I set down to the table here there ain't no chinks," Charlotte used to say. "If we could hev some cabbage, or some pork an' greens, how the light would stream in!"

Then they had to be more particular about their dress. They had always been tidy enough, but now it had to be something more; the widow, in the kindness of her heart, had made it possible, and the good folks in charge of the "Home," in the kindness of their hearts, tried to carry out the widow's designs.

But nothing could transform these two unpolished old women into two nice old ladies. They did not take kindly to white lace caps and delicate neckerchiefs. They liked their new black cashmere dresses well enough, but they felt as if they broke a commandment when they put them on every afternoon. They had always worn calico with long aprons at home, and they wanted to now; and they wanted to twist up their scanty gray locks into little knots at the back of their heads, and go without caps, just as they always had done.

Charlotte in a dainty white cap was pitiful, but Harriet was both pitiful and comical. They were totally at variance with their surroundings, and they felt it keenly, as people of their stamp always do. No amount of kindness and attention—and they had enough of both—sufficed to reconcile them to their new abode. Charlotte pleaded continually with her sister to go back to their old home.

"O Lord, Harriét, she would exclaim (by the way, Charlotte's "O Lord," which, as she used it, was innocent enough, had been heard with much disfavor in the "Home," and she, not knowing at all why, had been remonstrated with concerning it), "let us go home. I can't stay here no ways in this world. I don't like their vittles, an' I don't like to wear a cap; I want to go home and do different. The currants will be ripe, Harriét. O Lord, thar was almost a chink, thinking about 'em. I want some of 'em; an' the Porter apples will be gittin' ripe, an' we could have some apple-pie. This here ain't good; I want merlasses fur sweeting. Can't we get back no ways, Harriét? It ain't far, an' we could walk, an' they don't lock us in, nor nothin'. I don't want to die here; it ain't so straight up to heaven from here. O Lord, I've felt as if I was slantendicular from heaven ever since I've been here, an' it's been so awful dark. I ain't had any chinks. I want to go home, Harriét."

"We'll go to-morrow mornin'," said Harriet, finally;

"we'll pack up our things an' go; we'll put on our old dresses, an' we'll do up the new ones in bundles, an' we'll jest shy out the back way to-morrow mornin'; an' we'll go. I kin find the way, an' I reckon we kin git thar, if it is four-teen mile. Mebbe somebody will give us a lift."

And they went. With a grim humor Harriet hung the new white lace caps with which she and Charlotte had been so pestered, one on each post at the head of the bedstead, so they would meet the eyes of the first person who opened the door. Then they took their bundles, stole slyly out, and were soon on the high-road, hobbling along, holding each other's hands, as jubilant as two children, and chuck-ling to themselves over their escape, and the probable as-tonishment there would be in the "Home" over it.

"O Lord, Harriét, what do you s'pose they will say to them caps?" cried Charlotte, with a gleeful cackle.

"I guess they'll see as folks ain't goin' to be made to wear caps agin their will in a free kentry," returned Har-riet, with an echoing cackle, as they sped feebly and brave-ly along.

The "Home" stood on the very outskirts of the city, luckily for them. They would have found it a difficult un-dertaking to traverse the crowded streets. As it was, a short walk brought them into the free country road—free comparatively, for even here at ten o'clock in the morning there was considerable travelling to and from the city on business or pleasure.

People whom they met on the road did not stare at them as curiously as might have been expected. Har-riet held her bristling chin high in air, and hobbled along with an appearance of being well aware of what she was about, that led folks to doubt their own first opinion that there was something unusual about the two old women.

Still their evident feebleness now and then occasioned from one and another more particular scrutiny. When they had been on the road a half-hour or so, a man in a covered wagon drove up behind them. After he had passed them, he poked his head around the front of the vehicle and looked back. Finally he stopped, and waited for them to come up to him.

"Like a ride, ma'am?" said he, looking at once bewildered and compassionate.

"Thankee," said Harriet, "we'd be much obleeged."

After the man had lifted the old women into the wagon, and established them on the back seat, he turned around, as he drove slowly along, and gazed at them curiously.

"Seems to me you look pretty feeble to be walking far," said he. "Where were you going?"

Harriet told him with an air of defiance.

"Why," he exclaimed, "it is fourteen miles out. You could never walk it in the world. Well, I am going within three miles of there, and I can go on a little farther as well as not. But I don't see— Have you been in the city?"

"I have been visitin' my married darter in the city," said Harriet, calmly.

Charlotte started, and swallowed convulsively.

Harriet had never told a deliberate falsehood before in her life, but this seemed to her one of the tremendous exigencies of life which justify a lie. She felt desperate. If she could not contrive to deceive him in some way, the man might turn directly around and carry Charlotte and her back to the "Home" and the white caps.

"I should not have thought your daughter would have

let you start for such a walk as that," said the man. "Is this lady your sister? She is blind, isn't she? She does not look fit to walk a mile."

"Yes, she's my sister," replied Harriet, stubbornly: "an' she's blind; an' my darter didn't want us to walk. She felt reel bad about it. But she couldn't help it. She's poor, and her husband's dead, an' she's got four leetle children."

Harriet recounted the hardships of her imaginary daughter with a glibness that was astonishing. Charlotte swallowed again.

"Well," said the man, "I am glad I overtook you, for I don't think you would ever have reached home alive."

About six miles from the city an open buggy passed them swiftly. In it were seated the matron and one of the gentlemen in charge of the "Home." They never thought of looking into the covered wagon—and indeed one can travel in one of those vehicles, so popular in some parts of New England, with as much privacy as he could in his tomb. The two in the buggy were seriously alarmed, and anxious for the safety of the old women, who were chuckling maliciously in the wagon they soon left far behind. Harriet had watched them breathlessly until they disappeared on a curve of the road; then she whispered to Charlotte.

A little after noon the two old women crept slowly up the foot-path across the field to their old home.

"The clover is up to our knees," said Harriet; "an' the sorrel and the white-weed; an' there's lots of yaller butter-flies."

"O Lord, Harriét, thar's a chink, an' I do believe I saw one of them yaller butterflies go past it," cried Charlotte, trembling all over, and nodding her gray head violently.

Harriet stood on the old sunken door-step and fitted the

key, which she drew triumphantly from her pocket, in the lock, while Charlotte stood waiting and shaking behind her.

Then they went in. Everything was there just as they had left it. Charlotte sank down on a chair and began to cry. Harriet hurried across to the window that looked out on the garden.

"The currants air ripe," said she ; "*an'* them pumpkins hev run all over everything."

"O Lord, Harriét," sobbed Charlotte, "thar is so many chinks that they air all runnin' together!"

GENTIAN.

It had been raining hard all night; when the morning dawned clear everything looked vivid and unnatural. The wet leaves on the trees and hedges seemed to emit a real green light of their own; the tree trunks were black and dank, and the spots of moss on them stood out distinctly.

A tall old woman was coming quickly up the street. She had on a stiffly starched calico gown, which sprang and rattled as she walked. She kept smoothing it anxiously. "Gittin' every mite of the stiff'nin' out," she muttered to herself.

She stopped at a long cottage house, whose unpainted walls, with white window-facings, and wide sweep of shingled roof, looked dark and startling through being sodden with rain.

There was a low stone wall by way of fence, with a gap in it for a gate.

She had just passed through this gap when the house door opened, and a woman put out her head.

"Is that you, Hannah?" said she.

"Yes, it's me." She laid a hard emphasis on the last word; then she sighed heavily.

"Hadn't you better hold your dress up comin' through that wet grass, Hannah? You'll git it all bedraggled."

" I know it. I'm a-gittin' every mite of the stiff'nin' out on't. I worked half the forenoon ironin' on't yesterday, too. Well, I thought I'd got to git over here an' fetch a few of these fried cakes. I thought mebbe Alferd would relish 'em fur his breakfast; an' he'd got to have 'em while they was hot; they ain't good fur nothin' cold; an' I didn't hev a soul to send—never do. How is Alferd this mornin', Lucy?"

" 'Bout the same, I guess."

" 'Ain't had the doctor yit?"

" No." She had a little, patient, pleasant smile on her face, looking up at her questioner.

The women were sisters. Hannah was Hannah Orton, unmarried. Lucy was Mrs. Tollet. Alfred was her sick husband.

Hannah's long, sallow face was deeply wrinkled. Her wide mouth twisted emphatically as she talked.

" Well, I know one thing; ef he was my husband he'd *hev* a doctor."

Mrs. Tollet's voice was old, but there was a childish tone in it, a sweet, uncertain pipe.

" No; you couldn't make him, Hannah; you couldn't, no more'n me. Alferd was allers jest so. He ain't never thought nothin' of doctors, nor doctors' stuff."

" Well, I'd make him take somethin'. In my opinion he needs somethin' bitter." She screwed her mouth as if the bitter morsel were on her own tongue.

" Lor'! he wouldn't take it, you know, Hannah."

" He'd hev to. Gentian would be good fur him."

" He wouldn't tech it."

" I'd make him, ef I put it in his tea unbeknownst to him."

" Oh, I wouldn't dare to."

" Land ! I guess I'd dare to.   Ef folks don't know enough
to take what's good fur 'em, they'd orter be made to by
hook or crook.   I don't believe in deceivin' generally, but
I don't believe the Lord would hev let folks hed the faculty
fur deceivin' in 'em ef it wa'n't to be used fur good sometimes.   It's my opinion Alferd won't last long ef he don't
hev somethin' pretty soon to strengthen of him up an' give
him a start.   Well, it ain't no use talkin'.   I've got to git home
an' put this dress in the wash-tub agin, I s'pose.   I never
see such a sight—jest look at that !   You'd better give
Alferd those cakes afore they git cold."

" I shouldn't wonder ef he relished 'em.   You was real
good to think of it, Hannah."

" Well, I'm a-goin'.   Every mite of the stiff'nin's out.
Sometimes it seems as ef thar wa'n't no end to the work.
I didn't know how to git out this mornin', anyway."

When Mrs. Tollet entered the house she found her husband in a wooden rocking-chair with a calico cushion, by
the kitchen window.   He was a short, large-framed old
man, but he was very thin.   There were great hollows in
his yellow cheeks.

" What you got thar, Lucy ?"

" Some griddle-cakes Hannah brought."

" Griddle-cakes !"

" They're real nice-lookin' ones.   Don't you think you'd
relish one or two, Alferd ?"

" Ef you an' Hannah want griddle-cakes, you kin hev
griddle-cakes."

" Then you don't want to hev one, with some maple merlasses on it ?   They've kept hot ; she hed 'em kivered up."

" Take 'em away !"

She set them meekly on the pantry shelf; then she came back and stood before her husband, gentle deprecation in her soft old face and in the whole poise of her little slender body.

"What *will* you hev fur breakfast, Alferd?"

"I don' know. Well, you might as well fry a little slice of bacon, an' git a cup of tea."

"Ain't you 'most afeard of—bacon, Alferd?"

"No, I ain't. Ef anybody's sick, they kin tell what they want themselves 'bout as well's anybody kin tell 'em. They don't hev any hankerin' arter anythin' unless it's good for 'em. When they need anythin', natur gives 'em a longin' arter it. I wish you'd hurry up an' cook that bacon, Lucy. I'm awful faint at my stomach."

She cooked the bacon and made the tea with no more words. Indeed, it was seldom that she used as many as she had now. Alfred Tollet, ever since she had married him, had been the sole autocrat of all her little Russias; her very thoughts had followed after him, like sheep.

After breakfast she went about putting her house in order for the day. When that was done, and she was ready to sit down with her sewing, she found that her husband had fallen asleep in his chair. She stood over him a minute, looking at his pale old face with the sincerest love and reverence. Then she sat down by the window and sewed, but not long. She got her bonnet and shawl stealthily, and stole out of the house. She sped quickly down the village street. She was light-footed for an old woman. She slackened her pace when she reached the village store, and crept hesitatingly into the great lumbering, rank-smelling room, with its dark, newly-sprinkled floor. She bought a bar of soap; then she stood irresolute.

17

"Anything else this mornin', Mis' Tollet?" The propri-etor himself, a narrow-shouldered, irritable man, was wait-ing on her. His tone was impatient. Mrs. Tollet was too absorbed to notice it. She stood hesitating.

"*Is* there anything else you want?"

"Well—I don' know; but—p'rhaps I'd better—hev—ten cents' wuth of gentian." Her very lips were white; she had an expression of frightened, guilty resolution. If she had asked for strychnine, with a view to her own bodily de-struction, she would not have had a different look.

The man mistook it, and his conscience smote him. He thought his manner had frightened her, but she had never noticed it.

"Goin' to give your husband some bitters?" he asked, affably, as he handed her the package.

She started and blushed. "No—I—thought some would be good fur—me."

"Well, gentian is a first-rate bitter. Good-morning, Mis' Tollet."

"Good-morning, Mr. Gill."

She was trembling all over when she reached her house door. There is a subtle, easily raised wind which blows spirits about like leaves, and she had come into it with her little paper of gentian. She had hidden the parcel in her pocket before she entered the kitchen. Her husband was awake. He turned his wondering, half-resentful eyes tow-ards her without moving his head.

"Where hev you been, Lucy?"

"I—jest went down to the store a minit, Alferd, while you was asleep.'

"What fur?"

"A bar of soap."

Alfred Tollet had always been a very healthy man until this spring. Some people thought that his illness was alarming now, more from its unwontedness and consequent effect on his mind, than from anything serious in its nature. However that may have been, he had complained of great depression and languor all the spring, and had not attempted to do any work.

It was the beginning of May now.

"Ef Alferd kin only git up May hill," Mrs. Tollet's sister had said to her, "he'll git along all right through the summer. It's a dretful tryin' time."

So up May hill, under the white apple and plum boughs, over the dandelions and the young grass, Alfred Tollet climbed, pushed and led faithfully by his loving old wife. At last he stood triumphantly on the summit of that fair hill, with its sweet, wearisome ascent. When the first of June came, people said, "Alfred Tollet's a good deal better."

He began to plant a little and bestir himself.

"Alferd's out workin' in the garden," Mrs. Tollet told her sister one afternoon. She had strolled over to her house with her knitting after dinner.

"You don't say so ! Well, I thought when I see him Sunday that he was lookin' better. He's got through May, an I guess he'll pull through. I did feel kinder worried 'bout him one spell— Why, Lucy, what's the matter?"

"Nothin'. Why?"

"You looked at me dretful kind of queer an' distressed, I thought."

"I guess you must hev imagined it, Hannah. Thar ain't nothin' the matter." She tried to look unconcernedly at her sister, but her lips were trembling.

"Well, I don't know 'bout it. You look kinder queer now. I guess you walked too fast comin' over here. You allers did race."

"Mebbe I did."

"For the land's sake, jest see that dust you tracked in! I've got to git the dust-pan an' brush now, an' sweep it up."

"I'll do it."

"No; set still. I'd rather see to it myself."

As the summer went on Alfred Tollet continued to improve. He was as hearty as ever by September. But his wife seemed to lose as he gained. She grew thin, and her small face had a solemn, anxious look. She went out very little. She did not go to church at all, and she had been a devout church-goer. Occasionally she went over to her sister's, that was all. Hannah watched her shrewdly. She was a woman who arrived at conclusions slowly; but she never turned aside from the road to them.

"Look-a here, Lucy," she said one day, "I know what's the matter with you; thar's somethin' on your mind; an' I think you'd better out with it."

The words seemed propelled like bullets by her vehemence. Lucy shrank down and away from them, her pitiful eyes turned up towards her sister.

"Oh, Hannah, you scare me; I don't know what you mean."

"Yes, you do. Do you s'pose I'm blind? You're worrying yourself to death, an' I want to know the reason why. Is it anything 'bout Alferd?"

"Yes—don't, Hannah."

"Well, I'll go over an' give him a piece of my mind! I'll see—"

"Oh, Hannah, don't! It ain't him. It's me—it's me."

" What on airth hev you done?"

Mrs. Tollet began to sob.

" For the land sake, stop cryin' an' tell me."

" Oh, I—give him—gentian."

" Lucy Ann Tollet, air you crazy? What ef you did give him gentian? I don't see nothin' to take on so about."

" I—deceived him, an' it's been 'most killin' me to think on't ever since."

" What do you mean?"

" I put it in his tea, the way you said."

" An' he never knew it?"

" He kinder complained 'bout its tastin' bitter, an' I told him 'twas his mouth. He asked me ef it didn't taste bitter to me, an' I said, ' No.' I don' know nothin' what's goin' to become of me. Then I had to be so keerful 'bout putting too much on't in his tea, that I was afraid he wouldn't get enough. So I put little sprinklin's on't in the bread an' pies an' everythin' I cooked. An' when he'd say nothin' tasted right nowadays, an' somehow everything was kinder bitterish, I'd tell him it must be his mouth."

" Look here, Lucy, you didn't eat everythin' with gentian in it yourself?"

" Course I did."

" Fur the land sake!"

" I s'pose the stuff must hev done him good; he's picked right up ever since he begun takin' it. But I can't git over my deceivin' of him so. I've 'bout made up my mind to tell him."

" Well, all I've got to say is you're a big fool if you do. I declare, Lucy Ann Tollet, I never saw sech a woman! The idee of your worryin' over such a thing as that, when it's done Alferd good, too! P'rhaps you'd ruther he'd died?"

"Sometimes I think I hed 'most ruther."

"Well !"

In the course of a few days Mrs. Tollet did tell her husband. He received her disclosure in precisely the way she had known that he would. Her nerves received just the shock which they were braced to meet.

They had come home from meeting on a Sunday night. Mrs. Tollet stood before him ; she had not even taken off her shawl and little black bonnet.

"Alferd," said she, "I've got somethin' to tell you ; it's been on my mind a long time. I meant it all fur the best ; but I've been doin' somethin' wrong. I've been deceivin' of you. I give you gentian last spring when you was so poorly. I put little sprinklin's on't into everything you ate. An' I didn't tell the truth when I said 'twas your mouth, an' it didn't taste bitter to me."

The old man half closed his eyes, and looked at her intently ; his mouth widened out rigidly. "You put a little gentian into everything I ate unbeknownst to me, did you ?" said he. "H'm !"

"Oh, Alferd, don't look at me so ! I meant it all fur the best. I was afeard you wouldn't git well without you hed it, Alferd. I was dretful worried about you ; you didn't know nothin' about it, but I was. I laid awake nights a-worryin' an' prayin. I know I did wrong ; it wa'n't right to deceive you, but it was all along of my worryin' an' my thinkin' so much of you, Alferd. I was afeard you'd die an' leave me all alone ; an'—it 'most killed me to think on't."

Mr. Tollet pulled off his boots, then pattered heavily about the house, locking the doors and making preparations for retiring. He would not speak another word to his wife about the matter, though she kept on with her piteous little protestations.

Next morning, while she was getting breakfast, he went down to the store. The meal, a nice one—she had taken unusual pains with it—was on the table when he returned; but he never glanced at it. His hands were full of bundles, which he opened with painstaking deliberation. His wife watched apprehensively. There was a new teapot, a pound of tea, and some bread and cheese, also a salt mackerel.

Mrs. Tollet's eyes shone round and big; her lips were white. Her husband put a pinch of tea in the new teapot, and filled it with boiling water from the kettle.

"What air you a-doin' on, Alferd?" she asked, feebly.

"I'm jest a-goin' to make sure I hev some tea, an' somethin' to eat without any gentian in it."

"Oh, Alferd, I made these corn-cakes on purpose, an' they air real light. They 'ain't got no gentian on 'em, Alferd."

He sliced his bread and cheese clumsily, and sat down to eat them in stubborn silence.

Mrs. Tollet, motionless at her end of the table, stared at him with an appalled look. She never thought of eating anything herself.

After breakfast, when her husband started out to work, he pointed at the mackerel. "Don't you tech that," said he.

"But, Alferd—"

"I ain't got nothin' more to say. Don't you tech it."

Never a morning had passed before but Lucy Tollet had set her house in order; to-day she remained there at the kitchen-table till noon, and did not put away the breakfast dishes.

Alfred came home, kindled up the fire, cooked and ate

his salt mackerel imperturbably ; and she did not move or speak till he was about to go away again. Then she said, in a voice which seemed to shrink of itself, " Alferd !"

He did not turn his head.

" Alferd, you must answer me ; I'm in airnest. Don't you want me to do nothin' fur you any more ? Don't you never want me to cook anything fur you agin ?"

" No ; I'm afeard of gittin' things that's bitter."

" I won't never put any gentian in anything agin, Alferd. Won't you let me git supper ?"

" No, I won't. I don't want to talk no more about it. In futur I'm a-goin' to cook my vittles myself, an' that's all thar is about it."

" Alferd, if you don't want me to do nothin' fur you, meb-be—you'll think I ain't airnin' my own vittles ; mebbe— you'd rather I go over to Hannah's—"

She sobbed aloud when she said that. He looked startled, and eyed her sharply for a minute. The other performer in the little melodrama which this thwarted, arbitrary old man had arranged was adopting a *rôle* that he had not antici-pated, but he was still going to abide by his own.

" Mebbe 'twould be jest as well," said he. Then he went out of the door.

Hannah Orton was in her kitchen sewing when her sister entered.

" Fur the land sake, Lucy, what is the matter ?"

" I've left him—I've left Alferd ! Oh ! oh !"

Lucy Tollet gasped for breath ; she sank into a chair, and leaned her head against the wall. Hannah got some water.

" Don't, Lucy—there, there ! Drink this, poor lamb !"

She did not quite faint. She could speak in a few minutes. "He bought him a new tea-pot this mornin', Hannah, an' some bread an' cheese and salt mackerel. He's goin' to do his own cookin'; he don't want me to do nothin' more fur him; he's afeard I'll put gentian in it. I've left him ! I've come to stay with you !"

"You told him, then ?"

"I hed to ; I couldn't go on so no longer. He wouldn't let me tech that mackerel, an' it orter hev been soaked. It was salt enough to kill him."

"Serve him right ef it did."

"Hannah Orton, I ain't a-goin' to hev a thing said agin Alferd."

"Well, ef you want to stan' up fur Alferd Tollet, you kin. You allers would stan' up fur him agin your own folks. Ef you want to keep on carin' fur sech a miserable, set, un-feelin'—"

"Don't you say another word, Hannah—not another one ; I won't hear it."

"I ain't a-goin' to say nothin'; thar ain't any need of your bein' so fierce. Now don't cry so, Lucy. We shell git along real nice here together. You'll get used to it arter a little while, an' you'll see you air a good deal better off without him; you've been nothin' but jest a slave ever since you was married. Don't you s'pose I've seen it ? I've pitied you so, I didn't know what to do. I've seen the time when I'd like to ha' shook Alferd."

"Don't, Hannah."

"I ain't a-goin' to say nothin' more. You jest stop cryin', an' try an' be calm, or you'll be sick. Hev you hed any dinner ?"

"I don't want none."

"You've got to eat somethin', Lucy Ann Tollet. Thar

ain't no sense in your givin' up so. I've got a nice little piece of lamb, an' some pease an' string-beans, left over, an' I'm a-goin' to get 'em. You've got to eat 'em, an' then you'll feel better. Look-a here, I want to know ef Alferd drove you out of the house 'cause you give him gentian? I ain't got it through my head yet."

"I asked him ef he'd ruther hev me go, an' he said mebbe 'twould be jest as well. I thought I shouldn't hev no right to stay ef I couldn't git his meals for him."

"Right to stay! Lucy Ann Tollet, ef it wa'n't fur the grace of the Lord, I believe you'd be a simpleton. I don't understand no sech goodness; I allers thought it would run into foolishness some time, an' I believe it has with you. Well, don't worry no more about it; set up an' eat your dinner. Jest smooth out that mat under your feet a little; you've got it all scrolled up."

No bitter herb could have added anything to the bitterness of that first dinner which poor Lucy Tollet ate after she had left her own home. Time and custom lessened, but not much, the bitterness of the subsequent ones. Hannah had sewed for her living all her narrow, single life; Lucy shared her work now. They had to live frugally; still they had enough. Hannah owned the little house in which she lived.

Lucy Tollet lived with her through the fall and winter. Her leaving her husband started a great whirlpool of excitement in this little village. Hannah's custom doubled: people came ostensibly for work, but really for information. They quizzed her about her sister, but Hannah could be taciturn. She did their work and divulged nothing, except occasionally when she was surprised. Then she would let fall a few little hints, which were not at Lucy's expense.

They never saw Mrs. Tollet; she always ran when she heard any one coming. She never went out to church nor on the street. She grew to have a morbid dread of meeting her husband or seeing him. She would never sit at the window, lest he might go past. Hannah could not understand this; neither could Lucy herself.

Hannah thought she was suffering less, and was becoming weaned from her affection, because she did so. But in reality she was suffering more, and her faithful love for her imperious old husband was strengthening.

All the autumn and winter she stayed and worked quietly; in the spring she grew restless, though not perceptibly. She had never bewailed herself much after the first; she dreaded her sister's attacks on Alfred. Silence as to her own grief was her best way of defending him.

Towards spring she often let her work fall in her lap, and thought. Then she would glance timidly at Hannah, as if she could know what her thoughts were; but Hannah was no mind-reader. Hannah, when she set out for meeting one evening in May, had no conception whatever of the plan which was all matured in her sister's mind.

Lucy watched her out of sight; then she got herself ready quickly. She smoothed her hair, put on her bonnet and shawl, and started up the road towards her old home.

There was no moon, but it was clear and starry. The blooming trees stood beside the road like sweet, white, spring angels; there was a whippoorwill calling somewhere over across the fields. Lucy Tollet saw neither stars nor blooming trees; she did not hear the whippoorwill. That hard, whimsical old man in the little weather-beaten house ahead towered up like a grand giant between the white trees and this one living old woman ; his voice in her ears drowned out all the sweet notes of the spring birds.

When she came in sight of the house there was a light in the kitchen window. She crept up to it softly and looked in. Alfred was standing there with his hat on. He was looking straight at the window, and he saw her the minute her little pale face came up above the sill.

He opened the door quickly and came out. "Lucy, is that you?"

"Oh, Alferd, let me come home ! I'll never deceive you agin !"

"You jest go straight back to Hannah's this minute."

She caught hold of his coat. "Oh, Alferd, don't—don't drive me away agin ! It'll kill me this time ; it will ! it will !"

"You go right back."

She sank right down at his feet then, and clung to them. "Alferd, I won't go ; I won't ! I won't ! You sha'n't drive me away agin. Oh, Alferd, don't drive me away from home ! I've lived here with you for fifty year a'most. Let me come home an' cook fur you, an' do fur you agin. Oh, Alferd, Alferd !"

"See here, Lucy—git up ; stop takin' on so. I want to tell you somethin'. You jest go right back to Hannah's, an' don't you worry. You set down an' wait a minute. Thar !"

Lucy looked at him. "What do you mean, Alferd?"

"Never you mind ; you jist go right along."

Lucy Tollet sped back along the road to Hannah's, hardly knowing what she was about. It is doubtful if she realized anything but a blind obedience to her husband's will, and a hope of something roused by a new tone in his voice. She sat down on the door-step and waited, she did not know for what. In a few minutes she heard the creak of heavy boots, and her husband came in sight. He walked straight up to her.

"I've come to ask you to come home, Lucy. I'm a-feelin' kinder poorly this spring, an'—I want you ter stew me up a little gentian. That you give me afore did me a sight of good."

"Oh, Alferd!"

"That's what I'd got laid out to do when I see you at the winder, Lucy, an' I was a-goin' to do it."

AN OBJECT OF LOVE.

THERE were no clouds in the whole sky except a few bleak violet-colored ones in the west. Between them the sky showed a clear, cold yellow. The air was very still, and the trees stood out distinctly.

"Thar's goin' to be a heavy frost, sure enough," said Ann Millet. "I'll hev to git the squashes in."

She stood in the door, surveying the look outside, as she said this. Then she went in, and presently emerged with a little black shawl pinned closely over her head, and began work.

This was a tiny white-painted house, with a door and one window in front, and a little piazza, over which the roof jutted, and on which the kitchen door opened, on the rear corner. The squashes were piled up on this piazza in a great yellow and green heap.

"A splendid lot they *air*," said Ann. "I'd orter be thankful." Ann always spoke of her obligation to duty, and never seemed to think of herself as performing the duty itself. "I'd *orter* be thankful," said she always.

Her shawl, pinned closely over her hair and ears, showed the small oval of her face. The greater part of it seemed to be taken up by a heavy forehead, from under which her deep-set blue eyes looked with a strange, solemn expression. She looked alike at everything, the clear cold sky and the squashes, soberly and solemnly.

This expression, taken in connection with her little delicate old face, had something almost uncanny about it. Some people complained of feeling nervous when Ann looked at them.

"Thar's Mis' Stone comin'," said she. "Hope to goodness she won't stop an' hinder me! Lor' sakes! I'd orter hev more patience."

A tall, stooping figure came up the street, and paused at her gate hesitatingly.

"Good-evenin', Ann."

"Good-evenin', Mis' Stone. Come in, won't ye?"

Mrs. Stone came through the gate, walked up to the piazza, and stopped.

"Gettin' in your squashes, ain't you?"

"Yes. I didn't dare resk 'em out to-night, it's so cold. I left 'em out last year, an' they got touched, an' it about spoilt 'em."

"Well, I should be kinder afraid to resk 'em; it's a good deal colder than I hed any idea of when I come out. I thought I'd run over to Mis' Maxwell's a minute, so I jest clapped on this head-tie an' this little cape over my shoulders, an' I'm chilled clean through. I don' know but I've tuk cold. Yes; I'd take' em in. We got ourn in last week, such as they was. We ain't got more'n half as many as you hev. I shouldn't think you could use 'em all, Ann."

"Well, I do. I allers liked squashes, an' Willy likes 'em too. You'd orter see him brush round me, a-roundin' up his back an' purrin' when I'm a-scrapin' of 'em out of the shell. He likes 'em better'n fresh meat."

"Seems queer for a cat to like sech things. Ourn won't

touch 'em ; he's awful dainty. How nice an' big your cat looks a-settin' thar in the window !"

"He's a-watchin' of me. He jumped up thar jest the minute I come out."

"He's a good deal of company for you, ain't he?"

"Yes, he is. What on airth I should do this long winter that's comin', without him, I don' know. Everybody wants somethin' that's alive in the house."

"That's so. It must be pretty lonesome for you any-way. Ruth an' me often speak of it, when we look over here, 'specially in the winter season, some of them awful stormy nights we hev."

"Well, I don't mean to complain, anyway. I'd orter be thankful. I've got my Bible an' Willy, an' a roof over my head, an' enough to eat an' wear; an' a good many folks hev to be alone, as fur as other folks is concerned, on this airth. An' p'rhaps some other woman ain't lonesome be-cause I am, an' maybe she'd be one of the kind that didn't like cats, an' wouldn't hev got along half as well as me. No: I've got a good many mercies to be thankful fur—more'n I deserve. I never orter complain."

"Well, if all of us looked at our mercies more'n our trials, we'd be a good deal happier. But, sakes ! I must be goin'. I'm catchin' cold, an' I'm henderin' you. It's supper-time, too. You've got somethin' cookin' in the house that smells good."

"Yes ; it's some stewed tomarter. I allers like some-thin' I kin eat butter an' pepper on sech a night as this."

"Well, somethin' of that kind *is* good. Good-night, Ann."

"Good-night, Mis' Stone. Goin' to meetin' to-night?"

"I'm goin' ef Ruth don't. One of us has to stay with the children, you know. Good-night."

Mrs. Stone had spoken in a very high-pitched tone all the while. Ann was somewhat deaf. She had spoken loudly and shrilly, too ; so now there was a sudden lull, and one could hear a cricket chirping somewhere about the door.

Mrs. Stone, pulling her tiny drab cape tighter across her stooping, rounded shoulders, hitched rapidly down the street to her own home, which stood on the opposite side, a little below Ann's, and Ann went on tugging in her squashes.

" I'm glad she's gone," she muttered, looking after Mrs. Stone's retreating figure. " I didn't know how to be hendered a minute. I'd orter hev more patience."

She had to carry in the squashes one at a time. She was a little woman, and although she had been used to hard work all her life, it had not been of a kind to strengthen her muscles : she had been a dressmaker. So she stepped patiently into her kitchen with a squash, and out without one ; then in again with one. She piled them up in a heap on the floor in a corner.

" They'll hev to go up on that shelf over the mantel," said she, " to-morrow. I can't git 'em up thar to-night an' go to meetin' nohow."

She had a double shelf of unpainted pine rigged over the ordinary one for her squashes.

After the squashes were all in Ann took off her shawl and hung it on a nail behind the kitchen door. Then she set her bowl of smoking hot tomato stew on a little table between the windows, and sat down contentedly.

There was a white cloth on the table, and some bread and butter and pie beside the stew. Ann looked at it solemnly. " I'd orter be thankful," said she. That was her way of saying grace. Then she fell to eating with a relish.

18

This solemn, spiritual-looking old woman loved her food, and had a keen lookout for it. Perhaps she got a spiritual enjoyment out of it too, besides the lower material one. Perhaps hot stewed tomatoes, made savory with butter and pepper and salt, on a frosty November night, had for her a subtle flavor of home comfort and shelter and coziness, appealing to her imagination, besides the commoner one appealing to her palate.

Before anything else, though—before seating herself—she had given her cat his saucer of warm milk in a snug corner by the stove. He was a beautiful little animal, with a handsome dark striped coat on his back, and white paws and face.

When he had finished lapping his milk, he came and stood beside his mistress's chair while she ate, and purred —he rarely mewed—and she gave him bits of bread from her plate now and then. She talked to him too. " Nice Willy," said she, " nice cat. Got up on the window to see me bring in the squashes, didn't he? There's a beautiful lot of 'em, an' he shall hev some stewed for his dinner to-morrow, so he shall."

And the cat would purr, and rub his soft coat against her, and look as if he knew just what she meant.

There was a prayer-meeting in the church vestry that evening, and Ann Millet went. She never missed one. The minister, when he entered, always found her sitting there at the head of the third seat from the front, in the right-hand row—always in the same place, a meek, erect little figure, in a poor, tidy black bonnet and an obsolete black coat, with no seam in the whole of the voluminous back. That had been the style of outside garments when Miss Millet had laid aside dressmaking, and she had never gone a step further in fashions. She had stopped just where she was, and treated her old patterns as conservatively as she did her Bible.

She had had a pretty voice when she was young, people said, and she sang now in a thin sweet quaver the hymns which the minister gave out. She listened in solemn enjoyment to the stereotyped prayers and the speaker's remarks. He was a dull, middle-aged preacher in a dull country town.

After meeting Ann went up and told him how much she had enjoyed his remarks, and inquired after his wife and children. She always did. To her a minister was an unpublished apostle, and his wife and family were set apart on the earth. No matter how dull a parson labored here, he would always have one disciple in this old woman.

When Ann had walked home through the frosty starlight, she lit her lamp first, and then she called her cat. She had expected to find him waiting to be let in, but he was not. She stood out on her little piazza, which ran along the rear corner of her house by her kitchen-door, and called, "Willy! Willy! Willy!"

She thought every minute she would see him come bounding around the corner, but she did not. She called over and over and over, in her shrill, anxious pipe, "Willy! Willy! Willy! Kitty! Kitty! Kitty!"

Finally she went into the house and waited awhile, crouching, shivering with cold and nervousness, over the kitchen stove. Then she went outside and called again, "Willy! Willy! Willy!" over and over, waiting between the calls, trembling, her dull old ears alert, her dim old eyes strained. She ran out to the road, and looked and called, and down to the dreary garden-patch behind the house, among the withered corn-stalks and the mouldering squash-vines all white with frost. Once her heart leaped ; she thought she saw Willy coming ; but it was only a black cat which belonged to one of the neighbors. Then she went into the house and waited a little while ; then out again, calling shrilly, " Willy ! Willy !"

There were northern lights streaking the sky ; the stars shone steadily through the rosy glow ; it was very still and lonesome and cold. The little thin, shivering old woman standing out-doors, all alone in the rude, chilly night air, under these splendid stars and streaming lights, called over and over the poor little creature which was everything earthly she had to keep her company in the great universe in which she herself was so small.

" Willy ! Willy ! Willy !" called Ann. " Oh, where is that cat ? Oh dear ! Willy ! Willy !"

She spent the night that way. Mrs. Stone's daughter Ruth, who was up with a sick child, heard her.

" Miss Millet must have lost her cat," she told her mother in the morning ; " I heard her calling him all night long."

Pretty soon, indeed, Ann came over, her small old face wild and wan. " Hev you seen anything of Willy ?" she asked. " He's been out all night, an' I'm afraid somethin's happened to him. I never knowed him to stay out so before."

When they told her they had not, she went on to the next neighbor's to inquire. But no one had seen anything of the cat. All that day and night, at intervals, people heard her plaintive, inquiring call, " Willy ! Willy ? Willy ? Willy !"

The next Sunday Ann was not out at church. It was a beautiful day too.

" I'm goin' to run over an' see if Ann Millet's sick," Mrs. Stone told her daughter, when she returned from church. " She wa'n't out to meetin' to-day, and I'm afraid somethin's the matter. I never knew her to miss goin'."

So she went over. Miss Millet was sitting in her little wooden rocking-chair in her kitchen, when she opened the door.

" Why, Ann Millet, are you sick?"

" No, I ain't sick."

" You wa'n't out to meetin', an' I didn't know—"

" I ain't never goin' to meetin' agin."

" Why, what *do* you mean?"

Mrs. Stone dropped into a chair, and stared at her neighbor.

" I mean jest what I say. I ain't never goin' to meetin' agin. Folks go to meetin' to thank the Lord for blessin's, I s'pose. I've lost mine, an' I ain't goin'."

" What *hev* you lost, Ann?"

" 'Ain't I lost Willy?"

" You don't mean to say you're makin' such a fuss as this over a cat?"

Mrs. Stone could make a good deal of disapprobation and contempt manifest in her pale, high-featured face, and she did now.

" Yes, I do."

" Well, I ain't nothin' agin cats, but I must say I'm beat. Why, Ann Millet, it's downright sinful fur you to feel so. Of course you set a good deal by Willy; but it ain't as ef he was a human creature. Cats is cats. For my part, I never thought it was right to set by animals as ef they was babies."

" I can't hear what you say."

"I never thought it was right to set by animals as ef they was babies."

"I don't keer. It's comfortin' to have live creatures about you, an' I ain't never hed anything like other women. I ain't hed no folks of my own sence I kin remember. I've worked hard all my life, an' hed nothin' at all to love, an' I've thought I'd orter be thankful all the same. But I did want as much as a cat."

"Well, as I said before, I've nothin' agin cats. But I don't understand any human bein' with an immortal soul a-settin' so much by one."

"I can't hear what you say." Ann could usually hear Mrs. Stone's high voice without difficulty, but to-day she seemed deafer.

"I don't understand any human bein' with an immortal *soul* a-settin' so much by a *cat.*"

"You've got *folks,* Mis' Stone."

"I know I hev; but folks is trials sometimes. Not that my children are, though. I've got a good deal to be thankful for, I'll own, in that way. But, Ann Millet, I didn't think *you* was one to sink down so under *any* trial. I thought the Lord would be a comfort to you."

"I know all that, Mis' Stone. But when it comes to it, I'm *here,* an' I ain't *thar;* an' I've got hands, an' I want somethin' I kin touch." Then the poor soul broke down, and sobbed out loud, like a baby: "I ain't—never felt as ef I'd orter begrutch other—women their homes an' their folks. I thought—p'rhaps—I could git along better without 'em than—some; an' the Lord knowed it, an' seein' thar wa'n't enough to go round, he gave 'em to them that needed 'em most. I 'ain't—never—felt—as ef I'd orter complain. But—thar—was—cats—enough. I might 'a hed— that—much."

" You kin git another cat, Ann. Mis' Maxwell's got some real smart kittens, an' I know she wants to get rid of 'em."

" I don't *want* any of Mis' Maxwell's kittens; I don't never want any other cat."

" P'haps yourn will come back. Now don't take on so."

" What ?"

" P'rhaps yourn will come back."

" No, he won't. I'll never see him agin. I've felt jest that way about it from the first. Somebody's stole him, or he's been p'isoned and crawled away an' died, or he's been shot fur his fur. I heerd thar was a boy over the river makin' a cat-skin kerridge blanket, an' I went over thar an' asked him, an' he said he hadn't never shot a cat like Willy. But I don' know. Boys ain't brought up any too strict. I hope he spoke the truth."

" Hark ! I declar' I thought I heard a cat mew some-whar ! But I guess I didn't. I don't hear it now. Well, I'm sorry, Ann. I s'pose I've got to go ; thar's dinner to git, an' the baby's consider'ble fretty to-day. Why, Ann Millet, whar's your squashes ?"

" What ?"

" Where are your squashes ?"

" I throwed 'em away out in the field. Willy can't hev none of 'em now, an' I don't keer about 'em myself."

Mrs. Stone looked at her in horror. When she got home she told her daughter that Ann Millet was in a dreadful state of mind, and she thought the minister ought to see her. She believed she should tell him if she were not out to meeting that night.

She was not. This touch of grief had goaded that meek, reverential nature into fierceness. The childish earnestness which she had had in religion she had now in the other direction. Ann Millet, in spite of all excuses that could be made for her, was for the time a wicked, rebellious old woman. And she was as truly so as if this petty occasion for it had been a graver one in other people's estimation.

The next day the minister called on her, stimulated by Mrs. Stone's report. He did not find her so outspoken; her awe of him restrained her. Still, this phase of her character was a revelation to him. He told his wife, when he returned home, that he never should have known it was Ann Millet.

In the course of the call a rap came at the kitchen door.

Ann rose and answered it, hopping nervously across the floor. She returned to the minister with more distress in her face than ever.

"Nothin' but a little gal with a Malty cat," said she. "The children hev got wind of my losin' Willy, an' they mean it all right, but it seems as ef I should fly! They keep comin' and bringin' cats. They'll find a cat that they think mebbe is Willy, an' so they bring him to show me. They've brought Malty and white cats, an' cats all Malty. They've brought yaller cats and black, an' thar wa'n't one of 'em looked any like Willy. Then they've brought kittens that they knowed wa'n't Willy, but they thought mebbe I'd like 'em instead of him. They mean all right, I know; they're real tender-hearted; but it 'most kills me. Why, they brought me two little kittens that hadn't got their eyes open jest before you come. They was striped an' white, an' they said they thought they'd grow up to look like Willy. They were the Hooper children, an' they knowed him."

It would have been ludicrous if the poor old woman's distress had not been so genuine. However, Mr. Beal, the minister, was not a man to see the ridiculous side ; he could simply be puzzled, and that he was.

It was a case entirely outside his experience, and he did not know how to deal with it. He wondered anxiously what he had best say to her. Finally he went away without saying much of anything, he was so afraid that what he said might be out of proportion to the demands of the case.

It seemed to him bordering on sacrilege to treat this trouble of Ann Millet's like a genuine affliction, though, on the other hand, that treatment was what her state of mind seemed to require.

Going out the door, he stopped and listened a minute ; he thought he heard a cat mew. Then he concluded he was mistaken, and went on. He watched eagerly for Ann the next meeting night, but she did not come. It is doubtful whether or not she ever would have done so if she had not found the cat. She had a nature which could rally an enormous amount of strength for persistency.

But the day after the meeting, she had occasion to go down cellar for something. The cellar stairs led up to the front part of the house ; indeed, the cellar was under that part only. Ann went through her chilly sitting-room—she never used it except in summer—and opened the cellar door, which was in the front entry. There was a quick rush from the gloom below, and Willy flew up the cellar stairs.

"Lor' sakes!" said Ann, with a white, shocked face. "He has been down thar all the while. Now I remember. He followed me when I came through here to git my cloak that meetin' night, an' he wanted to go down cellar, an' I let him. I thought he wanted to hunt. Lor' sakes!"

She went back into the kitchen, her knees trembling. The cat followed, brushing against her and purring. She poured out a saucer of milk, and watched him hungrily lapping. He did not look as if he had suffered, though he had been in the cellar a week. But mice were plenty in this old house, and he had probably foraged successfully for himself.

Ann watched him, the white, awed look still on her face. " I s'pose he mewed an' I didn't hear him. Thar he was all the time, jest whar I put him ; an' me a-blamin' of the Lord, an' puttin' of it on him. I've been an awful wicked woman. I ain't been to meetin', an' I've talked, an'— Them squashes I threw away! It's been so warm they 'ain't froze, an' I don't deserve it. I hadn't orter hev one of 'em ; I hadn't orter hev anythin'. I'd orter offer up Willy. Lor' sakes ! think of me a-sayin' what I did, an' him down cellar !"

That afternoon Mrs. Stone looked across from her sitting-room window where she was sewing, and saw Ann slowly and painfully bringing in squashes one at a time.

"Look here, Ruth," she called to her daughter. "Jest you see. Ann Millet's bringing in them squashes she threw away. I don't believe but what she's come to her senses."

The next meeting night Ann was in her place. The minister saw her, rejoicing. After meeting he hurried out of his desk to speak to her. She did not seem to be coming to see him as usual.

When she looked up at him there was an odd expression on her face. Her old cheeks were flushing.

" I am rejoiced to see you out, Miss Millet," said the minister, shaking her hand.

" Yes.   I thought I'd come out to-night."

" I am so happy to see you are feeling better."

" The cat has come back," said Ann.

A GATHERER OF SIMPLES.

A DAMP air was blowing up, and the frogs were beginning to peep. The sun was setting in a low red sky. On
both sides of the road were rich green meadows intersected
by little canal-like brooks. Beyond the meadows on the
west was a distant stretch of pine woods, that showed dark
against the clear sky. Aurelia Flower was going along the
road towards her home, with a great sheaf of leaves and
flowers in her arms. There were the rosy spikes of hardhack; the great white corymbs of thoroughwort, and the
long blue racemes of lobelia. Then there were great
bunches of the odorous tansy and pennyroyal in with the
rest.

Aurelia was a tall, strongly-built woman; she was not
much over thirty, but she looked older. Her complexion
had a hard red tinge from exposure to sun and wind, and
showed seams as unreservedly as granite. Her face was
thin, and her cheek-bones high. She had a profusion of
auburn hair, showing in a loose slipping coil beneath her
limp black straw hat. Her dress, as a matter of fashion,
was execrable; in point of harmony with her immediate surroundings, very well, though she had not thought of it in
that way. There was a green under-skirt, and a brown
over-skirt and basque of an obsolete cut. She had worn it

just so for a good many years, and never thought of alter-
ing it. It did not seem to occur to her that though her
name was Flower, she was not really a flower in regard to
apparel, and had not its right of unchangeableness in the
spring. When the trees hung out their catkins, she flaunted
her poor old greens and browns under them, rejoicing, and
never dreamed but they looked all right. As far as dress
went, Aurelia was a happy woman. She went over the road
to-night at a good pace, her armful of leaves and blossoms
nodding; her spare, muscular limbs bore her along easily.
She had been over a good many miles since noon, but she
never thought of being tired.

Presently she came in sight of her home, a square unpainted building, black with age. It stood a little back
from the road on a gentle slope. There were three great
maple-trees in front of the house; their branches rustled
against the roof. On the left was a small garden; some
tall poles thickly twined with hops were prominent in it.

Aurelia went round to the side door of the house with
her armful of green things. The door opened directly into
the great kitchen. One on entering would have started
back as one would on seeing unexpected company in a
room. The walls were as green as a lady's bower with
bunches and festoons of all sorts of New England herbs.
There they hung, their brave blossoms turning gray and
black, giving out strange, half-pleasant, half-disgusting
odors. Aurelia took them in like her native air. "It's
good to get home," murmured she to herself, for there was
no one else: she lived alone.

She took off her hat and disposed of her burden; then
she got herself some supper. She did not build a fire in
the cooking-stove, for she never drank tea in warm weather.

Instead, she had a tumbler of root-beer which she had made herself. She set it out on one end of her kitchen-table with a slice of coarse bread and a saucer of cold beans. She sat down to them and ate with a good appetite. She looked better with her hat off. Her forehead was an important part of her face ; it was white and womanly, and her red-· dish hair lay round it in pretty curves ; then her brown eyes, under very strongly arched brows, showed to better advantage. Taken by herself, and not compared with other women, Aurelia was not so bad-looking ; but she never was taken by herself in that way, and nobody had ever given her any credit for comeliness. It would have been like looking at a jack-in-the-pulpit and losing all the impression that had ever been made on one by roses and hyacinths, and seeing absolutely nothing else but its green and brown lines : it is doubtful if it could be done.

She had finished her supper, and was sorting her fresh herbs, when the door opened and a woman walked in. She had no bonnet on her head : she was a neighbor, and this was an unceremonious little country place.

" Good-evenin', 'Relia," said she. There was an important look on her plain face, as if there were more to follow.

" Good-evenin', Mis' Atwood. Take a chair."

" Been herbin' again ?"

" Yes ; I went out a little while this afternoon."

" Where'd you go ?—up on Green Mountain ?"

" No ; I went over to White's Woods. There were some kinds there I wanted."

" You don't say so ! That's a matter of six miles, ain't it ? Ain't you tired ?"

" Lor', no," said Aurelia. " I reckon I'm pretty strong, or mebbe the smell of the herbs keeps me up ;" and she laughed.

So did the other. "Sure enough—well, mebbe it does. I never thought of that. But it seems like a pretty long tramp to me, though my bein' so fleshy may make a difference. I could have walked it easier once."

"I shouldn't wonder if it did make a difference. I ain't got much flesh to carry round to tire me out."

"You're always pretty well, too, ain't you, 'Relia?"

"Lor', yes; I never knew what 'twas to be sick. How's your folks, Mis' Atwood? Is Viny any better than she was?"

"I don't know as she is, much. She feels pretty poorly most of the time. I guess I'll hev you fix some more of that root-beer for her. I thought that seemed to 'liven her up a little."

"I've got a jug of it all made, down cellar, and you can take it when you go home, if you want to."

"So I will, if you've got it. I was in hopes you might hev it."

The important look had not vanished from Mrs. Atwood's face, but she was not the woman to tell important news in a hurry, and have the gusto of it so soon over. She was one of the natures who always dispose of bread before pie. Now she came to it, however.

"I heard some news to-night, 'Relia," said she.

Aurelia picked out another spray of hardhack. "What was it?"

"Thomas Rankin's dead."

Aurelia clutched the hardhack mechanically. "You don't mean it, Mis' Atwood! When did he die? I hadn't heard he was sick."

"He wasn't, long. Had a kind of a fit this noon, and died right off. The doctor—they sent for Dr. Smith from

Alden — called it sunstroke. You know 'twas awful hot, and he'd been out in the field to work all the mornin'. *I* think 'twas heart trouble; it's in the Rankin family; his father died of it. Doctors don't know everything."

"Well, it's a dreadful thing," said Aurelia. "I can't realize it. There he's left four little children, and it ain't more'n a year since Mis' Rankin died. It *ain't* a year, is it?"

"It ain't a year into a month and sixteen days," said Mrs. Atwood, solemnly. "Viny and I was countin' of it up just before I come in here."

"Well, I guess 'tisn't, come to think of it. I couldn't have told exactly. The oldest of those children ain't more than eight, is she?"

"Ethelind is eight, coming next month: Viny and I was reckinin' it up. Then Edith is six, and Isadore is five, and Myrtie ain't but two, poor little thing."

"What do you s'pose will be done with 'em?"

"I don't know. Viny an' me was talking of it over, and got it settled that *her* sister, Mis' Loomis, over to Alden, would *hev* to hev 'em. It'll be considerable for her, too, for she's got two of her own, and I don't s'pose Sam Loomis has got much. But I don't see what else can be done. Of course strangers ain't goin' to take children when there is folks."

"Wouldn't *his* mother take 'em?"

"What, old-lady Sears? Lor', no. You know she was dreadful put out 'bout Thomas marryin' where he did, and declared he shouldn't hev a cent of her money. It was all her second husband's, anyway. John Rankin wasn't worth anything. She won't do anything for 'em. She's livin' in great style down near the city, they say. Got a nice house, and keeps help. She might hev 'em jest as well as not, but she won't. She's a hard woman to get along with, anyhow. She nagged both her husbands to death, an' Thomas never had no peace at home. Guess that was one reason why he was in such a hurry to get married. Mis' Rankin was a good-tempered soul, if she wasn't quite so drivin' as some."

"I do feel dreadfully to think of those children," said Aurelia.

"'Tis hard ; but we must try an' believe it will be ruled for the best. I s'pose I must go, for I left Viny all alone."

"Well, if you must, I'll get that root-beer for you, Mis' Atwood. I shall keep thinking 'bout those children all night."

A week or two after that, Mrs. Atwood had some more news ; but she didn't go to Aurelia with it, for Aurelia was the very sub-essence of it herself. She unfolded it gingerly to her daughter Lavinia—a pale, peaked young woman, who looked as if it would take more than Aurelia's root-beer to make her robust. Aurelia had taken the youngest Rankin child for her own, and Mrs. Atwood had just heard of it. "It's true," said she ; "I see her with it myself. Old-lady Sears never so much as sent a letter, let alone not coming to the funeral, and Mis' Loomis was glad enough to get rid of it."

Viny drank in the story as if it had been so much nourishing jelly. Her too narrow life was killing her as much as anything else.

Meanwhile Aurelia had the child, and was actively happy, for the first time in her life, to her own *naïve* astonishment, for she had never known that she was not so before. She had naturally strong affections, of an outward rather than an inward tendency. She was capable of much enjoyment

19

from pure living, but she had never had anything of which to be so very fond. She could only remember her father as a gloomy, hard-working man, who never noticed her much. He had a melancholy temperament, which resulted in a tragical end when Aurelia was a mere child. When she thought of him, the same horror which she had when they brought him home from the river crept over her now. They had never known certainly just how Martin Flower had come to die ; but folks never spoke of him to Aurelia and her mother, and the two never talked of him together. They knew that everybody said Martin Flower had drowned himself ; they felt shame and a Puritan shrinking from the sin.

Aurelia's mother had been a hard, silent woman before ; she grew more hard and silent afterwards. She worked hard, and taught Aurelia to. Their work was peculiar ; they hardly knew themselves how they had happened to drift into it ; it had seemed to creep in with other work, till finally it usurped it altogether. At first, after her husband's death, Mrs. Flower had tried millinery : she had learned the trade in her youth. But she made no headway now in sewing rosebuds and dainty bows on to bonnets ; it did not suit with tragedy. The bonnets seemed infected with her own mood ; the bows lay flat with stern resolve, and the rosebuds stood up fiercely ; she did not please her customers, even among those uncritical country folk, and they dropped off. She had always made excellent root-beer, and had had quite a reputation in the neighborhood for it. How it happened she could not tell, but she found herself selling it ; then she made hop yeast, and sold that. Then she was a woman of fertile brain, and another project suggested itself to her.

She and Aurelia ransacked the woods thereabouts for medicinal herbs, and disposed of them to druggists in a neighboring town. They had a garden also of some sorts— the different mints, thyme, lavender, coriander, rosemary, and others. It was an unusual business for two women to engage in, but it increased, and they prospered, according to their small ideas. But Mrs. Flower grew more and more bitter with success. What regrets and longing that her husband could have lived and shared it, and been spared his final agony, she had in her heart, nobody but the poor woman herself knew ; she never spoke of them. She died when Aurelia was twenty, and a woman far beyond her years. She mourned for her mother, but although she never knew it, her warmest love had not been called out. It had been hardly possible. Mrs. Flower had not been a lovable mother; she had rarely spoken to Aurelia but with cold censure for the last few years. People whispered that it was a happy release for the poor girl when her mother died ; they had begun to think she was growing like her husband, and perhaps was not " just right."

Aurelia went on with the business with calm equanimity, and made even profits every year. They were small, but more than enough for her to live on, and she paid the last dollar of the mortgage which had so fretted her father, and owned the whole house clear. She led a peaceful, innocent life, with her green herbs for companions ; she associated little with the people around, except in a business way. They came to see her, but she rarely entered their houses. Every room in her house was festooned with herbs ; she knew every kind that grew in the New England woods, and hunted them out in their season and brought them home ; she was a simple, sweet soul, with none of the morbid mel-

ancholy of her parents about her. She loved her woi k, and
the greenwood things were to her as friends, and the heal-
ing qualities of sarsaparilla and thoroughwort, and the sweetness of thyme and lavender, seemed to have entered into
her nature, till she almost could talk with them in that way.
She had never thought of being unhappy; but now she
wondered at herself over this child. It was a darling of a
child; as dainty and winsome a girl baby as ever was. Her
poor young mother had had a fondness for romantic names,
which she had bestowed, as the only heritage within her
power, on all her children. This one was Myrtilla—Myrtie
for short. The little thing clung to Aurelia from the first,
and Aurelia found that she had another way of loving besides the way in which she loved lavender and thoroughwort. The comfort she took with the child through the next
winter was unspeakable. The herbs were banished from
the south room, which was turned into a nursery, and a
warm carpet was put on the floor, that the baby might not
take cold. She learned to cook for the baby—her own
diet had been chiefly vegetarian. She became a charming
nursing mother. People wondered. "It does beat all how
handy 'Relia is with that baby," Mrs. Atwood told Viny.

Aurelia took even more comfort with the little thing when
spring came, and she could take her out with her; then she
bought a little straw carriage, and the two went after herbs
together. Home they would come in the tender spring
twilight, the baby asleep in her carriage, with a great sheaf
of flowers beside her, and Aurelia with another over her
shoulder.

She felt all through that summer as if she were too happy
to have it last. Once she said so to one of the neighbors.
" I feel as if it wa'n't right for me to be so perfectly happy,"

said she. " I feel some days as if I was walkin' an' walkin' an'
walkin' through a garden of sweet-smellin' herbs, an' nothin'
else ; an' as for Myrtie, she's a bundle of myrtle an' cam-
phor out of King Solomon's garden.   I'm so afraid it can't
last."

Happiness had seemed to awake in Aurelia a taint of her
father's foreboding melancholy.   But she apparently had
no reason for it until early fall.   Then, returning with Myrtie one night from a trip to the woods, she found an old
lady seated on her door-step, grimly waiting for her.   She
was an old woman and tremulous, but still undaunted and
unshaken as to her spirit.   Her tall, shrunken form was
loaded with silk and jet.   She stood up as Aurelia approached, wondering, and her dim old eyes peered at her
aggressively through fine gold spectacles, which lent an additional glare to them.

" I suppose you are Miss Flower ?" began the old lady,
with no prefatory parley.

" Yes," said Aurelia, trembling.

" Well, my name's Mrs. Matthew Sears, an' I've come
for my grandchild there."

Aurelia turned very white.   She let her herbs slide to the
ground.   " I—hardly understand—I guess," faltered she.
" Can't you let me keep her ?"

" Well, I guess I won't have one of my grandchildren
brought up by an old yarb-woman—not if I know it."

The old lady sniffed.   Aurelia stood looking at her.   She
felt as if she had fallen down from heaven, and the hard
reality of the earth had jarred the voice out of her.   Then
the old lady made a step towards the carriage, and caught
up Myrtie in her trembling arms.   The child screamed with
fright.   She had been asleep.   She turned her little fright-

ened face towards Aurelia, and held out her arms, and cried,
" Mamma ! mamma ! mamma !" in a perfect frenzy of terror.
The old lady tried in vain to hush her. Aurelia found her
voice then. " You'd better let me take her and give her
her supper," she said, " and when she is asleep again I will
bring her over to you."

" Well," said the old lady, doubtfully. She was glad to
get the frantic little thing out of her arms, though.

Aurelia held her close and hushed her, and she subsided into occasional convulsive sobs, and furtive, frightened
glances at her grandmother.

" I s'pose you are stopping at the hotel ?" said Aurelia.

" Yes, I am," said the old lady, stoutly. " You kin bring
her over as soon as she's asleep." Then she marched off
with uncertain majesty.

Some women would have argued the case longer, but Aurelia felt that there was simply no use in it. The old lady
was the child's grandmother : if she wanted her, she saw no
way but to give her up. She never thought of pleading, she
was so convinced of the old lady's determination.

She carried Myrtie into the house, gave her her supper, washed her, and dressed her in her little best dress.
Then she took her up in her lap and tried to explain to her
childish mind the change that was to be made in her life.
She told her she was going to live with her grandmother,
and she must be a good little girl, and love her, and do just
as she told her to. Myrtie sobbed with unreasoning grief,
and clung to Aurelia ; but she wholly failed to take in the
full meaning of it all.

She was still fretful, and bewildered by her rude waken-
ing from her nap. Presently she fell asleep again, and
Aurelia laid her down while she got together her little ward-

robe. There was a hop pillow in a little linen case, on which Myrtie had always slept; she packed that up with the other things.

Then she rolled up the little sleeping girl in a blanket, laid her in her carriage, and went over to the hotel. It was not much of a hotel—merely an ordinary two-story house, where two or three spare rooms were ample accommodation for the few straggling guests who came to this little rural place. It was only a few steps from Aurelia's house. The old lady had the chamber of honor—a large square room on the first floor, opening directly on to the piazza. In spite of all Aurelia's care, Myrtie woke up and began to cry when she was carried in. She had to go off and leave her screaming piteously after her. Out on the piazza she uttered the first complaint, almost, of her life to the hostess, Mrs. Simonds, who had followed her there.

"Don't feel bad, 'Relia," said the woman, who was almost crying herself. "I know it's awful hard, when you was taking so much comfort. We all feel for you."

Aurelia looked straight ahead. She had the bundle of little clothes and the hop pillow in her arms; the old lady had said, in a way that would have been funny if it had not been for the poor heart that listened, that she didn't want any yarb pillows, nor any clothes scented with yarbs nuther.

"I don't mean to be wicked," said Aurelia, "but I can't help thinking that Providence ought to provide for women. I wish Myrtie was *mine*."

The other woman wiped her eyes at the hungry way in which she said "mine."

"Well, I can't do anything; but I'm sorry for you, if that's all. You'd make enough sight better mother for

Myrtie than that cross old woman. I don't b'lieve she
more'n half wants her, only she's *sot*. She doesn't care
anything about having the other children ; she's going to
leave them with Mis' Loomis ; but she says her grandchildren ain't going to be living with strangers, an' she ought
to hev been consulted.   After all you've done for the child,
to treat you as she has to-night, she's the most ungrateful—
I know one thing ; I'd charge her for Myrtie's board—a
good price, too."

"Oh, I don't want anything of that sort," said poor Aurelia, dejectedly, listening to her darling's sobs.   "You go
in an' try to hush her, Mis' Simonds.   Oh !"

"So I will.   Her grandmother can't do anything with
her, poor little thing !   I've got some peppermints.   I do
believe she's spankin' her—the—"

Aurelia did not run in with Mrs. Simonds ; she listened
outside till the pitiful cries hushed a little ; then she went
desolately home.

She sat down in the kitchen, with the little clothes in her
lap.   She did not think of going to bed ; she did not cry nor
moan to herself ; she just sat there still.   It was not very
late when she came home—between eight and nine.   In
about half an hour, perhaps, she heard a sound outside that
made her heart leap—a little voice crying pitifully, and saying, between the sobs, "Mamma ! mamma !"

Aurelia made one spring to the door.   There was the
tiny creature in her little nightgown, shaking all over with
cold and sobs.

Aurelia caught her up, and all her calm was over.   "Oh,
you darling ! you darling ! you darling !" she cried, covering
her little cold body all over with kisses.   "You sha'n't leave
me—you sha'n't ! you sha'n't !   Little sweetheart—all I've

got in the world. I guess they sha'n't take you away when you don't want to go. Did you cry, and mamma go off and leave you? Did they whip you? They never shall again — never! never! There, there, blessed, don't cry; mamma'll get you all warm, and you shall go to sleep on your own little pillow. Oh, you darling! darling! darling!"

Aurelia busied herself about the child, rubbing the little numb limbs, and getting some milk heated. She never asked how she came to get away; she never thought of anything except that she had her. She stopped every other minute to kiss her and croon to her; she laughed and cried. Now she gave way to her feelings; she was almost beside herself. She had the child all warm and fed and comforted by the kitchen fire when she heard steps outside, and she knew at once what was coming, and a fierce resolve sprang up in her heart: they should not have that child again to-night. She cast a hurried glance around; there was hardly a second's time. In the corner of the kitchen was a great heap of herbs which she had taken down from the walls where they had been drying; the next day she had intended to pack them and send them off. She caught up Myrtie and covered her with them. "Lie still, darling!" she whispered. "Don't make a bit of noise, or your grandmother will get you again." Myrtie crouched under them, trembling.

Then the door opened; Mr. Simonds stood there with a lantern. "That little girl's run away," he began—"slipped out while the old lady was out of the room a minute. Beats all how such a little thing knew enough. She's here, ain't she?"

"No," said Aurelia, "she ain't."

"You don't mean it?"

"Yes."

"Ain't you seen her, though?"

"No."

Mr. Simonds, who was fat and placid, began to look grave. "Then, all there is about it, we've got to have a hunt," said he. "'Twon't do to have that little tot out in her nightgown long. We hadn't a thought but that she was here. Must have lost her way."

Aurelia watched him stride down the yard. Then she ran after him. "Mr. Simonds!" He turned. "I told you a lie. Myrtie's in the corner of the kitchen under a heap of herbs."

"Why, what on earth—"

"I wanted to keep her so to-night." Aurelia burst right out in loud sobs.

"There, 'Relia! It's a confounded shame. You shall keep her. I'll make it all right with the old lady somehow. I reckon, as long as the child's safe, she'll be glad to get rid of her to-night. She wouldn't have slept much. Go right into the house, 'Relia, and don't worry."

Aurelia obeyed. She hung over the little creature, asleep in her crib, all night. She watched her every breath. She never thought of sleeping herself — her last night with Myrtie. The seconds were so many grains of gold-dust. Her heart failed her when day broke. She washed and dressed Myrtie at the usual time, and gave her her breakfast. Then she sat down with her and waited. The child's sorrow was soon forgotten, and she played about as usual. Aurelia watched her despairingly. She began to wonder at length why they did not come for her. It grew later and later. She would not carry her back herself, she was resolved on that.

It was ten o'clock before any one came; then it was Mrs. Simonds. She had a strange look on her face.

"Relia," she said, standing in the door and looking at her and Myrtie, "you ain't heard what has happened to our house this mornin', hev you?"

"No," said Aurelia, awed.

"Old Mis' Sears is dead. Had her third shock: she's had two in the last three years. She was took soon after Mr. Simonds got home. We got a doctor right off, but she died 'bout an hour ago."

"Oh," said Aurelia, "I've been a wicked woman."

"No you ain't, Aurelia; don't you go to feeling so. There's no call for the living to be unjust to themselves because folks are dead. You did the best you could. An' now you're glad you can keep the child; you can't help it. I thought of it myself the first thing."

"Oh, I was such a wicked woman to think of it myself," said Aurelia. "If I could only have done something for the poor old soul! Why didn't you call me?"

"I told Mr. Simonds I wouldn't; you'd had enough."

There was one thing, however, which Aurelia found to do —a simple and touching thing, though it probably meant more to her than to most of those who knew of it.

On the day of the funeral the poor old woman's grave was found lined with fragrant herbs from Aurelia's garden —thyme and lavender and rosemary. She had cried when she picked them, because she could not help being glad, and they were all she could give for atonement.

AN INDEPENDENT THINKER.

ESTHER GAY'S house was little and square, and mounted
on posts like stilts. A stair led up to the door on the
left side. Morning-glories climbed up the stair-railing,
the front of the house and the other side were covered
with them, all the windows but one were curtained with
the matted green vines. Esther sat at the uncurtained
window, and knitted. She perked her thin, pale nose up
in the air, her pointed chin tilted upward too; she held her
knitting high, and the needles clicked loud, and shone in
the sun. The bell was ringing for church, and a good
many people were passing. They could look in on her, and
see very plainly what she was doing. Every time a group
went by she pursed her thin old lips tighter, and pointed
up her nose higher, and knitted more fiercely. Her skinny
shoulders jerked. She cast a sharp glance at every one
who passed, but no one caught her looking. She knew
them all. This was a little village. By and by the bell
had stopped tolling, and even the late church-goers had
creaked briskly out of sight. The street, which was narrow
here, was still and vacant.

Presently a woman appeared in a little flower-garden in
front of the opposite house. She was picking a nosegay.
She was little and spare, and she bent over the flowers

with a stiffness as of stiff wires. It seemed as if it would take mechanical force to spring her up again.

Esther watched her. "It's dretful hard work for her to git around," she muttered to herself.

Finally, she laid down her knitting and called across to her. "Laviny!" said she.

The woman came out to the gate with some marigolds and candytuft in her hand. Her dim blue eyes blinked in the light. She looked over and smiled with a sort of helpless inquiry.

"Come over here a minute."

"I—guess I—can't."

Esther was very deaf. She could not hear a word, but she saw the deprecating shake of the head, and she knew well enough.

"I'd like to know why you can't, a minute. You kin hear your mother the minute she speaks."

The woman glanced back at the house, then she looked over at Esther. Her streaked light hair hung in half-curls over her wide crocheted collar, she had a little, narrow, wrinkled face, but her cheeks were as red as roses.

"I guess I'd better not. It's Sunday, you know," said she. Her soft, timid voice could by no possibility reach those deaf ears across the way.

"What?"

"I—guess I'd better not—as long as it's *Sunday*."

Esther's strained attention caught the last word, and guessed at the rest from a knowledge of the speaker.

"Stuff," said she, with a sniff through her delicate, up-tilted nostrils. "I'd like to know how much worse 'tis for you to step over here a minute, an' tell me how *she* is when I can't hear across the road, than to stop an' talk comin'

out o' meetin'; you'd do that quick enough. You're strain-
in', Laviny Dodge."

Lavinia, as if overwhelmed by the argument, cast one
anxious glance back at the house, and came through the
gate.

Just then a feeble, tremulous voice, with a wonderful quality of fine sharpness in it, broke forth behind her,

"Laviny, Laviny, where be you goin'? Come back here."

Lavinia, wheeling with such precipitate vigor that it suggested a creak, went up the path.

"I wa'n't goin' anywhere, mother," she called out.
"What's the matter?"

"You can't pull the wool over my eyes. I *seed* you
a-goin' out the gate."

Lavinia's mother was over ninety and bedridden. That
infinitesimal face which had passed through the stages of
beauty, commonplaceness, and hideousness, and now arrived at that of the fine grotesqueness which has, as well as
beauty, a certain charm of its own, peered out from its great
feather pillows. The skin on the pinched face was of a
dark-yellow color, the eyes were like black points, the tiny,
sunken mouth had a sardonic pucker.

"Esther jest wanted me to come over there a minute.
She wanted to ask after you," said Lavinia, standing beside
the bed, holding her flowers.

"Hey?"

"She *jest* wanted me to come over an' tell her how you
was."

"How I was?"

"Yes."

"Did you tell her I was miser'ble?"

"I didn't go, mother."

" I *seed* you a-goin' out the gate."

" I came back. She couldn't hear 'thout I went way over."

" Hey ?"

" It's all right, mother," screamed Lavinia. Then she went about putting the flowers in water.

The old woman's little eyes followed her, with a sharp light like steel.

" I ain't goin' to hev you goin' over to Esther Gay's, Sabbath day," she went on, her thin voice rasping out from her pillows like a file. "She ain't no kind of a girl. Wa'n't she knittin' ?"

" Yes."

" Hey ?"

" Yes, she was knittin', mother."

" Wa'n't knittin' ?"

" Y-e-s, she was."

" I knowed it. Stayin' home from meetin' an' knittin'. I ain't goin' to hev you over thar, Laviny."

Esther Gay, over in her window, held her knitting up higher, and knitted with fury. " H'm, the old lady called her back," said she. " If they want to show out they kin, I'm goin' to do what I think's right."

The morning-glories on the house were beautiful this morning, the purple and white and rosy ones stood out with a soft crispness. Esther Gay's house was not so pretty in winter—there was no paint on it, and some crooked outlines showed. It was a poor little structure, but Esther owned it free of encumbrances. She had also a pension of ninety-six dollars which served her for support. She considered herself well to do. There was not enough for anything besides necessaries, but Esther was one who had always looked upon necessaries as luxuries. Her sharp eyes saw the farthest worth of things. When she bought a half-cord of pine wood with an allotment of her pension-money, she saw in a vision all the warmth and utility which could ever come from it. When it was heaped up in the space under the house which she used for a wood-shed, she used to go and look at it.

"Esther Gay does think so much of her own things," people said.

That little house, which, with its precipitous stair and festoons of morning-glories, had something of a foreign pict-uresqueness, looked to her like a real palace. She paid a higher tax upon it than she should have done. A lesser one had been levied, and regarded by her as an insult. "My house is worth more'n that," she had told the assessor with an indignant bridle. She paid the increased tax with cheerful pride, and frequently spoke of it. To-day she often glanced from her knitting around the room. There was a certain beauty in it, although it was hardly the one which she recognized. It was full of a lovely, wavering, gold-green light, and there was a fine order and cleanness which gave a sense of peace. But Esther saw mainly her striped rag-carpet, her formally set chairs, her lounge covered with Brussels, and her shining cooking-stove.

Still she looked at nothing with the delight with which she surveyed her granddaughter Hatty, when she returned from church.

"Well, you've got home, ain't you?" she said, when the young, slim girl, with her pale, sharp face, which was like her grandmother's, stood before her. Hatty in her meet-ing-gown of light-brown delaine, and her white meeting-hat trimmed with light-brown ribbons and blue flowers was not pretty, but the old woman admired her.

"Yes," said Hatty. Then she went into her little bed-room to take off her things. There was a slow shyness about her. She never talked much, even to her grand-mother.

"You kin git you somethin' to eat, if you want it," said the old woman. "I don't want to stop myself till I git this heel done. Was Henry to meetin'?"

"Yes."

"His father an' mother?"

"Yes."

Henry was the young man who had been paying atten-tion to Hatty. Her grandmother was proud and pleased; she liked him.

Hatty generally went to church Sunday evenings, and the young man escorted her home, and came in and made a call. To-night the girl did not go to church as usual. Esther was astonished.

"Why, ain't you goin' to meetin'?" said she.

"No; I guess not."

"Why? why not?"

"I thought I wouldn't."

The old woman looked at her sharply. The tea-things were cleared away, and she was at her knitting again, a little lamp at her elbow.

Presently Hatty went out, and sat at the head of the stairs, in the twilight. She sat there by herself until meet-ing was over, and the people had been straggling by for some time. Then she went down-stairs, and joined a young man who passed at the foot of them. She was gone half an hour.

"Where hev you been?" asked her grandmother, when she returned.

20

" I went out a little way."

" Who with ?"

" Henry."

" Why didn't he come in ?"

" He thought he wouldn't."

" I don't see why."

Hatty said nothing. She lit her candle to go to bed. Her little thin face was imperturbable.

She worked in a shop, and earned a little money. Her grandmother would not touch a dollar of it; what she did not need to spend for herself, she made her save. Lately the old woman had been considering the advisability of her taking a sum from the saving's bank to buy a silk dress. She thought she might need it soon.

Monday, she opened upon the subject. " Hatty," said she, " I've been thinkin'—don't you believe it would be a good plan for you to take a little of your money out of the bank an' buy you a nice dress ?"

Hatty never answered quickly. She looked at her grandmother, then she kept on with her sewing. It was after supper, her shop-work was done, and she was sitting at the table with her needle. She seemed to be considering her grandmother's remark.

The old woman waited a moment, then she proceeded : "I've been thinkin' — you ain't never had any real nice dress, you know — that it would be a real good plan for you to take some money, now you've got it, an' buy you a silk one. You ain't never had one, an' you're old enough to."

Still Hatty sewed, and said nothing.

" You might want to go somewhar," continued Esther, " an'—well, of course, if anythin' should happen, if Henry—

It's jest as well not to hev' to do everythin' all to once, an' it's consider'ble work to make a silk dress— Why don't you say somethin'?"

" I don't want any silk dress."

" I'd like to know why not?"

Hatty made no reply.

" Look here, Hatty, you an' Henry Little ain't had no trouble, hev' you?"

" I don't know as we have."

" What?"

" I don't know as we have."

" Hatty Gay, I know there's somethin' the matter. Now you jest tell me what 'tis. Ain't he comin' here no more?"

Suddenly the girl curved her arm around on the table, and laid her face down on it. She would not speak another word. She did not seem to be crying, but she sat there, hiding her little plain, uncommunicative face.

" Hatty Gay, ain't he comin'? *Why* ain't he comin'?"

Hatty would give the old woman no information. All she got was that obtained from ensuing events. Henry Little did not come; she ascertained that. The weeks went on, and he had never once climbed those vine-wreathed stairs to see Hatty.

Esther fretted and questioned. One day, in the midst of her nervous conjectures, she struck the chord in Hatty which vibrated with information.

" I hope you want too forrard with Henry, Hatty," said the old woman. " You didn't act too anxious arter him, did you? That's apt to turn fellows."

Then Hatty spoke. Some pink spots flared out on her quiet, pale cheeks.

" Grandma," said she, " I'll tell you, if you want to know,

what the trouble is. I wasn't goin' to, because I didn't want to make you feel bad; but, if you're goin' to throw out such things as that to me, I don't care. Henry's mother don't like you, there!"

"What?"

"Henry's mother don't like you."

"Don't like me?"

"No."

"Why, what hev I done? I don't see what you mean, Hatty Gay."

"Grace Porter told me. Mrs. Little told her mother. Then I asked him, an' he owned up it was so."

"I'd like to know what she said."

Hatty went on, pitilessly, "She told Grace's mother she didn't want her son to marry into the Gay tribe anyhow. She didn't think much of 'em. She said any girl whose folks didn't keep Sunday, an' stayed away from meetin' an' worked, wouldn't amount to much."

"I don't believe she said it."

"She did. Henry said his mother took on so he was afraid she'd die, if he didn't give it up."

Esther sat up straight. She seemed to bristle out suddenly with points, from her knitting-needles to her sharp elbows and thin chin and nose. "Well, he kin give it up then, if he wants to, for all me. I ain't goin' to give up my principles fir him, nor any of his folks, an' they'll find it out. You kin git somebody else jest as good as he is."

"I don't want anybody else."

"H'm, you needn't have 'em then, ef you ain't got no more sperit. I shouldn't think you'd want your grandmother to give up doin' what's right yourself, Hatty Gay."

"I ain't sure it is right."

"Ain't sure it's right. Then I s'pose you think it would be better for an old woman that's stone deaf, an' can't hear a word of the preachin', to go to meetin' an' set there, doin' nothin' two hours, instead of stayin' to home an' knittin', to airn a leetle money to give to the Lord. All I've got to say is, you kin think so, then. I'm a-goin' to do what's right, no matter what happens."

Hatty said nothing more. She took up her sewing again ; her grandmother kept glancing at her. Finally she said, in a mollifying voice, "Why don't you go an' git you a leetle piece of that cake in the cupboard ; you didn't eat no supper hardly."

"I don't want any."

"Well, if you want to make yourself sick, an' go without eatin, you kin."

Hatty did go without eating much through the following weeks. She laid awake nights, too, staring pitifully into the darkness, but she did not make herself ill. There was an unflinching strength in that little, meagre body, which lay even back of her own will. It would take long for her lack of spirit to break her down entirely ; but her grandmother did not know that. She watched her and worried. Still she had not the least idea of giving in. She knitted more zealously than ever Sundays ; indeed, there was, to her possibly distorted perceptions, a religious zeal in it.

She knitted on week-days too. She reeled off a good many pairs of those reliable blue-yarn stockings, and sold them to a dealer in the city. She gave away every cent which she earned, and carefully concealed the direction of her giving. Even Hatty did not know of it.

Six weeks after Hatty's lover left, the old woman across the way died. After the funeral, when measures were taken for the settlement of the estate, it was discovered that all the little property was gone, eaten up by a mortgage and the interest. The two old women had lived upon the small house and the few acres of land for the last ten years, ever since Lavinia's father had died. He had grubbed away in a boot-shop, and earned enough for their frugal support as long as he lived. Lavinia had never been able to work for her own living; she was not now. "Laviny Dodge will have to go to the poorhouse," everybody said.

One noon Hatty spoke of it to her grandmother. She rarely spoke of anything now, but this was uncommon news.

"They say Laviny Dodge has got to go to the poor-house," said she.

"What?"

"They say Laviny Dodge has got to go to the poor-house."

"I don't believe a word on't."

"They say it's so."

That afternoon Esther went over to ascertain the truth of the report for herself. She found Lavinia sitting alone in the kitchen crying. Esther went right in, and stood looking at her.

"It's so, ain't it?" said she.

Lavinia started. There was a momentary glimpse of a red, distorted face; then she hid it again, and went on rocking herself to and fro and sobbing. She had seated herself in the rocking-chair to weep. "Yes," she wailed, "it's so! I've got to go. Mr. Barnes come in, an' said I had this mornin'; there ain't no other way. I've—got—to go. Oh, what would mother have said!"

Esther stood still, looking. "A place gits run out afore you know it," she remarked.

"Oh, I didn't s'pose it was quite so near gone. I thought mebbe I could stay—as long as I lived."

"You'd oughter hev kept account."

"I s'pose I hed, but I never knew much 'bout money-matters, an' poor mother, she was too old. Father was real sharp, ef he'd lived. Oh, I've got to go! I never thought it would come to this!"

"I don't think you're fit to do any work."

"No; they say I ain't. My rheumatism has been worse lately. It's been hard work for me to crawl round an' wait on mother. I've got to go. Oh, Esther, it's awful to think I can't die in my own home. Now I've got—to die in the poorhouse! I've—got—to die in the poorhouse!"

"I've got to go now," said Esther.

"Don't go. You ain't but jest come. I ain't got a soul to speak to."

"I'll come in agin arter supper," said Esther, and went out resolutely, with Lavinia wailing after her to come back. At home, she sat down and deliberated. She had a long talk with Hatty when she returned. "I don't care," was all she could get out of the girl, who was more silent than usual. She ate very little supper.

It was eight o'clock when Esther went over to the Dodge house. The windows were all dark. "Land, I believe she's gone to bed," said the old woman, fumbling along through the yard. The door was fast, so she knocked. "Laviny, Laviny, be you gone to bed? Laviny Dodge!"

"Who is it?" said a quavering voice on the other side, presently.

"It's me. You gone to bed?"

"It's you, Mis' Gay, ain't it?"

"Yes. Let me in. I want to see you a minute."

Then Lavinia opened the door and stood there, her old knees knocking together with cold and nervousness. She had got out of bed and put a plaid shawl over her shoulders when she heard Esther.

"I want to come in jest a minute," said Esther. "I hadn't any idee you'd be gone to bed."

The fire had gone out, and it was chilly in the kitchen, where the two women sat down.

"You'll ketch your death of cold in your night-gown," said Esther. "You'd better git somethin' more to put over you."

"I don't keer if I do ketch cold," said Lavinia, with an air of feeble recklessness, which sat oddly upon her.

"Laviny Dodge, don't talk so."

"I don't keer. I'd ruther ketch my death of cold than not; then I shouldn't have to die in the poorhouse." The old head, in its little cotton night-cap, cocked itself sideways, with pitiful bravado.

Esther rose, went into the bedroom, got a quilt and put it over Lavinia's knees. "There," said she, "you hev that over you. There ain't no sense in your talkin' that way. You're jest a-flyin' in the face of Providence, an' Providence don't mind the little flappin' you kin make, any more than a barn does a swaller."

"I can't help it."

"What?"

"I—can't help it."

"Yes, you kin help it, too. Now, I'll tell you what I've come over here for. I've been thinkin' on't all the arternoon, an' I've made up my mind. I want you to come over and live with me."

Lavinia sat feebly staring at her. "Live with you!"

"Yes. I've got my house an' my pension, an' I pick up some with my knittin'. Two won't cost much more'n one. I reckon we kin git along well enough."

Lavinia said nothing, she still sat staring. She looked scared.

Esther began to feel hurt. "Mebbe you don't want to come," she said, stiffly, at last.

Lavinia shivered. "There's jest—one thing—" she commenced.

"What?"

"There's jest one thing—"

"What's that?"

"I dunno what— Mother— You're real good; but— Oh, I don't see how I kin come, Esther!"

"Why not? If there's any reason why you don't want to live with me, I want to know what 'tis."

Lavinia was crying. "I can't tell you," she sobbed; "but, mother— If—you didn't work Sundays. Oh!"

"Then you mean to say you'd ruther go to the poor-house than come to live with me, Lavinia Dodge?"

"I—can't help it."

"Then, all I've got to say is, you kin go."

Esther went home, and said no more. In a few days she, peering around her curtain, saw poor Lavinia Dodge, a little, trembling, shivering figure, hoisted into the poor-house covered wagon, and driven off. After the wagon was out of sight, she sat down and cried.

It was early in the afternoon. Hatty had just gone to her work, having scarcely tasted her dinner. Her grand-mother had worked hard to get an extra one to-day, too, but she had no heart to eat. Her mournful silence, which seemed almost obstinate, made the old woman at once

angry and wretched. Now she wept over Lavinia Dodge
and Hatty, and the two causes combined made bitter
tears.

"I wish to the land" she cried out loud once—"I wish
to the land I could find some excuse ; but I ain't goin' to
give up what I think's right."

Esther Gay had never been so miserable in her life as
she was for the three months after Lavinia Dodge left her
home. She thought of her, she watched Hatty, and she
knitted. Hatty was at last beginning to show the effects
of her long worry. She looked badly, and the neighbors
began speaking about it to her grandmother. The old
woman seemed to resent it when they did. At times she
scolded the girl, at times she tried to pet her, and she
knitted constantly, week-days and Sundays.

Lavinia had been in the almshouse three months, when
one of the neighbors came in one day and told Esther that
she was confined to her bed. Her rheumatism was worse,
and she was helpless. Esther dropped her knitting, and
stared radiantly at the neighbor. "You said she was an
awful sight of trouble, didn't you ?" said she.

"Yes ; Mis' Marvin said it was worse than takin' care of
a baby."

"I should think it would take about all of anybody's
time."

"I should. Why, Esther Gay, you look real tickled
'cause she's sick !" cried the woman, bluntly.

Esther colored. "You talk pretty," said she.

"Well, I don't care ; you looked so. I don't s'pose you
was," said the other, apologetically.

That afternoon Esther Gay made two visits : one at the
selectmen's room, in the town-hall, the other at Henry Lit-

tle's. One of her errands at the selectmen's room was concerning the reduction of her taxes.

" I'm a-payin' too much on that leetle house," said she, standing up, alert and defiant. " It ain't wuth it." There was some dickering, but she gained her point. Poor Esther Gay would never make again her foolish little boast about her large tax. More than all her patient, toilsome knitting was the sacrifice of this bit of harmless vanity.

When she arrived at the Littles', Henry was out in the yard. He was very young; his innocent, awkward face flushed when he saw Esther coming up the path.

"Good arternoon," said she. Henry jerked his head.

"Your mother to home?"

" Ye—s."

Esther advanced and knocked, while Henry stood staring. Presently Mrs. Little answered the knock. She was a large woman. The astonished young man saw his mother turn red in the face, and rear herself in order of battle, as it were, when she saw who her caller was; then he heard Esther speak.

" I'm a-comin' right to the p'int afore I come in," said she. " I've heard you said you didn't want your son to marry my granddaughter because you didn't like some things about me. Now, I want to know if you said it."

"Yes; I did," replied Mrs. Little, tremulous with agitation, red, and perspiring, but not weakening.

"Then you didn't have nothin' again' Hatty, you nor Henry? 'Twa'n't an excuse?"

" I ain't never had anything against the girl."

" Then I want to come in a minute. I've got somethin' I want to say to you, Mrs. Little."

" Well, you can come in—if you want to."

After Esther had entered, Henry stood looking wistfully at the windows. It seemed to him that he could not wait to know the reason of Esther's visit. He took things more soberly than Hatty ; he had not lost his meals nor his sleep ; still he had suffered. He was very fond of the girl, and he had a heart which was not easily diverted. It was hardly possible that he would ever die of grief, but it was quite possible that he might live long with a memory, young as he was.

When his mother escorted Esther to the door, as she took leave, there was a marked difference in her manner. "Come again soon, Mis' Gay," he heard her say , "run up any time you feel like it, an' stay to tea. I'd really like to have you."

"Thank ye," said Esther, as she went down the steps. She had an aspect of sweetness about her which did not seem to mix well with herself.

When she reached home she found Hatty lying on the lounge. "How do you feel to-night?" said she, unpinning her shawl.

"Pretty well."

"You'd better go an' brush your hair an' change your dress. I've been over to Henry's an' seen his mother, an' I shouldn't wonder if he was over here to-night."

Hatty sat bolt upright and looked at her grandmother. "What do you mean?"

"What I say. I've been over to Mrs. Little's, an' we've had a talk. I guess she thought she'd been kind of silly to make such a fuss. I reasoned with her, an' I guess she saw I'd been more right about some things than she'd thought for. An' as far as goin' to meetin' an' knittin' Sundays is concerned— Well, I don't s'pose I kin knit

any more if I want to. I've been to see about it, an' Laviny Dodge is comin' here Saturday, an' she's so bad with
her rheumatiz that she can't move, an' I guess it'll be all I
kin do to wait on her, without doin' much knittin'. Mebbe
I kin git a few minutes evenin's, but I reckon 'twon't
amount to much. Of course I couldn't go to meetin' if I
wanted to. I couldn't leave Laviny."

"Did she say he—was coming?"

"Yes ; she said she shouldn't wonder if he was up."

The young man did come that evening, and Esther retired to her little bedroom early, and lay listening happily
to the soft murmur of voices outside. Lavinia Dodge arrived Saturday. The next morning, when Hatty had gone
to church, she called Esther. "I want to speak to you
a minute," said she. "I want to know if— Mr. Winter
brought me over, and he married the Ball girl that's been
in the post-office, you know, and somethin' he said— Esther
Gay, I want to know if you're the one that's been sendin'
that money to me and mother all along?"

Esther colored, and turned to go. "I don't see why you
think it's me."

"Esther, don't you go. I know 'twas ; you can't say
'twa'n't."

"It wa'n't much, anyhow."

"'Twas to us. It kept us goin' a good while longer. We
never said anythin' about it. Mother was awful proud, you
know, but I dunno what we should have done. Esther,
how could you do it?"

"Oh, it wa'n't anythin'. It was extra money. I airn'd
it."

"Knittin' ?"

Esther jerked her head defiantly. The sick woman began to cry. "If I'd ha' known, I would ha' come. I wouldn't have said a word."

"Yes, you would, too. You was bound to stan' up for what you thought was right, jest as much as I was. Now, we've both stood up, an' it's all right. Don't you fret no more about it."

"To think—"

"Land sakes, don't cry. The tea's all steeped, and I'm goin' to bring you in a cup now."

Henry came that evening. About nine o'clock Esther got a pitcher and went down to the well to draw some water for the invalid. Her old joints were so tired and stiff that she could scarcely move. She had had a hard day. After she had filled her pitcher she stood resting for a moment, staring up at the bright sitting-room windows. Henry and Hatty were in there: just a simple, awkward young pair, with nothing beautiful about them, save the spark of eternal nature, which had its own light. But they sat up stiffly and timidly in their two chairs, looking at each other with full content. They had glanced solemnly and bashfully at Esther when she passed through the room; she appeared not to see them.

Standing at the well, looking up at the windows, she chuckled softly to herself. "It's all settled right," said she, "an' there don't none of 'em suspect that I'm a-carryin' out my p'int arter all."

IN BUTTERFLY TIME.

"SEEMS to me the butterflies is dretful thick this season, Becca."

"Yes, they do seem to be consider'ble thick, mother."

"I never see 'em so thick. Thar's hull swarms on 'em: lots of them common yaller ones, an' leetle rusty red ones; an' thar's some of them big spotted ones, ain't thar? Near's I kin see through my specs, thar's one now a-settin' on that head of clover."

"Yes, there is one, mother."

"Thar's lots of grasshoppers too. The grasshoppers air a-risin' up around my feet, an' the butterflies air flyin' up in my face out of the flowers. Law, hev we got to the bars a'ready? I hadn't no idee on't. Be keerful about lettin' on 'em down, Becca."

The younger of the two old women let down the bars which separated the blooming field which they had been traversing from the road, and they passed through.

"S'pose you'd better put 'em up agin, Becca, though thar ain't any need on't, as I see. Thar ain't nothin' in the field to git out but the butterflies an' the grasshoppers, an' they'll git out if they want to, whether or no. Let me take holt."

"There ain't any need of it, mother."

"Yes, I will, too, Becca Wheat. I'm jest as strong in my arms as ever I was. You ain't no call to think I ain't."

"I don't think so, mother; I know you're real strong."

"I allers was pretty strong to lift—stronger'n you."

The bars up, the two women kept on down the road. It was bordered by stone walls and flowering bushes. Ahead, just as far as they could see, was one white house. They were going there to a women's prayer-meeting.

The older of the two kept a little ahead of the younger, trotting weakly through the short, dusty grass. Her small, old head in a black straw bonnet bobbed in time to every step; her sharp, yellow little face peeped out of the bonnet, alert and half aggressive. She wore a short black shawl tightly drawn over her narrow, wiry back, and held her hands folded primly in front over the two ends.

The other woman, her daughter, pacing dreamily behind, was taller and slenderer. Her face was pale and full, but slightly wrinkled, with a sweet, wide mouth. The pleasant expression about it was so decided that it was almost a smile. Her dress was slightly younger, a hat instead of a bonnet, and no shawl over her black calico afternoon dress.

As they drew nearer to the house the old woman peered anxiously ahead through her spectacles.

"See any one thar, Becca?"

"I should think two women jest went in. I couldn't tell who they was."

"You'd orter wear your spectacles, Becca; your eyesight ain't so good as mine was at your age. She's got her front room open for the meetin'. I kin see the curtains flappin'."

Quite a strong soft wind was blowing. As they went up the front walk between the phlox bushes with their purplish-pink heads, the green curtains with a flowery border swung out of the windows of Mrs. Thomas's best room, the one on the right of the front door.

The door stood open, and a mildly curious face or two showed through the windows.

"Thar's old Mis' Wheat an' Becca," said some one in a whisper to Mrs. Thomas, and she came to the door.

There was a solemn composure on her large, comfortable face. "Good-afternoon, Mis' Wheat," said she; "good-afternoon, Becca. Walk in."

They walked in with staid demeanor, and took their seats. The chairs were set close to the walls around the room. There were nine or ten women there with good, grave faces. One old woman sat close to the mantel-shelf, and Mrs. Wheat took a vacant chair beside her.

"How d'ye do, Mis' Dill?" whispered she, reaching out her little skinny hand.

The other shook it stiffly. She was as small as Mrs. Wheat, but her little face was round, and her chin had a square decision in its cut, instead of a sharp one. She had a clean, nicely folded white handkerchief in her lap, and she wiped her spectacles carefully with it and looked through them at Mrs. Wheat before replying.

"I'm enjoyin' pretty good health jest now, thankee, Mis' Wheat," whispered she.

Mrs. Wheat's eyes snapped. "You do seem to be lookin' pretty middlin' for one of your age," said she.

Mrs. Dill gave a stony look at her.

The meeting began then. The good women read in the Bible and prayed, one after another, the others silent on their knees beside her. Their husbands and sons in the hay-fields, the children in the district school, the too light-minded though innocent village girls, the minister wrest-

21

ling with his dull sermon faithfully in his shabby study, the whole world, were remembered in their homely petitions. The south wind sang in at the windows ; a pine-tree around the corner of the house soughed ; the locusts cried shrilly over in the blossoming fields ; and their timid prayers went up.

Old Mrs. Wheat, in her corner, on her knees, listened with an outward show of reverence, but she was inwardly torn with jealousy. She was the last one called upon to take part ; even old Mrs. Dill was preferred before her. But she had her revenge; when she did get her chance to speak, long and weary was the time she kept her devout sisters on their aching knees.

She had been storing up a good deal to say while the others were praying, and now she said it. For church and town and commonwealth, for missions at home and abroad, her shrill cry went up. Lastly she prayed, with emphatic quavers, for old Mrs. Dill. "O Lord," pleaded she, "remember, we pray thee, this aged handmaiden at my side. May she long enjoy what blessin's are left to her in her age an' decrepitood. Sanctify her trials unto her, an' enable her to look away from the feebleness an' want of strength which is now her lot on this airth, to that better country where the wicked cease from troubling and the weary air at rest."

When the prayer was ended, Mrs. Dill rose softly from her knees and sat down. Her face was absolutely immovable as she met Mrs. Wheat's glance when the meeting dispersed.

The two old ladies were left alone in the best room for a little while. Mrs. Thomas, who was Mrs. Dill's daughter, wanted to see Becca about something, so she called her out into the sitting-room.

"You an' Mis' Wheat can visit a little while, while Becca an' I are out here," said she.

Mrs. Dill looked at her daughter when she said this, as if inclined to decline the proposal. Then an expression of stubborn fortitude came over her face, and she settled herself solidly in her chair.

The two looked primly at each other when they were left alone.

"How is Mis' Thomas?" said Mrs. Wheat; "and how is Adoniram?"

"They air both well, thank ye."

"I s'pose Adoniram is to work?"

"Hayin'."

"I thought I ketched a glimpse of him in the field over thar when I come in. Adoniram grows old, don't he?"

"I don't know."

"I sot lookin' at him in meetin' last Sabbath, an' thinkin' how dretfully he was altered. I hope he'll be spared to you as long as you live, Mis' Dill. It's consider'ble better on your account that he hain't never got married, ain't it?"

Mrs. Dill reddened, and stiffened her chin a little. "Thar's a good many folks don't git married, Mis' Wheat, men, an' women too, sometimes."

"Becca could 'a got married dozens of times, if she'd wanted to, Mis' Dill."

"I s'pose so."

"See here, Mis' Dill, s'pose we come to the p'int. You're allers kinder flingin' at me, an' I know well enough what it means. You've allers blamed me 'cause you thought I come betwixt my Becca an' your Adoniram, an' I didn't as I knows on."

"Oh no; course you didn't."

"I s'pose you don't believe it, Mis' Dill?"

"No; I ain't forgot how Adoniram come home from your house, jest about this time o' year, a matter o' forty year ago."

"I don't know what you mean."

Mrs. Dill sat up straight in her chair, and talked with slow emphasis. Her eyes never winked.

"Jest about this time in the afternoon, an' this time o' year, 'bout forty year ago, Adoniram come home from your house. They'd got the hay in the day before, so he had a leetle restin' spell, an' he went right over thar. I knowed where he'd gone well enough, though he made up an arrant after a rake to Deacon White's. I knowed he'd stop to Becca's before he got home. She'd been off visitin', an' he hadn't seen her for a week. She'd jest got home that mornin'. Well, Adoniram went, an' he come home. I was a-goin' through the front entry when he come in through the settin'-room. He was jest as pale as death. I asked him what the matter was, an' he wouldn't say nothin'. The door stood open in here, an' he come in an' dropped into a cheer by the table, an' put his head down on it. I coaxed an' coaxed, an' finally I got it out of him. He'd been over to Becca's, an' you'd treated him so he couldn't ever go agin. He said you didn't like him, an' that was the end on't. Becca couldn't go agin her mother's wishes, an' he wasn't ever goin to ask her to. Adoniram had jest joined the church that spring, an' he'd jest as soon cut his hand off as to lead Becca to disobey her parents. He's allers had a strong feelin' that marriages made that way wa'n't blessed. I've heerd him say so a good many times. So—"

"I'd like to know what I ever did to mistreat Adoniram, Mis' Dill."

" He never told me the hull perticklars. Thar was somethin' 'bout a butterfly."

" Lor, I remember. 'Twa'n't nothin' — nothin' at all. Young folks air so silly ! I remember jest as well as ef 'twas yisterday. Adoniram an' Becca was out in the yard in front of the house. Becca had it all laid out in flower-beds jest as it is now, an' thar was swarms of butterflies round 'em. They was out thar in the yard, an' I was in the settin'-room winder. They was kinder foolin,' an' all of a sudden Adoniram he begun chasin' a butterfly. It was one of them great blue-spotted ones. He caught it mighty spry, an' was a-givin' it to Becca, when I said somethin' out o' the winder. I don't know jest what it 'twas. I thought 'twas dretful silly for him to waste his time ketchin' butterflies, an' Becca had some sewin' I wanted her to do. I s'pose 'twas somethin' 'bout that."

" You didn't think Adoniram was good enough for Becca ; that was the hull on't."

" That wa'n't it, Mis' Dill. I don't see how you come to think such a thing."

" You'd jest set your heart on havin' her git that rich Arms feller ; you know you had. But she didn't ; she didn't git anybody."

Mrs. Dill's thin voice quavered and shook, and her little bony form trembled all over, but the spirit within her manifested itself bravely through shakes and quavers.

" You air misjudgin' of me, Mis' Dill, an' you ain't showin' a Christian spirit. You'll be sorry for it when you come to think it over. You'll see 'twas all jest the way I said 'twas, 'an I didn't mean nothin'. Let alone anything else, it's awful cruel to ketch butterflies ; you know that, Mis' Dill."

"You've done a crueler thing than ketchin' butterflies, Martha Wheat."

" Well, Mis' Dill, we'd better not talk 'bout this any longer. 'Tain't jest becomin' after the meetin' we've jest had to git to disputin'. Thar's Becca."

Going home along the green-bordered road and across the flowery field, Rebecca Wheat noticed that something seemed to have disturbed her mother. The nervous old woman fretted and fidgeted. In the middle of the field she stopped short, and almost danced up and down with feeble, childish wrath.

"Why, what is the matter, mother?"

"Them pesky butterflies!" ejaculated her mother, waving her trembling hands. "I'd like to poison their honey for 'em."

"Let me go on ahead, mother; then they won't bother you so much. I kin kinder brush them away."

"Well, you may, ef you're a mind ter. Say, Becca— speakin' of butterflies brings it to mind. You never thought I was ter blame 'bout separatin' you 'an Adoniram Dill, did you?"

The old daughter looked pleasantly into her old mother's face. " I didn't blame anybody, mother. I didn't think you used to like Adoniram very well; but it's all over now."

"You didn't take it to heart much, did you, Becca?"

"Not enough to hurt me any, I guess. Do you mind the butterflies so much with me ahead?"

"No, I guess I don't. I've kinder been thinkin' on't over lately, an' ef I was kinder sharp 'bout that butterfly business, an' hindered you an' Adoniram's makin' a match on't, I ain't above sayin' I might hev been a leetle more keerful. Adoniram's turned out pretty well. Mis' Higgins told me yisterday that he'd jest bought that ten-acre lot of Deacon White's. I guess he must hev been layin' up money. Well, Becca, I dessay you air better off than you would be ef you'd been married. It's pretty resky."

Rebecca, plodding before her mother, looked ahead at the familiar landscape, with that expression of strong, pleasant patience which the years seemed to have brought out in relief on her face, like the chasing on silver. It made her more attractive than she had been in her youth, for she had never been pretty.

She and her mother reached the comfortable house, with three great elms in front of it, where they lived, two hours before sunset.

About an hour later Adoniram Dill also went home from his labor across the fields. He was a tall, muscular old man, with a strong-featured, beardless face. He was so straight and agile that he looked, the width of a field away, like a young man. When he came nearer, one saw his iron-gray hair, the deep seams, and the old brown tint of his face, with a start of surprise.

Supper was not quite ready, so after he had washed his face and hands at the kitchen sink he went into the sitting-room, and sat down in a calico-covered rocking-chair with a newspaper. His mother looked in presently, and saw him there.

She stood in the entry-door and beckoned him solemnly. "Come into the parlor a minute," she whispered; "I've got somethin' I want to tell you, an' the children will be racin' in here."

Adoniram rose and followed her in obediently.

She shut the parlor door and looked round at him. " Adoniram, what do you think? Mis' Wheat was over to the meetin' this arternoon, and she an' me hed a little talk arter the others was gone, an' she brought up that old affair of you an' Becca agin."

" There ain't any use bringin' it up, mother."

" She says she didn't mean a thing when she talked to you so about that butterfly business. She jest thought you hadn't orter be wastin' your time doin' sech cruel things as ketchin' butterflies, an' she wanted Becca to come in an' do some sewin'. That's what she said. I let her know I didn't believe a word on't. I told her right to her face that she thought you wa'n't good enough for Becca, an' she wanted her to hev that rich Arms feller."

"Seems to me I'd have let it all gone, mother."

" I war'n't goin' to let it all go, Adoniram. I'm slow-spoken, an' I don't often speak, but once in a while I've got to. She's the most aggervatin'—I don't know what you would hev done with her ef you hed merried Becca. You'd hed to hev her arter Mr. Wheat died. She ain't never liked me. She tried to be dretful nice to me to-day, 'cause she'd got an axe to grind; but she'd got so much spite in her she couldn't help it showin' out a leetle. Why, she kerried it into the prayer-meetin', she did, Adoniram. She *prayed* for me, 'cause I was so old an' broken down, an' she's three year older'n me. I think it's awful to show out that way in a prayer-meetin'."

" P'rhaps she didn't mean anything."

" Yes, she did. I knew jest what she meant by the hull on't, Adoniram Dill. She's got kinder sick livin' thar alone with Becca, without any man to split up kindlin'-wood an' bring in water, an' she's tryin' to git you back agin. She jest the same as said she hedn't no objections to it. I guess she thinks you've been doin' pretty well, too. She thinks it would be a mighty nice thing now to hev you step in thar with your money an' wait on 'em. I see through her."

"P'rhaps it ain't so, mother."

"Yes, 'tis. Adoniram Dill, you don't mean to say you'd hev any idee of marryin' Becca Wheat, arter you've been treated as you hev?"

"You ain't heard me say any such thing, mother."

"I thought you looked kinder queer. You wouldn't, would you, Adoniram?"

"Not if it didn't seem for—the best. I don't—know."

All of a sudden Adoniram Dill sat down beside the little parlor table and leaned his head on it as he had forty years ago.

"What's the matter?" his mother asked, with a scared start, looking at him with awed eyes. It was almost like a coming back of the dead, this rising of her son's youth from its snowy and grassy grave in her sight. "Oh, Adoniram, you poor boy, you ain't felt jest the same way about her all these years? It's awful. I hadn't any idee on't."

"Never mind, mother. Jane's callin' us to supper; you go right along, an' I'll come in a minute."

"Thar ain't any need of your havin' any more frettin' about it, anyhow, Adoniram. Her mother's willin', an' I ain't a doubt but Becca is. I've seen her look kinder down-hearted sometimes; for all she's so good an' uncomplain-in', I guess she's been worried as well as some other folks. You jest slick up arter supper, an' go right over an' ask her. Thar ain't no reason at all why you shouldn't. You ain't nuther of you so very old, not more'n sixty. An' I don' know as Mis' Wheat 'll be so very bad to git along with. I dessay she's meant all right."

Adoniram said nothing. He rose with an effort, and went out to supper with his mother, who kept gazing at him with loving, questioning eyes.

" Ain't you goin' ?" she whispered when they were in the sitting-room again.

" I guess not to-night, mother."

" Well, mebbe *'tis* jest as well to wait till to-morrer. I don't want Mis' Wheat to think you was in too much of a rush."

After his mother had gone to bed, and out-of-doors the summer night was complete with all its stars, he sat down alone on the front door-step, and thought. He felt like a wanderer returned to some beautiful, dear country, the true home of his heart, which he had thought to never see again. To-night the golden gates of youth swung open with sweet music for Adoniram Dill, with his gray locks and his hard, seamed face, and he entered in, never knowing he was any different.

The steadiness with which he had kept to his ideas of duty for the last forty years gave his happiness, now that the long strain was over, an almost unearthly, holy charac- ter. It was truly the reward of virtue. The faithful old man who had taken what he considered to be the right course for himself and the woman he loved, without ques- tion or appeal to that mandate of obedience which he read so literally, was capable at sixty of being as freely happy as a child.

The sordid motives which had possibly actuated Becca's mother to withdraw her opposition at last did not fret him at all. He was far above it. That hard, shrill voice which had rung out of that sitting-room window for him for the last forty years was still. The voice had truly said cruel things, more cruel than its owner would own to now. The poor, honest young man had gone away that day with the full and settled understanding that his sweetheart's mother was bitterly opposed to him, and that must be the end of it all. He never dreamed of such a thing as urging her to marry him without her mother's consent.

So he had never been since in that front yard, full of roses and pinks and butterflies.

He and Rebecca had met in the village society like kindly acquaintances for all these years.

Adoniram, looking across the little country church Sunday after Sunday as the years went on, might have seen the woman growing old who should have grown old by his side, with bitter regret, and Rebecca, with patient sadness, have marked his entrance among all the congregation ; but no one had known.

The day after the meeting Adoniram had to drive over to the store on business. On his way back he passed a house where an aged sister of Mrs. Wheat's lived, and saw, with a start, the latter's thin face at a window. " I wonder if Becca's home?" said he. Then he drove on quicker, with a gathering resolution.

About four o'clock he was going across lots through the field towards the Wheats'. He had on his Sunday coat. When about half-way across he saw a woman's figure approaching. Soon he saw it was Rebecca. He stood in the narrow footpath, between the tall clover and daisies and herd's-grass which came up to his knees, and waited.

She greeted him, when she reached him, in her usual good, placid way. " How do you do, Mr. Dill ?"

" I was comin' to see you, Becca."

She looked at him, and the calm lines in her face changed a little. " I'll go back. I was going after mother, that was all ; but she won't be in any hurry."

" No, there ain't any need of your goin' back. I can say what I wanted to jest as well here, an' then you can keep right on after your mother. Becca, supposin' 'twas forty year ago, an' you an' me was here, an' your mother was willin', what would you say ef I asked you to marry me ?"

Great tears stood in her eyes. "Oh, Adoniram, it wouldn't be fair."

" Don't you think your mother would be willin' ?"

"I don't think she's so set agin it as she was, but 'twouldn't be fair. I'm sixty year old, Adoniram."

" So'm I, Becca."

She shook her head. "No, Adoniram, it ain't any use. It might have been different once. Now, after all this time, when I'm old an' broken down, an' the fault of all the trouble on my side of the house, I ain't goin' to be so mean as to let you marry me. It ain't fair."

Adoniram gave one step forward, and caught his old sweetheart in his arms. " I've been waitin' for you forty year, Becca, an' there ain't nothin' more comin' betwixt us. Don't you say anything more about its not bein' fair."

" You know mother'll hev to live with us."

" I'll try an' make her jest as happy as I can."

The clover and the grasses rustled in the wind, and the butterflies came flying around the old man and his old sweetheart standing there. It would have made no difference to them if they had been waiting in their little chrysalis coffins a hundred years or so, they were butterflies now. There were yellow ones and little rusty red ones, and now and then a gorgeous large one with blue spots on his black wings. Seeing one of these made Adoniram remember something swiftly.

"Want me to ketch a butterfly for you, Becca?"

"I've got one now you caught forty year ago."

AN UNWILLING GUEST.

"I've been lookin' in the pantry, an' you ain't got a bit of cake in the house. I'm goin' to work an' make you a good loaf of cup-cake before I go home."

"Oh! I wouldn't, Mis' Steele; it'll be too much work."

"Work! I guess I ain't quite so feeble but I can make a loaf of cup-cake."

"You've got on your nice silk dress."

"H'm! I ain't afraid of this old silk. Where's the eggs?"

"There ain't a bit of need of our havin' any cake—Lawson an' me don't eat much cake, anyway. Besides, he can make it."

"Guess he ain't much time to make cake whilst he's plantin'. Besides, 'twould drive me crazy to have a man messin' round. Where'll I find some eggs?"

"I don't believe there's any in the house. You're real good to offer, Mis' Steele, but I don't believe there's any need on't."

"Where'd the eggs be if there was any in the house?"

"I guess he keeps 'em in a little brown basket in front of the window in the pantry."

"Here's the basket, but there ain't any eggs in it. Don't you s'pose I could find some out in the barn?"

"You don't want to go huntin' round in the barn with that good dress on."

"Guess I sha'n't hurt it any."

Mrs. Steele stalked out of the room, the little basket dangling from her hand. Her black-silk dress rattled and her new, shiny shoes creaked. She had on some jingling chains and bracelets, and long gold ear-rings with little balls attached, which swung and bobbed and tinkled as she walked.

Susan Lawson, at the window, could not see her, as she was faced the other way, but she listened to the noise of her departure. She heard two doors slam, and the creaking steps very faint in the distance.

"Oh dear!" said she. She pressed her lips together and leaned her head back. The clock ticked loud; a sunbeam, with a broad slant of dancing motes in it, streamed in the window. Susan's old face looked like porcelain in the strong light, which seemed to almost shine through it. Her skin was thin and clear, and stretched tightly over the delicate face-bones. There was a faint pink on the cheeks.

"Oh dear!" she said, the second time, when she heard the creaking footsteps nearer and louder. "Did you find the eggs?" asked she, meekly, when the door opened.

"Yes, I found the eggs, an' I found somethin' else. For pity's sake, Susan, what does Lawson mean by havin' so many cats in that barn?"

"I know it. I've said all I could to have him get rid of some of 'em."

"Well, I guess I'd say, an' keep a-sayin', till he did. I don't believe I'm stretchin' it a mite when I say I saw fifty out there just now. I hadn't any more'n shut the sink-room door before the evilest-lookin' black cat I ever saw popped its head out of a hole in the wall. Then I went a few steps farther, an' two or three scud like a whirlwind right under my feet. Much as half a dozen flew out of one corner when I went in to look for eggs. I declare I thought they'd scratch my eyes out; I was actually afraid of 'em. They were as black as minks, and they had the greenest eyes! The barn's alive with 'em. I don't see what Lawson's thinkin' of."

"I know there's a lot; there was the last of my bein' about, when I used to go out there, an' I s'pose there's more now."

"Why don't Lawson kill some of 'em?"

"I've talked to him about it till I've got tired of it. Two years ago he did get so far's to load the gun one afternoon an' go out in the barn. But I listened, an' it didn't go off. I guess he was kinder afraid on't; to tell the truth, he don't know much about fire-arms."

"Well, if I was a man, an' couldn't fire a gun, I wouldn't tell of it. I'd risk it, but I could shoot some of them cats. I guess my barn wouldn't be overrun with 'em if I knew it."

Mrs. Steele carried the eggs into the pantry; then she came back with a resolute look on her large face with its beetling nose. "Where is that gun?" asked she.

"Oh, Mis' Steele, you don't—"

"I ain't goin' to have you so overrun with cats if I can help it. If Lawson can't fire a gun, I can. The amount of it is, if one cat's killed, the rest'll leave, and I'll risk it but I can hit one. I ain't afraid to try, anyhow. Where's the gun?"

Susan turned white. "Oh, Mis' Steele, don't."

"Where's the gun?"

"You'll get killed. Oh, you will! you will! Don't— please don't."

"Get killed! I should laugh. What do you s'pose I'm goin' to do—point it at myself instead of the cat? Where is it?"

Mrs. Steele stood in front of the other woman, her large, short-waisted figure, in its smooth, shiny black silk, thrown back majestically on her heels, and looked at her imperiously.

Susan felt as if her answer were a thread, and Mrs. Steele had a firm clutch on it, and was pulling it surely out of her soul. She had to let it go.

"It's in the back chamber," said she. "Oh, don't!"

"You just sit still, an' not worry."

Susan clutched the arms of her chair with her little bony hands, and sat listening. She heard the footsteps on the back stairs, ascending and descending, then, after an interval of agonized suspense, the sharp report of the gun.

Her heart beat so heavily that it made her tremble all over. She sat thus, her poor little house of life all ajar with the heavy working of its enginery, and waited. Two, three minutes passed, and Mrs. Steele did not come. Five minutes passed. Susan began to scream : "Mis' Steele, oh, Mis' Steele, are you killed? Mis' Steele, answer! Why don't you answer? Mis' Steele, are you killed? Oh! oh! Here I am, an' can't stir a step; p'rhaps she's bleedin' to death out there. Oh, where's Lawson? Lawson! Lawson! come—come quick! Mis' Steele's killed! Mis' Steele! Mis' Steele!"

"Susan Lawson, what are you hollerin' so for?" said Mrs. Steele, suddenly. Susan had not heard her enter amid her frantic outcries.

"Oh, Mis' Steele, you ain't killed?" she said, faintly.

"Killed? I'd laugh if I couldn't shoot a cat without get-

22

tin' killed. What have you gone an' got into such a stew
for?"

"You was so long!"

"I thought p'rhaps I'd get aim at another, but I didn't."

"Did you kill one?"

"I guess so. She ran, but I guess she was hurt pretty
bad."

Susan peered round at her. "Why, you look awful white,
Mis' Steele. You ain't hurt, are you?" Susan was shivering now so that she could scarcely speak. Her eyes looked
wild; her thin lips were parted, and she panted between her
words.

"Hurt, no; how should I be hurt? I've been lookin'
kinder pale for a few days, anyway; quite a number's spoke
of it."

"Why, Mis' Steele, what's that on your dress?"

"What?"

"All over the back of it. Why, Mis' Steele, you're all
covered with dust. Where hev you been? Come up here,
an' let me brush it off There's hay-seed, too. It's too
bad—on this nice dress."

"Land! I guess 'twon't hurt it any. I must ha' rubbed
against something out in the barn. That's enough. I'm
goin' to put my shawl on, an' that will cover it up. I'll
take it off an' give it a good cleanin' when I get home.
Come to think it over, I don't know's I'd better stop to
make that cake to-night, if you don't care much about it.
I'll come over an' do it to-morrow. It's a little later than
I thought for, an' I've got to bake bread for supper."

"I wouldn't stop, Mis' Steele. It ain't any matter about
the cake, nohow."

"She goes kinder stiff," thought Susan, watching Mrs.

Steele in her black silk and cashmere long shawl going out of the yard. "How beautiful an' green the grass is gettin'! I'm thankful she wa'n't hurt."

In the course of a half-hour Jonas Lawson, Susan's husband, came up from the garden, where he had been planting pease. The woman at the window watched the tall, soberly moving figure. The broad yard was covered with the most beautiful spring grass, and the dandelions were just beginning to blossom. Susan watched her husband's spreading feet anxiously. "There! he's stepped on that dandelion; I knew he would," said she.

Lawson opened the door slowly and entered. "Who was it fired a gun a little while ago?" said he. His arms hung straight at his sides, his long face was deeply furrowed, the furrows all running up and down. He dropped his lower jaw a good deal when he spoke, and his straight black beard seemed to elongate.

"Oh, Lawson, it was Mis' Steele. She skeered me 'most to death."

Lawson stood listening to the story. "The gun kicked, most likely," said he, soberly, when Susan mentioned the dust on Mrs. Steele's black silk. "It's apt to. It ain't a very safe gun; I'm 'most afraid of it myself. I reckon she got knocked over."

"Oh dear! do you s'pose it hurt her much, Lawson?"

"Shouldn't be surprised if she was pretty lame to-morrow."

"Oh dear! I wish she hadn't touched it."

"I heard the gun, an' I thought I'd come up as soon as I got that row of pease planted, an' see if there was anythin' the matter. I knew you couldn't do nothin' to help yourself, if anybody was to kill you."

Lawson plodded about, getting tea ready. Susan had been unable to walk for several years, and all the domestic duties had devolved upon him. She had taught him how to cook, and he did fairly well, although he was extremely slow and painstaking. Susan had been very quick herself, and sometimes it fretted her to watch him.

"It took him jest three hours and a half to make a pan of ginger-bread this mornin'," she told Mrs. Steele one day. "It was real good, but it seemed as if I should fly, seein' him do it. He measured the flour over ten times—I counted." She was all of a nervous quiver telling it.

Nobody knew the real magnitude of the trial which the poor vivacious soul had to bear, sitting there in her calico-covered rocker, with her stiff feet on a little wooden stool, from morning till night, day after day. She fluttered and beat under Providence as a bird would under a man's hand; but she was held down relentlessly in that chair, and would be till the beating and fluttering stopped.

Lawson turned her chair about, as was the custom, that she might watch him preparing the meal.

He spread the cover on the table and placed the plates; then he was in the pantry a long time fumbling about.

"What are you doing, Lawson?" Susan asked, trying to peer around the corner.

"I—can't seem to see the knives anywhere. It's curious. I allers put 'em in one place."

"Ain't they in the knife-box?"

"They—appear to be gone, box and all." Lawson spoke in a tone of grave perplexity, and fumbled on.

"Ain't you found 'em yet!"

"No, I—don't seem to see 'em yet. It's curious."

"Oh dear! push me in there, an' let me see if I can't see

'em. Mis' Steele came in here an' righted up things," said Susan, after sitting in the pantry and staring vainly at the shelves; "she must have put 'em somewhere else."

They spread their bread-and-butter with Lawson's jack-knife that night.

"Mis' Steele means real well," said Lawson, laboring with the narrow blade, "but it seems as if she kinder upsets things sometimes."

"I ain't goin' to hear a word again' Mis' Steele. She put 'em up somewhere; they're safe enough."

"Oh, I ain't no doubt of it, Susan; we'll come across 'em. I don't mean a thing again' Mis' Steele."

Lawson, after he had cleared away the tea things, fumbled again in the pantry.

"What are you huntin' for now?" Susan called out.

"Nothin' but my shavin' things. I don't seem to see 'em. It's curious."

"Ain't they in the corner of the top shelf, where they allers are?"

"I don't seem to see 'em there. I guess mebbe Mis' Steele set 'em somewhere else. It ain't no matter. I was kinder thinkin' of shavin' an' goin' to meetin', but mebbe it's jest as well I didn't. I feel kinder stiff to-night."

"Seems as if you ought to go to meetin'. You're sure they ain't right there?"

"I don't see 'em. I guess Mis' Steele must ha' put 'em up. Well, it don't make no odds."

Lawson sat down and read the paper.

The next day Mrs. Steele came over, and revealed the knives and the shaving apparatus in the top drawer of a bureau in the kitchen.

"There wa'n't nothin' in there," said she, "an' I thought you could use it for a kind of sideboard."

That day Mrs Steele made the cup-cake and broached a plan.

"You be ready, Susan," said she, standing with her bonnet and shawl on, taking leave ; "I'm comin' over with the horse an' wagon to-morrow, to take you to my house."

"Oh, no, Mis' Steele !"

"You needn't say a word. You're comin', an' you're goin' to make me a good long visit."

"Oh, I can't !"

"Can't ? I don't see any reason why you can't."

"I can't leave Lawson."

"Goodness ! if Lawson can't take care of himself six weeks, I should think 'twas a pity."

"Oh, Mis' Steele, I couldn't stay six weeks."

"Don't you say another word about it. I'm comin' over to-morrow, an' you be ready."

"I couldn't git into the wagon."

"Me an' Lawson can lift you in. Don't you say a word. You ain't goin' to sit in that chair without any change a day longer, if I can help it. You be ready."

"Oh, Mis' Steele."

But she was out in the yard, looking back at the window, and nodding emphatically.

When Lawson came in from his planting he found Susan crying.

"What's the matter? ain't you feelin' as well as common to-day?" he inquired, with long-drawn concern.

"Oh, Lawson, what do you think ? Mis' Steele's comin' over with her horse an' covered wagon to-morrow, an' take me over to her house, and keep me six weeks."

"Don't you feel as if you wanted to go?" Lawson said, with a look of slow wonder.

"I'm scared to death. You don't think about it; nobody thinks nothin' about it: how I've been sittin' here in this house nigh on to ten year, an' what an awful thing it is for me to think of goin' out of it."

"Don't you feel as if it might do you good?"

"Good! I've been lookin' at that grass out there. I feel as if I'd stayed in this house so long that I'm rooted, jest as the grass is in the yard. An' now they're goin' to take me up root an' all, an' I'm only a poor little old worn-out woman, an' I can't stan' it; I—can't—stan' it!" Susan sobbed hysterically.

"It seems to me, I'd tell her I couldn't come, if I felt so about it," said Lawson, his face lengthening, and the long furrows in it.

"There's them lilacs an' them flowerin' almonds gettin' ready to blow under the window here. An' the yard's greener than I ever see it this time o' year."

"The grass round Mis' Steele's place is uncommon forrard; I noticed it goin' by there the other day."

"What do you s'pose I care about her grass? You can't git along alone, Lawson, neither."

"Oh, I shall do well enough! I can make me some pies."

"Yes, you won't make a thing but mince-pies, an' git sick, I'll warrant."

"I was calculatin' to make some apple-pies."

"Mis' Steele made some cup-cake to-day, an' I expect nothin' but that 'll make you sick, now I'm goin' away. It's rich. She put a cup of butter and two whole cups of sugar in it. I didn't know how to have her, butter's so high, but I couldn't say nothin'. She was real good to do it."

In the night Susan aroused Lawson; she had thought of another tribulation connected with her prospective visit.

"Lawson," said she, "I've thought of somethin' else. I can't go, nohow."

"What is it?" asked Lawson, with his usual steady gravity—not even his sudden awakening could alter that.

"I ain't got a bonnet that's fit to wear. I ain't been out to meetin' for ten year, you know; an' I ain't hed a sign of a bonnet for all that time."

"Is the one you hed when you was taken sick worn out?"

"Worn out? No; but it don't look nothin' like the bonnets they wear nowadays. It's as flat as a saucer, an' Mis' Steele's is high in front as a steeple. I ain't goin' to ride through the town in such a lookin' thing. I've got some pride left."

But for all poor Susan Lawson's little feminine pride concerning attire, for all her valid excuses and her tearful, sleepless night, she went. She tied on nervously the flat Neapolitan bonnet, with its little tuft of feathery green grass, which had flourished bravely in some old millinery spring; the strings also were grass green.

Lawson and Mrs. Steele carried her out between them in her chair. Poor Susan in her old bonnet, coming out into the sweet spring world, was like the feeble blossoming of some ancient rose which had missed the full glory of the resurrection. The spring, which one thinks of as an angel, was the same, but the rose and the old woman were different. The old woman felt the difference, if the rose did not.

"Oh, dear! I ain't what I used to be," she groaned, as they hoisted her, all trembling with fear, into the wagon. "I can't do as I used to, an' my bonnet is all behind the times."

Mrs. Steele's vehicle was a "covered wagon." There was no opening except in front; the black curtains buttoned closely over the back and sides. Susan sat, every nerve rigid, on the glossy back seat, and clutched the one in front firmly. Mrs. Steele sat there driving in a masterly way, holding the lines high and taut, her shoulders thrown back. The horse had been, though he was not now, a spirited animal.

Years ago a long stable at the right of Mrs. Steele's house had been well filled with horses. Mr. Steele had been an extensive dealer in them, and had thus acquired the wealth which his widow now enjoyed. She had always been well conversant with her husband's business, and now she liked to talk wisely about horses, though she had only one of their noble stock left.

"Ain't you afraid, Mis' Steele?" Susan kept asking, nervously.

"Afraid! Why, I've drove this horse ever since John died."

"Then you're used to him?"

"I should hope I was. He's rather smart, but he's a pretty fair horse. He's been a little lame lately, but he's gettin' over it all right. He interfered goin' down that steep hill by Sam Basset's one time, last February, an' hurt him. Two year ago I thought he had a spavin, but it didn't amount to nothin'. John always thought a good deal of this horse; he valued him pretty high."

Susan looked with her wide, wondering eyes at a small galled spot on the horse's back, and thought innocently that that was the fraudulent spavin.

She watched timorously every motion of the animal, and felt such a glad sense of safety that she did not repine, as she had expected, when she was carried over Mrs. Steele's threshold by Mrs. Steele and her hired man.

But the repining came. Susan was quite prostrated from her unusual exertion, and had to lie in bed for several days. Stretched out there in Mrs. Steele's unfamiliar bedroom, staring at the unfamiliar walls, that terrible, anticipated home-sickness attacked her.

"I don't want you to think I ain't grateful," she told Mrs. Steele, who found her crying one day, "but I do kinder wish, if I'm goin' to be sick, that I was to home in my own bed."

"You ain't goin' to be sick," pronounced Mrs. Steele, with cheerful alacrity; "an' if you was, you're a good deal better off here."

In a few days Susan was able to sit up. Mrs. Steele arranged her complacently in a stuffed easy-chair beside her sitting-room window.

"There, Harrison," she told her hired man that night, "that poor soul in there is goin' to take a little comfort for a few weeks, if I can bring it about."

Harrison Adams, the hired man, had come into the service of the Steeles in his boyhood. Now he was married, and lived at a short distance; but he still carried on the farm for Mrs. Steele. She was not a woman to live idly. She could not deal in horses, but she could make a few acres profitable, and she did.

This man was all the servant she kept. She managed her house herself. She was a fine cook, and Susan, during her visit, could complain of no lack of good living. The house was comfortable, too; indeed, it was grand compared with the guest's own domicile.

But all this made no impression on Susan. The truth

was that she had become so accustomed to her own poor little pebbles, and loved them so, that she thought they were
diamonds.

Seated there in Mrs. Steele's soft easy-chair, she would
sigh regretfully for her hard creaking rocker at home. She
tasted Mrs. Steele's rich food, and longed for some of Lawson's cooking. She looked out of that pleasant front window on the broad road, with the spring garlands flinging
over it and the people passing, and muttered, " It ain't half
so pleasant as my window to home." Mrs. Steele's fine
sitting-room, with its brave Brussels and its springy hair-
cloth, what was it to her own beloved kitchen, with the
bureau in the corner, the table and stove and yellow chairs,
and its voice—the clock ?

On the morning of the day when the six weeks were up,
Susan woke in a tumult of joyful anticipation. Nothing was
said, but she supposed that her going home that day was an
understood thing. So, after breakfast, she sat waiting for
her hostess to mention it. Mrs. Steele was busy in the
kitchen all the morning, the sweet, rich smell of baking
cake floated into the sitting-room.

" Mebbe she thinks we'd better not go till afternoon ; she
seems pretty busy," Susan thought, patiently.

But when the afternoon was spinning out, and Mrs. Steele
sat sewing and said nothing, Susan's heart sank.

" Mis' Steele," she said, timidly, " don't you think we'd better go before much later ? I'm afraid it 'll be growin' damp."

" Go where ?"

" Why, go home."

" Go home ?"

"Why, I thought I was goin' home to-day ; it's six weeks
since I came."

"Oh, you ain't goin' home yet a while; you're goin' to stay till you get better. Your visit ain't half out yet."

"Oh, Mis' Steele, you're real good, but I feel as if I must git home."

"Now, Susan Lawson, I should like to know what earthly reason you have for wantin' to go home. You can't do nothin' when you get there."

"I feel as if I'd oughter get home. I've left Lawson a long spell now."

"Nonsense!—a man that can cook as well as he can!"

"He won't make nothin' but mince-pies, an' get sick."

"I didn't see but he looked well enough when he was here last week. You ain't goin', so don't you say another word about it. You're goin' to stay here, where you can be took care of an' have things as you'd ought to."

"You're real good," Mis' Steele.

Susan turned her face towards the window. There were tears in her eyes, and she saw the trees all wavering, the grassy front yard seemed to undulate.

Mrs. Steele watched her sharply. "I declare I'm 'most mad with her!" she said to herself when she went into the kitchen to get tea. "Seems as if anybody might know when they was well off."

June came, and poor Susan Lawson still visited. Her timid entreaties and mild protests had availed nothing against Mrs. Steele's determined kindness. Once she had appealed to Lawson, but that had been fruitless.

"She doesn't want to go," Mrs. Steele had assured him, following him to the door. "She'll be all off the notion of it to-morrow. Don't you do nothin' about it."

"Well, jest as you say, Mis' Steele," Lawson had replied, and gone home undisturbedly and eaten his solitary pie for tea.

In the second week of June, on Sunday afternoon, Susan was all alone in the house. Mrs. Steele had gone to church. It was a lovely day. The June roses were in blossom; there were clumps of them in the front yard. Susan, at her window, poked her head out into the sweet air, and stared about.

This poor old troubled face at the window, and the beautiful day armed against grief with roses and honey and songs, confronted each other.

Then the old woman began complaining, as if to the other.

"Oh," she muttered, "there's roses and everything. It's summer, an' I ain't to home yet. I'm a poor old woman, that's what I am—a poor old woman with a longin' to get home, an' no legs. Oh, what shall I do? Oh dear! oh dear me!"

Harrison Adams came strolling up the road. He was not a constant church-goer. Susan eyed his swinging arms in their clean white Sunday shirt-sleeves, and his dark red face with its sun-bleached blond mustache.

"Harrison!" she called. Her voice quavered out shrilly. "Won't you please come up to the window a minute?" she cried out again, when he stopped and looked around inquiringly.

"Anything wrong?" he asked, standing under the window and smiling.

"I want you to harness up an' take me home."

"Why, Mis' Steele's got the horse," the young man said, staring at her.

"Can't you git one somewhere—can't you?"

"Why, Mis' Steele 'll carry you when she gets home. 'Twon't be more'n half an hour."

"No, she won't—she won't!" Susan's voice rose into a wail. "She won't; an' I want to go home."

"Why, she would if you asked her — wouldn't she?" Harrison looked at her apprehensively. He began to think there was something wrong with her head.

"I've asked an' asked her."

"Well, I should think it was pretty work if she wouldn't let you go home when you wanted to."

"Mis' Steele means all right. I ain't goin' to hear a word again' her. She's done everything for me, an' more, too; but she don't know how gold ain't yaller an' honey ain't sweet when anybody's away from home and wantin' to be there. She means all right."

"Well, I don' know but she does; but it seems pretty hard lines if you can't go home when you want to," said the young fellow, growing indignant and sympathetic.

"Can't you git me home somehow? I've got to git home; I can't stan' it any longer. It seems as if I should die." She began sobbing.

Harrison stood looking at her; her little frail, quivering shoulders, her head with its thin, yellow-gray hair, her narrow, knotty hands, which covered her poor weeping face, her peaked elbows, which seemed pricking through the sleeves, those pitiful, stiff, helpless feet on the cricket. Before this young man, with all his nerves and muscles, all his body-servants ready to obey joyfully and strongly his commands, this woman seemed like a little appealing skeleton, who, deprived of her own physical powers, and left stranded in an element where they were necessary, besought the assistance of his.

"I don' know," said he. "I'm perfectly willin' to carry you home, if we can fix it. But you see the horse is gone."

"Ain't there another you can git?"

"Nobody's but White's over there. They've gone to meetin', but I can get into the barn, I guess. But I don' know 'bout takin' you with him. He's an awful smart horse, jumpin' at everything. They don't drive him to meetin' because the women-folks are so scared of him. He ran away last spring, an' one of the boys was throwed out an' had his arm broke. I ain't afraid but what I can hold him, but you might get uneasy."

"I ain't afraid. Harness him up quick."

"Well, I'll do just as you say. I can hold him fast enough, an' there ain't any danger really. I'll go an' see if I can get into the barn."

"Hurry, or she'll be home."

That black, plunging horse had to be securely tied to the stone post while Harrison lifted Susan in. Then he un-fastened him, and sprang for his life to the seat. Then they flew.

"Don't you be afraid, Mis' Lawson," said Harrison, the veins swelling out on his forehead, his extended arms like steel. "I can hold him."

"I ain't afraid."

Harrison glanced at her. That old wasted face looked above fear. Her eyes were fixed ahead, and rapt.

"You're pretty spunky," said he.

"I've allers been scared of horses, but I'm goin' home now, an' I don't care for nothin' else."

The horse was somewhat subdued by the time they reached the Lawson place.

Susan gave a cry of rapture when they came in sight of it. Then she leaned forward and looked. Just a low, poorly kept cottage, with a grassy yard sloping to the road to the ordinary eye; but no one knew, no mortal could ever know, what that poor homesick soul saw there.

As they drove into the yard one of the black cats peered around the open door of the barn; her wild green eyes shone.

"How bright that cat looks!" said Susan, admiringly.

Presently Lawson opened the side door. He had an apron on, and his hands were white with flour.

"Oh, Lawson, I've got home!"

"I was jest makin' a few apple-pies," said he, going out to the buggy. "I don't calculate to do such things Sunday, but I was drove yesterday, hayin', an' I got short. How do you do, Susan?"

When Susan was safely in the kitchen, seated in her old beloved chair, she leaned her head back, and closed her eyes with a happy sigh. "Oh!" she said, "I 'ain't never set in a chair so easy as this!"

Lawson stood looking uneasily at a bowl on the table. "I reckon I'll set this up," said he; "it's a little mince-meat I had. I brought it out, but I didn't really think I'd use it; I thought I'd make a few apple-pies."

"I'd make the mince ones, Lawson; I guess they'd taste good. You need somethin' hearty whilst you're hayin'."

"Well, perhaps it would be a good idea for me to."

"Lawson, them cherry-trees out in front of the house are loaded with cherries, ain't they?"

Lawson stared at her. "There ain't a cherry on 'em this year," said he; "I've been wonderin' what ailed 'em. Porter thinks it's that frost we had, when they were blowed out."

"You'd better go an' look again by and by. I guess

you didn't look very sharp; the trees was red with 'em. Them blush-roses is beautiful, too."

"Why, there ain't one rose on the bushes."

"I rather guess I know when I see 'em."

23

A SOUVENIR.

"NANCY, why don't you show Paulina *that?*"

"Now, Charlotte, it ain't worth showing."

"Now do show me what it is: you've got my curiosity all roused up," said Paulina. She cocked up her face at the other two women, who were taller. She was very small and lean; she wore her black hair heavily frizzed, and had on a fine black silk dress, and a lace bonnet with some red flowers. Charlotte, otherwise Mrs. Steadman, was very proud to take her about, she was so airy and well dressed. She was Mrs. Jerome Loomis, an out-of-town lady, a cousin of her late husband's, who was visiting her for a few days. She had taken her over to call on her sister Nancy, Mrs. Weeks, this afternoon. She herself had on nothing better than a plain black-and-white checked gingham; it was a warm afternoon, but she had realized keenly her reflected grandeur as she had walked up the street with her well-dressed guest. She was a tall, spare woman, and usually walked with a nervous stride, but to-day, all unconsciously, she nipped, and teetered, and swung her limp gingham skirts with just the same air that Paulina did her black silk one. It was a nervous imitation. Mrs. Steadman was incapable of anything else: she was not a weak woman. Her mind, being impressed, simply produced a reflex action in her body. She would have despised herself if she had known it, because of the very pride which led her into it.

The call had been made, and the three women were standing in Mrs. Weeks's entry taking leave.

Paulina went on, coaxingly: "Now do show it to me. What is it? I know it is something beautiful, or your sister wouldn't have said anything about it."

Paulina had a protruding upper jaw, and when she smiled her mouth stretched far back. She smiled a good deal when she talked. She jerked her head too, and moved her eyes. She affected a snapping vivacity of manner, or else she had it naturally. She did not know which it was herself, but she admired it in herself.

Mrs. Weeks, who looked a deal like her sister, except that she was paler, and her hair was grayer, and she wore spectacles, colored up faintly.

"'Tain't worth seein'," said she, deprecatingly; "but as long's Charlotte's spoke of it, I don't mind showin' it to you."

Then she opened the door opposite the sitting-room, and with an air at once solemn and embarrassed, motioned her callers to precede her.

Paulina bobbed her head about engagingly. "Dear me, which is it? There are so many pretty things here I never could tell which you meant."

Mrs. Weeks was innocently proud of her best parlor. She had so much faith in its grandeur that she was almost afraid of it herself. Every time she opened the door its glories smote her freshly, and caused her to thrill with awe and delight. Until the last two years she had been used to the commonest and poorest things in the way of furniture; indeed, this parlor had not been finished and plastered till lately. To have it completed and furnished had been the principal longing of her life; now it was accomplished by dint of the closest work and economy; it was the perfect flower, as it were, of all her wishes and fancies. When she had her parlor she had always meant to have something good, she had said, and now it was superlatively good to her simple eyes. There was a gilded paper on the walls, and a Brussels carpet with an enormous flower pattern on the floor. The furniture was covered with red plush —everybody else in town had hair-cloth, plush was magnificent audacity. Every chair had a tidy on its back; there was a very large ruffled lamp-mat for the marble-top table; there were mats for the vases on the shelf, and there was a beautiful rug in front of the fireplace.

Paulina darted towards it, her silk and her stiff white skirt rattling. "*Is* this it?"

"*This*," said Mrs. Steadman, pointing impressively at the wall.

"Oh! Why, Mrs. Weeks, where did you get it? who made it?"

"She made it," said her sister; "an' she wa'n't long about it either."

"Why, you don't mean it! How could you ever have had the patience? All those little fine, beautiful flowers are made of—"

"*Hair.* Yes, every one of 'em. Jest look close. Thar's rose-buds, an' lilies, an' pansies, an' poppies, an' acorns, besides the leaves."

"I see. Oh, that *dear* little rose-bud in that corner made out of sandy hair! And that acorn is so natural! and that sprig of ivy! Mrs. Weeks, I don't see how you can do such things."

Even Nancy Weeks's mild nature could not hinder her from straightening herself up a little out of mere self-respect as she gazed at her intricate handiwork with her admiring guests.

" I made the whole wreath," said she, " out of my folks' hair—out of the Wilsons'—Charlotte an' me was Wilsons, you know. I had a good many locks of 'em 'way back. I had some of my great-grandmother's hair, an' my grandmother's. That little forget-me-not in the corner's made out of my great-grandmother's—I didn't hev much of that —an' that lily's grandmother's. She was a light-favored woman, an' her hair turned a queer kind of a yeller-gray. I had a great piece of it mother cut off after she died. It worked in real pretty. Then I had a lot of my mother's, an' some of my sister's that died, an' a child's that mother lost when he was a baby, and a little of my uncle Solomon White's, mother's brother's, an' some of my father's. Then thar's some of the little boy's that Charlotte lost."

" They're all dead whose hair is in it ?" said Paulina, with awed and admiring interest.

Nancy looked at her sister.

" Well, thar's one in it that ain't dead," said Charlotte, hesitatingly, returning her sister's look. " Nancy wanted some hair that color dreadfully. None of the Wilsons' was sandy. That reddish rose-bud you spoke of was made out of it."

" Whose was it ?" asked Paulina, curiously.

" Oh, well—somebody's."

" Well," said Paulina, with a sigh, " it's beautiful, and it must have been a sight of work. I don't see how you ever had the patience to do it. You're a wonderful woman."

" Oh, no ! It wa'n't so very much to do after you got at it."

" It's such an ornament, and apart from that it must be such a comfort to you to have it."

" That's what I tell Nancy. Of course it makes a handsome picture to hang on the wall. But I should think full as much of keepin' the hair so; it's such a nice way."

" That oval frame is elegant, too."

After her callers had gone, Nancy, with simple pleasure and self-gratulation, thought over what they had said. This innocent, narrow-minded, middle-aged woman felt as much throbbing wonder and delight over her hair wreath as any genius over one of his creations. As far as happiness of that kind went she was just as well off as a Michael Angelo or a Turner; and as far as anything else, she was just as good a woman for believing in hair wreaths.

She had toiled hard over this one; seemingly, nothing but true artistic instinct, and delight in work, could have urged her on. It was exceedingly slow, nervous work, and she was a very delicate woman. Many a night she had lain awake with her tired brain weaving the hair roses and lilies which her fingers had laid down.

Paulina spoke to Charlotte on their way home about her sister's looking so frail.

" I know it," said Charlotte. "Nancy never had any backbone, an' she's worked awful hard. I s'pose it's more'n she ought to do, makin' all those fancy fixin's; but she's crazy to do 'em, can't seem to let 'em alone; an' she does have a real knack at it."

" That hair wreath was beautiful," assented the other; "but I should have been afraid it would have worn on her."

When they got home, Mrs. Steadman's daughter Emmeline had tea ready. She was a capable young woman; she took in dressmaking, and supported herself and mother, and had all she could do. She was rather pretty; tall and slender like her mother; with a round face, and a mouth with an odd, firm pucker to it when she talked, that strangers took for a smile; she had very rosy cheeks.

There was a prayer-meeting in the church vestry that evening, and after tea Mrs. Steadman proposed going, with her company and her daughter. Emmeline demurred a little. She guessed she wouldn't go, she said.

"Why not?" asked her mother, sharply. She still kept a tight rein over this steady, dutiful daughter of hers. "You don't expect anybody to-night?"

Her mother said "anybody" with a regard for secrecy; she meant Andrew Stoddard.

Emmeline colored very red. "No, I don't," she said, quickly; "I'll go." She was not engaged to the young man, and felt sensitive. It seemed to her if she should stay at home for him, and he should not come, and her mother and her cousin should suspect her of it, she could not bear it; besides, she did not really expect him; there was nothing but the chance he might come to keep her. So she put on her hat, and went to the meeting with her mother and Mrs. Loomis.

She wondered when she got home if he had been there, but there was no way of finding out. He had to drive from a town six miles farther up the river to see her. He was the son of the country storekeeper there, and acted himself as head clerk. He was a steady, fine-looking young man, though he had the name of being rather fiery-tempered. People thought he was a great catch for Emmeline. He had been to see her some six weeks now. She hoped he would ask her to marry him: she could not help it; for she had grown fond of him.

Her mother was sure that he would—in fact, she hardly knew but he had. Emmeline herself was not so sure ; she had never a very exalted opinion of herself, and was more certain of her own loving than she was of anybody else's.

When Sunday night came she stayed at home from meeting, without any comment from her mother, who put on her best bonnet and shawl, and went alone. Paulina Loomis had gone home the day before.

Emmeline had put the little front room, which served alike as dressmaker's shop and parlor, in the nicest order. It was a poor little place, anyway. There was a worn rag-carpet, some cane-seated chairs, and one black wooden rocker covered with chintz. An old-fashioned bureau stood against the wall ; and of a week-day a mahogany card-table, made square by having its two leaves up, was in the centre of the room. Emmeline used this last for cutting.

To-day she had put down the leaves, and moved it back against the wall, between the two front windows. Then she had got the best lamp out of the closet, and set it on the table. It was a new lamp, with a pretty figured globe, one she had bought since Andrew began coming to see her. She had picked a bunch of flowers out in her garden, too, and arranged them in a gilt-and-white china vase, and set it beside the lamp. There were balsams, and phlox, and lark-spur, and pinks, and some asparagus for green. She had tucked all her work and her patterns out of sight in the bureau drawers, swept and dusted, and got out a tidy to pin on the rocking-chair. Then she had put on her best dress, and sat down to wait. She thought, perhaps, he would come before her mother went to church ; but he did not. So she sat there alone in the fading light, waiting. Every time she heard a team coming, she thought it was his ; but it would roll past, and her heart would sink. At last the people began to flock home from meeting, and her mother's tall, stooping, black figure came in through the gate. She thought Andrew was there, so she went straight through the long narrow entry to the kitchen ; Emmeline knew why she did. After a while she opened the door from the kitchen cautiously, and peered into the dark room : she had a lamp out there.

"There's nobody in here, mother," said Emmeline ; "you needn't be afraid."

"Didn't he come ? I thought I didn't hear any talkin'."

"No ; nobody's been here."

"Why, I wonder what's the reason ?"

"I s'pose there's some good one," replied Emmeline, puckering up her lips firmly. "I'm tired ; I guess I'll go to bed."

If she felt badly she did not show it, except by her silence at her mother's wondering remarks ; but she had always been very reticent about Andrew, not often speaking his name. She did not cry any after she went to bed—indeed, she could not, for her mother slept with her ; her father was dead.

The weeks went on, and Emmeline got ready for Andrew a good many times, half-surreptitiously. She would put sundry little ornamental touches to the room, or herself, hoping her mother would not observe them ; but he never came. The neighbors began to notice it, and to throw out various hints and insinuations to Mrs. Steadman. They never said anything to Emmeline. She was so still, they did not dare to. Her mother met them frostily. Emmeline didn't care if Andrew Stoddard didn't come. She guessed she should laugh to see *her* fretting over him. She even hinted, in her rampant loyalty, that p'rhaps there was some reason folks didn't dream of why he didn't come. Mebbe he'd been given to understand he wasn't wanted.

One afternoon she came home from one of the neighbors' with some news. She had seen a woman who lived next to the Stoddards, and Andrew had gone West.

"Has he?" said Emmeline, and went on sewing.

"You're a queer girl," said her mother. She liked Emmeline to be dignified and reticent about it to other people, but she felt aggrieved that she did not unbend and talk it over with her.

About this time her sister Nancy was taken sick with a slow fever. She lingered along a few weeks; the fever left her, but she had no strength to rally; then she died. It was a hard blow to Charlotte. She had been very fond of her sister, and had an admiration for her which was somewhat singular, since she herself was much the stronger character of the two. She had seemed to feel almost as much satisfaction in Nancy's fine parlor and fancy-work as if they had been her own. Perhaps she consoled herself in that way for not having any of her own, and maintained to herself her dignity among her neighbors.

After her sister's death she began to think that some of these fine things ought, by right, to belong to her.

"Nancy earned 'em jest as much by savin' as Thomas did by workin'," she told Emmeline. "It wouldn't be nothin' more'n fair for her sister to have 'em." But Thomas Weeks had in him capabilities of action of which people generally did not suspect him.

He was a little, spare, iron-gray, inoffensive-looking man, but he had been a small tyrant over his mild-visaged, spectacled wife. Now she was dead he had definite plans of his own, which matured as soon as decency would permit, and which did not include his giving his deceased wife's sister his fine red-plush furniture. She visited him often and hinted, but he smiled knowingly, and talked about something else.

Nancy had been dead about six months, when, one afternoon, Mrs. Steadman saw him drive past in a shiny buggy with a lady. Her suspicions were aroused, and she talked, and worried, and watched. She found out he had a new hat and coat, and was having the house painted, and the sitting-room and kitchen papered. Everybody said he was going to get married, but nobody seemed to know to whom. At last it came out. He came to church one Sunday with his bride—a short, stout, sallow woman in middle-aged bridal finery, no more like poor Nancy than a huckleberry bush is like a willow sapling. She was a widow from a neighboring town, and reputed to have quite a snug little property— four or five thousand dollars.

Emmeline and her mother sat just across the aisle from the newly wedded couple. Mrs. Steadman had given one startled, comprehensive glance at them when they turned into the pew. After that she did not look at them again, but sat straight and rigid, holding her chin so stiffly against her long neck that it looked like a double one, pursing up her lips as if to keep back a rushing crowd of words which were clamoring behind them.

She told Emmeline, when they got home, that it was all she could do not to speak right out in meeting and tell Thomas Weeks just what she thought of him.

"I'd like to get right up," said she, "an' ask him 'f he remembered it was hardly six months since my poor sister was laid away, an' 'f he'd ever heerd of such a thing as common decency an' respect for folks' memory, an' 'f he didn't think it was treatin' some folks pretty hard to bring another woman in to use their dead sister's things, when he'd never given them a penny's worth of 'em."

As far as the results went, Charlotte might just as well have spoken out in meeting, and accused her recreant brother-in-law openly. She had always been a woman who talked a great deal, and could not help making funerals for all her woes, and now there was not a woman in the town with whom she did not discuss Thomas's second marriage, and her own grievances in connection therewith. They all sympathized with her : women always do in such cases.

She warmed up on the subject to everybody who came into the shop. Emmeline kept quietly sewing, giving her opinions on her work when asked for them, but not saying much besides. Her mother did not understand her ; privately she thought her unfeeling. Emmeline had not heard a word from Andrew Stoddard all this time. For a while she had had a forlorn hope of a letter, but it had died away now. Outwardly she was living just as she always had before he had come ; but the old homely ways, whose crooks she had thought she knew by heart, were constantly giving her a feeling of pain and strangeness. She was not imaginative nor self-conscious ; she never really knew how unhappy she was, or she would have been unhappier. She kept steadily at work, and ate and slept and went about as usual ; she never dreamed of its being possible for her to do anything else, but the *difference* was all the time goading her terribly.

Her mother's fretting over the affair had disturbed her actively more than anything else ; she was almost glad now to have it turned into another channel. And this new one threatened to be well worn indeed before Mrs. Steadman should leave it. She scolded and cried in it. She was divided between grief and indignation.

Poor Nancy's few articles of finery rankled more and more in her mind. She journeyed up to Thomas's house evening after evening to see if there were a light in the best parlor; report said that they used it common now. She came home trembling: there was one.

"To think of their usin' poor Nancy's best plush furniture like that!" she said; "settin' in them stuffed chairs every evenin' jest as if they was wooden ones; they won't last no time at all. An' to think how hard she worked an' saved to get 'em, an' how choice she was of 'em. Then thar's all them tidies an' mats an' rugs, an' that beautiful hair wreath made out of my folks' hair!"

This last seemed to disturb Charlotte more than anything else. She had not a doubt, she said, but what working on it had hastened Nancy's death, and to think that that other woman should have it!

One Friday evening Mrs. Steadman started for meeting. Emmeline did not go. She had some work she was hurrying on, and her mother, contrary to her usual habit, did not urge her to; indeed she rather advocated her staying at home.

About half an hour after her mother left, Emmeline laid down her work—it had grown too dark for her to see without lighting a lamp. As she sat at the window, a moment in the dusk, she saw a figure hurrying up which she did not think could be her mother's, it came so fast and flurriedly; besides, it was not time for meeting to be out.

But when the gate opened she saw it was. Her mother

scuttled up the steps into the entry, and opened the shop door cautiously.

"Emmeline, anybody here?"

"No."

She came in then. She had something under her arm. "Light the lamp, Emmeline—quick! See what I've got!"

Emmeline got up and lighted the lamp. "Why, mother!" said she, aghast. Her mother was holding the hair wreath, in its oval gilt frame, with an expression of mingled triumph and terror. "Why, mother, how did you get it?"

"Get it? I walked into the house an' took it," said Charlotte, defiantly. "I don't care; I meant to have it. Nancy made it, an' worked herself 'most to death over it, an' it's made out of my folks' hair, an' I had a right to it."

"Why, mother, how did you ever dare?"

"I peeked into the vestry, an' saw 'em both in thar on one of the back seats. Then I run right up to the house. I knew, unless they did different from what they used to, I could git in through the shed. An' I did. I went right through the kitchen an' sittin'-room into the parlor. It made me feel bad enough. That plush furniture's gettin' real worn, usin' it so common; the nap's all rubbed off on the edges, an' the tidies are dirty. I saw a great spot on that Brussels carpet, too, where somebody'd tracked in. It don't look much as it used to. I could have sat right down an' cried. But I was afraid to stop long, so I jest took this picture down an' come off. I didn't see a soul. I s'pose you think I've done an awful thing, Emmeline?"

"I'm afraid you'll have some trouble about it, mother."

"*I* ain't afraid."

In spite of her bravado, she was afraid. She tucked away the wreath out of sight up-stairs, and when Thomas

Weeks came to the door the next day, she answered his ring with an inward trepidation. She had an inclination to run out of the back door, and leave Emmeline to encounter him, but she resisted it.

She came off victorious, however. Even Thomas Weeks succumbed before the crushing arguments and the withering sarcasms, tumbling pell-mell over each other, which she brought to bear upon him.

" He says I may keep it," she told Emmeline when she went in. " He guesses Mis' Weeks don't set no great store by it, an' he don't care. He was awful toppin' at first, but he begun to look kind of 'shamed, an' wilted right down after I'd talked to him awhile. I told him jest what I thought of the whole business from beginnin' to end."

After that the hair wreath was hung up in state in the front room, and openly displayed. Everybody upheld Charlotte in taking it, and she felt herself quite a heroine. Nothing delighted her more than to have people speak about it and admire it.

One day she was descanting on its beauties to one of the neighbors, when a question arose which attracted Emmeline's attention.

"Whose hair is that reddish rose-bud made out of?" asked the woman.

Mrs. Steadman gave a warning " Hush !" and a scared glance at her daughter. Emmeline saw it. After the woman had gone she went up to the wreath, and looked at it closely. "Mother," said she, "whose hair is in that rose-bud ?"

Mrs. Steadman shrank before her daughter's look.

" Mother, you *didn't* go to my drawer and take that out ! I missed it ! How did you know I had it ?"

" Now, Emmeline, thar ain't no reason for you to get so mad. I went to your drawer one day for something, an' happened to see it. An' poor Nancy wanted some hair that color dreadfully, an' she didn't really want to go out of the family, an' we all thought—"

" Mother, did *he* know it?"

" Now, Emmeline, it's ridiculous for you to fire up so. I s'pose he did. You remember that last Friday night when Paulina was here last summer, an' we all went to meetin'? He came that night, and we warn't to home, and Nancy was settin' on her door-step when he drove by, an' she had to call him in an' show him the wreath. An' I s'pose she let on 'bout his hair bein' in it. I told her she was awful silly; but she said he kinder cornered her up, an' she couldn't help it. I scolded her for it. She said he seemed kinder upset."

" Mother, that was the reason."

" Reason for what?"

" The reason he stopped coming, and—everything."

" Emmeline Steadman, I don't believe it. 'Tain't likely a fellar'd get so mad as that jest 'cause somebody'd made a rose-bud out of his hair to put in a wreath; 'taint reasonable. I should think he'd been rather pleased than anything else."

" Oh, mother, don't you see? He — gave it to me, and he thought that was all I cared for it, to give it to Aunt Nancy to put in a hair wreath. And he is awful sensitive and quick-tempered."

" I should think he was, to get mad at such a thing as that; I can't believe he did!"

" I *know* he did!"

" Well, there ain't any call for you to feel huffy about it.

I'm sorry I did it: I'm sure I wouldn't if I'd dreamed it was goin' to make any trouble. I didn't have any idea he was such a fire-an'-tow kind of a fellar as that. I guess it's jest as well we didn't have him in the family; thar wouldn't have been no livin' with him."

That night Emmeline wrote a letter to Andrew Stoddard. She sat up for the purpose, pretending she had some work to finish, after her mother had gone to bed. She wrote the sort of letter that most New England girls in her standing would have written. She began it "Dear Friend," touched very lightly on the subject of the hair, just enough to explain it, then decorously hoped that if any misunderstanding had interrupted their friendship it might be done away with ; she should always value his very highly. Then she signed herself his true friend "Emmeline E. Steadman."

Nobody knew what tortures of suspense Emmeline suffered after she had sent her poor little friendly letter. She sewed on quietly just as usual. Her mother knew nothing about it.

She began to go regularly to the post-office, though not at mail times. She would make an errand to the store where it was, and, after she was through trading, inquire quietly and casually if there were a letter for her.

One morning she came home from one of those errands, dropped down in a chair, and covered her face with her hands. Her mother was frightened: she was mixing bread: they were both out in the kitchen.

"Emmeline, what *is* the matter?"

Emmeline burst into a bitter cry: "He's married. Mrs. Wilson told me just now. Mrs. Adams told her: she lives next to his folks."

24

"Why, Emmeline, I didn't know you cared so much about that fellar as all that!"

"I didn't!" said Emmeline, fiercely; "but I—wrote to him, an' what's he goin' to think? I'd died first, if I'd known. Oh, if you'd only let that lock of hair alone! You brought all this trouble on me!"

"Well, Emmeline Steadman, if you want to talk so to the mother that's done for you what I have, on account of a fellar that's showed pretty plain he didn't care any great about you, you can."

Emmeline said no more, but, with a look of despair, rose to go up-stairs.

"I've told you I am sorry I took it."

"I think you'd better be," said Emmeline, as she went through the door.

She did no more work that day; she stayed up-stairs, and would see nobody: she did not care now what people thought. Mrs. Steadman grew more and more conscience-stricken and worried; she went for the night mail herself, with a forlorn hope of something, she did not know what.

When she got back she came directly up-stairs into the room where Emmeline was. "Emmeline," said she, in a shaking voice, "here's a letter for you; I guess it's from *him.*"

Emmeline took it and opened it, her face set and un-moved; she had it all settled that the letter was to tell her of his marriage. She read down the first page, her face changing with every word. Her mother watched her breath-lessly, as if she too were reading the letter by reflection in her daughter's face.

At last Emmeline looked up at her mother. She was radiant; she was trying to keep from smiling, lest she be-

tray too much; but she could not help it. She looked
blissful and shamefaced together.

"Mother—he ain't married after all ; and he says it's all
right about the hair ; and—he's coming home !"

Charlotte's face was as radiant as her daughter's, but
she said, " Well, what do you think now? After you've
been such an ungrateful girl, blaming your mother, an' talkin'
to her as you did this mornin', I should think you'd be
ashamed. You don't deserve it !"

Emmeline got off the bed ; with her letter in her hand
she went over to her mother, and kissed her shyly on her
soft, old cheek. " I'm real sorry I spoke so, mother."

AN OLD ARITHMETICIAN.

A STRONG, soft south wind had been blowing the day before, and the trees had dropped nearly all their leaves. There were left only a few brownish-golden ones dangling on the elms, and hardly any at all on the maples. There were many trees on the street, and the fallen leaves were heaped high. Mrs. Wilson Torry's little door-yard was ankle-deep with them. The air was full of their odor, which could affect the spirit like a song, and mingled with it was the scent of grapes.

The minister had been calling on Mrs. Torry that afternoon, and now he stood facing her on the porch, taking leave. He was very young, and this was his first parish. He was small and light and mild-looking ; still he had considerable nervous volubility. The simple village women never found him hard to entertain.

Now, all at once, he made an exclamation, and fumbled in his pocket for a folded paper. "There," said he, "I nearly forgot this. Mr. Plainfield requested me to hand this to you, Mrs. Torry. It is a problem which he has been working over ; he gave it to me to try, and wanted me to propose, when I called, that you should see what you could do with it."

She seized it eagerly. "Well, I'll see what I can do ;

but you an' he mustn't make no great calculations on me. You know I don't know anything about the 'rithmetic books an' the rules they hev nowadays ; but I'm willin' to try."

"Oh, you'll have it done while Mr. Plainfield and I are thinking of it, Mrs. Torry."

"You ain't neither of you done it, then ?"

"He had not at last accounts, and—I have not," replied the young man, laughing, but coloring a little.

The old lady's eyes gleamed as she looked at him, then at the paper. "I dare say I can't make head nor tail of it," said she, "but I'll see what I can do by an' by."

She had something of a childish air as she stood there. She was slender, and so short that she was almost dwarfed ; her shoulders were curved a little by spinal disease. She had a small, round face, and a mouth which widened out innocently into smiles as she talked. Her eyes looked out directly at one, like a child's ; over them loomed a high forehead with bulging temples covered with deep wrinkles.

"You have always been very fond of mathematics, haven't you, Mrs. Torry ?" said the minister, in his slow retreat.

"Lor', yes. I can't remember the time when I wa'n't crazy to cipher."

"Arithmetic is a very fascinating study, I think," remarked the minister, trying to slide easily off the subject and down the porch steps.

"'Tis to me. An' there's somethin' I was thinkin' about this very forenoon—seein' all them leaves on the ground made me, I s'pose. It's always been a sight of comfort to me to count. When I was a little girl I'd most rather count than play. I used to sit down and count by the hour together. I remember a little pewter porringer I had, that I used to fill up with beans an' count 'em. Well, it come into my head this forenoon what a blessed privilege it would be to count up all the beautiful things in this creation. Just think of countin' all them red an' gold-colored leaves, an' all the grapes an' apples in the fall; an' when it come to the winter, all the flakes of snow, an' the sparkles of frost; an' when it come to the spring, all the flowers, an' blades of grass, an' the little, new, light-green leaves. I don' know but you'll think it ain't exactly reverent, but it does seem to me that I'd rather do that than sing in the other world. Mebbe somebody does have to do the countin'; mebbe it's singin' for some."

She stared up into the warm, blue air, in which the bare branches of the trees glistened, with a sweet, solemn wonder in her old face.

The minister, in a bewildered way, pondered all the old woman had said, as he rustled down the street. Later, Mr. Plainfield (the young high-school teacher) and he would have a discussion over it. They often talked over Mrs. Wilson Torry.

After her caller had gone, the old woman entered the house. On the left of the little entry was the best room, where she had been entertaining the minister; on the right, the kitchen. A young girl was in there eating an apple. She looked up when Mrs. Torry stood in the door.

"He's gone, ain't he?" said she.

"Why, Letty, when did you come?"

"A few minutes ago. School's just out. I came in the back door, and heard him talking, so I kept still."

"Why didn't you come in and see him?"

"Oh, I didn't want to see him. What you got there, grandma?"

"Nothin' but a sum the minister brought me to do. He an' Mr. Plainfield have been workin' over it."

"Couldn't they do it?"

"Well, he said they hadn't neither of 'em done it yet."

"Is it awful hard?"

"I don' know. I ain't looked at it yet."

"Let me see. He didn't get it out of any of our books, I know. We never had anything like this."

"I s'pose it's one he come across somewhere. I guess I'll sit down an' look at it two or three minutes."

An old bureau stood against the wall; on it were arranged four religious newspapers in the exact order of their issues, the latest on top, Farmers' almanacs for the last four years filed in the same way, and a slate surmounted by an old arithmetic. The pile of newspapers was in the middle; the slate and almanacs were on either end.

Letty, soberly eating her apple, watched her grandmother getting out the arithmetic and slate. She was a pretty young girl; her small, innocent face, in spite of its youthful roundness and fairness, reminded people of Mrs. Torry's.

"I don't think much of Mr. Plainfield anyhow," said she, as the click of her grandmother's pencil on the slate began; "and he knows I don't. He overheard me telling Lizzie Bascom so to-day. He came right up behind us on the street, and I know he heard. You ought to have seen his face."

"I don't see what you've got agin him," remarked Mrs. Torry, absently, as she dotted down figures.

"I haven't much of anything that I know of against him, only I don't think he's much of a teacher. He can't do examples as quickly as you, I know, and I don't think a man has any business to be school-teaching if he can't do examples as quickly as an old lady."

Mrs. Torry stopped her work, and fixed her round, unwinking eyes full on the girl's face.

"Letty Torry, there's some things you don't understand. You never will understand 'em, if you live to be as old as Methuselah, as far as that's concerned. But you'll get so you know the things *air*. Sometimes it don't make any difference if anybody's ignorant, an' ain't got any book-learnin'; air old, an' had a hard-workin' life. There'll be somethin' in 'em that everybody else ain't got; somethin' that growed, an' didn't have to be learned. I've got this faculty; I can cipher. It ain't nothin' agin Mr. Plainfield if he ain't got it; it's a *gift.*" Her voice took on a solemn tone and trembled. Letty looked at her with childish wonder. "Well," said she, with a subdued manner, "he has no right to teach, anyhow, without it. I guess I'll have another apple. I was real hungry."

So Letty ate another apple silently, while her grandmother worked at the problem again.

She did not solve it as easily as usual. She worked till midnight, her little lamp drawn close to her on the kitchen table; then she went to bed, with the answer still in doubt.

"It ain't goin' to do for me to set up any longer," said she, forlornly, as she replaced the slate on the bureau. "I shall be sick if I do. But I declare I don't see what's got into me. I hope I ain't losin' my faculty."

She could not sleep much. The next morning, as soon as their simple breakfast was eaten and Letty had gone to school, she seated herself with her slate and pencil.

When Letty came home at noon she found her grandmother still at work, and no dinner ready.

"I do declare!" cried the old woman. "You don't mean to say you're home, Letty! It *ain't* twelve o'clock, is it?"

"Course it is; quarter past."

"I ain't got one mite of dinner ready, then. I've been so took up with the sum I hadn't no idea how the time was goin'. I don' know what you will do, child."

"Oh, I'll get some bread and milk, grandma; just as soon have it as anything else. Got the problem done?"

"No, I ain't. I feel real bad about your dinner. I'll kindle up a fire now an' fry you an egg—there be time enough."

"I'd rather have bread and milk."

After Letty had gone to school for the afternoon, and Mrs. Torry had been working fruitlessly for an hour longer, she dropped her pencil.

"I declare," said she, "I'm afraid I am losin' my faculty!"

Tears stood in her eyes. "I won't give up that I am, anyhow," said she, and took the pencil again.

When Letty returned, in the latter part of the afternoon, she scarcely knew it, with the full meaning of the word. She saw her, but her true consciousness was so full of figures that Letty's fair face could only look in at the door.

Letty ran in hastily; a young girl was waiting for her outside. "Oh, grandma," cried Letty, "Lizzie's going to Ellsworth to do an errand for her mother; she's coming back on the last train. Can't I go with her?"

Her grandmother stared at her for a minute and made no answer.

"She's got tickets for both of us. Can't I go, grandma?"

"Yes."

Letty smoothed her hair a little and put on her best hat ; then she went.

"Good-by," said she, looking back at the intent old figure ; but she got no answer.

"Grandma's so taken up with an example she's got that she doesn't know anything," she told her friend when she was outside. "She didn't answer when I said good-by ; she forgot to get dinner to-day too."

Mrs. Torry worked on and on. She never looked up nor thought of anything else until it grew so dark that she could not see her figures. "I'll have to light the lamp," said she, with a sigh.

After it was lighted she went to work again. She never thought of wanting any supper, though she had eaten nothing since morning.

The kitchen clock struck seven—Letty should have been home then—eight, and nine, but she never noticed it. A few minutes afterwards some one knocked on the door. She ciphered on. Then the knocks were repeated, louder and quicker.

"Somebody's knockin', I guess," she muttered, and opened the door. Mr. Plainfield stood there. He was a handsome young man with rosy cheeks ; he was always smiling. He looked past her into the room inquiringly. "Is Letty at home?" said he.

"Letty?"

"Yes, Letty. Is she at home?"

"Why, yes, she's here. Letty!"

"Has she gone to bed?"

"Why, yes, I guess she has." Mrs. Torry opened the door at the foot of the stairs. "Letty! Letty!"

"I guess she must be asleep," said she, turning to the

young man, who had stepped into the kitchen. " Want me to go up an' see? Did you want anything pertickler?"

He hesitated. " If you had—just as soon—I—had something special—"

The old lady climbed the steep, uncarpeted stairs, feebly, with a long pat on every step. She came down faster, reckless of her trembling uncertainty. " She ain't there! Letty's gone! Where is she?"

" You knew she went to Ellsworth with Lizzie ?"

" No, I didn't.

" Why, she said something to you about it, didn't she ?"

" I don' know whether she did or not."

" Lizzie just told me that she missed her in the depot. She left her there for a minute while she went back for something she had forgotten. When she came back she was gone. The train was all ready, and Lizzie thought she must be on it, so she got on herself. She did not see her in the depot here, and has been crying about it, and afraid to tell till just now. I came right over as soon as I knew about it."

" Oh, Letty! Letty! Where's Letty? Oh, Mr. Plainfield, you go an' find her! Go right off! You will, won't you? Letty allers liked you."

" I always liked Letty," said the young man, brokenly. " I'll find her—don't you worry."

" You'll go right off now ?"

" Of course I will ; I won't wait a minute."

" Oh, Letty, Letty! Where is she? What shall I do? That little bit of a thing—and she was always one of the frightened kind—out all alone ; an' it's night! She never went to Ellsworth alone in her hull life. She didn't know nothin' about the town, an' she didn't have a cent of money in her pocket."

"I'll send Mrs. Bascom over to stay with you," Mr. Plainfield called back as he hurried off.

Soon Mrs. Bascom came, poking her white, nervous face in the door inquiringly. "She ain't come?"

"No. Oh, Mis' Bascom, what shall I do?"

"Oh, Mis' Torry, I do feel so bad about it I don't know what to do. If Lizzie had only told before! but there she was up-stairs crying, and afraid to tell. I've been scolding her, but she felt so bad I had to stop. She called me, an' told me finally; an' I guess twa'n't long before Mr. Plainfield started off to find out if she *was* home. It was lucky he was boarding with us. He'll find her if anybody can; he's as quick as lightning. He turned white's a sheet when I told him."

"Oh, Mis' Bascom!"

"Now, don't give up so, Mis' Torry. He'll find her. She can't be very far off. You'll see her walking in here first thing you know. He's got a real fast team, an' he's started for Ellsworth now. He went past me like a streak when I was coming up the road. He'll have her back safe and sound before morning."

"Oh, Letty! Letty! Oh, what shall I do? It's my own fault, every mite of it's my own fault. 'Tis; you don't know nothin' about it. The minister brought me a sum, he an' Mr. Plainfield had been workin' on, to do, yesterday afternoon, an' I jest sat and ciphered half the night, an' all day. I didn't know no more what Letty asked me, when she came in from school, than nothin' at all. I didn't more'n half know when she come. I didn't know nothin' but them figgers, an' now Letty's lost, an' it's my fault."

"Why, you might have let her gone if you'd known."

"I guess I shouldn't let her gone all alone with your Lizzie, to come home after dark in the last train, little delicate thing as she was. I guess I shouldn't; an' I guess I should have started up an' done something, if I'd known, when she wasn't here at train time. I didn't get the sum done, an' I'm glad of it; it seems to me jest as if I was losin' my faculty as I'm growin' older, an' I hope I am."

"Now, don't talk so, Mis' Torry. Sit down an' try to be calm. You'll be sick."

"I guess there ain't much bein' calm. I tell you what 'tis, Mis' Bascom, I've been a wicked woman. I've been thinkin' so much of this faculty I've had for cipherin' that I've set it afore everything—I hev. Only yesterday that poor child didn't hev any dinner but crackers an' milk, 'cause I was so took up with the sum that I forgot it. An' she was jest as patient as a lamb about it; said she'd rather hev crackers an' milk than anything else. Oh, dear! dear!"

"Don't cry, Mis' Torry."

"I can't help it. It don't make no difference what folks are born with a faculty for—whether it's cipherin', or singin', or writin' poetry—the love that's betwixt human beings an' the help that's betwixt 'em ought to come first. I've known it all the time, but I've gone agin it, an' now I've got my pay. What shall I do?"

Mrs. Bascom remained with her all night, but she could not pacify her in the least. She was nearly distracted herself. She was fearful that her Lizzie might be blamed.

The next day people flocked to the house to inquire if there were any news from Letty, and to comfort her grandmother. Sympathy seemed fairly dripping like fragrant oil from these simple, honest hearts; but the poor old woman got no refreshing influence from it. She kept on her old strain in their ears. She had lost Letty, and it was all her own fault, and what should she do? Mr. Plainfield did not come home. The minister took his place in school. Nothing was heard until noon; then a telegram from the teacher came. He thought he was on Letty's track, he said; they should hear again.

Next day there was a second message: Letty was safe; coming home as soon as possible. The following day passed then, and not another word came. The old grandmother's faith and hope seemed to have deserted her. She knew Letty was not found; she never would be found. She and Mr. Plainfield were both lost now. Something dreadful had happened to both of them.

"The worst of it is," she told Mrs. Bascom one afternoon, with a fierce indignation at herself, "I can't help thinkin' about that awful sum now after all that's happened. Them figgers keep troopin' into my head right in the midst of my thinkin' about Letty. It's all I can do to let that slate alone, an' not take it off the bureau. But I won't—I won't if it kills me not to. An' all the time I jest despise myself for it: a-lettin' my faculty for cipherin' get ahead of things that's higher an' sacreder. I do think I've lost my faculty now, an' I 'most hope I hev. But it won't make no difference 'bout Letty now. Oh dear! dear! What shall I do?"

On the fourth day after Letty's disappearance, between six and seven o'clock in the evening, Mrs. Torry was sitting alone in her kitchen. The last sympathizer had gone home to eat her supper.

The distressed old woman had drunk a cup of tea; that was all she would touch. The pot was still on the stove.

There was a soft yellow light from the lamp over the room. The warm air was full of the fragrance of boiling tea.

Mrs. Torry sat looking over at the bureau. She would have looked the same way if she had been starving and seen food there.

"Oh," she whispered, "if—I could—only work on that sum a little while, it does seem as if 'twould comfort me more'n anything. O Lord! I wonder if I was to blame? 'Twas the way I was made, an' I couldn't help that. P'rhaps I should hev let Letty gone, an' she'd been lost, anyway. I wonder if I hev lost my faculty?"

She sat there looking over at the slate. At last she rose and started to cross the room. Midway she stopped.

"Oh, what am I doin'? Letty's lost, an' I'm goin' to ci-pherin'! S'pose she should come in an' ketch me? She'd be so hurt she'd never get over it. She wouldn't think I cared anything about her."

She stood looking at the slate and thinking for a mo-ment. Then her face settled into a hard calm.

"Letty won't come back—she won't never come back. I might as well cipher as anything else."

She went across the room, got the slate and pencil, and returned to her seat. She had been ciphering for a minute or so when a sound outside caused her to start and stop. She sat with mouth open and chin trembling, listening. The sound came nearer; it was at the door. Of all the sweet sounds which had smote that old woman's ears since her birth—songs of birds, choral hymns, Sabbath bells— there had been none so sweet as this. It was Letty's thin, girlish treble just outside the door which she heard.

For a second, as she sat listening, her face was rapt, an-gelic; in spite of its sallowness and wrinkles it might have

figured in an altar-piece. Then it changed. The slate was
in her lap. What would Letty think?

It was all passing swiftly; the door-latch rattled; she
slipped the slate under her gingham apron, and sat still.

"Oh, poor grandma!" cried Letty, running in; "you've
been frightened 'most to death about me, haven't you?"
She bent over her grandmother and laid her soft, pretty
cheek against hers.

"Oh, Letty! I didn't think you'd ever come back."

"I have; but I did have the dreadfulest time. I got
carried 'way out West on an express train. Just think of
it! I got on the wrong train while I was·waiting for Lizzie. I was frightened almost to death. But Mr. Plainfield
telegraphed ahead. He found out where I was going, and
they took me to a hotel; and then he came for me. You
haven't said anything to Mr. Plainfield, grandma."

The young man was standing smiling behind Letty. She
looked astonished when her grandmother did not rise to
speak to him, but sat perfectly still as she uttered some
broken thanks.

"Why, grandma, you ain't sick, are you?" said she.

"No—I ain't sick," said her grandmother, with a meek
tone.

When Mr. Plainfield left, in a few moments, Letty gave a
half-defiant, half-ashamed glance at her grandmother, and
followed him out, closing the door.

When she returned Mrs. Torry was standing by the table
pouring out a cup of tea for her. The slate was in its usual
place on the bureau.

"Grandma," said Letty, blushing innocently, "I thought
I ought to say something to Mr. Plainfield, you know. I
hadn't, and I knew he heard what I said to Lizzie that day.

I thought I ought to ask his pardon, when he had done so much for me. I've made up my mind that I do like him. There's other things besides doing arithmetic examples."

"I guess there is, child. Them things is all second. I think I'd rather have a man who hadn't got any special faculty, if I was goin' to git married."

"Nobody said anything about getting married, grandma."

Pretty soon Letty went to bed. She was worn out with her adventures.

"Ain't you going too, grandma?" asked she, turning around, lamp in hand, at the foot of the stairs.

"Pretty soon, child; pretty soon. I've—got a little some-thin' I want to do first."

The grandmother sat up till nearly morning working over the problem. Once in a while she would lay down her slate and climb up-stairs and peep into Letty's little, peaceful girl-chamber to see if she were safe.

"If I have got that dear child safe, an' ain't lost my fac-ulty, it's more'n I deserve," muttered she, as she took her slate the last time.

The next evening the minister came over. "So, Letty's come," he said, when Mrs. Torry opened the door.

"Yes, Letty's come, and—I've got that sum you gave me done."

25

A CONFLICT ENDED.

In Acton there were two churches, a Congregational and a Baptist. They stood on opposite sides of the road, and the Baptist edifice was a little farther down than the other. On Sunday morning both bells were ringing. The Baptist bell was much larger, and followed quickly on the soft peal of the Congregational with a heavy brazen clang which vibrated a good while. The people went flocking through the street to the irregular jangle of the bells. It was a very hot day, and the sun beat down heavily; parasols were bobbing over all the ladies' heads.

More people went into the Baptist church, whose society was much the larger of the two. It had been for the last ten years—ever since the Congregational had settled a new minister. His advent had divided the church, and a good third of the congregation had gone over to the Baptist brethren, with whom they still remained.

It is probable that many of them passed their old sanctuary to-day with the original stubborn animosity as active as ever in their hearts, and led their families up the Baptist steps with the same strong spiritual pull of indignation.

One old lady, who had made herself prominent on the opposition, trotted by this morning with the identical wiry vehemence which she had manifested ten years ago. She wore a full black silk skirt, which she held up inanely in front, and allowed to trail in the dust in the rear.

Some of the stanch Congregational people glanced at her amusedly. One fleshy, fair-faced girl in blue muslin said to her companion, with a laugh: "See that old lady trailing her best black silk by to the Baptist. Ain't it ridiculous how she keeps on showing out? I heard some one talking about it yesterday."

"Yes."

The girl colored up confusedly. "Oh dear!" she thought to herself. The lady with her had an unpleasant history connected with this old church quarrel. She was a small, bony woman in a shiny purple silk, which was strained very tightly across her sharp shoulder-blades. Her bonnet was quite elaborate with flowers and plumes, as was also her companion's. In fact, she was the village milliner, and the girl was her apprentice.

When the two went up the church steps, they passed a man of about fifty, who was sitting thereon well to one side. He had a singular face—a mild forehead, a gently curving mouth, and a terrible chin, with a look of strength in it that might have abashed moûntains. He held his straw hat in his hand, and the sun was shining full on his bald head.

The milliner half stopped, and gave an anxious glance at him; then passed on. In the vestibule she stopped again.

"You go right in, Margy," she said to the girl. "I'll be along in a minute."

"Where be you going, Miss Barney?"

"You go right in. I'll be there in a minute."

Margy entered the audience-room then, as if fairly brushed in by the imperious wave of a little knotty hand, and Esther Barney stood waiting until the rush of entering people was over. Then she stepped swiftly back to the side of the man seated on the steps. She spread her large black parasol deliberately, and extended the handle towards him.

" No, no, Esther ; I don't want it—I don't want it."

" If you're determined on setting out in this broiling sun, Marcus Woodman, you jest take this parasol of mine an' use it."

" I don't want your parasol, Esther. I—"

" Don't you say it over again. Take it."

" I won't—not if I don't want to."

" You'll get a sun-stroke."

" That's my own lookout."

" Marcus Woodman, you take it."

She threw all the force there was in her intense, nervous nature into her tone and look ; but she failed in her attempt, because of the utter difference in quality between her own will and that with which she had to deal. They were on such different planes that hers slid by his with its own momentum ; there could be no contact even of antagonism between them. He sat there rigid, every line of his face stiffened into an icy obstinacy. She held out the parasol towards him like a weapon.

Finally she let it drop at her side, her whole expression changed.

" Marcus," said she, " how's your mother ?"

He started. " Pretty well, thank you, Esther."

" She's out to meeting, then ?"

" Yes."

" I've been a-thinking—I ain't drove jest now—that maybe I'd come over an' see her some day this week."

He rose politely then. " Wish you would, Esther. Mother'd be real pleased, I know."

"Well, I'll see—Wednesday, p'rhaps, if I ain't too busy. I must go in now; they're 'most through singing."

"Esther—"

"I don't believe I can stop any longer, Marcus."

"About the parasol—thank you jest the same if I don't take it. Of course you know I can't set out here holding a parasol; folks would laugh. But I'm obliged to you all the same. Hope I didn't say anything to hurt your feelings?"

"Oh no; why, no, Marcus. Of course I don't want to make you take it if you don't want it. I don't know but it would look kinder queer, come to think of it. Oh dear! they are through singing."

"Say, Esther, I don't know but I might as well take that parasol, if you'd jest as soon. The sun is pretty hot, an' I might get a headache. I forgot my umbrella, to tell the truth."

"I might have known better than to have gone at him the way I did," thought Esther to herself, when she was seated at last in the cool church beside Margy. "Seems as if I might have got used to Marcus Woodman by this time."

She did not see him when she came out of church; but a little boy in the vestibule handed her the parasol, with the remark, "Mr. Woodman said for me to give this to you."

She and Margy passed down the street towards home. Going by the Baptist church, they noticed a young man standing by the entrance. He stared hard at Margy.

She began to laugh after they had passed him. "Did you see that fellow stare?" said she. "Hope he'll know me next time."

"That's George Elliot ; he's that old lady's son you was speaking about this morning."

"Well, that's enough for me."

"He's a real good, steady young man."

Margy sniffed.

"P'rhaps you'll change your mind some day."

She did, and speedily, too. That glimpse of Margy Wilson's pretty, new face—for she was a stranger in the town—had been too much for George Elliot. He obtained an introduction, and soon was a steady visitor at Esther Barney's house. Margy fell in love with him easily. She had never had much attention from the young men, and he was an engaging young fellow, small and bright-eyed, though with a nervous persistency like his mother's in his manner.

"I'm going to have it an understood thing," Margy told Esther, after her lover had become constant in his attentions, "that I'm going with George, and I ain't going with his mother. I can't bear that old woman."

But poor Margy found that it was not so easy to thrust determined old age off the stage, even when young Love was flying about so fast on his butterfly wings that he seemed to multiply himself, and there was no room for anything else, because the air was so full of Loves. That old mother, with her trailing black skirt and her wiry obstinacy, trotted as unwaveringly through the sweet stir as a ghost through a door.

One Monday morning Margy could not eat any breakfast, and there were tear stains around her blue eyes.

"Why, what's the matter, Margy ?" asked Esther, eying her across the little kitchen-table.

"Nothing's the matter. I ain't hungry any to speak of,

that's all. I guess I'll go right to work on Mis' Fuller's bonnet."

"I'd try an' eat something if I was you. Be sure you cut that velvet straight, if you go to work on it."

When the two were sitting together at their work in the little room back of the shop, Margy suddenly threw her scissors down. "There!" said she, "I've done it; I knew I should. I've cut this velvet bias. I knew I should cut everything bias I touched to-day."

There was a droll pucker on her mouth; then it began to quiver. She hid her face in her hands and sobbed. "Oh, dear, dear, dear!"

"Margy Wilson, what is the matter?"

"George and I—had a talk last night. We've broke the engagement, an' it's killing me. An' now I've cut this velvet bias. Oh, dear, dear, *dear*, dear!"

"For the land's sake, don't mind anything about the velvet. What's come betwixt you an' George?"

"His mother—horrid old thing! He said she'd got to live with us, and I said she shouldn't. Then he said he wouldn't marry any girl that wasn't willing to live with his mother, and I said he wouldn't ever marry me, then. If George Elliot thinks more of his mother than he does of me, he can have her. I don't care. I'll show him I can get along without him."

"Well, I don't know, Margy. I'm real sorry about it. George Elliot's a good, likely young man; but if you didn't want to live with his mother, it was better to say so right in the beginning. And I don't know as I blame you much: she's pretty set in her ways."

"I guess she is. I never could bear her. I guess he'll find out—"

Margy dried her eyes defiantly, and took up the velvet again. " I've spoilt this velvet. I don't see why being disappointed in love should affect a girl so's to make her cut bias."

There was a whimsical element in Margy which seemed to roll uppermost along with her grief.

Esther looked a little puzzled. " Never mind the velvet, child : it ain't much, anyway." She began tossing over some ribbons to cover her departure from her usual reticence. " I'm real sorry about it, Margy. Such things are hard to bear, but they can be lived through. I know something about it myself. You knew I'd had some of this kind of trouble, didn't you?"

" About Mr. Woodman, you mean ?"

" Yes, about Marcus Woodman. I'll tell you what 'tis, Margy Wilson, you've got one thing to be thankful for, and that is that there ain't anything ridickerlous about this affair of yourn. That makes it the hardest of anything, according to my mind—when you know that everybody's laughing, and you can hardly help laughing yourself, though you feel 'most ready to die."

" Ain't that Mr. Woodman crazy ?"

" No, he ain't crazy ; he's got too much will for his common-sense, that's all, and the will teeters the sense a little too far into the air. I see all through it from the beginning. I could read Marcus Woodman jest like a book."

" I don't see how in the world you ever come to like such a man."

"Well, I s'pose love's the strongest when there ain't any good reason for it. They say it is. I can't say as I ever really admired Marcus Woodman much. I always see right through him ; but that didn't hinder my thinking so much of him that I never felt as if I could marry any other man. And I've had chances, though I shouldn't want you to say so."

"You turned him off because he went to sitting on the church steps?"

"Course I did. Do you s'pose I was going to marry a man who made a laughing-stock of himself that way?"

"I don't see how he ever come to do it. It's the funniest thing I ever heard of."

"I know it. It seems so silly nobody 'd believe it. Well, all there is about it, Marcus Woodman's got so much mulishness in him it makes him almost miraculous. You see, he got up an' spoke in that church meeting when they had such a row about Mr. Morton's being settled here— Marcus was awful set again' him. I never could see any reason why, and I don't think he could. He said Mr. Morton wa'n't doctrinal; that was what they all said; but I don't believe half of 'em knew what doctrinal was. I never could see why Mr. Morton wa'n't as good as most ministers —enough sight better than them that treated him so, any-way. I always felt that they was really setting him in a pulpit high over their heads by using him the way they did, though they didn't know it.

"Well, Marcus spoke in that church meeting, an' he kept getting more and more set every word he said. He always had a way of saying things over and over, as if he was making steps out of 'em, an' raising of himself up on 'em, till there was no moving him at all. And he did that night. Finally, when he was up real high, he said, as for him, if Mr. Morton was settled over that church, he'd never go inside the door himself as long as he lived. Somebody spoke out then—I never quite knew who 'twas, though I suspected—an' says, 'You'll have to set on the steps, then, Brother Woodman.'

" Everybody laughed at that but Marcus. He didn't see nothing to laugh at. He spoke out awful set, kinder gritting his teeth, ' I will set on the steps fifty years before I'll go into this house if that man's settled here.'

" I couldn't believe he'd really do it. We were going to be married that spring, an' it did seem as if he might listen to me ; but he wouldn't. The Sunday Mr. Morton begun to preach, he begun to set on them steps, an' he's set there ever since, in all kinds of weather. It's a wonder it 'ain't killed him ; but I guess it's made him tough."

" Why, didn't he feel bad when you wouldn't marry him ?"

" Feel bad ? Of course he did. He took on terribly. But it didn't make any difference ; he wouldn't give in a hair's breadth. I declare it did seem as if I should die. His mother felt awfully too—she's a real good woman. I don't know what Marcus would have done without her. He wants a sight of tending and waiting on ; he's dreadful babyish in some ways, though you wouldn't think it.

" Well, it's all over now, as far as I'm concerned. I've got over it a good deal, though sometimes it makes me jest as mad as ever to see him setting there. But I try to be reconciled, and I get along jest as well, mebbe, as if I'd had him—I don't know. I fretted more at first than there was any sense in, and I hope you won't."

" I ain't going to fret at all, Miss Barney. I may cut bias for a while, but I sha'n't do anything worse."

" How you do talk, child !"

A good deal of it was talk with Margy ; she had not as much courage as her words proclaimed. She was capable of a strong temporary resolution, but of no enduring one. She gradually weakened as the days without her lover went on, and one Saturday night she succumbed entirely. There was quite a rush of business, but through it all she caught a conversation between some customers—two pretty young girls.

"Who was that with you last night at the concert ?"

"That—oh, that was George Elliot. Didn't you know him ?"

"He's got another girl," thought Margy, with a great throb.

The next Sunday night, coming out of meeting with Miss Barney, she left her suddenly. George Elliot was one of a waiting line of young men in the vestibule. She went straight up to him. He looked at her in bewilderment, his dark face turning red.

"Good-evening, Miss Wilson," he stammered out, finally.

"Good-evening," she whispered, and stood looking up at him piteously. She was white and trembling.

At last he stepped forward suddenly and offered her his arm. In spite of his resentment, he could not put her to open shame before all his mates, who were staring curiously.

When they were out in the dark, cool street, he bent over her. "Why, Margy, what does all this mean ?"

"Oh, George, let her live with us, please. I want her to. I know I can get along with her if I try. I'll do everything I can. Please let her live with us."

"Who's *her ?*"

"Your mother."

"And I suppose *us* is you and I ? I thought that was all over, Margy ; ain't it ?"

"Oh, George, I am sorry I treated you so."

"And you are willing to let mother live with us now ?"

"I'll do anything. Oh, George !"

" Don't cry, Margy. There—nobody's looking—give us a kiss. It's been a long time ; ain't it, dear? So you've made up your mind that you're willing to let mother live with us ?"

" Yes."

" Well, I don't believe she ever will, Margy. She's about made up her mind to go and live with my brother Edward, whether or no. So you won't be troubled with her. I dare say she might have been a little of a trial as she grew older."

" You didn't tell me."

" I thought it was your place to give in, dear."

" Yes, it was, George."

" I'm mighty glad you did. I tell you what it is, dear, I don't know how you've felt, but I've been pretty miserable lately."

" Poor George !"

They passed Esther Barney's house, and strolled along half a mile farther. When they returned, and Margy stole softly into the house and up-stairs, it was quite late, and Esther had gone to bed. Margy saw the light was not out in her room, so she peeped in. She could not wait till morning to tell her.

" Where have you been ?" said Esther, looking up at her out of her pillows.

" Oh, I went to walk a little way with George."

" Then you've made up ?"

" Yes."

" Is his mother going to live with you ?"

" No ; I guess not. She's going to live with Edward. But I told him I was willing she should. I've about made up my mind it's a woman's place to give in mostly. I s'pose you think I'm an awful fool."

"No, I don't; no, I don't, Margy. I'm real glad it's all right betwixt you and George. I've seen you weren't very happy lately."

They talked a little longer; then Margy said "Good-night," going over to Esther and kissing her. Being so rich in love made her generous with it. She looked down sweetly into the older woman's thin, red-cheeked face. "I wish you were as happy as I," said she. "I wish you and Mr. Woodman could make up too."

"That's an entirely different matter. I couldn't give in in such a thing as that."

Margy looked at her; she was not subtle, but she had just come out triumphant through innocent love and sub-mission, and used the wisdom she had gained thereby.

"Don't you believe," said she, "if you was to give in the way I did, that he would?"

Esther started up with an astonished air. That had nev-er occurred to her before. "Oh, I don't believe he would. You don't know him; he's awful set. Besides, I don't know but I'm better off the way it is."

In spite of herself, however, she could not help thinking of Margy's suggestion. Would he give in? She was hard-ly disposed to run the risk. With her peculiar cast of mind, her feeling for the ludicrous so keen that it almost amount-ed to a special sense, and her sensitiveness to ridicule, it would have been easier for her to have married a man un-der the shadow of a crime than one who was the deserving target of gibes and jests. Besides, she told herself, it was possible that he had changed his mind, that he no longer cared for her. How could she make the first overtures? She had not Margy's impulsiveness and innocence of youth to excuse her.

Also, she was partly influenced by the reason which she had given Margy: she was not so very sure that it would be best for her to take any such step. She was more fixed in the peace and pride of her old maidenhood than she had realized, and was more shy of disturbing it. Her comfortable meals, her tidy housekeeping, and her prosperous work had become such sources of satisfaction to her that she was almost wedded to them, and jealous of any interference.

So it is doubtful if there would have been any change in the state of affairs if Marcus Woodman's mother had not died towards spring. Esther was greatly distressed about it.

"I don't see what Marcus is going to do," she told Margy. "He ain't any fitter to take care of himself than a baby, and he won't have any housekeeper, they say."

One evening, after Marcus's mother had been dead about three weeks, Esther went over there. Margy had gone out to walk with George, so nobody knew. When she reached the house—a white cottage on a hill—she saw a light in the kitchen window.

"He's there," said she. She knocked on the door softly. Marcus shuffled over to it—he was in his stocking feet—and opened it.

"Good-evening, Marcus," said she, speaking first.

"Good-evening."

"I hadn't anything special to do this evening, so I thought I'd look in a minute and see how you was getting along."

"I ain't getting along very well; but I'm glad to see you. Come right in."

When she was seated opposite him by the kitchen fire, she surveyed him and his surroundings pityingly. Everything had an abject air of forlornness; there was neither

tidiness nor comfort. After a few words she rose energetically. "See here, Marcus," said she, "you jest fill up
that tea-kettle, and I'm going to slick up here a little for
you while I stay."

"Now, Esther, I don't feel as if—"

"Don't you say nothing. Here's the tea-kettle. I might
jest as well be doing that as setting still."

He watched her, in a way that made her nervous, as she
flew about putting things to rights; but she said to herself
that this was easier than sitting still, and gradually leading
up to the object for which she had come. She kept wondering if she could ever accomplish it. When the room was
in order, finally, she sat down again, with a strained-up look
in her face.

"Marcus," said she, "I might as well begin. There was
something I wanted to say to you to-night."

He looked at her, and she went on :

"I've been thinking some lately about how matters used
to be betwixt you an' me, and it's jest possible—I don't
know—but I might have been a little more patient than I
was. I don't know as I'd feel the same way now if—"

"Oh, Esther, what do you mean ?"

"I ain't going to tell you, Marcus Woodman, if you can't
find out. I've said full enough ; more'n I ever thought I
should."

He was an awkward man, but he rose and threw himself
on his knees at her feet with all the grace of complete
unconsciousness of action. "Oh, Esther, you don't mean,
do you ?—you don't mean that you'd be willing to—marry
me ?"

"No ; not if you don't get up. You look ridickerlous."

"Esther, do you mean it ?"

"Yes. Now get up."

"You ain't thinking—I can't give up what we had the trouble about, any more now than I could then."

"Ain't I said once that wouldn't make any difference?"

At that he put his head down on her knees and sobbed.

"Do, for mercy sake, stop. Somebody 'll be coming in. 'Tain't as if we was a young couple."

"I ain't going to till I've told you about it, Esther. You ain't never really understood. In the first of it, we was both mad; but we ain't now, and we can talk it over. Oh, Esther, I've had such an awful life! I've looked at you, and— Oh, dear, dear, dear !"

"Marcus, you scare me to death crying so."

"I won't. Esther, look here—it's the gospel truth : I ain't a thing again' Mr. Morton now."

"Then why on earth don't you go into the meeting-house and behave yourself?"

"Don't you suppose I would if I could? I can't, Esther —I can't."

"I don't know what you mean by can't."

"Do you s'pose I've took any comfort sitting there on them steps in the winter snows an' the summer suns? Do you s'pose I've took any comfort not marrying you? Don't you s'pose I'd given all I was worth any time the last ten year to have got up an' walked into the church with the rest of the folks?"

"Well, I'll own, Marcus, I don't see why you couldn't if you wanted to."

"I ain't sure as I see myself, Esther. All I know is I can't make myself give it up. I can't. I ain't made strong enough to."

"As near as I can make out, you've taken to sitting on

the church steps the way other men take to smoking and drinking."

"I don't know but you're right, Esther, though I hadn't thought of it in that way before."

"Well, you must try to overcome it."

"I never can, Esther. It ain't right for me to let you think I can."

"Well, we won't talk about it any more to-night. It's time I was going home."

"Esther—did you mean it?"

"Mean what?"

"That you'd marry me any way?"

"Yes, I did. Now do get up. I do hate to see you looking so silly."

Esther had a new pearl-colored silk gown, and a little mantle like it, and a bonnet trimmed with roses and plumes, and she and Marcus were married in June.

The Sunday on which she came out a bride they were late at church; but late as it was, curious people were lingering by the steps to watch them. What would they do? Would Marcus Woodman enter that church door which his awful will had guarded for him so long?

They walked slowly up the steps between the watching people. When they came to the place where he was accustomed to sit, Marcus stopped short and looked down at his wife with an agonized face.

"Oh, Esther, I've—got—to stop."

"Well, we'll both sit down here, then."

"*You?*"

"Yes; I'm willing."

"No; you go in."

"No, Marcus; I sit with you on our wedding Sunday."

26

Her sharp, middle-aged face as she looked up at him was fairly heroic. This was all that she could do : her last weapon was used. If this failed, she would accept the chances with which she had married, and before the eyes of all these tittering people she would sit down at his side on these church steps. She was determined, and she would not weaken.

He stood for a moment staring into her face. He trembled so that the bystanders noticed it. He actually leaned over towards his old seat as if wire ropes were pulling him down upon it. Then he stood up straight, like a man, and walked through the church door with his wife.

The people followed. Not one of them even smiled. They had felt the pathos in the comedy.

The sitters in the pews watched Marcus wonderingly as he went up the aisle with Esther. He looked strange to them ; he had almost the grand mien of a conqueror.

A PATIENT WAITER.

"Be sure you sweep it clean, Lily."

"Yes, 'm. I ain't leavin' a single stone on it."

"I'm 'most afraid to trust you. I think likely as not he may come to-day, an' not wait to write. It's so pleasant, I feel jest as if somebody was comin'."

"I'm a-sweepin' it real clean, Aunt Fidelia."

"Well, be pertickler. An' you'd better sweep the sidewalk a little ways in front of the yard. I saw a lot of loose stones on it yesterday."

"Yes, 'm."

The broom was taller than the child, but she was sturdy, and she wielded it with joyful vigor. Down the narrow path between the rows of dahlias she went. Her smooth yellow head shone in the sun. Her long blue gingham apron whisked about her legs as she swept.

The dahlias were in full bloom, and they nodded their golden and red balls gently when the child jostled them. Beyond the dahlias on either side were zinnias and candytuft and marigolds. The house was very small. There was only one window at the side of the front door. A curved green trellis stood against the little space of house wall on the other side, and a yellow honeysuckle climbed on it.

Fidelia Almy stood in the door with a cloth in her hand.

She had been dusting the outside of the door and the threshold, rubbing off every speck punctiliously.

Fidelia stood there in the morning light with her head nodding like a flower in a wind. It nodded so all the time. She had a disease of the nerves. Her yellow-gray hair was crimped, and put up carefully in a little coil, with two long curls on either side. Her long, delicate face, which always had a downward droop as it nodded, had a soft polish like ivory.

When Lily Almy, who was Fidelia's orphan niece, whom she was bringing up, had reached the gate with her broom, she peered down the road ; then she ran back eagerly.

"Oh, Aunt Fidelia," she said, in a precise, slow voice, which was copied from her aunt's, "there's a man comin'. Do you s'pose it's him ?"

"What kind of a lookin' man ?" Fidelia's head nodded faster ; a bright red spot gleamed out on either cheek.

"A real handsome man. He's tall, and he's got reddish whiskers. And he's got a carpet bag."

"That's the way he looks."

"Oh, Aunt Fidelia, do you s'pose it's him."

"'Tain't very likely to be."

"Here he is."

Fidelia ran into the house, and knelt down by the parlor window, just peering over the sill. Her whole body seemed wavering like her head ; her breath came in great gasps. The man, who was young and handsome, walked past.

Lily ran in. "'Twa'n't him, was it ?" said she.

"I didn't much expect it was. I've always thought he'd come on a Tuesday. I've dreamed 'bout his comin' Tuesday more times than I can tell. Now I'm goin' to fix the flowers in the vases, and then I'm goin' down to the post-office. I feel jest as if I might git a letter to-day. There was one in the candle last night."

Fidelia moved, nodding, among her flowers in her front yard. She gathered up her purple calico apron, and cut the flowers into it.

"You run out into the garden an' git some sparrow-grass for green," she told Lily, "an' pick some of that striped grass under the parlor window, an' some of them spider-lilies by the fence."

The little white-painted mantel-shelf in Fidelia's parlor was like an altar, upon which she daily heaped floral offerings. And who knows what fair deity in bright clouds she saw when she made her sacrifice?

Fidelia had only two vases, tall gilt and white china ones, with scrolling tops; these stood finely in the centre, holding their drooping nosegays. Beside these were broken china bowls, cream jugs without handles, tumblers, wine-glasses, saucers, and one smart china mug with "Friendship's Offering" in gold letters. Slightly withered flowers were in all of them. Fidelia threw them out, and filled all the vessels with fresh ones. The green asparagus sprays brushed the shelf, the striped grass overtopped the gay flowers.

"There," said Fidelia, "now I'm goin' to the post-office."

"If anybody comes, I'll ask him in here, an' tell him you'll be right back, sha'n't I?" said Lily.

"Tell him I'll be back in jest a few minutes, an' give him the big rockin'-chair."

The post-office was a mile away, in the corner of a country store. Twice a day, year out and year in, Fidelia journeyed thither.

"It's only Fidelia Almy," people said, looking out of the

windows, as the poor solitary figure with its nodding head went by through summer suns and winter winds.

Once in a while they hailed her. " See if there's any thing for me, won't you, Fidelia ?"

At last it was an understood thing that Fidelia should carry the mail to the dozen families between her house and the post-office. She often had her black worked bag filled up with letters, but there was never one of her own. Fidelia Almy never had a letter.

" That woman's been comin' here the last thirty years," the postmaster told a stranger one day, " an' she ain't never had a letter sence I've been here, an' I don't believe she ever did before."

Fidelia used to come in a little before the mail was distributed, and sit on an old settee near the door, waiting. Her face at those times had a wild, strained look ; but after the letters were all in the boxes it settled back into its old expression, and she travelled away with her bag of other people's letters, nodding patiently.

On her route was one young girl who had a lover in a neighboring town. Her letters came regularly. She used to watch for Fidelia, and run to meet her, her pretty face all blushes. Fidelia always had the letter separated from the others, and ready for her. She always smiled when she held it out. " They keep a-comin'," she said one day, " an' there don't seem to be no end to it. But if I was you, Louisa, I'd try an' git him to settle over here, if you ain't married before long. There's slips, an' it ain't always safe trustin' to letters."

The girl told her lover what Fidelia had said, with tender laughter and happy pity. " Poor thing," she said. " She had a beau, you know, Willy, and he went away thirty years ago, and ever since then she's been looking for a letter from him, and she's kind of cracked over it. And she's afraid it'll turn out the same way with me."

Then she and her sweetheart laughed together at the idea of this sad, foolish destiny for this pretty, courageous young thing.

To-day Fidelia, with her black broadcloth bag, worked on one side with a wreath and on the other with a bunch of flowers, walked slowly to the office and back. As the years went on she walked slower. This double journey of hers seemed to tire her more. Once in a while she would sit down and rest on the stone wall. The clumps of dusty way-side flowers, meadow-sweet and tansy, stood around her; over her head was the blue sky. But she clutched her black letter-bag, and nodded her drooping head, and never looked up. Her sky was elsewhere.

When she came in sight of her own house Lily, who was watching at the gate, came running to meet her.

"Oh, Aunt Fidelia," said she, "Aunt Sally's in there."

"Did she take off her shoes an' let you brush 'em before she went in ?"

"She wouldn't. She went right straight in. She jest laughed when I asked her to take her shoes off. An', Aunt Fidelia, she's done somethin' else. I couldn't help it."

"What ?"

"She's been eatin' some of Mr. Lennox's plum-cake up. I couldn't stop her, Aunt Fidelia. I told her she mus'n't."

"You didn't say nothin' 'bout Mr. Lennox, did you ?"

"No, I didn't, Aunt Fidelia. Oh, did you get a letter !"

"No ; I didn't much think I would to-day. Oh dear ! there's Sally eatin' cake right in the front entry."

A stout old woman, with a piece of cake in her hand,

stood in the front door as Fidelia and Lily came up between the dahlias.

"How d'ye do, Fidelia?" cried she, warmly.

"Pretty well, thank you. How do you do, Sally?" Fidelia answered. She shook hands, and looked at the other with a sort of meek uneasiness. "Hadn't you jest as soon step out here whilst you're eatin' that cake?" asked she, timidly. "I've jest swept the entry."

"No; I ain't goin' to step out there an inch," said the other, mumbling the cake vigorously between her old jaws. "If you ain't the worst old maid, Fidelia! Ain't seen all the sister you've got in the world for a year, an' wantin' her to go out-doors to eat a piece of cake. Hard work to git the cake, too."

"It don't make any difference," said Fidelia. "I'm real kind o' used up every time I sweep nowadays, that's all."

"Better stop sweepin', then; there ain't no need of so much fussin'. It's more'n half that's got your nerves out of kilter—sweepin' an' scrubbin' from mornin' till night, an' wantin' folks to take off their shoes before they come in, as if they was goin' into a heathen temple. Well, I ain't goin' to waste all my breath scoldin' when I've come over to see you. How air you now, Fidelia?"

"I'm 'bout the same as ever." Fidelia, following her sister into the parlor, stooped slyly to pick up some crumbs which had fallen on the entry floor.

"Just as shaky, ain't you? Why, Fidelia Almy, what in creation have you got this room rigged up so fur?"

"Rigged up how?"

"Why, everything covered up this way. What hev you got this old sheet over the carpet fur?"

"It was fadin' dreadfully."

"Fadin'! Good land! If you ain't got every chair sewed up in caliker, an' the pictures in old piller-cases, an'— Fidelia Almy, if you ain't got the solar lamp a-settin' in a little bag!"

" The gilt was gittin' real kind o' tarnished."

"Tarnished! An' every single thing on the table—the chiner card-basket an' Mrs. Hemans's Poems pinned up in a white rag! Good land! Well, I've always heard tell that there was two kinds of old maids—old maids an' consarned old maids—an' I guess you're one of the last sort. Why, what air you cuttin' on so fur?"

Fidelia gathered up all her trembling meekness and weakness into a show of dignity. "Things are all fadin' and wearin' out, an' I want to keep 'em decent as long as I last. I ain't got no money to buy any more. I ain't got no husband nor sons to do for me, like you, an' I've got to take care of things if I hev anything. An'—I'm goin to."

Her sister laughed. "Well, good land! I don't care. Cover up your things if you want to. There ain't no need of your gittin' riled. But this room does look enough to make a cat laugh. All them flowers on the mantel, an' all those white things. I declare, Fidelia Almy, it does look jest as if 'twas laid out. Well, we won't talk no more about it. I'm goin' out to hev a cup of tea. I put the teapot on, an' started the fire."

Poor Fidelia had a distressing day with her visiting sister. All her prim household arrangements were examined and commented on. Not a closet nor bureau drawer escaped inspection. When the guest departed, at length, the woman and the child looked at each other with relief.

" Ain't you glad she's gone?" asked Lily. She had been pink with indignation all day.

" Hush, child ; you mustn't. She's my sister, an' I'm always glad to see her, if she is a little tryin' sometimes."

" She wanted you to take the covers off an' let the things git spoiled before Mr. Lennox comes, didn't she ?"

" She don't know nothin' about that."

" Are you goin' to make another plum-cake to-night, Aunt Fidelia ?"

" I don' know. I guess we'd better sweep first."

The two worked hard and late that night. They swept every inch of floor which that profane dusty foot had trod. The child helped eagerly. She was Fidelia's confidante, and she repaid her confidence with the sweetest faith and sympathy. Nothing could exceed her innocent trust in Fidelia's pathetic story and pathetic hopes. This sad human experience was her fairy tale of childhood. That recreant lover, Ansel Lennox, who had left his sweetheart for California thirty years ago, and promised falsely to write and return, was her fairy prince. Her bright imagination pictured him beautiful as a god.

" He was about as handsome a young man as you ever see," said poor Fidelia. And a young Apollo towered up before Lily's credulous eyes. The lapse of thirty years affected the imagination of neither ; but Lily used to look at her aunt reflectively sometimes.

" I wish you could have some medicine to make you stop shakin' before that handsome Mr. Lennox comes," she said once.

" I'm in hopes that medicine I'm takin' will stop it," said Fidelia. " I think, mebbe, it's a little better now. I'm glad I thought to put that catnip in ; it makes it a good deal more quietin'."

On the narrow ledge of shelf behind Fidelia's kitchen

sink stood always a blue quart bottle of medicine. She prepared it herself from roots and herbs. She experimented and added new ingredients, and swallowed it with a touching faith that it would cure her. Beside this bottle stood another of sage tea ; that was for her hair. She used it plentifully every day in the hope that it would stop the gray hairs coming, and bring back the fine color. Fidelia used to have pretty golden hair.

Lily teased her to make the sage tea stronger. "You've been usin' it a dreadful long time, Aunt Fidelia," said she, "an' your hair's jest as gray as 'twas before."

"Takes quite a long time before you can see any difference," said Fidelia.

Many a summer morning, when the dew was heavy, she and Lily used to steal out early and bathe their faces in it. Fidelia said it would make people rosy and keep away the wrinkles.

"It works better on me than it does on you, don't it ?" asked pink-and-white Lily, innocently, once. The two were out in the shining white field together. The morning lit up Lily as it did the flowers. Her eyes had lovely blue sparkles in them ; her yellow hair, ruffled by the wind, glittered as radiantly between one and the light as the cobweb lines across the grasses. She looked wonderingly at her aunt, with her nodding gray head, plunging her little yellow hands into the dewy green things. Those dull tints and white hairs and wrinkles showed forth so plainly in the clear light that even the child's charming faith was disturbed a little. Would the dew ever make this old creature pretty again ?

But—"You can't expect it to work in a minute," replied Fidelia, cheerfully. And Lily was satisfied.

"I guess it'll work by the time Mr. Lennox comes," she said.

Fidelia was always neat and trim in her appearance, her hair was always carefully arranged, and her shoes tidy; but summer and winter she wore one sort of gown—a purple calico. She had a fine black silk hung away in the closet up-stairs. She had one or two good woollens, and some delicate cambrics. There was even one white muslin, with some lace in neck and sleeves, hanging there. But she never wore one of them. Her sister scolded her for it, and other people wondered. Fidelia's child-confidante alone knew the reason why. This poor, nodding, enchanted princess was saving her gay attire till the prince returned and the enchantment ceased, and she was beautiful again.

"You mustn't say nothin' about it," Fidelia had said; "but I ain't goin' to put on them good dresses an' tag 'em right out. Mebbe the time 'll come when I'll want 'em more."

"Mr. Lennox 'll think that black silk is beautiful," said Lily, "an' that white muslin."

"I had that jest after he went away, an' I ain't never put it on. I thought I wouldn't; muslin don't look half so nice after the new look gits off it."

So Lily waited all through her childhood. She watched her aunt start forth on her daily pilgrimages to the post-office, with the confident expectation that one of these days she would return with a letter from Mr. Lennox. She regarded that sacred loaf of plum-cake which was always kept on hand, and believed that he might appear to dispose of it at any moment. She had the sincerest faith that the time was coming when the herb medicine would quiet poor Fidelia's tremulous head, when the sage tea would turn all the gray hairs gold, and the dew would make her yellow, seamy cheeks smooth and rosy, when she would put on that magnificent black silk or that dainty girlish muslin, and sit in the parlor with Mr. Lennox, and have the covers off the chairs, and the mantel-piece blooming with flowers.

So the child and the woman lived happily with their beautiful chimera, until gradually he vanished into thin air for one of them.

Lily could not have told when the conviction first seized her that Mr. Lennox would never write, would never come; that Aunt Fidelia's gray hair would never turn gold, nor her faded cheeks be rosy; that her nodding head would nod until she was dead.

It was hardly until she was a woman herself, and had a lover of her own. It is possible that he gave the final overthrow to her faith, that it had not entirely vanished before. She told him all about Mr. Lennox. She scarcely looked upon it as a secret to be kept now. She had ascertained that many people were acquainted with Fidelia Almy's poor romance, except in its minor details.

So Lily told her lover. "Good Lord!" he said. "How long is it since he went?"

"Forty years now," said Lily. They were walking home from meeting one Sunday night.

"Forty years! Why, there ain't any more chance of hearing anything from him— Did he have any folks here?"

"No. He was a clerk in a store here. He fell in love with Aunt Fidelia, and went off to California to get some more money before he got married."

"Didn't anybody ever hear anything from him?"

"Aunt Fidelia always said not; but Aunt Sally told me

once that she knew well enough that he got married out there right after he went away ; she said she heard it pretty straight. She never had any patience with Aunt Fidelia. If she'd known half the things— Poor Aunt Fidelia ! She's getting worse lately. She goes to the post-office Sundays. I can't stop her. Every single Sunday, before meeting, down she goes."

"Why, she can't get in."

"I know it. She just tries the door, and comes back again."

"Why, dear, she's crazy, ain't she ?"

"No, she ain't crazy ; she's rational enough about every-thing else. All the way I can put it is, she's just been point-ed one way all her life, and going one way, and now she's getting nearer the end of the road, she's pointed sharper and she's going faster. She's had a hard time. I'm going to do all I can for her, anyhow. I'll help her get ready for Mr. Lennox as long as she lives."

Fidelia took great delight in Lily's love affair. All that seemed to trouble her was the suspicion that the young man might leave town, and the pair be brought to letter-writing.

"You mind, Lily," she would say ; "don't you let Valen-tine settle anywhere else before you're married. If you do, you'll have to come to writin' letters, an' letters ain't to be depended on. There's slips. You'd get sick of waitin' the way I have. I ain't minded it much ; but you're young, an' it would be different."

When Valentine Rowe did find employment in a town fifty miles away, poor Fidelia seemed to have taken upon herself a double burden of suspense.

In those days she was much too early for the mails, and waited, breathless, in the office for hours. When she got a letter for Lily she went home radiant; she seemed to forget her own disappointment.

Lily's letters came regularly for a long time. Valentine came to see her occasionally too. Then, one day, when Lily expected a letter, it did not come. Her aunt dragged herself home feebly.

"It ain't come, Lily," said she. "The trouble's begun. You poor child, how air you goin' to go through with it?"

Lily laughed. "Why, Aunt Fidelia!" said she, "what are you worrying for? I haven't missed a letter before. Something happened so Valentine couldn't write Sunday, that's all. It don't trouble me a mite."

However, even Lily was troubled at length. Weeks went by, and no letter came from Valentine Rowe. Fidelia tottered home despondent day after day. The girl had a brave heart, but she began to shudder, watching her. She felt as if she were looking into her own destiny.

"I'm going to write to Valentine," she said, suddenly, one day, after Fidelia had returned from her bootless journey.

Fidelia looked at her fiercely. "Lily Almy," said she, "whatever else you do, don't you do that. Don't you force yourself on any feller, when there's a chance you ain't wanted. Don't you do anything that ain't modest. You'd better live the way I've done."

"He may be sick," said Lily, pitifully.

"The folks he's with would write. Don't you write a word. I didn't write. An' mebbe you'll hear to-morrow. I guess we'd better sweep the parlor to-day."

This new anxiety seemed to wear on Fidelia more than her own had done. She now talked more about Valentine Rowe than Mr. Lennox. Her faith in Lily's case did not seem as active as in her own.

"I wouldn't go down to the post-office, seems to me," Lily said one morning—Fidelia tottered going out the door ; "you don't look fit to. I'll go by an' by."

"I can go well enough," said Fidelia, in her feeble, shrill voice. "You ain't goin' to begin as long as I can help it." And she crawled slowly out of the yard between the rows of dahlias, and down the road, her head nodding, her flabby black bag hanging at her side.

That was the last time she ever went to the post-office. That day she returned with her patient, disappointed heart for the last time.

When poor Fidelia Almy left her little house again she went riding, lying quietly, her nodding head still forever. She had passed out of that strong wind of Providence which had tossed her so hard, into the eternal calm. She rode past the post-office on her way to the little green grave-yard, and never knew nor cared whether there was a letter for her or not. But the bell tolled, and the summer air was soft and sweet, and the little funeral train passed by ; and maybe there was one among the fair, wide possibilities of heaven.

The first day on which Fidelia gave up going to the post-office, Lily began going in her stead. In the morning Fidelia looked up at her pitifully from her pillow, when she found that she could not rise.

"You'll have to go to the office, Lily," she whispered ; "an' you'd better hurry, cr you'll be late for the mail."

That was the constant cry to which the poor girl had to listen. It was always, "Hurry, hurry, or you'll be late for the mail."

Lily was a sweet, healthy young thing, but the contagion of this strained faith and expectation seemed to seize upon her in her daily tramps to the post-office. Sometimes, going along the road, she could hardly believe herself not to be the veritable Fidelia Almy, living life over again, beginning a new watch for her lost lover's letter. She put her hand to her head to see if it nodded. She kept whispering to herself, "Hurry, hurry, or you'll be late for the mail."

Fidelia lay ill a week before she died, and the week had nearly gone, when Lily flew home from the office one night, jubilant. She ran in to the sick woman. "Oh, Aunt Fidelia!" she cried, "the letter's come!"

Fidelia had not raised herself for days, but she sat up now erect. All her failing forces seemed to gather themselves up and flash and beat, now the lifeward wind for them blew. The color came into her cheeks, her eyes shone triumphant. "Ansel's—letter!"

Lily sobbed right out in the midst of her joy: "Oh, poor Aunt Fidelia! poor Aunt Fidelia! I didn't think—I forgot. I was awful cruel. It's a letter from Valentine. He's been sick. The folks wrote, but they put on the wrong state—Massachusetts instead of Vermont. He's comin' right home, an' he's goin' to stay. He's goin' to settle here. Poor Aunt Fidelia! I didn't think."

Fidelia lay back on her pillow. "You dear child," she whispered, "you won't have to."

Valentine Rowe came the morning of the day on which she died. She eagerly demanded to see him.

"You're a-goin' to settle here, ain't you?" she asked him. "Don't you go away again before you're married; don't you do it. It ain't safe trustin' to letters; there's slips."

The young man looked down at her with tears in his honest eyes. "I'll settle here sure," said he. "Don't you worry. I'll promise you."

27

Fidelia looked up at him, and shut her eyes peacefully. "The dear child!" she murmured.

Along the middle of the afternoon she called Lily. She wanted her to put her head down, so she could tell her something.

"Them dresses," she whispered, "up-stairs. You'd better take em' an' use 'em. You can make that white one over for a weddin' dress. An' you'd better take the covers off the things in the parlor when you're married, an'—eat the plum-cake."

Near sunset she called Lily again. "The evenin' mail," she whispered. "It's time for it. You'd better hurry, or you'll be late. I shouldn't be—a bit—surprised if the letter came to night."

Lily broke down and cried. "Oh, dear, poor aunty!" she sobbed. The awful pitifulness of it all seemed to overwhelm her suddenly. She could keep up no longer.

But Fidelia did not seem to notice it. She went on talking. "Ansel Lennox—promised he'd write when he went away, an' he said he'd come again. It's time for the evenin' mail. You'd better hurry, or you'll be late. He—promised he'd write, an'"—she looked up at Lily suddenly; a look of triumphant resolution came into her poor face—"*I ain't goin' to give it up yet.*"

A CONQUEST OF HUMILITY.

Two o'clock had been the hour set for the wedding. It was now four, and the bridegroom had not yet appeared. The relatives who had been bidden to the festivities had been waiting impatiently in the two square front rooms of Maria Caldwell's house, but now some had straggled out into the front yard, from which they could look up the road to better advantage.

They were talking excitedly. A shrill feminine babble, with an undertone of masculine bass, floated about the house and yard. It had been swelling in volume from a mere whisper for the last half-hour—ever since Hiram Caldwell had set out for the bridegroom's house to ascertain the reason for his tardiness at his own wedding.

Hiram, who was a young fellow, had gotten into his shiny buggy with a red, important face, and driven off at a furious rate. He was own cousin to Delia Caldwell, the prospective bride. All the people assembled were Thayers or Caldwells, or connections thereof. The tardy bridegroom's name was Lawrence Thayer.

It was a beautiful summer afternoon. The air was hot and sweet. Around the Caldwell house it was spicy sweet with pinks ; there was a great bed of them at the foot of the green bank which extended under the front windows.

Some of the women and young girls pulled pinks and sniffed them as they stood waiting. Mrs. Erastus Thayer had stuck two or three in the bosom of her cinnamon-brown silk dress. She stood beside the gate; occasionally she craned her neck over it and peered down the road. The sun was hot upon her silken shoulders, the horizontal wrinkles shone, but she did not mind.

"See anything of him?" some one called out.

"No. I'm dreadful afraid somethin' has happened."

"Oh, mother, what do you think's happened?" asked a young girl at her side, hitting her with a sharp elbow. The girl was young, slim, and tall; she stooped a little; her pointed elbows showed redly through her loose white muslin sleeves; her face was pretty.

"Hush, child! I don't know," said her mother.

The girl stood staring at her with helpless, awed eyes.

At last the woman in cinnamon-brown silk turned excitedly about. "He's comin'!" she proclaimed, in a shrill whisper.

The whisper passed from one to another.

"He's coming!" everybody repeated. Heads crowded together at the window; all the company was in motion.

"It ain't Lawrence," said a woman's voice, disappointedly. "It ain't nobody but his father, with Hiram."

"Somethin' *has happened*," repeated Mrs. Thayer. The young girl trembled and caught hold of her mother's dress; her eyes grew big and wild. Hiram Caldwell drove up the road. He met the gaze of the people with a look of solemn embarrassment. But he was not so important as he had been. There was a large, white-headed old man with him, who drew the larger share of attention. He got lumberingly out of the buggy when Hiram drew rein at the gate.

Then he proceeded up the gravel walk to the house. The people stood back and stared. No one dared speak to him except Mrs. Erastus Thayer. She darted before him in the path ; her brown silk skirts swished.

"Mr. Thayer," cried she, "what is the matter ? Do tell us ! What has happened ?"

"Where's Delia?" said the old man.

"Oh, she's in the bedroom out of the parlor. She ain't been out yet. Mr. Thayer, for mercy's sake, what is the matter? What has happened to him ?"

David Thayer waved her aside, and kept straight on, his long yellow face immovable, his gaunt old shoulders resolutely braced, through the parlor, and knocked at the bedroom door.

A nervously shaking woman in black silk opened it. She screamed when she saw him. "Oh, Mr. Thayer, it's you! What is the matter? where is he ?" she gasped, clutching his arm.

A young woman in a pearl-colored silk gown stood, straight and silent, behind her. She had a tall, full figure, and there was something grand in her attitude. She stood like a young pine-tree, as if she had all necessary elements of support in her own self. Her features were strong and fine. She would have been handsome if her complexion had been better. Her skin was thick and dull.

She did not speak, but stood looking at David Thayer. Her mouth was shut tightly, her eyes steady. She might have been braced to meet a wind.

There were several other women in the little room. Mr. Thayer looked at them uneasily. "I want to see Delia an' her mother, an' nobody else," said he, finally.

The women started and looked at each other ; they then

left. The old man closed the door after them and turned to Delia.

Her mother had begun to cry. " Oh dear ! oh dear !" she wailed. " I knew somethin' dreadful had happened."

"Delia," said he, " I don't know what you're goin' to say. It ain't very pleasant for me to tell you. I wish this minute Lawrence Thayer didn't belong to me. But that don't better matters any. He does, an' somebody's got to tell you."

" Oh, is he dead ?" asked Delia's mother, brokenly.

" No, he ain't dead," said the old man ; " an' he ain't sick. I don't know of anything that ails him except he's a fool. He won't come—that's the whole of it."

"Won't come !" shrieked the mother. Delia stood stiff and straight.

"No, he won't come. His mother an' I have been talkin' an' reasonin' with him, but it hasn't done any good. I don't know but it'll kill his mother. It's all on account of that Briggs girl : you might as well know it. I wish she'd never come near the house. I've seen what way the wind blew for some time, but I never dreamed it would come to this. I think it's a sudden start on his part. I believe he meant to come, this noon, as much as could be ; but Olive came home, an' they were talkin' together in the parlor, an' I see she'd been cryin'. His mother an' I got ready, an' when he didn't come down-stairs she went up to see where he was. He had his door locked, an' he called out he wasn't goin' ; that was all we could get out of him. He wouldn't say another word, but we knew what the trouble was. His mother had noticed how red Olive's eyes were when she went back to the shop. She'd been takin' on, I suppose, an' so he decided, all of a sudden, he'd back out. There ain't any

excuse for him, an' I ain't goin' to make up any. He's
treated you mean, Delia, an' I'd rather have cut off my
right hand than had it happened; that's all I can say about
it, an' that don't do any good."

Mrs. Caldwell stepped forward suddenly. "I should
think he had treated her mean!" she said—her voice rose
loud and shrill. "I never heard anything like it. If I had
a son like that, I wouldn't tell of it. That Briggs girl! He
ought to be strung up. If you an' his mother had had any
sort of spunk you'd made him come. You always babied
him to death. He's a rascal. I'd like to get hold of him,
that's all; I—"

Delia caught her mother by the arm. "Mother, if you
have any sense, or feeling for me, don't talk so loud: all
those folks out there will hear."

The older woman's shrill vituperation flowed through the
daughter's remonstrance and beyond it. "I would like to
show him he couldn't do such things as this without gettin'
some punishment for it. I—"

"Mother!"

Mrs. Caldwell changed her tone suddenly. She began
to cry weakly. "Oh, Delia, you poor child, what will you
do?" she sobbed.

"It isn't going to do any good to go on so, mother."

"There's all them folks out there. Oh dear! What
will they say? I wouldn't care so much if it wa'n't for all
them Thayers an' Caldwells. They'll jest crow. Oh dear!
you poor child!"

Delia turned to Mr. Thayer. "Somebody ought to tell
them," said she, "that—there won't be any—wedding."

"Oh, Delia, how can you take it so calm?" wailed her
mother.

"I suppose so," asserted the old man; "but I declare I can't tell 'em such a thing about a son of mine. I feel as if I'd been through about all I could."

"The minister would be a good one, wouldn't he?" said Delia.

Mr. Thayer took up with the suggestion eagerly. He opened the door a chink, and asked one of the waiting officious guests to summon the minister. When he came he gave him instructions in an agitated whisper; then retreated. The trio in the bedroom became conscious of a great hush without; then the minister's solemnly inflected voice broke upon it. He was telling them that the wedding was postponed. Then there was a little responsive murmur, and the minister knocked on the door.

"Shall I tell them when it will take place?—they are inquiring," he whispered.

Delia heard him. "You can tell them it will never take place," said she, in a clear voice.

The minister stared at her wonderingly. "Oh!" groaned her mother. Then the minister's voice rose again, and directly there were a creaking and rustling, and subdued clatter of voices. The guests were departing.

After a little, Delia approached the door as if she were going out into the parlor.

"Oh, Delia, don't go! wait till they're all gone!" wailed her mother. "All them Thayers and Caldwells!"

"They are gone, most of them. I've stood in this hot little room long enough," said Delia, and threw open the door. Directly opposite was a mahogany table with the wedding presents on it. Three or four women, among them Mrs. Erastus Thayer and her daughter, were bending over them and whispering.

When the door opened they turned and stared at Delia
standing there in her pearl-colored silk, with some drooping white bridal flowers on her breast. They looked stiff
and embarrassed. Then Mrs. Thayer recovered herself and
came forward.

"Delia," said she, in a soft whisper, "dear girl."

She put her arm around Delia, and attempted to draw
her towards herself; but the girl released herself, and gave
her a slight backward push.

"Please don't make any fuss over me, Mrs. Thayer," said
she; "it isn't necessary."

Mrs. Thayer started back, and went towards the door.
Her face was very red. She tried to smile. Her daughter
and the other woman followed her.

"I'm real glad she can show some temper about it," she
whispered, when they were all out in the entry. "It's a
good deal better for her."

"Ask her why he didn't come," one of the women whispered, nudging her.

"I'm kind of afraid to. I'll stop and ask Hiram on my
way home; mebbe Mr. Thayer told him."

"Delia, in her bridal gear, stood majestically beside one
of the parlor windows. She was plainly waiting for her
guests to go. They kept peering in at her, while they whispered among themselves. Presently Mrs. Thayer's daughter came across the room tremblingly. She had hesitated
on the parlor threshold, but her mother had given her a
slight push on her slender shoulders, and she had entered
suddenly. She kept looking back as she advanced towards
Delia.

"Mother wants to know," she faltered, in her thin girlish
pipe, "if—you wouldn't rather—she'd—take back that toi-

let set she brought. She says she don't know but it will make you feel bad to see it."

"Of course you can take it."

"Mrs. Emmons says she'll take her mats too, if you'd like to have her."

"Of course she can take them."

The young girl shrank over to the table, snatched up the toilet set and mats, and fled to her mother.

When they were all gone, David Thayer approached Delia. He had been sitting on a chair by the bedroom door, holding his head in his hands.

"I'm goin' now," said he. "If there's anything I can do, you let me know."

"There won't be anything," said Delia. "I shall get along all right."

He shook her hand hard in his old trembling one. "You're more of a man than Lawrence is," said he. He was a very old man, and his voice, although it was still deep, quavered.

"There isn't any use in your saying much to him," said Delia. "I don't want you to, on my account."

"Delia, don't you go to standin' up for him. He don't deserve it."

"I ain't standing up for him. I know he's your son, but it doesn't seem to me there's a great deal to stand up for. What he's done is natural enough; he's been carried away by a pretty face ; but he has shown out what he is."

"I don't blame you a bit for feelin' so, Delia."

"I don't see any other way to feel ; it's the truth."

"Well, good-bye, Delia. I hope you won't lay up anything again' his mother an' me. We'll always think a good deal of you."

"I haven't any reason to lay up anything against you that I know of," said Delia. Her manner was stern, although she did not mean it to be. She could not, as it were, relax her muscles enough to be cordial. All the strength in Delia Caldwell's nature was now concentrated. It could accomplish great things, but it might grind little ones to pieces.

"Well, good-bye, Delia," said the old man, piteously. He was himself a strong character, but he seemed weak beside her.

After he had gone, Delia went into the bedroom to her mother. Mrs. Caldwell was sitting there crying. She looked up when her daughter entered.

"Oh, Delia," she sobbed, "what are you goin' to do?—what are you goin' to do?"

"I am going to take off this dress, for one thing."

"I don't see what you will do. There you've got this dress and your black silk, two new silk dresses, and your new brown woollen one, and your new bonnet and mantle, all these new things, and the weddin'-cake."

"I suppose I can wear dresses and bonnets just as well if I ain't married; and as for the wedding-cake, we'll have some of it for supper."

"Delia Caldwell!"

"What's the matter, mother?"

Delia slipped off the long shimmering skirt of her pearl-colored silk, shook it out, and laid it carefully over a chair.

"Are you crazy?"

"Not that I know of. Why?"

"You don't act natural."

"I'm acting the way that's natural to me."

"What are you going to do? Oh, you poor child!"

Mrs. Caldwell laid hold of her daughter's hand as she passed near her, and attempted to pull her to her side.

"Don't, please, mother," said Delia.

Her mother relinquished her hold, and sobbed afresh. "I won't pity you if you don't want me to," said she? "but it's dreadful. There's—another—thing. You've lost your school. Flora Strong's spoke for it, an' she won't want to give it up."

"I don't want her to. I'll get another one."

Delia put on a calico dress, and kindled a fire, and made tea as usual. She put some slices of wedding-cake on the table : perhaps her will extended to her palate, and kept it from tasting like dust and ashes to her. Her mother drank a cup of tea between her lamentations.

After supper Delia packed up her wedding gifts and addressed them to their respective donors. There were a few bits of silver, but the greater number of the presents were pieces of fancy-work from female relatives. She folded these mats and tidies relentlessly with her firm brown fingers. There was no tenderness in her touch. She felt not the least sentiment towards inanimate things.

"I think they're actin' awful mean to want to grab these things back so quick," said her mother, her wrath gaining upon her grief a little.

"It goes well with the rest," said Delia.

Among the gifts which she returned was a little embroidered tidy from Flora Strong, the girl who had been engaged to teach her former school.

Flora came over early the next morning. She opened the door, and stood there hesitating. She was bashful before the trouble in the house. "Good-morning, Mrs. Caldwell ; good-morning, Delia," she faltered, deprecatingly. She had a thin, pretty face, with very red lips and cheeks. She fumbled a little parcel nervously.

"Good-mornin', Flora," said Mrs. Caldwell. Then she turned her back, and went into the pantry.

Delia was washing dishes at the sink. She spoke just as she always did. "Good-morning," said she. "Sit down, won't you, Flora?"

Then Flora began. "Oh, Delia," she burst out, "what made you send this back?—what made you? You didn't think I'd take it?"

"Take what?"

"This tidy. Oh, Delia, I made it for you! It doesn't make any difference whether—" Flora choked with sobs. She dropped into a chair, and put her handkerchief over her face. Mrs. Caldwell heard her, and began weeping, as she stood in the pantry. Delia went on with her dishes.

"Oh, Delia, you'll—take it back, won't you?" Flora said, finally.

"Of course I will, if you want me to. It's real pretty."

"When I heard of it," the girl went on—"I don't know as you want me to speak of it, but I've got to—I felt as if —I declare I'd like to see Lawrence Thayer come up with. I'll never speak to him again as long as I live. Delia, you aren't standing up for him, are you? You don't care if I do say he's—a villain?"

"I hope she don't," wailed her mother in the pantry.

"No," said Delia, "I don't care."

Then Flora offered to give up the school. She pleaded that she should take it, but Delia would not. She could get another, she said.

That afternoon, indeed, she went to see the committee. She had put the house to rights, pinned Flora's tidy on the big rocking-chair in the parlor, and dressed herself carefully in a blue-sprigged muslin, one of her wedding gowns. Passing down the hot village street, she saw women sewing at their cool sitting-room windows. She looked up at them and nodded as usual. She knew of a school whose teacher had left to be married, as she had done. She thought the vacancy had possibly not been filled. Very little of the vacation had passed. Moreover, the school was not a desirable one : the pay was small, and it was three miles from the village. Delia obtained the position. Early in September she began her duties. She went stanchly back and forth over the rough, dusty road day after day. She had the reputation of being a very fine teacher, although the children were a little in awe of her. They never came to meet her and hang about her on her way to the schoolhouse. Her road lay past the Thayer house, where she would have been living now had all gone well. Occasionally she met Lawrence ; she passed him without a look. Quite often she met Olive Briggs, who worked in a milliner's shop, and boarded at Lawrence's father's. She always bowed to her pleasantly. She had seen her in the shop, although she had no real acquaintance with her. The girl was pretty, with the prettiness that Delia lacked. Her face was sweet and rosy and laughing. She was fine and small, and moved with a sort of tremulous lightness like a butterfly. Delia, meeting her, seemed to tramp.

Everybody thought Lawrence and Olive Briggs would be married. They went to evening meetings together, and to ride. Lawrence had a fine horse. Delia was at every evening meeting. She watched her old lover enter with the other girl, and never shrank. She also looked at them riding past.

" Did you see them, Delia?" her mother asked in a fluttering voice one afternoon. She and Delia were sitting at
the front windows, and Lawrence and Olive had just whirled
by the house.

" Yes."

" You kept so still, I didn't know as you did."

People kept close watch over Lawrence and Olive and
Delia. Lawrence was subjected to a mild species of ostra-
cism by a certain set of the village girls, Delia's mates—
honest, simple young souls ; they would not speak to him
on the street. They treated Olive with rough, rural stiffness
when they traded with her in the one milliner's shop. She
was an out-of-town girl, and had always been regarded
with something of suspicion. These village women had a
strong local conservatism. They eyed strangers long before
they admitted them.

As for Delia, the young women friends of her own age
treated her with a sort of deferential sympathy. They
dared not openly condole with her, but they made her aware
of their partisanship. As a general thing no one except a
Thayer or a Caldwell alluded to the matter in her presence.
The relatives of the two families were open enough in expressing themselves, either with recrimination or excuse
for Lawrence, or with sympathy or covert blame for Delia.
She heard the most of it, directly or indirectly. Like many
New England towns, this was almost overshadowed by the
ramifications of a few family trees. A considerable por-
tion of the population was made of these Thayers and Caldwells—two honorable and respectable old names. They
were really, for the most part, kindly and respectable people, conscious of no ill intentions, and probably possessed of
few. Some of them expostulated against receiving back

those vain bridal gifts, but Delia insisted. Some of them were more willing to give than she to receive their honest and most genuine sympathy however ungracefully they might proffer it.

Still the fine and exquisite stabs which Delia Caldwell had to take from her own relations and those of her forsworn bridegroom were innumerable. There are those good and innocent-hearted people who seem to be furnished with stings only for those of their own kind; they are stingless towards others. In one way this fact may have proved beneficial to Delia: while engaged in active defence against outside attacks, she had no time to sting herself.

She girded on that pearl-colored silk as if it were chain armor, and went to merrymakings. She made calls in that fine black silk and white-plumed wedding bonnet. It seemed at times as if she were fairly running after her trouble; she did more than look it in the face.

It was in February, when Delia had been teaching her new school nearly two terms, that Olive Briggs left town. People said she had given up her work and gone home to get ready to be married.

Delia's mother heard of it, and told her. "I should think she'd be awful afraid he wouldn't come to the weddin'," she said, bitterly.

"So should I," assented Delia. She echoed everybody's severe remarks about Lawrence.

It might have been a month later when Flora Strong ran in one morning before school. "I've just heard the greatest news!" she panted. "What do you think—she's jilted him?"

"Jilted whom?"

"Olive Briggs—she's jilted Lawrence Thayer. She's

going to be married to another fellow in May. I had it from Milly Davis ; she writes to her. It's so."

" I can't believe it," Mrs. Caldwell said, quivering.

"Well, it's so. I declare I jumped right up and down when I heard of it. Delia, aren't you glad ?"

" I don't know what difference it can make to me."

" I mean aren't you glad he's got his pay ?"

"Yes, I am," said Delia, with slow decision.

" She wouldn't be human if she wasn't," said her mother. Mrs. Caldwell was cold and trembling with nervousness. She stood grasping the back of a chair. " But I'm afraid it ain't so. Are you sure it's so, Flora ?"

" Mrs. Caldwell, I know it's so."

Delia on her way to school that morning looked at the Thayer house as she passed. " I wonder how *he* feels," she said to herself. She saw Lawrence Thayer, in her stead, in the midst of all that covert ridicule and obloquy, that galling sympathy, that agony of jealousy and betrayed trust. They distorted his face like flames ; she saw him writhe through their liquid wavering.

She pressed her lips together, and marched along. At that moment, had she met Lawrence, she would have passed him with a fiercer coldness than ever, but if she had seen the girl she would have been ready to fly at her.

The village tongues were even harder on Lawrence than they had been on her. The sight of a person bending towards the earth with the weight of his just deserts upon his shoulders is generally gratifying and amusing even to his friends. Then there was more open rudeness among the young men who were Lawrence's mates. They jeered him everywhere. He went about doggedly. He was strong in silence, but he had a sweet womanish face which showed

28

the marks of words quickly. He was still very young. Delia was two years older than he, and looked ten. Still, Lawrence seemed as old in some respects. He was a quiet, shy young man, who liked to stay at home with his parents, and never went about much with the young people. Before Olive came he had seldom spoken to any girl besides Delia. They had been together soberly and steadily ever since their school-days.

Some people said now, "Don't you suppose Lawrence Thayer will go with Delia again?" But the answer always was, "She won't look at him."

One Sunday afternoon, about a year after Olive Briggs's marriage, Mrs. Caldwell said to Delia, as they were walking home from church, "I jest want to know if you noticed how Lawrence Thayer stared at you in meetin' this afternoon?"

"No, I didn't," said Delia. She was looking uncommonly well that day. She wore her black silk, and had some dark-red roses in her bonnet.

"Well, he never took his eyes off you. Delia, that feller would give all his old shoes to come back, if you'd have him."

"Don't talk so foolish, mother."

"He would—you depend on it."

"I'd like to see him," said Delia, sternly. There was a red glow on her dull, thick cheeks.

"Well, I say so too," said her mother.

The next night, when Delia reached the Thayer house on her way from school, Lawrence's mother stood at the gate. She had a little green shawl over her head. She was shivering; the wind blew up cool. Just behind her in the yard there was a little peach-tree all in blossom.

She held out her hand mutely when Delia reached her. The girl did not take it. " Good-evening," said she, and was passing.

" Can't you stop jest a minute, Delia?"

" Was there anything you wanted?"

" Can't you come into the house jest a minute? I wanted to see you about somethin'."

" I don't believe I can to-night, Mrs. Thayer."

"There ain't anybody there. There was somethin' I wanted to see you about."

The green shawl was bound severely around her small, old face with its peaked chin. She reached out her long, wrinkled hand over the gate, and clutched Delia's arm softly.

" Well, I'll come in a minute." Delia followed Mrs. Thayer past the blooming peach-tree into the house.

The old woman dragged forward the best rocking-chair tremblingly. " Sit down, dear," said she. Then she seated herself close beside her, and, leaning forward, gazed into her face with a sort of deprecating mildness. She even laid hold of one of her hands, but the girl drew it away softly. There was a gentle rustic demonstrativeness about Lawrence's mother which had always rather abashed Delia, who was typically reserved. " I wanted to speak to you about Lawrence," said the old woman. Delia sat stiffly erect, her head turned away. " I can't bear to think you are always goin' to feel so hard towards him, Delia. Did you know it?"

Delia half arose. " There isn't any use in bringing all this up again, Mrs. Thayer; it's all past now."

" Sit down jest a minute, dear. I want to talk to you. I know you've got good reason to blame him; but there's some excuse. He wa'n't nothin' but a boy, an' she was sweet-lookin', an' she took on dreadful. You'd thought she was goin' to die. It's turned out jest the way I knew 'twould. I told Lawrence how 'twould be then. I see right through her. She meant well enough. I s'pose she thought she was in love with Lawrence ; but she was flighty. She went home and saw another fellow, an' Lawrence was nowhere. He didn't care so much as folks thought. Delia, I'm goin' to tell you the truth : he thought more of you than he did of her the whole time. You look as if you thought I was crazy, but I ain't. She jest bewitched him a little spell, but you was at the bottom of his heart always —you *was*, Delia." The old woman broke into sobs.

Delia rose. "I'd better go. There isn't any use in bringing this up, Mrs. Thayer."

"Don't go, Delia—don't. I wanted to tell you. He got to talkin' with me a little the other Sabbath night. It's the first time he's said a word, but he felt awful bad, an' I questioned him. Says he, ' Mother, I don't dream of such a thing as her havin' of me, or carin' anything about me again ; but I do feel as if I should like to do somethin' if I could, to make up to her a little for the awful wrong I've done her.' That was jest the words he said. Delia, he ain't such a bad boy as you think he is, after all. You hadn't ought to despise him."

"He'll have to do something to show I've got some reason not to, then," said Delia. She looked immovably at the old woman, who was struggling with her sobs. She told her mother of the conversation after she got home.

"You did jest right," said Mrs. Caldwell. "I wouldn't knuckle to 'em if I was in your place." She was getting tea. After they had finished the meal, and sat idly at the table for a few minutes, she looked across at her daughter suddenly, with embarrassed sharpness. " Speakin' about Lawrence, you wouldn't feel as if you ever could take him, anyhow, would you ?" said she.

" Mother, what are you talking about ?"

In a few weeks the anniversary of Delia's defeated wedding came. She spoke of it herself after dinner. She and her mother were making currant-jelly.

"Why, it's my wedding-day, mother," said she. " I ought to have put on my wedding-gown, and eaten some weddingcake, instead of making jelly."

" Don't talk so, child," said her mother. Sometimes Delia's hardihood startled her.

Delia was pressing the currants in a muslin bag, and the juice was running through her fingers, when there was a loud knock at the door.

"Why, who's that, her mother said, fluttering. She ran and peeped through the sitting-room blinds. " It's Mrs. 'Rastus Thayer," she motioned back, " an' Milly."

" I'll go to the door," said Delia. She washed her hands hurriedly, and went. She noticed with surprise that the two visitors were dressed in their Sunday best, Mrs. Thayer in her nicely kept cinnamon-brown silk, and Milly in her freshly starched white muslin. They had an air of constrained curiosity about them as they entered and took their seats in the parlor.

Delia sat down with them and tried to talk. Pretty soon her mother, who had prinked a little, entered ; but just as she did so there was another knock. Some of the Caldwell cousins had come this time. They also were finely dressed, and entered with that same soberly expectant air. They were hardly seated before others arrived. Delia, go-

ing to the door this time, saw the people coming by twos
and threes up the street. They flocked in, and she brought
chairs. Nothing disturbed her outward composure; but
her mother grew pale and tremulous. She no longer tried
to speak; she sat staring. At two o'clock the rooms were
filled with that same company who had assembled to see
Delia wedded two years before.

They sat around the walls in stiff silence; they seemed
to be waiting. Delia was not imaginative, nor given to
morbid fancies; but sitting there in the midst of that mys-
terious company, in her cotton gown, with her hands stained
with currant juice, she began to fairly believe that it was a
dream. Were not these people mere phantoms of the familiar village folk assembling after this truly fantastic manner, and sitting here in this ghostly silence? Was not the
whole a phantasmagoria of the last moments of her sweet
old happiness and belief in truth? Was not she herself,
disenchanted, with her cotton gown and stained hands, the
one real thing in it?

The scent of the pinks came in the window, and she noticed that. "How real it all is?" she thought. "But I
shall wake up before long." It was like one of those
dreams in which one clings stanchly to the consciousness
of the dream, and will not sink beneath its terrors.

When Lawrence Thayer entered she seemed to wake violently. She half rose from her seat, then sank down again.
Her mother screamed.

Lawrence Thayer stood by the parlor door, where everybody in the two rooms could hear him. His gentle, beardless face was pale as death, but the pallor revealed some
strong lines which his youthful bloom had softened. He
was slender, and stooped a little naturally; now he was

straight as a reed. He had a strange look to these people who had always known him.

"Friends," he began, in a solemn, panting voice, "I—have—asked you to come here on the anniversary of the day on which Delia Caldwell and I were to have been married, to make to her, before you all, the restitution in my power. I don't do it to put myself before you in a better light : God, who knows everything, knows I don't : it's for *her*. I was a coward, and mean, and it's going to last. Nothing that I can do now is going to alter that. All I want now is to make up to her a little for what she's been through. Two years ago to-day she stood before you all rejected and slighted. Now look at me in her place."

Then he turned to Delia, with a stiff motion. It was like solemn, formal oratory, but his terrible earnestness gave it heat. "Delia Caldwell, I humbly beg your pardon. I love you better than the whole world, and I ask you to be my wife."

"I never will." It was as if Delia's whole nature had been set to these words ; they had to be spoken. She had risen, and stood staring at him so intently that the whole concourse of people vanished in blackness. She saw only his white face. All the thoughts in her brain spread wings and flew, swiftly circling. She heard what he said, and she heard her own thoughts with a strange double consciousness. All those days came back—the sweet old confidences, the old looks and ways. That pale speaking face was Lawrence's—Lawrence's ; not that strange other's who had left her for that pink-faced girl. This revelation of his inner self, which smote the others with a sense of strangeness, thrilled her with the recognition of love. " A coward and mean." Yes, he had been, but— Yes, there was some excuse for him—there was. Is not every fault wedded to its own excuse, that pity may be born into the world? "He was as honest in what he was saying as a man could be. He could have had no hope that she would marry him. He knew her enduring will, her power of indignation. This was no subtle scheme for his own advantage. Even these people would not think that. They would not, indeed, believe him capable of it. The system of terrible but coolly calculated ventures for success was one with which this man would not be likely to grapple. He was honest in this. There sat all the Thayers and Caldwells. How they would talk, and laugh at him!

Lawrence turned to go. He had bowed silently when she gave him her quick answer. There was a certain dignity about him. He had in reality pulled himself up to the level of his own noble, avowed sentiments.

Delia stood gazing after him. She looked so relentless that she was almost terrible. One young girl, staring at her, began to cry.

Mrs. Erastus Thayer sat near the door. Delia's eyes glanced from Lawrence to her face. Then she sprang forward.

"You needn't look at him in that way," she cried out. "I am going to marry him. Lawrence, come back."

THE END.